Hellzapoppin'

Heide Goody & Iain Grant

Pigeon Park Press

Paperback ISBN: 978-0-9933149-8-8
Ebook ISBN: 978-0-9933149-9-5

Cover artwork and design copyright © Mike Watts 2015
(www.bigbeano.co.uk)

Published by Pigeon Park Press

www.pigeonparkpress.com
info@pigeonparkpress.com

Chapter 1 – The day Father Eustace arrived

"Well, mates, this is a bit of a stumper," said Rutspud, looking up.

"Did I not tell you so?" said Frogspear, hissing through his fangs, black spittle flying from the corners of his mouth.

"Take it slow, brother," shrugged Bootlick, his fat, boneless shoulders rolling like beetles under a blanket. "It's just one soul."

Frogspear shook his laughing stick frantically, the tiny bones rattling from within.

"Devils must concern themselves with details, as we all know."

"I bet they don't have these kinds of problems in the seventh circle," said Rutspud.

It was part of Rutspud's general philosophy that the sixth circle of Hell got all the oddballs, troublemakers and awkward cases. It was all that bastard Dante's fault for creating the idea of stupid circles in the first place. Before the management read Inferno, Hell was just, well, Hell, but once someone in charge had got hold of a copy, then it was circle this and circle that. He didn't complain about it. Firstly, because here, the lava fields and obsidian spires were as magnificent as any in all Perdition. Secondly, because, even though demons were not allowed friendships, he couldn't hope for a better pair of deadly enemies than Frogspear and Bootlick anywhere else. And thirdly, if he did complain, it

3

would only earn him a thorough scourging and a decade working in the cesspit of idle flatterers.

"But what is one to do?" said Frogspear.

"Grab some righteous lunch," suggested Bootlick.

Rutspud ignored him and addressed the man bound to the flaming wheel above them.

"Mr Ixion?"

"What?" the man shouted back.

"On a scale of one to 'mercy, for the love of God, mercy', how much agony are you in?"

"Pah!" spat Ixion. "Zero."

"Zero?"

"Zero!"

Rutspud looked at Frogspear.

"You've turned the temperature up?"

"Most assuredly."

"And down?"

"T'was a freezing wheel for much of topside's seventeenth century."

"You've spun it."

"Every other mortal week."

"How fast?"

"Until such time as his lungs exploded from the top of his head."

"Hooks? Rats? Acid?"

"Do you take me for a fool, Rutspud? I have attempted every course. He has endured this now for over seven thousand years. He cares not."

"We need to truck on down to the team huddle," said Bootlick. "We're late."

"Technically, since time doesn't exist here, we can't be late. Besides, when have you ever cared about being late?" said Rutspud.

"I heard there could be biscuits. Dig what I'm puttin' down?"

"Will you help me or nay?" squealed Frogspear. He gave a nervous shake of his laughing stick. "My infernal appraisal approaches and my torment targets amount to a piteous baggage."

"I just want a biscuit, one time," said Bootlick. "You dig?"

"I fear the villainous performance improvement process," said Frogspear. "Assertiveness coaching. Progress checks. Oh nonny, nonny."

"Sounds swell!" said Bootlick.

Rutspud rolled his eyes. He was good at rolling his eyes. He had sly but very expressive eyes.

"Oh, yes, the benefits of performance improvement. It's like giving a new hat to a man about to have his head chopped off." He shrugged. "I don't know, Frogspear. I guess you'll have to let him down."

"What?" said Ixion.

"I said we'll have to let you down," called Rutspud. "Take you off your wheel."

"You can't do that!"

"No point keeping you up there, is there?"

At a flick of Rutspud's hand, a band of Frogspear's imps swarmed over Ixion to remove his chains.

"But I'm Ixion!" the ancient king cried frantically. "I'm the man on the wheel of fire!"

"You don't want us to take you down?"

"It's *my* wheel!"

Rutspud grinned at Frogspear.

"Problem solved. Do it, boys."

Chains that were more rust and centuries of dried blood than they were iron fell stiffly away and Ixion tumbled to the ground.

"No! No!" he shouted, leaping vainly for the wheel that was already being hoisted out of reach.

Ixion's screams of desperation and grief brought some instant relief to Frogspear.

"Thanks, boon companions. Now, let us get to that meeting."

"Biscuits, man," said Bootlick.

Bootlick, Frogspear and Rutspud walked over to the conference room in the Kafka-designed Sixth Circle Management Centre. Actually, only Rutspud really walked, striding like a man with a song in his heart. It was a nasty little song, with lots of hand gestures, but a song nonetheless. Bootlick didn't so much walk as continually avoid falling, his lazy webbed feet flopping in front of him, always just in time to stop his considerable bulk slamming into the floor. Frogspear skittered along on his hoof-claws with the sound and energy of a caffeine-fuelled typist.

The three demons pushed their way past the damned bureaucrats, doomed to wander for eternity with deliveries for offices that definitely existed but could never be reached, and entered the conference room to find all but three of the dentist's seats round the saw-edged table taken.

"Alas!" said Frogspear. "We are late."

"Word got out about them biscuits," whispered Bootlick.

Rutspud slipped into a seat and tried to look as if he had been there for positively hours, whatever they were.

At the head of the table, their overseer, the spindly and nail-bearded Scabass, finished gouging some last minute notes into the back of a damned soul who served as his jotter block and jabbed his quill in the creature's rump.

The thirteen demons around the table fell silent, so that the only sound to be heard was the lava bubbling beneath the iron grille flooring. The lava kept the floor delightfully red hot and provided the room with its only light.

"We are quorate at last," said Scabass, relishing the hard 't's. "So, we can begin."

Bootlick coughed and raised his hand.

"Hey, man, heard a rumour we might see some *biscuit* action."

"Correct. There was a rumour. I started it. We have four items on the agenda before we come to our regular team-building exercise. First, I have it on good authority that Lord Peter is to begin a new round of departmental inspections and that we could come under scrutiny. He is going to want to see evidence of our key deliverables and of competencies at both an individual and organisational level."

"Say what?" said Bootlick.

"He is desirous to ascertain what we do and whether we have proven satisfactory," said Frogspear.

Lord Peter was the ruler of all Hell. Not long ago, Satan had been the Boss, but then there had been the 'unpleasantness', and Satan had departed for unknown parts and Lord Peter had stepped in. Some said Peter was the most wicked of the damned mortals. Others said Peter was a fallen saint, cast out of Heaven for trying to seize the throne of the Almighty. Some said that he was actually Satan and had just had some work done. The truth would probably never be known, especially by the grunts like Rutspud who worked directly with Hell's 'clients'. Whoever the new Boss was (or whether he was just the old one in disguise), Hell had become, under his rule, a minefield of corporate initiatives and painfully personal accountability.

"I, for one, welcome Lord Peter's visit," said Scabass, though it was obvious he was lying.

"Even if we're performing below target?" asked Codmince, who was the meeting's minutes-taker.

"What's important," said Scabass, "is that the management" – he gestured at himself with chisel-tipped fingers – "are seen to be dealing with failings appropriately." He consulted his jotter block. "Such as we are seeing in your team, Bootlick."

"Say *what*?" said Bootlick, sitting bolt upright, or as much as he could with a body that was almost entirely boneless.

"You've had three consecutive appraisals that rate you as 'inadequate'," said Scabass.

"Two, man. Just two."

"But you haven't returned your Improvement Action Plan paperwork by the mutually agreed deadline," said Scabass, "so it's an automatic fail on your next observation."

"No way with that deadline, man. Never agreed to it. And those forms blew my wig. There were over ten thousand pages of them."

"Don't whine or bleat. It's unprofessional."

"Cut me a break. I bust my conk in a tricky area."

"And an important one," said Scabass. "The banquet hall is a flagship for what Hell does. All those people with extremely long chopsticks or knives and forks and whatever, all unable to get the food to reach their mouths. Meanwhile, up in Heaven, an identical room where the blessed use the outsized instruments *to feed each other*. It speaks to people philosophically. It truly means something."

"Ain't that the truth," said Bootlick. "But it's sure hard to get them to stick to the script. They dig right on in with their fingers when I'm not looking."

"Then you find a solution."

"I've been all over that. Moved to soup and spoons, but they just hold them spoons further down. Solid blow my top trying to punish these cats for greed, but they just too damned smart to fall for it. They tell me they on hunger strike now. Man, they good for nothin' ..."

Bootlick's words wilted away as Scabass held up a hand for silence.

"Don't decorate your failure with trimmings, Bootlick. You don't deliver. How can the sixth circle allow you to continue in this fashion when others are doing such sterling work? It wouldn't be fair to them."

His long fingers reached for a panel of toggle switches set into the table before him.

"Take it slow, man!"

Scabass fixed Bootlick with an expression that was probably meant to be kind and patrician, but simply looked hungry.

"You can't have your cake and eat it, Bootlick, so you will have to step up to the plate and face the music."

Bootlick frowned.

"Say what?"

"The music," said Scabass and flicked a switch.

Like a pouncing spider, a metal contrivance of steel arms dropped onto Bootlick. Pincers grabbed, blades buzzed and, Rutspud saw, there was even a corkscrew and a tin-opener in there which screwed and opened respectively.

The device was one of the creations from Belphegor's demonic workshops, the Research and Development unit for all Hell, and it worked with the startlingly efficiency of all Belphegor's designs. It was so efficient, Bootlick didn't even have time to scream as the machine chopped and ripped him apart which, Rutspud reflected silently, had a certain mercy. Rutspud watched the bloody dismemberment with a carefully maintained neutral expression. Any demonstration of feelings of sadness or loss would be, at best, mocked or, more likely, seen as a request to follow Bootlick into the mincer.

Rutspud wiped something wet from his cheek. It wasn't a tear.

The machine quickly retracted, leaving a conical pile of body parts and miscellaneous innards on the chair.

Scabass made a note on his jotter block. The jotter block whimpered.

"Codmince, you will pick up Bootlick's duties."

"In addition to my own?" asked the demon, alarmed.

"Of course. Your team are delivering top-graded torture so, clearly, you have capacity to take on more."

"But, sir ..."

Codmince fell silent as Scabass's fingers drifted close to the panel of switches.

"Good," said Scabass.

Scabass ran through the targets, quotas and performances of the other demons around the table. The general theme was the same as always. If you were performing poorly then you would need to be punished. If you were performing well then you were obviously underworked and needed to take on more. Every demon was on a horrific treadmill of being increasingly burdened to the point of destruction. The demons referred to it as the 'Peter Principle' in honour of their supreme ruler who had instigated it.

None of them were safe, not even Rutspud, and he felt his guts tighten as Scabass came to him.

"Rutspud," he grinned, showing teeth like tin tacks. "Our star player. I see from the data that you continue to impress. Unprecedented levels of wailing and gnashing of teeth from your team. Your clients report agony levels that we might have thought unsustainable. Even the tough cases that have defeated lesser demons have caved in under your management. Who was that one we sent you last time? Indomitable spirit, kept going on about cleanliness and pie charts."

"Nightingale, sir."

"That's right. I hear she's almost insane with the horror of her plight these days. Almost," said Scabass, wagging his finger at the demons assembled. "Very important that. Taken to the brink of madness but never tipped over into a place we cannot reach them. Keep it up."

"Thank you, sir," said Rutspud.

"And Frogspear ..." said Scabass.

"Yes, sire?"

"Significant improvements since the last meeting. Few client interfaces measured as inadequate. You have, surprisingly, taken on board what we've said and turned things around."

"I am most grateful for the observation, sire," said Frogspear. His laughing stick quivered lightly in his hand.

"Thing is ..." said Scabass.

"Yes, sire?"

Scabass nodded grimly to himself as though emotionally torn.

"Thing is, I just don't like you."

He flicked a switch, and the demon-blender dropped and plunged its tools of dissection into Frogspear. Rutspud, sitting next to him, was treated to a close-up of the whole visceral spectacle. When the machine lifted away, Rutspud saw that, in his last moments, Frogspear had reached out and grabbed him. Frogspear's severed hand and forearm clung now to Rutspud's wrist. Rutspud prised the hand away and gently deposited it on the pile of parts.

"This organisation does not tolerate failure," said Scabass. "Or annoying sycophantic twats. Now, the census. Lord Peter wants a full headcount of the damned and the demons in Hell."

"Why, sir?" asked Pigcrack.

"Hell now functions on an ethos of total accountability at all levels. The fear is that some individuals are being missed out."

"Hiding, you mean?"

"Perhaps," said Scabass. "Which reminds me. We're still looking for a new motto for Hell that encapsulates our core values. The new favourite is *Every Damned Soul Matters*. I think it says something about the personal touch and our commitment to all. Opinions?"

There were plenty of enthusiastic noises of agreement.

"I preferred the old one," said Rimpurge.

Scabass nodded.

"*If No One Saw You Do It, It Didn't Happen*? Yes, the thinking is that, while that motto reflected our need for rigorous data-recording and evidencing, others rather unprofessionally interpreted it as *What Your Boss Doesn't Know Won't Hurt You.*"

Which, Rutspud thought, pretty much summed up every demon's view of life in Hell. The only freedom one had was in the gaps in The Management's omniscience.

"No additional comments?" asked Scabass. "No? Very well. Make a note of that, Codmince. Then, all that remains is the – oh, I almost forgot." Scabass pushed a grey chit of card along the table to Rutspud. "You've a new client to collect."

Rutspud looked at the rough-printed writing on the card.

"The more the merrier," he said, groaning inwardly.

"Indeed. And *now* the team-building exercise. Grab a handful, lads."

All the demons except Rutspud gleefully leapt at the pile of remains on Bootlick's and Frogspear's chairs.

"I've got Frogspear's teeth," said Pigcrack. "These were very good teeth. I'll trade them for mine."

"I'll trade them for my teeth and my gills," said Codmince.

"Who in Hell needs gills?"

Ah, yes, thought Rutspud, bidding his best enemies a silent farewell. Team-building: building a new team out of the remains of the old. Rimpurge grabbed the last remaining ... remains.

"Does anyone mind if I take Bootlick's tail?"

"That's not his tail," said Rutspud.

Brother Manfred, performing his Lan Que Wai exercises on the grassy slopes above St Cadfan's, held the firm belief that he could always form a pretty good idea about the upcoming day before morning prayers. Visitors to St Cadfan's often expressed the view that life on a small Welsh island must be predictable and dull, but Manfred, whose curriculum vitae might have listed past jobs as diverse as Unicycling Grand Master of Bavaria and fencing coach to a crown prince, knew better. Each day since he'd been hastily appointed acting abbot of the monastery had held more challenges than he really required, but this day promised to be exceptional.

Beyond the squat granite monastery and its walled garden, down on the beach far below, one of his brothers, Stephen, was chasing a naked man along the shoreline.

Yes, Manfred decided, today was likely to prove interesting.

As Manfred turned gracefully into Left Strike Tiger, Brother Stephen pounced on the naked man and they tumbled into the surf together. The naked man leapt up and ran off while Stephen floundered and shouted. The weather of late had been particularly cold, and the island offered little shelter from the onslaught of the westerly winds that tormented anyone who stepped outside. Manfred imagined that the sea-sodden monk's words were as foul as his likely mood.

Manfred moved into White Crane Spreads Its Wings and admitted that this matter was something for an acting abbot to deal with, sooner rather than later. Stephen's cries, carried by the cool wind, reached Manfred's ears.

"Help me! Someone! Help!"

"Coming, brother." Manfred stretched out in a final salutation, slipped his shoes back on and walked down to the beach.

Stephen, shivering, watched as Brother Manfred walked calmly down to the beach. There was never any urgency in Manfred's actions. Stephen jiggled a little in an effort to will Manfred to speed up. The placid smile and the laid back bouncing of Manfred's grey corkscrew curls seemed an affront to the urgency of the situation.

"He's getting away!" he called.

Manfred watched the figure running along the shingle as the sea sucked at his feet.

"It is a small island," he said, his light German accent hissing the sibilants like a polite kettle coming to the boil. "There are not so many places that he can go, no? So, who is your new friend, Brother Trevor?"

"Stephen," said Stephen automatically.

"Of course," said Manfred, in equally automatic reply.

Stephen had, for many years, lived with the curse that he looked like a 'Trevor', even though no one could define what a 'Trevor' looked like.

"I think it's the new abbot."

"I thought he was holed up in the hotel on the mainland."

Stephen pointed at the rowing boat rolling in the choppy waters twenty feet from shore.

"I guess he got tired of waiting."

Bad weather had prevented the supply boat coming out to the island for the past two months. The last e-mail that Brother Sebastian had received from Owen the boatman had said the new abbot, Father Eustace Pike, had taken up reluctant residence in the Gwesty Ty Newydd Hotel in Aberdaron.

"Not even the craziest of birdwatchers try to make the crossing in these conditions," said Stephen.

"Only the craziest of monks."

The naked man was busily scaling a short cliff at the east end of the beach in his efforts to get away from him.

"He's quite spritely for an old guy," said Stephen.

"So," said Manfred, "why were you chasing him?"

"Because he ran away, brother."

"And why do you suppose he ran away?"

"Because he's confused? I don't know. He must have hypothermia or something."

"Quite," said Manfred. "We shall do all we can to help him. Let us go and get the blankets, ropes and some herbal tea."

"What's the herbal tea for?"

"I'm a little thirsty, brother. You could perhaps use some too."

Stephen followed Manfred up to monastery, shaking his head at the unflustered temporary abbot.

If you can keep your head when all around are losing theirs, you probably haven't understood the situation, thought Stephen, and then shrugged. At least he was better than the last abbot, who had set fire to the monastery, brought half of it tumbling to the ground, and tried to murder the bridesmaid of a visiting wedding party. Everything was relative.

Stephen sat in front of the fire in the warming room and sipped on a camomile tea.

"I don't know why you're so keen on this stuff," he said to Manfred. "It tastes like rotten weeds."

"It is one of the few things that we can call sustainable, here on the island," said Manfred. "Those camomile flowers were grown in my herb garden."

"Oh, so we could never run out?" Stephen picked a wrinkled petal from between his teeth. "Shame."

Brother Sebastian, the monastery procurator and universally referred to as Bastian the Banker in recognition, or perhaps condemnation, of his devious handling of the monastery finances, came in with a fresh habit for Stephen.

"Sir's swimming costume."

"Thank you," said Stephen tartly and began to change. "Oh, did I tell you guys I've been sleepwalking again?"

Manfred peered at him in concern.

"Was this last night?" said Bastian. "I thought I saw something on the garden web-cams."

"Yes. That's why I went out early, to see if I could tell where I'd been."

"Do you think where you go is important?" asked Manfred.

Stephen shrugged.

"There was mud on my feet again," he said.

Manfred nodded.

"You haven't been feeling quite yourself for a while now. When we can get some supplies from the mainland, I will order you some pumpernickel bread. I think you will find it most sustaining."

"I don't honestly think this is something that health food can remedy, Manfred," said Bastian.

"Oh, really, Herr Cynic?"

"Really. I was reading the financial pages last night, but then got distracted by this blog which said that sleepwalking is usually caused by an over-active and under-utilised brain, unable to shut down even though the body has clocked off for the day. If anything, Trevor needs –"

"Stephen," said Stephen automatically.

"*Stephen* needs something to occupy his mind. Not pumpernickel."

"Maybe I do need something more to occupy my mind," said Stephen, eventually. "Perhaps I'm lacking purpose."

Manfred took the mug from Stephen.

"Right now your purpose is to help find the new abbot, so get dressed. I think the human body is a work of beauty, but I don't think we need two naked monks running round the island, eh?"

Minutes later, the three of them had walked up the slope behind the monastery to get a good view of the island. Stephen carried a pile of blankets. Bastian hefted a long coil of rope over his shoulder. They gazed around, hoping to spot some clue as to where the naked abbot might be hiding.

"How exactly are we going to find Father Eustace?" asked Stephen.

"I have an idea," said Manfred. "You two remain here with the supplies, and scan the island for any sign of movement. I will go to several key places along the pathways and construct some snares."

"Did you just say *snares*?" asked Stephen. "Like animal traps?"

"I am definitely coming with you, brother," said Bastian.

"There is no need for worry," said Manfred. "I am quite experienced in these matters. They will be non-lethal, of course. We don't want the poor fellow to die of exposure, so speed is of the essence."

"Really?" said Stephen. "And yet, mysteriously, there was time for tea."

"There's always time for tea," said Manfred, shaking his head at Stephen's naivety. "Come along, Bastian."

Stephen was uncomfortable with the idea of snares, but was unable to think of a better idea. He carefully scanned round the island and then settled down on the pile of blankets in the lee of a large boulder as he waited for the others to conclude their business.

There was a wrinkled lump inside the pocket of his habit which investigation revealed to be a paper bag of jelly babies. This was a pleasant surprise. Habits weren't exactly communal, but Bastian had clearly brought him a habit previously worn by Brother Bernard. The old goat had a famously sweet tooth. Sweets were in very short supply on Bardsey, and they weren't Stephen's, but he reasoned that a morning being battered by the elements might justify a tiny stolen treat. He popped a jelly baby into his mouth with a satisfied murmur.

Stephen rocked forward out of his sheltering hollow and strained to see what Manfred was doing. It looked as though he was down by the old north path, sharpening some sticks with a knife, which didn't seem right. It was clear from Bastian's emphatic hand gestures that he, too, doubted the wisdom in this.

Stephen helped himself to another jelly baby and gazed down at the sea. On a precarious cliff side in a narrow cove below, a long-legged sea bird with a ridiculous yellow comb battled the winds to construct its nest. The poor creature looked the wrong shape for flying, like a child's drawing of a bird, and it seemed to have picked one of the most inhospitable corners of the island to make its home.

"Still. At least *you've* got a sense of purpose," said Stephen.

Down the hillside, Manfred had tied a rope into a loop and was fastening the free end to a gatepost. Bastian was throwing his arms in the air.

There was a tiny noise behind him, like a footstep on stone.

Stephen stayed very still and waited. After a few moments, a hand appeared tentatively over his shoulder and took a jelly baby from the packet. It snatched back, and Stephen didn't dare to look around. He heard appreciative smacking sounds coming from close by. He held his breath. He held the packet a little higher, offering the sweets without looking. The hand crept over his shoulder again, and Stephen grasped the wrist.

A high keening wail erupted, removing the need for Stephen to alert Manfred and Bastian to this new development.

"Shush," he said, his ears ringing. "Nobody wants to hurt you. We're just worried that you'll hurt yourself, running around in the cold like that."

He found that he could easily manhandle the older man. From the scrapes on his limbs and the wild look in his eye, the fellow looked like he'd been through Hell to get here and had no strength left. Stephen pulled him gently forward and grabbed a blanket from the pile. Moments later, he had wrapped the abbot in a tight cocoon of blankets and fed him a jelly baby in an attempt to prevent any more wailing.

"Sorry to manhandle you, Father Abbot," said Stephen. "It seems very disrespectful. I hope you can forgive me. We like to treat our abbot well, really we do. Whatever you heard about the unfortunate business with the old abbot is – well, it's probably true, but it wasn't our fault."

Stephen realised he was babbling and clamped his lips tightly shut.

Manfred and Bastian came running up the hill, dropping the rope and squatting down to greet the abbot.

"I'm very pleased to make your acquaintance, Father Eustace," said Manfred. "I am Manfred, the prior of St Cadfan's."

Manfred reached out a hand towards the abbot, but realised that both arms were firmly pinned inside the blanket.

"I have been acting as abbot while we waited for you to arrive. I am certain that you will soon be restored to health and will want to take up your position."

Manfred gave the abbot's shoulder an encouraging squeeze.

"Right, that's enough kowtowing to the new boss," said Bastian. "The man's already at his wits' end without you blethering at him."

Indeed, there was only bewilderment in the abbot's eyes. His frantic gaze shifted between their faces and the keening noise started up again. Stephen rapidly produced a jelly baby and popped it into the abbot's mouth.

"Let's get him along to prior's house," said Bastian. "And, Stephen, you're on jelly baby duty."

Father Eustace had munched his way through the entire bag of jelly babies on the descent back to the monastery and so, once the new abbot was ensconced, Manfred and Stephen went to find Brother Bernard, the only likely source of the abbot-calming sweets. Manfred led him into the refurbished wing of the monastery. The collapse of parts of the old monastery the year before had uncovered some cellar rooms that had been blocked off, undisturbed, for centuries. The cellar was refurbished and the rooms above rebuilt with funds from the insurance payouts on some of the monastery's delightful tapestries lost in the terrible fire. Manfred was sure that the tapestries weren't worth quite as much as Bastian's inventive insurance claim but some matters were better not scrutinised too closely.

Manfred hoped to personally reconstruct the tapestries from photographs at some point but, in the meantime, his creative juices were poured into overseeing the interior design and decoration of the new rooms, particularly the visitors' centre and guest rooms.

"Bernard's been working on the mural for the visitors' centre."

"You held that design competition," said Stephen.

"Yes," said Manfred, a little stiffly. "The winning design was *Birds Through The Ages.*"

"Ah, a good link to the birdwatching thing. And I'm sure they'll find it restful to have a nature scene outside the – Jesus Christ!"

Stephen actually flinched away from the eight-foot flamingos curving over the archway in front of them. Sharply stylised and painted in the brightest of pinks, the flamingos glared at them with blankly unnerving eyes.

"Stunning, isn't it?" said Manfred.

"I am literally stunned," croaked Stephen.

Beyond the archway, the elderly brothers Bernard and Huey were working on the mural along both sides of the corridor. The cantankerous duo were some of the oldest brothers on the island and Stephen was surprised to see the pair of them engaged in anything as *energetic* as painting. One definite advantage of giving these two this task was that the smell of drying paint almost masked the smell of Brother Huey's feet. The monk's calloused feet bore more resemblance to sea-weathered rocks than actual human feet, and he did insist on wearing those open-toed sandals that clearly hadn't been washed in decades. Brother Huey was applying some dappling to the pale underbelly of an osprey coming in for the kill, talons outstretched, wings arced out behind. It was an image that invoked a primal fear in Stephen and gave him the irrational urge to scream and duck. Brother Bernard was finishing off a scene of six vultures craning over the bloodily realised carcass of a gazelle. Bright eyes stared from the painting. Even the dead gazelle was looking at him.

"This painting competition," said Stephen. "Many entries?"

"One," said Manfred. "Mine."

"And the judging panel?"

"Me. Just me. No one else was interested. Do you like it?"

"Like is an interesting word," said Stephen. "There are many shades of 'like'. This is very interesting, Brother Bernard. Very, um, visceral."

Brother Bernard straightened up, his back audibly creaking.

"I wanted to add some nice little squirrels. You know, with nuts. But Father Manfred here –"

"Just 'brother', please," said Manfred.

"– said it wasn't accurate. Pah! I think the visitors coming down here to the education rooms and the library would like to see some little squirrels nibbling on their nuts. What do you think, Brother Trevor?"

"Stephen."

"Stephen."

"Library?" said Stephen.

"Yes," said Manfred. "We've moved the boxes into a room down there. The old room was too damp and entirely unsuitable, let me tell you. Ah!"

"What?" said Stephen.

Manfred gave Stephen a wide smile, creases multiplying in his much-lived-in face.

"We need a librarian," he said.

"Yes?"

"You said you were in lack of purpose and direction."

"Oh. I'm not sure if ..."

"And didn't you study classical languages at university, brother?"

"I'm a bit rusty though."

"So maybe relearning the ropes will occupy your mind, stop the sleepwalking, no?"

Stephen could only smile politely in the face of such reasoned argument. Manfred slapped him on the shoulder.

19

"Go. You take a look while I talk to Brother Bernard here about his jelly babies."

"Jelly babies?" said Bernard suspiciously.

Stephen walked down the sloping corridor, past walls containing pencil sketches that hinted at the terrors that were still awaiting the painting skills of the two elderly monks, until he found the new library. It was one of the recently discovered underground rooms and while some of the chambers further along were nothing more than stone-lined holes, unfit for human access until they had been secured and reinforced, this large low room had been transformed with plasterboard walls, wooden flooring and a splash of pastel paint into a very pleasant space.

Currently, large cardboard boxes, more than thirty of them, filled the room. There were no shelves yet, but Stephen could instantly see how a thoughtful librarian might lay out the monastery's books, both modern and ancient, to the best effect.

"Okay," he said, nodding to himself. "We could do this."

He opened the nearest box and carefully lifted out a copy of the magnificent *Ventum Inter Salices*, which he remembered from his university days. And, here, a slim volume of *Flabellis Ripam Fluminis*. And ...

"Oh, my goodness. *Quinquaginta Umbras Cinereo*. I thought this was banned."

Stephen was about to open that salacious book when a further tome caught his eye. It was either particularly well preserved or was not half the age of some of the other books. However, it was otherwise the epitome of a monastic codex. It was a foot tall, a hand's width deep and bound in red age-darkened leather. A fat clasp held it closed and, on its cover, within an embossed garland of flames, was the title: *Librum Magnum Daemonum*.

"The Big Book of Demons?"

Stephen actually knew a little of demonology and the occult. As a teenage lad, like every teenage lad since the dawn of time, he had developed a number of all-consuming obsessions. His passions shifted slowly but conscientiously from *Dungeons & Dragons*, to the horror novels of HP Lovecraft, to ancient history and, finally, to beer, pool and why girls didn't go for guys like him. Somewhere along the way, he and his then best mate, Darren, had become briefly but utterly devoted to the study of the occult. They knew their *Lesser Key of Solomon* from their *Necronomicon*, their *Petit Albert* from their *Arbatel de Magia Veterum* and, in all that time, he had never heard of the *Librum Magnum Daemonum*.

Stephen lifted the heavy book out of the box and set it down as carefully as he could on the top of another box. He reached tentatively for the clasp, remembering the mostly fictional accounts of sorcerers, spiritualists and general meddlers whose brains were fried and faces melted by gazing upon the contents of the *wrong book*. Mostly fictional ...

"Right," he said to the book. "If you so much as try to steal my soul or eat my face, I will hang you in the lavatorium and use you for toilet paper."

The book did nothing, which was both what Stephen wanted and expected. He undid the clasp and opened the book to a random page.

It was a hand-written work and clearly no more than one or two hundred years old. The narrow-ruled pages and black cursive writing suggested something more like a Victorian accounts ledger than a book of demonology, but a brief glance at the Latin script disabused him of that notion.

Stephen mentally girded his loins and read out loud with all the speed and fluency of a six year old discovering the works of Janet and John.

"The demon... Rut...spud. Okay, Rutspud. The demon, Rutspud, is seen as a soldier all in red with the horns of... *haedi*? ...oh, a young goat. He is a cruel demon, a torturer who delights in the work of his... hands. In his... *hortos*... garden!... are a thousand rooms and a thousand beds and in each there is a new and vile torture such that the inferno... Hell... will hold new surprises for all the damned, no matter how long their torments..."

Rutspud sauntered down to the Soul Allocation Office, the song in his heart having shifted for the time being into a melancholy minor key and with more reflective and thoughtful hand gestures. The demon at the counter spiked his chit and gazed up at the towering racks above them.

"*Potter, B*," he said, clicking his tongue as he searched.

Rutspud had heard that the filing system at Soul Allocation was so archaic and esoteric that there were souls who had been left dangling there for centuries. Perhaps for those with a fear of heights, that was Hell enough. Maybe this was one area that Lord Peter's census might clear up.

"Ah," said the clerk loudly, and began cranking the handle that rotated one of the many columns. "This is yours."

The demon dragged one of the damned off the lower peg and, with a practised motion, slung it over the counter to land at Rutspud's feet.

The damned soul struggled to its feet and inspected the scraped knees below its ragged smock.

"Potter, eh?" said Rutspud, snarling for the sake of effect, because first impressions counted even when you weren't feeling up to it.

"Yes," said Potter, meeting Rutspud's eye.

Rutspud frowned.

"Man?"

"Woman."

"Damn," said Rutspud. "I thought 'woman' and then talked myself out of it. Right, woman, this way. I've left my whip at home, so you'll just have to imagine it for the time being."

The damned woman followed Rutspud, not seemingly out of any sense of obedience or fear, but because there wasn't anything better to do.

"So, what's your major crime?" asked Rutspud.

"Anthropomorphic animals," said Potter.

"Say what?"

"I wrote stories with animals as the main characters."

"Uh-huh. With pictures?"

"Yes."

"Woah," said Rutspud, grinning despite himself. "They must have had a stickler on the judgement panel the day you came through. Did they accuse you of claiming to be God's equal? A would-be creator of life?"

"Yes, they did."

"Ha! I can see it now. So, what did they give you?"

"Twenty years in the Pit of Carnivorous Rodents."

"Yeah? How did that pan out?"

"I knitted them little waistcoats and taught them how to dance."

"Didn't they just rip up the waistcoats and eat you?"

"Yes. But I'm patient. Anyway, who are you?"

"I'm Rutspud."

Rutspud heard Potter stop abruptly. He turned. The expression on her face, previously a blend of indifference, resignation and arrogance, was now one of mounting fear.

"So, you've heard of me," he said.

Potter was shaking her head.

"No?" he said.

"I don't deserve this," she quavered. "I'm not that bad. I'm not ..."

"You made tailored outfits for the horrors of the pit," said Rutspud.

From some distant chamber there came a sudden cry of anguish and pain, a fulsome many-voiced chord of shrieks, wails and bellows. Potter shuddered.

"No ..."

"Your new home beckons," said Rutspud, snatching hold of her wrist and dragging her along.

The last few hundred yards to Rutspud's cave wound through a labyrinth of narrow passages. The walls of the maze were dotted with an eclectic array of torture implements, curved and spiked works of wood and iron, many of them dotted with the scraps of flesh of those who had not been careful enough as they squeezed by.

"I know your reputation," whimpered Potter. "Surely, I am beneath you."

"Flattery. Not had that before." Rutspud propelled her forward to a heavy gate. The hollers of the tortured were loud now, close.

"There must be some mistake," whimpered Potter.

"Dancing rats," replied Rutspud. "Get in."

He levered open the gate a foot and thrust Potter inside. The damned woman – it was a woman, wasn't it? He'd already forgotten – stumbled and fell to her knees in his hall of tortures. Trembling, she raised herself up and looked around what might be her home for the remainder of eternity.

This, Rutspud always felt, was his favourite bit. He just loved the looks on their faces.

Potter slowly took in the devices of metal and chain and leather, the bed of fire, the snooker table, the boiling pool and the damned souls contorted, stretched out or draped like dolls upon them. Her expression of horror froze, twisted, and almost broke her face in two as she processed what was in front of her.

"Er, you have a snooker table," she said, a tremor in her voice suggesting she expected it to transform into a baize-covered monstrosity at its very mention.

"Do we?" said Rutspud. "I hadn't noticed."

"And ..." She pointed. "That bubbling pot. Is that a jacuzzi?"

"It bears a passing resemblance, yes."

"And ... that's a running machine treadmill thingamajig, isn't it?"

"If you like."

"And ... a sunbed."

"Yes."

"So that really is a snooker table."

"Full size."

"And these are the terrors of your cave?"

"We also have a small library, a selection of popular board games, a small craft-making workshop, a fully-stocked bar and – excuse me – Tesla!"

The damned soul sitting at an organist's keyboard by the wall stopped playing and the piercing shrieks of torture ceased at once.

"Sorry," said Tesla.

"I shouldn't complain," said Rutspud to Potter. "I asked him to invent the scream-organ and invent it he did. Getting him to stop playing it is a job sometimes. Where was I?"

"I don't ..."

"You've landed on your feet, Potter."

"No, this is some trick, some ruse ..."

This drew a chuckle from the damned.

"You lot always say that when you first arrive," said Rutspud.

"But your job is to torture the damned," said Potter.

"Oh, you're one of those types, are you?"

"No. No. I mean, it's your calling isn't it?"

"Sure, but if I pretend to torture this lot and they pretend to suffer, it's a lot easier and everyone's happy."

"But I've seen inspectors," said Potter, "demons with clipboards. They observe the damned to ascertain if they're suffering or not."

"Which is where Bernhardt and Wilde come in. Every other Wednesday, they put us through our paces. Roleplaying. Method, a little Stanislavski. Really immersing ourselves in our roles so when the time comes, we can show them what real suffering looks like."

"What? But wait, there's no time in Hell. There are no Wednesdays."

"Of course there bloody are, if we say there are," said Boudicca, not breaking stride on the treadmill. "And Wailing Wednesday is right between Yoga Tuesday and Meat and Mead Thursday."

"Swear box," said Whitehouse from her armchair, pointing to a jam jar next to her knitting.

"'Bloody' is not a swear," said Boudicca, but hopped off the treadmill and put a flinty-looking coin in the jar nonetheless.

"Good lad," said Rutspud.

Boudicca growled at him.

"Good lass," he corrected himself.

"But," said Potter, flabbergasted, "this is amazing. An oasis of peace and mercy in this realm of infinite nightmares. A *good* demon. I would not have believed such a thing possible."

Every figure in the cave had become quite still and now stared at Potter and Rutspud. Nightingale paused in cleaning. Mama-Na let the punchbag swing free. Shipton dealt out no more cards. Cartland put down her book.

Rutspud took a deep breath. Potter was a newbie, and she had made the same mistake everyone made when they first arrived. He should go easy on her, but he had had a bad day. He had lost two friends who he would never be able to mourn.

He narrowed his eyes to two slits of utter malevolence. He did have very expressive eyes.

"I will say this to you once, Potter," he whispered. "This set up exists to serve me and me alone. Hell measures performance based on specific types of evidence not actual, genuine suffering. I work very hard to get the highest ratings and continually save my own hide."

He placed a hand on Potter's chest.

"If I could get better ratings by actually torturing you, I would. Don't delude yourself otherwise. But I've discovered that getting my clients to help me, to work with them, not against them, is the best way to get what I want."

"I understand," said Potter contritely. "It's worthwhile us all working together as a team, you might say."

Rutspud laughed grimly.

"Sure. A team. What is it they say? There's no 'I' in TEAM. But there is ME and there is the messed up MEAT. And you're the MEAT, okay?"

"Quite."

Rutspud slapped her on the shoulder.

"Good. Right. Mama-Na! Get this young man –"

"Nnn rar!" growled the damned Neanderthal.

"Sorry – woman a bunk. I'm off to –"

He was cut off by a shrill off-key alarm bell. The red warning light on the wall was also flashing.

"Tesla!" he shouted.

Tesla consulted a viewing tube.

"Demon approaching, Rutspud," he replied and took up on the scream-organ with gusto.

Rutspud gave everyone an appraising look.

"Ready for action stations," he said and slipped out.

The demon beyond the gate was one Rutspud had not met before, and yet there was something familiar about those huge flappy ears, those webbed feet, and those emaciated, fidgety fingers. Fingers he had seen recently, gripping his arm tightly.

"Oh," he said, sorrowfully. "Frogspear?"

The demon looked at him with blank eyes. They were Bootlick's eyes.

"Bootlick?"

Drool dribbled from the creature's wonky mouth.

"So, neither one nor the other," said Rutspud, regarding the hasty stitching and industrial stapling that held this creature together, joining Frogspear's leather hide with Bootlick's rubbery skin. "So, is it Bootspear now? Or Froglick?"

The demon didn't even twitch but simply stared through Rutspud.

"Did they even remember to put a brain in there? Frogboot? Lickspear?"

At this last, the patchwork demon blinked and focused on Rutspud.

"And hello to you," said Rutspud. "Lickspear, is it now? How are you feeling?"

"Seldom have I felt more mellow," said Lickspear and then looked up. "Hey nonny-nonny."

Rutspud shook his head at this travesty of his former friends.

"Why are you here?" he said.

"I must tell you why I'm here," said Lickspear with sudden urgency.

"Isn't that what I just said?"

"Look lively, Lord Peter is coming."

"Here?" coughed Rutspud. "You'd better come inside and explain this properly. Maybe a glass of something strong will help you pull yourself together."

"Pull all the bits together," nodded Lickspear. "Dig that. Might you, perchance, help me pick them up?"

Rutspud rolled his eyes and dragged Lickspear inside, gathering his ears, laughing stick, and appendix with his free hand.

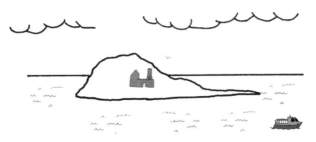

There was a loud cry from the corridor, which made Stephen jolt upright and lose his place in the book.

"He's vanished!" someone shouted.

Stephen stepped out into the corridor to find Brother Gillespie, the monastery's infirmarian, bent double, breathless, in front of Manfred.

"Who has vanished?" said Manfred.

The infirmarian, his handkerchief pressed against his enormous and constantly running nose, struggled to get his breath back to reply.

"The new abbot," he puffed. "I left him ... in his room and ..."

"He's run off again," said Stephen, approaching.

"No," said Brother Gillespie and sniffed back a gurgling stream of snot. "Window ... locked. I was outside the door the entire time."

"Impossible," said Stephen.

"So quick to limit the possibilities of God's creation," Manfred admonished him gently. He deftly tossed a bag of jelly babies he had borrowed from Brother Bernard from one hand to the other. "Lead on, Brother Gillespie. Show us this locked room mystery."

Brother Gillespie coughed and spluttered his way back up to the prior's house with Stephen and Manfred in his snotty wake. Stephen reflected on the unfortunate fact that he'd never seen the infirmarian in good health. While most of the time he thought it was an astonishingly bad advert for the monastery's healthcare, he could never shake the notion that Gillespie was hogging all the illnesses for himself and thus sparing everyone else.

"Here!" said Brother Gillespie, flinging wide the door to the abbot's bed chamber (a place that Manfred had never moved into during his temporary promotion).

Stephen and Manfred stepped into the room side by side. Here, the bed with barely rumpled sheets. Here, the rust-flowered mirror. Here, the damp spotted wash stand and the imposing walnut-veneered wardrobe. Here, the leaded windows that had been painted shut decades before and not opened since.

Stephen got down on hands and knees and looked under the bed.

"Chamber pot," he said.

"Well then," said Manfred, "we have a mystery such as might confound the famous Oberinspektor Derrick."

"Who?"

"But it is perhaps a mystery with only one solution."

Manfred stepped over to the wardrobe and rapped sharply on the door.

"Father Eustace?"

There was no reply from within. Manfred tried the handle. The door came open an inch and was then pulled shut from within.

"Not coming out!" snapped a muffled voice.

Manfred shrugged.

"So our abbot has retreated into his own private Narnia."

"What's wrong with him?" said Stephen.

"Shock, perhaps," said Brother Gillespie, who had been inspecting the contents of his hankie. "I checked him earlier. Blood pressure, heart rate and temperature; all fine. No sign of concussion or injury. In fact, if anything, the man's only issue was that he looked a little malnourished and underfed. My prescription would be a good hot meal or two. Plenty of fats, sugars and salts."

"Good," said Manfred. "Then all is well."

"What?" squeaked Stephen. "The man has shut himself inside a wardrobe!"

"Is he in any danger in there?"

Brother Gillespie sniffed and shook his head.

"I believe there's a pile of blankets in there. The abbot should be quite cosy."

"So, we're going to leave him there?"

"Yes. Come." Manfred moved to the door and then clicked his fingers at himself. "Almost forgot. I have for you the jelly babies, father. I'll leave them just outside the door."

Manfred deposited the paper bag on the stone floor in front of the wardrobe. Stephen, incredulous at the acting abbot's blasé attitude, followed the older men out of the door. As he left, there was a rustle and a slam and, when he looked back, the bag of sweets had gone and the wardrobe was making munching noises.

The eccentricity scale at St Cadfan's, always hovering in the upper reaches, had just risen a couple of notches.

Chapter 2 – The day the school party visited

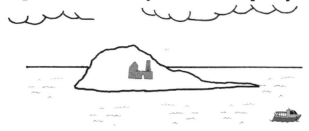

Stephen ripped the tape from the last box of books, feeling in that sound both a note of satisfaction and regret. Around him, glass-fronted shelves housed more than two hundred volumes, while five display cases held the finest works of illumination that the monks of St Cadfan's had produced in the last millennium. His library was almost complete, and it had taken far less time than he had feared. The constant rain of the last few weeks had helped, giving him little opportunity to go out and do much else (although muddy feet suggested that his sleeping mind had yet to receive that memo). It also provided a soundtrack of ceaseless patters, drips and trickles as it worked its way through the monastery stone.

A recent undertone to that background noise was the muttering of Brothers Huey and Bernard in the corridor outside. Their work on the visitor centre wall paintings had become more intense and more fraught as the date for their first scheduled visitors had approached. Nonetheless, Stephen was surprised when the corridor echoed with a shriek from Brother Bernard.

"Do that again and I'll do more than stamp on your bunions, you swine!"

Stephen was out the door in time to see Brother Huey spin his paintbrush in his hand like a flick knife.

"I'll snap your rotten spine before you do," growled the larger man.

"Brothers! Please!" called Manfred, approaching from the other direction.

Neither of the older monks was listening. Brother Huey stabbed violently, not at Brother Huey, but at his recent work on the wall. In return, Bernard slapped his heavier brush across Bernard's neighbouring work.

"Gah!" cried Bernard, smearing his hands over the still drying portions of Huey's artwork.

"Ark!" replied Huey, equally coherently, and pushed Bernard against the wall, rag-rolling Bernard's creations with the monk's considerable belly.

In the seconds it took Stephen and Manfred to run forward and separate them, a small tin of yellow gloss and a tube of red acrylic had been used as weapons, and the two artists looked like a pair of sweary Easter eggs.

"Enough!" said Brother Manfred sharply. "Come to your senses!"

Brother Huey huffed and shook himself from Stephen's grip.

"My apologies, brother."

Brother Bernard mumbled something wordless but vaguely contrite and tried to claw the paint from his bushy eyebrows.

"What in God's name came over you?" said Stephen, astonished more than upset.

"Ah," said Manfred and gestured to the wall, where the two monk's efforts of recent months had finally come together.

On the left, Brother Bernard had been working on a prehistoric scene in which yellow-eyed velociraptors stalked through a lush jungle while a feathered and scaly archaeopteryx glided overhead. Meanwhile, on the right, Brother Huey had been finishing off a representation of the fifth day of God's creation with a starburst of a hundred birds at its centre.

"Creation versus evolution?" said Stephen.

Manfred smiled.

"Well, gents. It's nice to see theological debate alive and well at St Cadfan's, however crudely it may be expressed."

Stephen contemplated the swirl of riotous colours in the borderland between the two pieces. Smears, spatters and violent splashes had created a dramatic inferno of expression, an explosion that reached outward towards dinosaurs and scriptural representation alike.

"It's quite good," he said cautiously.

"The act of creation itself," agreed Manfred.

"Is it?" said Brother Huey.

"It will certainly be a talking point," said Stephen.

Manfred clapped the artists on the shoulders.

"Nice work, gentlemen. Now, I must borrow Brother Stephen. We have a meeting in the chapter house to attend. You two can perhaps clean yourselves up. The boat will be arriving within the hour, bringing in our first visitors of the season."

"And my jelly babies?" said Brother Bernard.

Manfred nodded.

"I did ask Owen especially." He gazed at the artwork one last time. "Such passion, brothers."

Only when Brothers Manfred and Stephen were out of sight and earshot, did Huey turn to Bernard and grumble, "You still owe me a paintbrush for the one you stole."

"I told you," Bernard growled back, "this one is mine."

"Then you're a liar as well as a thief."

"Then why didn't you tell Brother Manfred?"

"I'd rather he thought ..."

"What? That we were arguing about creation? Who's the liar now?"

"Pah! You are an incorrigible old devil!"

"And you're not?" laughed Bernard coldly.

"At least I ..."

Huey stopped as something rolled under his foot.

"Is that your paintbrush?" said Bernard.

Huey sucked in his cheeks.

"Might be," he said, quietly.

"And this is Rutspud," said Scabass, maintaining the servile half-bow he had apparently adopted for the entire inspection.

"My lord," said Rutspud and threw himself on the floor, pulling the brainless Lickspear down beside him.

Lord Peter stepped over their prostrate bodies and into Rutspud's cave of tortures. Rutspud risked a glance up at them. Lord Peter's secretary, a fat man in a toga, with a laurel wreath of razor-blades on his head, passed his master a sheaf of notes. Lord Peter grunted and walked on.

Scabass dragged Rutspud to his feet.

"Everything is in order, isn't it, Rutspud?" he hissed.

"Of course, sir."

"His lordship seems pleased with the inspection so far and I hear there's a promotion coming up in Belphegor's offices."

"Really?"

"Really," Scabass snarled. "And if you screw up what little chance I have ..."

"Understood, sir," said Rutspud and scuttled inside with Lickspear, a hair's breadth ahead of Scabass's iron-spiked boots.

Lord Peter was gazing appraisingly at the Jacuzzi, where Boudicca and Mama-Na bobbed in the steam and froth, tears on their anguished cheeks.

"Unoriginal," said Lord Peter's secretary.

"Or classic?" suggested his master.

"Of course, lord," said the fat man, bobbing.

"I say, Demon," said Lord Peter.

"Yes, lord," said Rutspud, materialising at his side.

"This dial ..."

"Measures and controls the temperature, lord."

"Surely you keep it piping hot all the time?"

"No, lord. I've found that a smidgeon just above bearable is optimum. The unbearable is more unbearable if the bearable is just out of reach. Each person's threshold is different ..."

Lord Peter had already drifted over to the snooker table, recently converted into a rack. Bernhardt and Potter writhed, their torsos stretched beyond the capacity for screams.

"This green material they rest on. I find it somewhat unusual."

"Designed to encourage bedsores and keep wounds open as long as possible, lord," said Rutspud.

"And these holes around the perimeter?"

"To the drain the women's – I think they're women – the women's blood, lord."

Lord Peter strolled on, consulting the notes in his hands and only pausing to inspect Wilde (impaled on a giant spike) and Shipton (hung from the punchbag chain by her hair) and Cartland (hands wedged in workshop vices while imps ripped out her nails).

"This is not what I expected," said Lord Peter at last.

Lord Peter's human face – his healthy, handsome and carefree face – was a unique sight in Hell. And to see such a face in the greatest position of power was unnerving, like seeing a puppy with a rocket launcher. Rutspud could not read such a face.

"No, lord?" said Scabass, clearly as equally uncertain if this was a good thing or not.

"I hear of demons doing exemplary work and I expect to see bold new ideas and revolutionary thinking."

"I think the sixth circle is at the forefront of bold and revolutionary thinking, lord," wormed Scabass.

Lord Peter tapped the report in his hand.

"You've rated this demon's work as outstanding for the last three inspections. Climate for Suffering is rated as superb. Hope Management said to be flawless. The detail shown in this demon's Individual Torture Plans is extensive and yet he's also shown willingness to improvise if a torture session requires it. And yet ... there are no big ideas, only small improvements. I mean even this ..." Lord Peter gestured to Tesla who was twitching and groaning in the arcing light of his electric chair. "I've seen this kind of thing before."

Lord Peter casually stroked the keys of Tesla's scream-organ and an arpeggio of shrieks echoed through the chamber.

"What, pray tell, is this for?" asked Lord Peter, a frown on his face. "Artificially reproducing the cries of the damned, are we, demon?"

"Er, modelling, lord. How can the damned truly know what levels of agony they are to reach unless we show them?"

Lord Peter's inscrutable gaze lingered long on Rutspud.

"Nero, come," he said and walked out, his secretary in tow.

Rutspud looked warily to Scabass. Scabass was scratching his metal beard.

"So, was he happy with that or not?"

"I don't know, sir," said Rutspud honestly.

"If you've upset him, Rutspud ..."

Rutspud coughed and nudged his superior. The secretary, Nero, had returned.

Scabass smiled at the damned man.

"Yes?"

"His lordship wishes to see you both in his office at once."

"His office?" said Scabass. "In Pandemonium?"

"At once," said Nero firmly, and gestured for them to follow him.

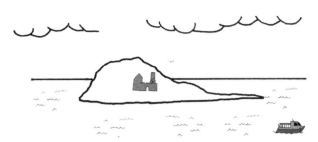

Brother Sebastian, monastery procurator and business manager, stood on the rocky shore as Owen the boatman tied up and lowered the gangplank. The seas had – Heavens be praised! – calmed enough to allow the crossing. Although the near ceaseless storms of the past months had passed, Bardsey had been treated to a symphonic suite of rain ever since. The current rains, dribbling down the clear plastic poncho Bastian wore over his habit, were a tolerable *andante*, slow and even. However, the dark clouds to the south west suggested a *fortissimo* finale might be imminent.

Two dozen little customers, swamped by their orange life vests, bumped around on deck. Customers? Bastian mentally chided himself. Guests. They were guests, he reminded himself (although, frankly, he should have been satisfied that his inner banker hadn't thought of them as 'marks').

The little blonde woman who led the party of *guests* ashore was not much taller than them. She stepped up to meet Bastian.

"Brother Sebastian?"

"Ms Well-Dunn," he said, shaking her hand. "Call me Bastian."

"Carol, please," giving him a smile of the kind to which he was rarely treated. "And these little angels – Jefri Rehemtulla! She does *not* want to sniff your seaweed! – are 4W from St Michael's Primary School."

Four taller women were methodically rounding up the eight- and nine-year old children and driving them up the beach, moving with the ponderous stoicism of world-weary riot police.

"I certainly am looking forward to today," said Carol.

"Well, you've come a long way. I hope you will find it value for money," said Bastian.

"Oh, payment!" said Carol and began to shuck off her rucksack.

"Later," Bastian assured her, although it was not easy for him to say. "Let's get on with the fun first."

Carol shrugged happily.

"My mother brought me here as a child. To see the birds, of course."

"Of course. Keen twitcher, are you?"

"Oh, I don't know. I'm not one of those mad people who stand in the elements for hours on end, binoculars at the ready, waiting to catch a glimpse of a bird that never appears."

Bastian looked at the gleam of excitement in her eye and the binoculars hanging around her neck.

"Of course you're not. Once you're all gathered together, if you want to follow the path to the monastery and we'll head up the hill to see what we can see."

Carol turned to her corralled class and her four assistants.

"Marion. Julie. Can you lead them up this way? Peroni Picken! What have I told you about twerking in public? Have some modesty!"

Bastian said hello to the children as they filed past. Their reply greetings were loud, false, and a shade too confident for Bastian's liking.

"Quite an outgoing bunch," Bastian said to Owen, as the stubble-cheeked boatman came up to meet him.

"A bunch of bloody tikes," said Owen.

"Is you being racist?" said one of the straggling schoolgirls.

Owen scowled at the girl. The woman bringing up the rear prodded her onward.

"Tough crossing?" Bastian asked Owen.

"Noisier than a flock of seagulls, that lot. And the same thieving mentality. I'm doing an inventory right now. If I'm missing a billhook or emergency flare, I'll let you know."

"Great."

"Oh, and I've half a mind to have a word with your fool abbot while I'm here. When I spoke to him in the pub the other month, I could tell he was getting impatient. He could have drowned, attempting the crossing in a rowing boat."

"We're just glad that he is alive and well."

"I suppose. Doesn't mean he's not an idiot."

"No. Although I'm sure he's going to bring some much-needed guidance and wisdom to St Cadfan's."

"Well, I wouldn't mind seeing him, anyway."

"Wouldn't we all."

"What?"

"Nothing."

It was, Manfred reflected sadly, the most hotly debated issue he had ever witnessed at one of the weekly monastic committee meetings. On one side of the long table was the conservative and cold-ridden Brother Gillespie and, sat across from him and pitted against him, the radical progressive, Brother Clement. The other monks, arranged around the sides of the long table in the chapter house, swayed in the tides of debate. Manfred could see that

Brothers Cecil, Roland and Vernon were clearly on Brother Gillespie's side, whereas Brothers Terry, Desmond, Henry and Lionel favoured Clement's viewpoint. Brother Willie's allegiances were less obvious, not least because the little old man's face was barely visible among the press of monks. Manfred, observing all from one end, stared up to the head of the table where Father Eustace sat, figuratively speaking.

"All I am saying," said Brother Gillespie, "is that one cannot tamper with tradition willy-nilly."

"But, brothers, we must recognise that times change and we must move on," countered Brother Clement. Brother Clement clicked rosary beads through his fingers as he spoke. They were like the ticking of his thoughts, rising and falling in tempo with his emotions.

"Change for change's sake," said Brother Gillespie with an emphatic nose blow.

Brother Henry gave a harrumph of support at this, although his attention remained firmly focussed on his book of Sudoku puzzles.

Brother Clement glowered, clicking a little faster on the prayer beads.

"Are you talking about what you want or what's good for this spiritual community?"

Brother Gillespie waved his hanky at Brother Clement. "Now, look here ..."

"And besides," said Brother Clement, "I think the change would bring an extra theological dimension to proceedings."

Manfred leaned forward. "Theological how exactly?" he asked.

"You see, it's the trinity, isn't it, dear brother?" said Brother Clement.

"Is it?"

"Yes." As St Cadfan's sacristan, Brother Clement was well-known for finding religious significance and meaning in the unlikeliest of places. "There's the three aspects: the chocolate, the nougat and the caramel and yet, at the same time, it's still one Mars Bar. As metaphors for God go, I think you'll agree it's quite elegant."

Manfred, despite himself, warmed to this argument.

"Very well," he said. "Perhaps it is worth making some compromise. We will, Brother Gillespie, continue to have Kit Kats at committee meetings, but also have a sample of fun-size Mars Bars."

"On a trial basis," insisted Brother Gillespie.

"How many Mars Bars?" asked Brother Clement.

Manfred closed his eyes.

"That is a matter to discuss another time, I think."

"Because they are only fun-size and exceedingly moreish."

"*I think*," said Manfred loudly, "we perhaps ought to move on from the matter of snacks to the items actually on the agenda."

'Agenda' was, Manfred knew, an entirely euphemistic term. His free-spirited ethos couldn't allow him to constrict his brothers to something as totalitarian and autocratic as a real pen and ink agenda. No, Manfred's agenda was an unwritten thought-cloud of intentions and wishes, more organic than a compost heap and probably about as helpful in the efficient running of the small island community. For all his liberal views, Manfred knew he had only himself to blame for the fact that an hour of meeting time had already been wasted in discussion over refreshments and for the fact that Brother Henry unashamedly did number puzzles throughout the entire thing and had turned up in his paisley pyjamas and terry towelling dressing-gown for the ninth week running.

"I am sure Father Eustace is keen to get to grips with the business of the monastery," said Manfred.

Everyone looked at the laptop positioned at the head of the table and the dark, blurry image on its screen. There was no movement on the screen or sound to be heard.

"It works, yes?" asked Manfred.

"I believe so," said Stephen. "Bastian fitted a new webcam in the wardrobe on Tuesday. I think the essential problem is that the interior of the abbot's wardrobe is quite dark."

"He has to come out at some point," said Brother Henry.

"Does he?" said Brother Clement. "There is, within the church, a grand tradition of ascetic hermits. St Simeon Stylites spent –"

"Thirty seven years sat on top of a pole," said Brother Henry. "We know. You've said. I don't think three weeks sat in the bottom of a wardrobe reaches the same level of profundity."

On the screen, a grey and grainy face lurched towards the camera.

"Bedpan!" shouted Father Eustace.

"Indeed," said Manfred, taking that as the cue to move on. "Now, as we enter a new chapter at St Cadfan's, with our new abbot installed, our refurbishments almost complete and our first visitors in months exploring the island as we speak, I wonder if we could consider a renewal of the social fabric of our monastery."

"Is this the team-building thing again?" said Brother Clement. "Pish and nonsense."

"I liked the abseiling we did last year," said Stephen.

"I believe Brother Sebastian suggested a poker night," said Brother Henry.

"I think letting Brother Sebastian organise a poker night would be the thin end of the wedge. Within the year, he'll have turned the monastery into a casino."

Stephen would have laughed, but he suspected Manfred was absolutely right.

"I was thinking perhaps group meditation," said Manfred. "Or some trust exercises."

"Why don't we simply have a good old pray together?" said Brother Clement, his beads clicking meaningfully. "We are monks after all."

Manfred sighed.

"I suppose. Father Abbot, do you have an opinion on this?" Manfred coughed loudly. "Father."

On the laptop screen, Father Eustace had an exploratory finger shoved firmly up his nose.

"We can see you, you know, father," said Manfred.

Father Eustace looked directly into camera and did a little facial shrug with his eyebrows.

"I don't think picking your nose is part of the ascetic hermitic tradition," said Brother Gillespie, giving his own dewy conk a thorough wiping.

"I'm sure Simeon Stylites's forefinger never invaded his nasal cavity," said Brother Clement.

"Thirty seven years without picking your nose?" said Stephen. "That's impressive."

"Filthy habit," yawned Brother Henry.

"At least he has one." Brother Clement glared pointedly at Brother Henry.

"Oh, a pun," said Brother Henry dryly. "For your information, I do own a habit. It's just that I'm equally comfortable in my dressing-gown. Habits. Dressing-gowns. They're essentially the same item."

"They are not," said Brother Clement, his clacking beads rising in tempo.

"As the weather improves," said Manfred, "we will be getting more visitors to the island. It would be nice if our personal appearance demonstrated a level of pride in St Cadfan's. The refurbishments to the building look amazing and so should we. I see the library is really coming together, Brother Trevor."

"Stephen," said Stephen. "I am very pleased with it. We have some wonderful books on display. Some very rare volumes and, actually, some I've never even heard of. I'm currently reading through the rather interesting *Librum Magnum Daemonum*."

Brother Gillespie coughed suddenly. Brother Gillespie coughed a lot, generally, but Stephen felt this was a *different* sort of cough, although he couldn't be sure why.

"Anyway," he continued slowly, "the whole area looks fantastic. The visitor centre is very impressive. We have artefacts on display and Brother Sebastian has installed computers and some big screens with links to the website so that physical visitors as well as internet browsers can see images from all the monastery's webcams."

"Not all of them, surely," said Brother Clement.

Stephen thought on it.

"The gardens, the cloisters, the church ... I think so."

"But not *all* of them?" said Brother Clement, pointing at the laptop screen on which a cross-eyed Father Eustace stared at something shapeless and moist on the tip of his finger.

"Oh," said Stephen.

"So can you smash bricks with your head?" asked the girl with the improbable name of Pixie Kaur.

"No." Bastian peered back down the island's one hill to check that everyone was still with them. A wending dragon of luminous green tabards stretched out behind him.

"Can you chop bits of wood with your hand?" continued Pixie. "You know, like, Hi-ya!"

"I've seen them do that," said Pixie's blonde friend, Araminta.

"I think you're confusing us with a different kind of monk, perhaps. Aren't you supposed to be looking for birds?"

Pixie held up one of the little camcorders that the teacher had distributed amongst the group. She panned it round for less than a second. "Nope. No birds."

"Keep looking," said Bastian.

Carol came scuttling up past the file of students to Bastian.

"Everything all right, Brother Sebastian?"

"Bastian, please. Yes. Well, I am a mite concerned about the weather."

The symphony of rain had continued unabashed all morning and, although they had yet to be subjected to a bombastic and torrential finale, the elements were subjecting them to a *largo* movement, slow perhaps but persistent, inescapable and soddening.

"Perhaps we need to make our way down for now," said Bastian.

"It is certainly getting a bit boggy underfoot," agreed Carol. "I did wonder about the state of the paths."

"Oh, they are well-worn but perfectly safe."

"Because if a child were to slip down the hill and tumble into the sea ..."

"Oh no, Ms Well-Dunn."

"... I could point out certain ideal candidates. You know, give them a nudge while I'm not looking. Then again, my name's on the trip paperwork, so best not. I think prison and losing my pension would be too high a price for bumping off Spartacus Wilson and company."

"My feet are wet and I'm cold," said the blonde girl.

43

Carol smiled at her.

"Araminta Dowling, is it my fault that you chose to come on this trip in leggings and strappy sandals?"

"Yes?"

"No. So, Brother Sebastian, lunch at the monastery then?" said Carol brightly. "I'll get this train turned around." And she marched back down the hill, shouting orders at her little charges.

On the way down to St Cadfan's, Pixie kept up her stream of questions, which at least partially distracted Bastian from the disappointment that the first organised school visit to St Cadfan's was not going as well as he imagined. On reflection, his rosy dreams of pleasant kiddy-winks, skipping straight out of the pages of Enid Blyton books, armed with rolls of banknotes to spend in the monastery gift shop, were probably unrealistic. Nonetheless, he had expected it to be better than this ...

"So, can you do that mind control thing?" asked Pixie.

"Sorry?" said Bastian.

"You know, 'these aren't the droids you're looking for'."

"I'm afraid I've no idea what you're on about."

"And, like, do you have a light saber?"

"A what? I'm sorry. We are a community of monks, men who have chosen to live together in the service of God."

The walls to the monastery gardens were less than a minute distant now but, for Bastian, they were too far away.

"Don't you like women?" asked Araminta.

"Of course we do," said Bastian.

"Have you got a wife?"

"No."

"A girlfriend?"

"No. We don't have wives or girlfriends."

"Are you, like, gay?" asked Pixie.

"No, I am not gay."

"Cos there's nothing wrong with being gay."

"I know that, Pixie," he said with forced calm. "I'm not gay."

"Ah," said Araminta suddenly. "You're one of them 'he-she's."

"A what?"

"A trannie," said Pixie. "Is that why you wear those dresses?"

"This is a habit," said Bastian, stooping slightly to pass through the archway in the garden wall. "It's a symbol of our role."

"Cos it looks like a dress."

"Or a big nightie," said Araminta. "Or a dressing-gown."

"It's not a dress or any kind of sleeping attire," said Bastian.

"That monk there's wearing slippers," said Pixie. "Are you lying to us?"

Bastian looked at the figure scurrying into the cloisters and contorted his weary face into something resembling a smile.

"No, girls. That's Brother Henry, and he *is* wearing a dressing-gown."

"Can *he* smash bricks with his head?"

"I don't know. Go ask him."

Technically speaking, Rutspud was not alive, not in any biological sense. And, in that respect, he had never lived or possessed such a thing as a life. But, in the absence of alternative vocabulary, Rutspud reckoned he had been 'alive' for something like ten thousand earth years, give or take a millennium. In that considerable time, he had seen much of Hell.

He had visited Hell's capital, Pandemonium, on a number of occasions, and stood in awe of its soaring towers, its unholy angles, and the delicious cosmic horror of a city constructed by mad architects with unhealthy imaginations. However, he had never previously stepped inside the Fortress of Nameless Dread, once the palace of Satan himself and, now, the heart of the new administration.

Rutspud, Scabass and Lord Peter's secretary rode up in the elevator together. It was fast and silent but for a faint metallic slicing sound, as though the lift itself were a giant guillotine blade, falling forever. The elevator bonged sourly as they reached their destination.

"Floor six-six-six," said Nero.

"Cute," said Rutspud.

"Shut your mouth," whispered Scabass. "Not a word from you."

Rutspud mimed zipping his mouth shut and immediately regretted it. It could, far too easily, be taken as a suggestion.

"If this thing goes badly for me," said Scabass, "I'm dragging you down with me."

Nero led them down a corridor of misaligned arches, the walls painted the reds and greys of an ulcerated intestine.

"This is the throne room of his former Satanic Majesty." Nero gestured casually to a pair of spiked double doors and a briefly glimpsed cathedral of fire beyond. "And this," he said, passing by the throne room to a frosted glass doorway further down the corridor, "is the Infernal Administrative Centre."

The glass doors slid open silently as they approached, and Nero ushered them into a space that was clean, too bright for Rutspud's liking and filled with the low-level hubbub of thousands of individuals doing their jobs and doing them well.

They walked through a vast conical chamber filled with desks topped with glowing screens at which damned souls sat with strange plastic earmuffs strapped to their heads.

"What is this place?" asked Scabass.

"Hell's call centre," said Nero. "Any invocations to Satan, demons or the powers of Hell come through here. Staffed entirely and perpetually by these damned individuals."

"What was their crime in life?" asked Scabass.

"They worked in call centres," shrugged Nero. "Through here."

A short way down a side corridor, Nero gestured at a row of plastic chairs.

"Wait here. You will be called for." Nero disappeared through a door.

With a lack of anything better to do, Rutspud and Scabass sat. The seats were too small for the ogreish Scabass, and his ferrous buttocks scraped the seat as he tried to get comfortable.

"For one of the damned, that Nero's an uppity creature."

"Are you going to put him in his place, sir?" said Rutspud.

"I think being Lord Peter's personal slave is punishment enough. Our lord is a cruel master. You see that?"

Scabass nodded towards a door beneath a sign that read, "Relaxation Centre."

"What is it?" said Rutspud.

"If Lord Peter hears of any demon who is struggling with his role, who finds his workload too tiresome and stressful to bear, they are made to spend time in there."

"This is Hell. How bad could it be?"

"Kittens. Lots of little fluffy kittens."

Rutspud shuddered.

"Have you ever seen a kitten?" said Scabass.

Rutspud nodded.

"Slugwrench and I found one once on the Plains of Leng. Horrible, horrible thing."

"It gets worse. You have to sit and stroke them until you are 'better'."

"The utter, utter bastard."

"And even worse still," said Scabass, "they make you listen to this thing called Enya."

"What is Enya?"

"Hope you never find out," said Scabass. "Our lord is a tyrant, such as Hell deserves, but his methods are sometimes beyond the pale. Listen."

"What?"

Scabass pinned Rutspud's lips together with his iron fingertips. Rutspud listened.

Through the wall behind them, he could just about hear Lord Peter and some demon in conversation.

"... went into that inspection utterly unprepared, Pumphog. I wanted detail in that overview."

"You told me you wanted me to make it concise," said the demon.

"That's right. Detail."

"Did you mean you wanted the document to be *precise*?"

"Precise. Concise. I needed details, Pumphog. I was made to look a fool."

"I'm sorry, lord."

"Are you?"

"Yes, sir," said Pumphog.

"And what do we do when we're sorry, Pumphog?" asked Lord Peter.

Rutspud strained his ears in the silence that followed.

"We seek forgiveness, don't we?" said Lord Peter.

"Please, lord," squeaked Pumphog.

"I think just one should do it, shouldn't it? Here."

As the demon began to next speak, Rutspud felt a sudden pressure in his ears, as though he had been plunged into unfathomable depths.

"Hail ... Mary, ... full ... of ... gra-!"

The was an explosive sound, simultaneously huge and silent, as though a ten megaton soap bubble had burst. It was like the smacking of God's lips. The painful pressure in Rutspud's ears vanished.

A door opened.

"Lord Peter will see you now," said Nero.

"Your mouth shut," said Scabass as they followed the secretary in. "Not a word."

Lord Peter's office was a large airy cube of a room. Behind Peter's desk, the entire wall was glass, with a balcony and the grand vista of Pandemonium beyond. A life-sized inverted crucifix hung on one wall. Next to the crucifix was a framed poster of a kitten dangling from a branch and the words, 'Hang in there'. The carpet beneath Rutspud's feet was made of some soft, shaggy fibre; totally nauseating to the touch.

Lord Peter glanced at some papers and brushed what appeared to be crumbs from its surface.

"Scabass. Rutspud," he said.

"Lord." The demons bowed deeply.

"I'll be brief and blunt," said Lord Peter. "The sixth circle is good and I do mean 'good'. There is room for development, but there is much to be praised."

"Thank you, lord," said Scabass, with obvious relief.

"And Rutspud's cave was the best of the best."

"Thank you, Lord," said Scabass.

"I *was* surprised by what I saw. I was expecting to see something bold and brash and new but, no, what I saw was the creative application of existing techniques."

"Thank you, Lord."

"Scabass, you are aware that, due to the, erm, departure of Lugtrout, a position of prominence has arisen in Infernal Innovation Programme."

"I am, my lord."

"I want some of the sixth circle's common sense applied to their crazy inventions."

"Of course, Lord," said Scabass, with a warmth and joy that Rutspud had never heard before.

"Very well. I am sure you will be able to find someone to take over Rutspud's duties."

Scabass's uncharacteristic warmth guttered and vanished.

"What?"

"Nero will take him there right now. Show his face around the place and such. But he can start as soon as is practicable."

Scabass glared down at Rutspud, a hundred questions and the pinpoints of fiery hatred in his eyes. Rutspud obediently remained silent. He did his best to look apologetic, although feared more than a little smugness might have crept into his very expressive eyes.

"Nero, Rutspud."

Lord Peter gestured to the door. Rutspud followed Lord Peter's secretary out into the corridor, himself followed by Scabass's throaty growl of fury.

"You seem tense, Scabass," he heard Lord Peter say.

"Lord?" said Scabass.

"Might I suggest that you're in need of some relaxation?"

Rutspud was sure he heard his now former boss say something about 'kittens' and then the door shut behind them.

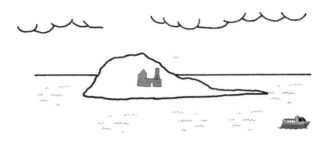

Bastian did his best to supervise the young students in the monastery visitor centre, although he might as well have tried to supervise the rain or the sea. In a confined space, the children had become a single, uncontrollable entity. Ostensibly given the task of using their camcorders to document the interior of the monastery, 4W seemed to have fallen to the ageless childhood activities of running, shouting and going about the earnest business of annoying each other and everyone around them.

Still, Bastian reflected, at least they were in out of the rain, which had now descended upon the monastery in force. St Cadfan's was a rather porous monastery and, unfortunately, the waters would by now be pooling on the floor of the almonry and other less secure parts of the monastery complex. The visitors' centre, being a more recent addition to the cellar rooms, was an unknown quantity and, although Bastian was ninety-nine percent – well, maybe eighty-percent – confident that the refurbished portions were watertight, he did worry that the as-yet untreated spaces further down the sloping corridor were quite possibly ankle-deep. Still, the children had been firmly instructed to stay away, and Bastian hoped that Carol Well-Dunn's stern voice and threats would hold the more curious in check.

While Bastian demonstrated the monastery's impressive website and on-line shop to a number of students, he could hear Carol and Manfred talking in the corridor. No doubt, Manfred was finding Carol's insights into the ornithological mural in the visitor centre refreshing, although after her twelfth detailed criticism of the paintings of the island's birds, Manfred had probably been 'refreshed' enough.

"I mean, it's lovely," she was saying, "but the kittiwake would never nest in such an exposed area. The wind would destroy the nest and the clutch of eggs."

"I see," said Manfred politely.

"Not that the kittiwake lays that many eggs at once."

"Is that so?" said Manfred.

"And what's this white bird with the yellow comb of feathers? Is that a real bird?"

"I found a picture of it in one of the library co–"

"Sparatacus! PJ! Jefri!" Carol suddenly yelled. "What did I just tell you? Up that end! There! Where I can see you!"

A hand tugged at Bastian's habit. Surprisingly, it wasn't Thor Lexworth-Hall, asking him for the umpteenth time if there was any food to be had.

"Is your monstarary haunted?" asked Pixie Kaur.

"Do you believe we live on after we die?" Bastian countered.

"Nah, I'm asking if you've got ghosts in the castle."

"Not that I'm aware of."

"I told you it was a man in a dungeon," said Araminta Dowling.

"What was?" asked Bastian.

"Cos I thought it was a ghost," said Pixie.

"What was?"

"Him," said Pixie and pointed at one of the large flat screens on the wall. Whereas the other screens displayed live images of the rain-sodden lawns, the silent apiaries and some soggy and miserable peacocks, this screen was taken up by the grey low-res image of Father Eustace, rocking back and forth in his wardrobe and seemingly singing to himself.

"Oh, my," said Bastian. "Yes, that's our, our abbot. He's on a sponsored sit-in."

"He looks like one of them mad people."

"All part of the act," Bastian assured her, without much conviction.

Stephen's plans to unpack and catalogue the final box of library books had been stymied somewhat by the arrival of a miniature film crew. Their mere sticky-fingered presence amongst his pristine glass cabinets and polished shelves was enough of a distraction. Then there was the bombardment of questions by a pre-teen video-journalist called Spartacus.

51

"Do you whip yourself?" he asked, holding a pencil as a pretend microphone while his cameraman, PJ, filmed.

"Whip?" said Stephen, standing over the *Librum Magnum Daemonum*, originally with the intention of reading some more, now just sheltering it from the dervishes of destruction.

"Or that thing where you stick nails in yourself?"

"Nails? What? Like mortifying of the flesh?"

"Yeah. I saw this film where this killer monk, real pasty he was, had all these pins and nails in his leg."

"No," said Stephen. "None of us are albino assassins ... yet!"

"Yeah, right," said Spartacus. "It's illegal to lie to children. We could sue you. What's that?"

Spartacus's pointing finger came perilously close to the Big Book of Demons.

"It's a very old book," said Stephen.

"Eoram inertia," Spartacus read out slowly. "What is that?"

"It's Latin," said Stephen.

"It sounds like Harry Potter words. Is it a magic book?"

Stephen sighed. "Well, sort of."

Spartacus looked at Stephen shrewdly. Stephen imagined that, given ten years and an extra two feet in height, that would be the look Spartacus would be giving men a second or two before smashing a pint glass in their faces.

"Are you wizards?"

"Why not?" Stephen muttered. "Yes, Spartacus. We're albino wizard assassin monks. You got me."

"Knew it," said PJ from behind his camcorder.

"Hey!" called a boy from the doorway. "Look what I've found!"

There was sufficient excitement in his voice to pull Spartacus and PJ away and out into the corridor without so much as a parting remark to Stephen. In fact, Stephen considered, that level of excitement probably indicated something forbidden, possibly dangerous, and, as a responsible man, he ought to follow them. But the peace and silence that they had left in the wake of their departure was too blissful to resist, and Stephen let them go. Out of sight, out of mind. Let them be someone else's problem.

"Now," he said, circling with his finger over the page to find his place. "Belphegor," he read, "prince of ... sloth seduces men by helping them make ... *ingeniosa* ... oh, ingenious devices to make them rich. His power is strongest in April. He tempts ... the foolish? ... into laziness and makes them fall asleep while they work. Monks – Ha! – are to beware his devices and ... *laqueum*? ... traps?"

The lift descended rapidly into the bowels of the Fortress of Nameless Dread. When it stopped, Rutspud imagined that he was probably several hundred storeys below what passed for ground level. The doors slid open.

The demon in the steam-powered wheelchair looked up from his notepad and peered at Rutspud through a pair of thick spectacles. Belphegor was uniformly purple in colour, apart from the grey whiskers that sprouted in clumps from his cheeks, brows and various warts upon his wrinkly, pot-bellied body. Hell's chief inventor and scientist had the essential appearance of a giant hairy raisin with arms and a head.

Rutspud bowed.

"Lord Belphegor, I am Rutpsud."

"I should hope so," croaked the ancient demon. "Otherwise one of us is in the wrong place. Lord Peter has informed me that you are to bring a breath of fresh air to my department."

"I am only here to serve, sir."

"I don't like suck-ups, Rutspud," said Belphegor. "Remember that. I prize honesty and intelligence. What do you think of this?"

He held up his notepad. A picture of a simple box with a button on top was surrounded by arcane symbols and scientific formulae.

"What is it, sir?" said Rutspud.

"My draft design for the despairatron. It causes the user to experience the sum total of all the suffering in Hell in real-time."

"That sounds terrible, sir."

"Thank you. Problem is, the despairatron is part of Hell's suffering matrix and, under the current design, that sum total of suffering includes the suffering inflicted by the despairatron itself. Hell's suffering plus Hell's suffering plus Hell's suffering ..."

"Positive feedback loop," nodded Rutspud.

"Quite. I'm not sure if it would simply deliver infinite suffering or blow up all creation. Still, there are ways to find out ... This way."

Belphegor pulled on one of the many levers on his wheelchair, and the contraption lurched sideways and down the smooth corridor. Rutspud followed, bathed in the miasma of fumes ejected by the machine's exhaust pipes.

"Does it run on coal, sir?" he asked.

"Shit," said Belphegor.

"Sorry?"

"This thing didn't start out as a wheelchair. I had set out to design a commode and just got carried away. What is it you think we do here?"

Belphegor had stopped at an opening where a gantry platform gave them a commanding view of a factory floor where forges roared, hammers beat sparks from metal sheets and a dozen machines pounded, moulded and welded.

"You make inventions," said Rutspud. "Machines."

"Why?"

"To make Hell a more efficient place. A better place."

"Wrong," cackled Belphegor.

"Sir?"

"We make Hell a lazier place. We invent things to do demons' jobs for them or to save the need for doing the job at all. Back when the old Boss first fell, there was nothing here but fire and darkness. Not even pitchforks. Each demon had nothing to rely on but his own strength, his own ... creativity. And now ... we exist in a Hell of devices and schemes and plans and a million and one targets and measures and assessments. The wheels of Hell grind ever faster, but the damned are still damned and Hell is still Hell. I am a duke of Hell, lord of sloth and, thanks to me, laziness abounds."

"I like lazy," said Rutspud.

Belphegor guffawed and slapped Rutspud on the back.

"Then you'll fit right in. Come." Belphegor trundled on down the corridor. "The Infernal Innovation Programme is your basic R&D set up, with three main work units. The three Ps, I call them: Places, Personnel and Particulars."

Belphegor trundled through a pair of swing doors into an office of draughtsman's desks, cardboard models and surveying equipment.

"Places," said Belphegor. "These guys handle the architecture."

"I thought Mulciber was architect of Hell, sir," said Rutspud.

"Sure, the big showy stuff. The looming towers. The castles of horrors. This place, though, does everything from city planning to centres of torturing excellence. Over there, that's Dante and Doré – words and pictures, I call 'em. They dream up all the really good stuff. Those guys gave us our nine circles of Hell, you know."

"Yes sir, I know!" Rutspud made a mental note to have a 'word' with Dante later.

Belphegor laughed, something wet and phlegmy rolling in the back of his throat.

"I know what you're thinking. How can the nine circles have existed in Hell before Dante there came up with them? Time is not as simple as that, Rutspud. Heck, there is no time in Hell. They invented the nine circles and 'voila!' – that's French for 'what the fuck is that?' by the way – there have always been nine circles."

"I see," said Rutspud, not seeing at all.

"Time is an imprecise thing, but we can't say the same thing about space. Like Heaven, Hell is of a fixed size and there's nothing we can do about that. The real challenge for these people is doing more with less. I tell you, we were lost until this guy came along."

Belphegor screeched to a halt in the midst of a work unit, where a thin fellow with beard and glasses busied over a clay and paper model construction he was working on. Rutspud looked at the designs hanging on fixtures and fittings all around. Black demons tessellated with white angels. Lizard creatures twisted and turned upon themselves. Castles in the air turned through impossible dimensions, turning up into down and making Rutspud's eyes water.

"What's this one, Escher?" said Belphegor.

"A Klein Bottle Hell," said the damned soul.

"I really don't know what he talks about half the time," Belphegor chuckled to Rutspud.

"Topographically, the inside of the structure is also the outside," the man patiently explained. "If the inmate tries to escape, they will only find themselves deeper inside."

"Escher here actually came to us on secondment from Heaven, but he then got himself into a bit of trouble," said Belphegor.

"Really?" asked Rutspud.

"I lost a staircase," said Escher.

"And so he's with us until he finds it," said Belphegor.

"And it's just a staircase?" said Rutspud.

"Not quite," said Escher.

"What's this one?" asked Rutspud.

He pointed at a complex sketch hanging on a wall. Images of a human and a demon, locked in a maze of twisting, illogical turns. Rutspud followed it with his finger.

"So, the person comes in here ... and then the demon tortures them here ... the person moves on and ... hey!"

"How about that?" said Belphegor. "The human transformed into their own demon of torture. The malleability of time working in our favour there. We're still looking forward to the arrival of the mortal who invented that one! Humans torturing themselves is our ultimate goal, speaking of which ..." Belphegor thrust his wheelchair forward through further swing doors.

"So if you do find that staircase, let me know," said Escher.

"And how will I know it when I see it?"

"Oh. You'll know it."

"Okay," Rutspud shrugged gamely and hurried to catch up with Belphegor.

He found himself in an office in which filing cabinets stretched hundreds of feet into the air. At a bank of central desks and on innumerable portable steps, seemingly identical, bespectacled men worked on manila files, checking, making notes and re-filing.

"The Jean-Paul Sartre Dating Agency," said Belphegor. "Working on the creed that 'Hell is other people', the Personnel unit pairs inmates to create that perfect match of utter hatred and horror. Some of the stuff is easy. Put a dozen racists of different ethnicities in a single pit and you've already got a thousand years of hilarious self-torture. Aloof intellectuals with football hooligans, communists with fascists, unrepentant gluttons with dieticians. Homoeopathists with Nazi scientists, that's one of my favourites. But JP truly excels in the field of finding those small, unobvious details that will truly set damned against damned without them ever knowing why they hate each other."

"And which one's Sartre, sir?" said Rutspud looking around.

"All of them," said Belphegor. "He's been paired up with a hundred versions of himself. Delicious stuff. Onward!"

Via the next set of doors, they entered a space that seemed to house a handful of incompatible features. To Rutspud's eyes, it appeared that a sadomasochist had set up shop in a carpenter's workshop, only then to be interrupted by a bloody war between a medieval army and every living creature in creation. Blades and blood, leather and chains, fur and feathers, sawdust and spikes all conspired to create a scene of thorough chaos. In the midst of it, two men pottered about, lost in their own work.

"Here's the office of Particulars," said Belphegor. "I know, I know, it may not look like much, but some of Hell's best ideas are produced here. You must know this chap."

Rutspud squinted at the man in a dark, blood-spattered tunic.

"Is that Bosch?"

"The very same."

"I think he designed some of my old colleagues."

"That'd be work colleagues with weird animal heads and a penchant for either eating people or sticking things up their arses, I should imagine."

"Sometimes both at the same time," Rutspud nodded.

"There's not much variation in his work," said Belphegor, "but, by Satan's balls, it's effective stuff."

"And who might that tweedy one humming to himself be, sir?"

"Lewis. Relatively new addition. We had truly high hopes for him, but he's had a lot of trouble adjusting."

"What's he making?"

"A wardrobe. That's all he does. He makes wardrobes. I don't know, we might have to give up on him."

"He looks utterly exhausted, sir."

"Yes, that will be his bedmate."

"Sir?"

"We've got him sharing a room with Clarence. Big male African lion. We thought it would make him happy ..."

A gagged and bound figure on a nearby torture rack groaned.

"No, Torquemada, I haven't forgotten about you," said Belphegor fondly. "Torquemada here is our crash test dummy. Nothing gets rolled out until it's been tried out on him. It's a small role but he's happy to contribute."

The ravaged and scarred man groaned wordlessly once more.

Belphegor spun his wheelchair round to face Rutspud.

"And that's it. Not all of it, but you get the gist. What do you think?"

"What do I think, sir? I think it's amazing. But ... but what would you want me to do?"

"Make sense of it all," said Belphegor. "These guys are ideas men. Recursive Hells and animal-headed demons are all great, but how should they be used? I gather your gift is the application of inventions to maximise personal laziness."

"It is," said Rutspud honestly.

"Then apply these inventions to the real problems in Hell. And maybe we can help make things easier for your lot in the sixth circle."

"Actually, sir," said Rutspud, "there is one issue I have with my own team of damned souls."

"Oh?"

"It's embarrassing, really. It's just ... I can't seem to tell which of them are men and which are women. As a demon, I've never really had much of a clue about this whole gender thing."

Belphegor gave him a haughty look.

"Do you need to know what sex they are?"

"Personal touch, sir. It's important."

"But, you know, obviously, that the female ones have ..." Belphegor mimed holding a pair of jiggling breasts.

"Well, yes. But some of them are hardly obvious and some of the men ... Well, look at Bosch."

Rutspud pointed at the Dutchman and his sagging fatty chest.

"Ah," said Belphegor. "Some boob versus moob confusion. Rutspud, I understand. I'll put our best minds onto it. In the meantime, let me show you something you'll like. It's a recent addition to our department."

"Sir?"

"I call it the creativity hub."

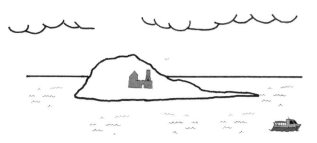

Spartacus Wilson had been looking forward to the school trip to Bardsey all term long. Naturally, he had absolutely no interest in bird-watching or going to some smelly Welsh island, but that wasn't what this school trip was about. School trips were never about the place you were going. School trips were about being on a coach with your mates, scoffing your packed lunch on the way there, and trying to cadge the better stuff off the spoilt kids. And then, at the end of the day, they were about spending all your pocket money on more sweets or some pointless tat, stuffing your face again on the way home, and waiting to see who would throw up over the kid next to them.

However, Jefri's discovery of three monks' habits could possibly have been the highlight of the entire day. Dressed up, with a coerced Thor Lexworth-Hall behind the camera, Spartacus, Jefri and PJ had already recorded a number of startling short films. *Kung Fu Monks* had been fun. *Wizard Mind Melt* had been mildly entertaining. And the discovery of some yet-to-be-installed roller blinds had made *Jedi Light Saber Massacre* a possibility. But now they had drifted down the corridor to the unrepaired and wonderfully dangerous looking end for what Spartacus had decided would be *Haunted Dungeon of Horrors*.

Miss Well-Dunn and the Learning Support Assistants were all busy elsewhere, and there was no one to complain about four boys, three of them almost swamped by oversized habits, ducking under the warning tape and into the old cellar. Around them, the fresh new plaster and paint gave way to ancient round-edge stone. The stone ceiling sagged above them and the floor beneath their feet was damp and potholed.

"We shouldn't be down here," said Thor.

"That's the point, monghead," said PJ, pressing on into the damp gloom. "It's forbidden."

"*The Haunted Dungeon of Forbidden Horrors*," said Spartacus. "Okay, first scene. Brother Thunderpants – that's you, Jefri – decides to see what's behind the forbidden door."

"What forbidden door?" said Jefri.

"That one," said Spartacus.

It was the only whole and complete door they had come across in the corridor. It was like a little church door, only a little church door that hadn't been cleaned in, like, a million years. Its surface glistened wetly, as though it were sweating.

"And ... action!"

Spartacus and PJ stood behind the camera with Thor, sniggering as Jefri stepped forward, raising his feet high to avoid tripping over his habit.

"It's really wet down here," he said.

"That's part of the forbidden horror," said Spartacus, and PJ made ghostly wailing sounds.

Jefri reached for the door handle.

"There's water coming out from under the door."

"That's ectoplasm," said Spartacus.

"What's that?" said Thor.

"Ghost puke. Go on, Jefri."

Jefri turned the handle and pulled. The door shifted half an inch. The trickle of water under the door was now a constant flow.

Jefri frowned and managed to say, "Er," before the door was thrust open from the inside and there was no more time for words.

Later, Bastian would not have been able to say if he was first alerted by the sound of screams or the sound of several thousand gallons of glutinous mud and rainwater emptying at once into the unrefurbished cellars. In truth, he was already out into the corridor and running before he consciously understood what was happening.

He collided with Stephen coming out of the library and, together, they ran down the slope to where it appeared that a sea of oxtail soup had decided to make an entrance. In the vile mire, more than a dozen figures bobbed and span. Coated inside a layer of sludge, it was hard to make out who or what the figures were, but Bastian grabbed the nearest screaming face and hauled its owner up the corridor to dryer ground.

Stephen had plunged in after the others and was already waist deep in the muck. He had a young man in his arms who seemed more intent on holding his camcorder aloft, out of the slime, than his head.

"Got it," the little boy panted once he was above the surface.

Bastian made to run back in a second time. He was overtaken by a grey-haired blur with a helmet on his head and a length of climbing rope around his waist. Brother Manfred, whose abseiling clobber clearly doubled as potholing rescue gear, dived in head first and vanished from sight but for his rope disappearing length by length into the muck.

"How many more are there?" Stephen demanded of the podgy camera-boy.

"F-four of us," the little boy coughed.

Four? thought Bastian, back in the soup. But there are dozens of them...

Bastian grabbed the nearest. The figure rolled over. Its empty eyesockets stared back at it him. The skull's death's head grin seemed to enjoy the look of shock on Bastian's face.

Bastian made a gargling sound of fright and stared at the bobbling corpses in the water. Dozens of them.

Later, when reflecting on those moments, Bastian realised that his first thought, once his mind had returned to sanity, was of the financial impact of the school trip being gate-crashed by a party of stiffs. Part of him would feel a deep-rooted shame at this. A more deep-rooted part of him was secretly proud of his pragmatism and foresight.

"Pull!" cried a voice from the dark.

The rope stiffened. Up the corridor, Brothers Huey and Bernard, aided by the burliest of Carol Well-Dunn's helpers, were hauling on Brother Manfred's line. Slipping and sliding in the gloop, Bastian got to a position where he and Stephen could also help. Tug by tug, they drew Manfred in until the Abominable Mud Man that was their prior stood before them, a tiny habit-wearing boy in each arm.

The two boys were grinning from ear to ear.

Within the hour, the four boys and the three muddy monks were washed, dried and sitting in fresh habits in the visitors' centre with Carol Well-Dunn. Manfred had brothers Huey and Bernard take the rest of the school party to the church to do brass rubbings and be treated to one of Brother Clements lengthy, although surprisingly engaging, talks about the figures represented in the stained-glass windows.

Meanwhile, the four boys had been given hot chocolate to help with the supposed shock, although the four of them seemed to be buzzing with excitement rather than cowering in terror. Two of them were playing on one of the computers, the ordeal seemingly forgotten.

Maybe the short attention spans of modern youth had their advantages, thought Bastian.

He drew Carol aside.

"I hope you understand ..." he said.

"In all honesty, Brother Sebastian ..." said Carol at the same time.

"... this is bad press for us ..."

"... people have lost their jobs over less ..."

"... and I'm not advocating lying ..."

"... I'm just being practical ..."

"I won't tell anyone, if you won't," they both said simultaneously.

They stared at one another for a long second and then smiled.

"So glad we are in accord," said Bastian.

"Me too," she said. "Now, I would like to talk to Brother Manfred a little further about the 'creative' representations in this delightful mural."

"Of course," said Manfred, who was still combing his drying curls. "For you, anything."

Bastian joined Stephen, who was perched on the edge of the computer desks and liberally feeding the boys some of the jelly babies that Owen the boatman had brought over that morning.

"The boys seem very happy right now," said Stephen.

"And are we okay?" Bastian asked.

Stephen nodded.

"As team-building exercises go, that was one of the best. Although I dread to think what I swallowed while I was in there."

"I think we're both going to need some medical advice."

"Are we going to have to call the police too?"

Bastian had no idea.

"There's a whole heap of questions to be answered here. An old room stuffed full of ... well, you know. How long have they been down there? Impossible to say."

"I found a severed hand once," said Spartacus Wilson, looking up with a hot chocolate moustache on his top lip.

"Pardon?" said Stephen.

"A hand. It was in the flowerbeds in the park."

"Really?" said Bastian. "And what happened?"

"We had a great time together but, in the end, it ran away."

"Sorry?"

"I was really cut up about it and mum said I should have therapy, but her boyfriend said he wasn't going to pay for it."

Bastian looked at the boy.

"I have no idea how to respond to that," he admitted. "Still, all's well that ends well. We just need to keep mum about this whole business, generally carry out some damage limitation and we can continue as normal."

"Done," said Thor. "Uploaded."

Stephen looked at the boy's computer screen.

"Oh."

"What?" said Bastian.

"You'd best take a look at this."

There was much to like about Belphegor's creativity hub. The pus-filled beanbags were really comfy, the lava plunge pools even more so. The ambient sounds of low-level torment provided the ideal background for personal thought and reflection. But, in Rutspud's opinion, the absolute revelation was this nebulous thing called 'internet'. It was a human construction, although directly accessible from Hell, and seemed to present an almost infinite array of text, image and sound. The internet might have been a human invention, but the tablet he viewed it on was one of Hell's own designs, as was the Windows Vista operating system and the Internet Explorer by which the internet was made visible.

Rutspud was a quick learner and, after very little instruction from one of the damned (who was to be locked in purgatory until he had read the entire internet), he was 'surfing' the 'web'.

Much of the internet seemed to be filled with cats (which Rutspud found terrifying) and naked people (which Rutspud found dull), but there was much to be enjoyed. Online shopping looked inviting, although neither Amazon nor IKEA seemed to deliver to Hell. Online casinos looked more interesting, except the websites required something called a credit card number which Rutspud did not possess. Video sharing websites were perhaps less engaging but, requiring neither an address nor financial details, were at least something Rutspud could make full use of.

Pop videos of semi-clad women were uninteresting. Videos of people getting smacked in the face in slow motion were hilarious. Videos of cats failing to jump over things and hurting themselves were creepy, but morally satisfying. Fun though it all was, Rutspud could feel Hell's non-time whizzing by, with himself no closer to coming up with ideas to impress Belphegor.

And then, after watching the amusing if bizarre *Midget Monks v The Pit of Mud Zombies* (posted by ThorLexiH), Rutspud clicked on an accompanying link.

"Bingo!" he declared.

He dragged his feet out of the volcanic foot spa, squirmed out of his cosy pus-bag and scampered back through to the chaotic workshop of Particulars.

"I've got it, sir," he said.

Belphegor raised his hairy eyebrows in query. The steam-powered commode puttered to itself.

"Got what, Rutspud?"

"I was watching this weird webcam of a man stuck in a wardrobe and it occurred to me... On Earth, they have these things called furniture shops."

"Yes?"

"Some of them are gargantuan, sir, selling aisle after aisle after aisle of flat pack beds and cabinets and wardrobes – yes, wardrobes – all with silly made up names like Bilköi and Rønti. And, and these are scary places to a lot of men – I think it's men. The ones with the hairy faces."

"Men," agreed Belphegor, "well, mostly."

"They're terrifying places. So large and yet so, so boring. And you can never find the exit. Let's do that."

"Open a boring furniture shop?"

"Not just that, sir," grinned Rutspud, his expressive eyes wide with excitement. "We take some of Lewis' wardrobes, open them up and, using Escher's mad geometry, make them like doorways into, I don't know, alternative worlds but – and here's the best part, sir – every world the damned go to will be *another furniture shop*."

"An inescapable and infinite maze of inescapable and infinite furniture shops," mused Belphegor, nodding. "That could work."

"Thank you, sir."

"So, when can you start, lad?"

Rutspud's eyes widened even further. He had big eyes and the capacity for some real bug-eyed widening.

"Seriously, sir? Thank you, sir. I can start whenever you like."

"Very well. Take some time to tie up your affairs in the sixth circle. We'll see you again when you're ready to start. Oh, and a couple of the boys came up with a fix for your personal problem."

"Really? Excellent."

Bosch passed Rutspud a cardboard box. Rutspud peeked at the contents.

"Oh."

It was a fair trek back to his cave of tortures in the sixth circle, and Rutspud had time aplenty to reflect on the great opportunity that had just been laid before him. Sure, he thought as he weaved his way through the narrow passages leading to his cavern, he wouldn't be in the beautiful sixth circle anymore, but the opportunity to be creative, useful and at least some distance from the ridiculous targets and measures he currently laboured under would be very welcome.

There was no sound from the scream-organ as he entered. Inside, everything was exactly as he left it. Wilde was still impaled on his spear. Potter and Bernhardt were still stretched out on the rack. Cartland was still having her nails ripped out on the vice.

Rutspud frowned.

"What are you all doing? The inspection's over."

"And break!" said Bernhardt loudly and with more than a smidgeon of anger.

Boudicca and Mama-Na climbed out of the Jacuzzi. Tesla stepped out of his Faraday cage of sparking electricity. Whitehouse peeled the fake sores from her face. Cartland unwound the vice and began collecting her false nails from the bench.

"I mean, this is excellent commitment guys," said Rutspud, "but, seriously, how long –"

"You just left!" said Bernhardt hotly. "We didn't know who was coming back or when. We were too scared to stop."

"But ... but ..."

Shipton unclipped the harness that connected her to the chains.

"Thou art a forgetful dæmon and a poor master t't' people in thy care."

"But didn't Lickspear sort things out once I was gone?"

"No," said Cartland. "That sodding moron –"

"Swear box," said Whitehouse.

"That sodding, badly-stitched moron lost one of his kidneys and went off to look for it."

"Found it, pops!" said Lickspear, entering the cave.

"No, Lickspear," said Rutspud. "That's a spider."

"Alas, surely not?"

"Pretty sure."

"You've never let us down like this before," said Bernhardt.

"Nnr anng!" said Mama-Na

"Swear box!" said Whitehouse.

"You lot are forgetting your place," said Rutspud darkly, drawing himself up to his full height, which wasn't really all that high. "If it wasn't for me, you would spend your time in torment."

"You think we enjoyed this?" said Potter.

Rutspud could see the pale tracks of dried tears on Potter's face.

"Don't test me," he said, although his heart wasn't in it. "You are the MEAT in my TEAM and that's all you are."

"We understand," said Tesla emptily. "I suppose we have some tidying up to do. Come on."

"Wait," said Rutspud. "Wait, please. I didn't want it to be like this. I've come with good news."

"This is Hell, there's never any good news," said Boudicca.

"I've got a promotion!"

Rutspud waited for the smiles and the cheers and the confetti, but there were none.

"What do you mean?" said Bernhardt.

"I've been asked to work for Belphegor."

"You're leaving us!" said Cartland. "And who will care for us? Who will take over here?"

"Oh, it's all about you, isn't it?" Rutspud sneered. "Lickspear can take over."

"Saints preserve us," said Wilde.

"I'll find some extra brains for him or something. It will be fine."

"This my kidney?" asked Lickspear.

"No, that's a spider. The same spider."

Cartland stepped forward.

"You are our lord, our ... owner. We are utterly in your power. But I think I speak for everyone when I say that is not good news. Not for us."

"Okay, okay. Tough crowd. Fine. Extra bit of good news. Belphegor gave me a solution to my gender-blindness problem. No more getting it wrong."

"Is that so?"

Rutspud grinned and opened the cardboard box.

"Now, Cartland. Man or woman?"

"Woman," she said, gesturing to her curves and her pink rags.

Rutspud slapped a sticker on her breast. It read, "Hi, I'm a woman."

"Done," said Rutspud. "Right. Who's next?"

Chapter 3 – The day Rutspud found the stairs

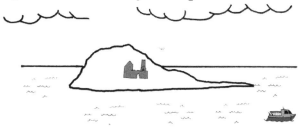

Stephen found Huey mopping up muddy footprints in the visitors' centre.

"Sleepwalking again," said Huey, with a curmudgeonly grunt. "I think you cover more ground at night than you do during the day. Then again –" He stretched and waggled his toes, sending a waft of foetid leather stink Stephen's way. "– if I wasn't cursed with every foot ailment under the sun, maybe my feet would take me off on some night-time perambulations."

Stephen looked down at the twelve polythene wrapped corpses laid out on the floor. The visitors' centre was currently in use as a makeshift morgue for the twelve bodies that had emerged during the school visit, although it might have been more accurate to describe the fleshless things as skeletons rather than bodies.

It troubled Stephen to see that he'd been walking amongst them. Why had his sleeping mind brought him here? He hoped that Brother Huey would hurry up with the mop before Manfred saw the mud. There had been some strong words used by the coroner's office about Manfred's devotion to cleanliness after he'd mentioned that he'd run the bones through the dishwasher to remove the worst of the mud.

The forensic osteoarchaeologist had determined that the skeletons were centuries old, while Bastian was still attempting to write her title onto a name badge for the visit. She had stood up from her examination and told the monks that they were free to deal with the remains in the way that they felt most appropriate.

"It's unlikely that they pose any risk to you, although it's difficult to be certain without being able to examine whatever soft tissue may have been present," she'd said, with a sideways glance at Manfred. "If I were you, I'd get them reburied as soon as it's practical and convenient. I've got some colleagues from Bangor University who'd be interested to come and take a look in the meantime, and more than one particularly enthusiastic amateur who called our office. You're not obliged to entertain any of them, of course, but the PhD students do like access to any new specimens."

The monks had welcomed the various visitors who had examined, measured and photographed the bones over the past few days. Among the visitors was local Arthurian nut, Ewan Thomas, who took all and any evidence to conclude that these were the bones of King Arthur's knights, even citing the cleanliness of the bones as a symbol of their virtuous nature. But, eventually, the visitors left and all was quiet.

"Where's Bernard?" asked Stephen.

"Pfff. Lazy oaf's having a lie-in," said Huey. "I gave him a shout, but he was out cold. Is it true they might have been plague victims?"

"What?"

"The skeletons."

"Where on earth did you get that idea?" asked Stephen.

"Those students were talking," said Huey. "The ones from Bangor. They said that there might have been bits of ... body that went down the drain in the dishwasher. They said that there might be smallpox, anthrax, plague or anything."

"Bastian made sure Manfred cleaned the dishwasher out with bleach afterwards."

"But it makes sense with them all being jumbled together like that. It must have been a plague pit, surely?"

"That's a bit far-fetched," said Stephen. "But I've been planning to have a good look through the old records in the library, see if I can find any clues about the bodies. I'm sure there'd be some record if the Black Death ever came to Bardsey. In the meantime, maybe we should be careful about starting rumours."

Huey pursed his lips and mopped on with the expression of someone who had decided how things were and wasn't about to change his mind.

Bastian sighed and beckoned to Manfred as he entered the room.

"It's had three million views," said Bastian, pointing at the screen. "Three million! If I refresh the website, you'll see the count going up."

"We're talking about the YouTube video made by our young visitors?" asked Manfred.

"*Midget Monks v The Pit of Mud Zombies*, what else?" said Bastian. "You should see some of the comments. The ones that are coherent, that is."

Manfred leaned over his shoulder to read.

"*Check out the div in the helmet at 8:34.* Oh, that's me! Do you think I should say hello?"

"No, definitely not! Never mind that. Look at all this discussion about plague pits!" said Bastian. "We'll never shake off this sort of damage. We need an emergency plan for putting the lid on all this somehow."

"That's a bit dramatic, Bastian."

"You know that the television networks are picking up this story now?"

Manfred stared at the screen, deep in thought.

"They do say that there's no such thing as bad publicity," he said. "I think we could work with this, make it into something positive."

"This I have to hear," said Bastian. "A positive spin on a plague pit? I'm all ears."

"Forget the plague pit," said Manfred. "As long as nobody dies, that will soon be forgotten. But those bones are lovely and clean now. No, what I was thinking about was an ossuary."

"An ossuary?"

"An ossuary. There's that lovely one in Rome."

"The Capuchin Crypt."

"And the catacombs in Paris. They have all the different bones arranged ornamentally," said Manfred, leaning across to open up another browser window on Bastian's computer. "Take a look at the way they have worked so effectively with the medium to show a powerful yet still reverential image."

He clicked through some images, and stopped on one that he jabbed at with a finger.

"This skeleton here represents justice, reminding people that they are all alive for just a short while, and they will all be judged by God when they die. See the scales he's holding, all made from bones!"

"So, you want to do something like this?" asked Bastian like someone approaching a lit firework.

"Something like this, but perhaps we can bring things up to date a little bit," said Manfred, rocking back on his heels thoughtfully. "Show the younger generation some of the classic scenes from the bible."

"If it doesn't have mind-melting Jedis or zombie transsexuals, I don't think it's going to speak to the sort of young people we hosted the other day," said Bastian, but he saw that Manfred was elsewhere, visualising works of art made possible with bone. He returned to the YouTube screen and pressed refresh with an angry scowl.

Rutspud had slipped into the habit of taking his work back to the cave. He found that several of the damned enjoyed knowing what he was doing, and if they could help him to shine in front of his new colleagues, he was all for it. Tesla, in particular, had been very busy. With whatever parts Rutspud had been able to smuggle out of the lab, or gather from elsewhere, he had constructed the device that Rutspud now weighed in his hand. It was vaguely gun-shaped, but where Rutspud expected a pointy bit for bullets to emerge from, there was a bulbous trumpet-shape, which made

Wilde titter inexplicably and say it reminded him of a young man he knew in Chelsea. Cartland had quilted the hand-grip for it, and had to be tied onto the snooker table again to stop her making a little cosy for when it was not in use.

"Why is the end part like this?" asked Rutspud. "It looks all wrong for making things go where you want them."

"We're firing rays," said Tesla.

"Rays."

"Yes. And we want to make sure that we get the coverage needed. If you are to condense an entire person, then the rays must cover the whole of their body or they might end up with a huge pair of feet that didn't shrink."

Rutspud's eyes lit up with delight at the possibilities.

"We could make something a little more targeted," Tesla continued, "in a chamber perhaps, if you would permit me access to the lab."

"Not going to happen," said Rutspud firmly. "We need to pretend that I made this, at least for now. So, if we fire this at one of the damned, we can make them smaller. How much smaller?"

Telsa shrugged.

"Let's find out."

Shortly afterwards, Rutspud placed the box onto Belphegor's lap with a hopeful smile.

"See? We can fit all six of them into a small box. Lewis made them some new living quarters in the cupboard where we keep the leftover demon body parts. Think of the space we can free up! It gives us a brand new way to deal with Hell's capacity problems."

Belphegor nodded and put a hand on the box that was moving around, as if the contents were greatly agitated.

"The device that you used, what's the technology?" he asked.

"Rays. It uses rays," said Rutspud, hoping that he could keep his eyes from looking too *shifty* and hoping the Belphegor didn't ask what 'rays' were.

"You built it yourself?" asked Belphegor.

"Yes, of course. Well, mostly," said Rutspud. He had a feeling that Belphegor wasn't fooled.

"This is interesting. Really interesting. Tell me, how you did you decide on these particular subjects for your first test?"

"Musicians?" Rutspud said. "Obvious, isn't it? Most people seem to think that all pop stars are tiny and, in real life, you know, stars of the 'small screen' – whatever that is – so it's not such a shocker when you see them. But open the box, and you'll see the added bonus."

Belphegor lifted the lid to reveal five angry-looking figures staring up at him.

"They look pretty healthy, these guinea pigs of yours," he said.

"You the man?" squeaked one of them.

"I'm in charge of this lab, yes," said Belphegor, lifting him out on his hand. "No need to pitch a purple haze."

The squeaker didn't bother replying but stamped a diminutive foot by way of protest.

"Man, you believe this shit?" he said. "We sound freaky and not the good kind of freaky. Music is my religion, man. We wan' our voices back."

Belphegor opened his mouth to reply but another voice joined in.

"Fuckin' Smurfs! That's what we sound like!"

Belphegor, eyed the tiny speaker with the spiked hair and bondage trousers. "Yes, I remember the Smurfs. One of our finer contributions to earth's cultural milieu, I always thought. So is it a problem, young man? Your voice very much matches your size now, surely?"

"Aw, c'mon," said a woman strolling forwards and striking a languid pose. "It's not so bad for Karen here, she sounds just the same as she always did, but the rest of us have lost all of our fucking *grit*. We're supposed to sound *rough* goddammit."

"Right on, Janis."

"Fascinating," said Belphegor, dropping Jimi Hendrix back into the box and closing the lid. "There's a psychological side-effect in play here. You've found a new way to apply torment, lad. The boss will be very pleased. Take them off and show them their new quarters while I go and have a word with maintenance about the temperature in this place."

Rutspud could barely contain his glee. He suspected that Belphegor knew he'd enlisted the help of Tesla, but hadn't they all said that they valued his laziness? They probably *expected* him to delegate his work to the damned. The trial of the new device couldn't have gone better, so Rutspud was hopeful that he could enjoy a blissful, if brief, hiatus from the constant worry of how he was going to demonstrate improvement in the next round of evaluations.

Rutspud eyed the demon before him. Hodshift the engineer bristled with ears. Where a human might have a covering of hair on the upper extremities, Hodshift had layers of ears. They varied in size, shape and species of donor, so the overall effect was chaotic, but what each had in common was a pencil tucked behind it.

Some of the ears had no natural grip for a pencil, so Hodshift's hands spent a good deal of their time catching pencils that fell from his head and attempting to secure them.

"So you're saying that the rise in temperature's because of us shrinking these six souls?" Rutspud asked.

Hodshift nodded, causing a cascade of pencils. Somehow he caught them all.

"It's yer basic gas laws. Learn them early on in Infernal Engineering. Pressure of a gas is direckly proportional to the temperature."

"But this isn't gas, it's ... souls," said Rutspud.

"Same difference," said Hodshift. "Make it smaller, it gets hotter. Goes for anything."

"But just these six caused the temperature to go up everywhere?"

"What yer dealin' wiv is a delicate e-co-lo-gy," said Hodshift, sounding out the last word carefully. "S'like a rainforest."

"What's a rainforest?"

"No idea. There's consequences if you mess with this stuff. Consequences. No offence, squire, but I fink you need to see what us engineers're up against," he said.

Hodshift led Rutspud to the wall of the Infernal Innovation cave, just to the left of the store cupboard where the tiny pop stars were exploring their new home. He held up an electronic pass to a place on the cave wall and, with a beep, a door swung open.

"I didn't know that was there," said Rutspud.

"You, mate, are about to go be'ind the scenes. Not many demons get to see this."

Hodshift ushered him through. Rutspud found himself in a clean, concrete conduit that led far into the distance in either direction. Metal pipes and coloured wires took up most of the space, but there was room enough for two demons to walk side by side.

"What is all this?" he asked, pointing at the dozens of pipes, some as thick as a man's waist, others much smaller.

Hodshift pointed at the pipes in turn and reeled them off.

"That's yer basic lava. That's the liquid fire for the lakes. The smaller ones are, let's see, brimstone, steam and marsh gas. Wires are fer the electrics and the communications."

Rutspud put his hand on a red screw valve.

"So you look after these things? Make sure it all keeps, er, flowing?"

"Yes," said Hodshift, taking Rutspud's hand and removing it pointedly from the valve. "Dangerous work, you might say. Bleeding air out of the lava pipe isn't for the faint hearted. You need to listen carefully to tell when the lava's about to blow, or you'll be blasted to buggery. Well, you would if we weren't already there, yeah."

Rutspud looked at Hodshift's enormous crop of ears and acknowledged with a small nod that he was the person for the careful listening job.

"We're always having to balance things," Hodshift continued. "S'posed to be a closed system, you see. Trouble is, we have to keep everything going as it is, and there's always *something* comes along that upsets the apple cart. Not saying that everyone's doing that shrinking thing you got there, mind, that's new. Still, there's always something. Mostly it's just the influx of new souls."

"Surely Hell expects new souls though?" Rutspud asked.

Hodshift gave a small bark of laughter.

"You'd think so, wouldn't you?" he said. "It don't stack up on the engineering side though. You take a closed system like we've got here and you keep on adding more energy and mass in the form of new souls. Leads to overheating like you wouldn't believe. Basic design flaw in my opinion. And don't even get me started on the problem of dealing with entropy in a set-up that's s'posed to last fer all time!"

"Entropy?"

"I said, don't get me started, sunshine!"

They walked along the corridor to a section where it widened out. Bays set into the walls held dials, levers and racks of equipment. Rutspud eyed the spares that were piled up on metal shelving and wondered what Tesla could conjure with access to these supplies. Hodshift gave a low whistle as he scanned the displays.

"Look," he said, pointing to a dial that showed a needle trembling into the red section. "We've got a situation right now. The outlying lava pools in level six are boiling over. Pound to a penny, that's part of the temperature spike you've caused down here. I'm going to have to get over there with an emergency crew. Here's a spare pass that will let you through the doors, you can find yer own way back, can't you?"

Rutspud nodded.

"That way back there," Hodshift pointed. "Fourth door on the right, if you get to the boiler room, you've gone too far. Now, you'll make sure that shrink-a-ma-jig device gets put somewhere safe, won't you? If you want to use it again, there's a form you'll need to fill in."

"Oh, where do I find the form?" asked Rutspud.

"Bottom of the lake of fire," said Hodshift and ambled off along the corridor.

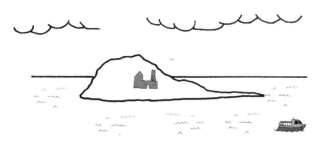

Manfred walked through St Cadfan's with his sketch book and a pencilled list. He stopped Brother Clement in the corridor.

"Ah, brother," said Manfred. "I am certain you will want to volunteer for this small improvement I'm proposing."

"Is this about the biscuits again?" said Brother Clement, his rosary beads beginning to click.

"No, no," said Manfred. "These are my plans for the St Cadfan's ossuary."

"An ossuary? With bones?"

"Yes. It could turn us into a real tourist destination. These are the plans I've sketched out."

He opened the pad and showed Brother Clement a page.

"See, this one is the feeding of the five thousand."

"Five thousand skulls?" said Brother Clement looking at the image.

"Yes. We can hinge their jaws to show them eating." Manfred cast an arm wide to show the scale and impact that the display would have. "This will be the unique selling point of the St Cadfan's ossuary – we will animate some of the displays, bring it right up to date."

Manfred flipped the page.

"This one shows Jesus turning water into wine. I'm thinking of installing a little pump behind the scenes so that we can have actual wine flowing around a circuit. Well, coloured water anyway."

"Hang on," said Brother Clement. "You've only got twelve skeletons. How will you do all of these? They look as though they'll need hundreds."

"Ah, you make an excellent observation, brother," said Manfred, closing the sketch pad. "Which is where the volunteering part comes in."

He pulled out a list with names.

"How would you feel about signing up here to donate your bones after your death?" he asked.

Brother Clement stared at him for a long moment while he processed the question.

"My bones? My bones!" he sputtered. "That's ghoulish and horrible and I can't believe you're asking."

Brother Clement scurried off, his beads clacking with nervous speed, like a holy Geiger counter. Manfred sighed and crossed out another name on his list. He scanned through the list and saw that the only remaining possibility was Brother Bernard. He hadn't seen him all day, so he went to the dormitories to look for him.

He knocked lightly on the door and listened for an answer. He heard nothing, so he gently opened the door and peered inside. The small window high in the wall still had its curtains closed, so there was only just enough light for Manfred to ascertain that Bernard was still in bed.

"Are you feeling all right, brother?" he asked, stepping forward. "It's past midday."

Manfred opened the curtains and approached the bed. Bernard lay perfectly still with his mouth slightly open. Manfred's stomach did a small flip.

"Brother Bernard?" he enquired tremulously. "Care to wake up?"

He tapped the older monk's shoulder firmly but Bernard was unresponsive. Manfred touched Bernard's forehead. It was cold.

Manfred cleared his throat.

"Wait there," he said, holding up an assertive hand. "Don't move! I'm going to fetch Brother Gillespie."

He dropped his papers and ran from the room. Moments later he came back in, picked up the list of names, looked thoughtfully at it for a moment and put a question mark at the side of Bernard's name.

Rutspud was lost.

He'd spent a bit of time poking around the interesting-looking shelves, and trying to make a mental inventory so that he could ask Tesla what the things all did. Then he hadn't been able to resist taking a look further along the corridor. He found a great many doors, but was nervous of opening them without knowing where he was. He came to a door that was even thicker than the others. It was warm to the touch and had a window set within it. Rutspud peered through the grimed glass and saw a multitude of demons feeding a gigantic, towering furnace. The demons shovelled unidentifiable chunks from a huge pile into an access hatch. He peered up and saw that a similar arrangement was just visible on a platform above this team. Another access hatch and another team of shovelling demons. Rutspud wondered how far up and down this furnace stretched, with layers of demons constantly fuelling it.

"Hell is indeed full of surprises," he said to himself.

He turned away. It was time to go back to Belphegor's laboratory.

Rutspud made his way along the corridor and tried to remember which of the doors was the right one. This one, surely? He held up Hodshift's pass and the door swung open. Instead of the Infernal Innovation lab, he saw another corridor. However, it did look familiar. Here were the pipes for the liquid fire and marsh gas that they had followed on their little tour.

Rutspud kept his eyes on the pipes as he walked on. He just need to find a place where he would find that original configuration of pipes that Hodshift had shown him.

"Lava, fire, brimstone, steam and gas," he repeated to himself along the corridor but, within minutes, he has switched to "Eeny, meeny, miney, mo," and tried opening doors at random.

The last door he opened before a bend in the tunnel revealed a short corridor and a staircase. Rutspud, eager to get home, would have ignored the staircase, but there was something unusual about it. At first glance, it had appeared to be a normal staircase, formed from metal struts and steps but then, for a moment, Rutspud imagined that it was simply a trick, a picture of stairs painted on the corridor wall.

Rutspud blinked and the stairs popped from two dimensions back into three. It was really there but ...

He approached it cautiously and took hold of the rail in his hand.

"Weird," he said, looked up the staircase and found himself staring *down* into an infinite abyss of concentric spirals.

"Woah!" he yelled and, eyes screwed shut, clung onto the rail to stop himself falling. Nothing happened.

"Trippy bloody staircase," he muttered and, with eyes still shut, stepped away.

He foot hit the next step down. He didn't recall climbing any steps. He stepped back and down again. And again.

He opened his eyes. Rutspud was climbing up the stairs, the evidence of his eyes and his senses contradicting one another. He abruptly understood.

"Escher!" he growled.

With a horrible, nauseous inevitability, he climbed more steps than he could be bothered to count, taking great care to pay no close attention to the stairs beneath his feet which – horror above horrors – circled clockwise and anticlockwise *at the same time*.

After an immeasurable length of time, the quality of light changed about him; instead of the familiar dull red glow, there was a greyish, washed-out look to things here. There was also, he noted, a chill in the air. He slowed as he turned the last bend of the spiral and stepped out into a stone tunnel.

Having stepped away from the staircase, Rutspud gave his feet a tentative glance to be sure that he was back on solid ground. His feet did nothing alarming, so he looked around more closely. He was in a tunnel, but one made from stone blocks, not hewn from bedrock as the ones below. Perhaps he had emerged into a castle or fortress of one of Hell's many fiefdoms. He might be significantly far from home and soon at the mercy of a Duke of Hell who didn't take kindly to trespassers.

The cold stone tunnel soon gave way to a corridor of smooth walls, painfully sharp lights and the most garishly bright wall paintings Rutspud had ever had the misfortune to see. Beaked creatures like, but not like, the tengu, roc and Ziz of Hell, stared out at Rutspud from a disturbingly alien landscape.

Rutspud scuttled hurriedly into a side room which, at first, put him in mind of Lord Peter's office. It was disgustingly neat and tidy, with the foul softness underfoot.

"Satan's balls!" he moaned.

He was in the Fortress of Nameless Dread. And, by the displays of books around this room, he had obviously stumbled into Lord Peter's private library.

"Gotta go," he told himself and was about to do so when his attention was drawn by a large book open on the table next to him. It was written in Latin, the language of the priesthood and, thus, of many of Hell's residents. Rutspud looked at the open page and gave a small gasp of surprise as he saw what was written there.

The demon, Rutspud, is seen as a soldier all in red with the horns of a young goat. He is a cruel demon, a torturer who delights in the work of his hands.

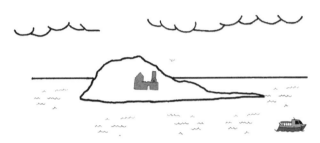

Manfred entered the locutory to tell Bastian about Bernard but found, to his frustration, that Bastian was conducting one of those internet video call things.

"I can assure you that the island will be perfectly safe for your visit," said Bastian, addressing a frowning woman via the webcam. "The authorities have given us the all-clear to resume all of our usual activities, and we'll have everything ready to welcome your bird-watching club."

"But the bodies!" said the woman. "Our members are most unhappy at the prospect of staying in an environment where dead bodies can just ... appear."

"Recent renovations had apparently disturbed an old burial site. It was flood water that caused the sudden mudslide that you've no doubt seen on YouTube."

"It's on YouTube? I only read about it in the Mail."

"Did you? Oh. Well, I can assure you that Bardsey hardly ever sees anything so dramatic."

"Oh, I don't know," said Manfred, "there was the inferno and all those deaths last year."

"What was that?" said the woman sharply.

"Nothing, nothing at all," said Bastian with a fierce look at Manfred. "My colleague has a colourful sense of humour, but he's just leaving. Now, maybe you'd like to tell me about your catering needs for next week?"

"Catering can wait," said the woman. "I heard that there might be plague on the island, and I'm certain that our members will be equally nervous about that."

Manfred tried to gesture to Bastian that he had an urgent message. Bastian's eyes flickered towards him for a moment, but he gave his focus back to the woman on the screen.

"I gather these rather fanciful rumours have appeared on the internet, and in the press, apparently," he said, "but they are groundless, utterly groundless. I can assure you that our community of monks are all fine, and the coroner's office is satisfied with the measures that have been taken."

Manfred shook his head at Bastian and mimed a throat-cutting gesture to illustrate that the monks were not, in fact, all fine.

"What's that man doing?" asked the woman. "Is he saying that someone has died?"

"Yes," said Manfred. "Brother Bernard has died."

Bastian glowered at Manfred.

"You mean Brother Bernard, our elderly acquaintance from Douarnenez Abbey in France?" he said, waggling his eyebrows at Manfred.

"Oh. Yes, that's the one," said Manfred, with a smile at the woman on the webcam. "Nice man. We will miss him. You can be assured, madam, that this monastery will look after the health of your members most carefully. I take a great deal of personal pride in keeping the place extremely clean. I even ran the bones through the dishwasher to be sure that they wouldn't mess the place up."

Manfred gave her his most charming smile, which had been known to break down many barriers, especially when accompanied by a little twinkling of the eyes.

Manfred thought afterwards that perhaps the quality of the webcam was to blame for not transmitting his smile to full effect. The woman unleashed a torrent of rage about health and safety and insisted that she would not be subjecting her members to the horrors of a kitchen where they might find human remains next to the cutlery. Bastian had his head buried in his hands as Manfred gently closed the door behind him.

Stephen descended to the library to get a bit of personal space. He'd just left a band of monks in the cloisters grimly dissecting the news of Brother Bernard's death. Bernard, like four fifths of the monks on Bardsey, had been at least seventy years old, but there had not been a natural death on the island in Stephen's time there, and the news had hit him hard. Brother Henry's tasteless jokes about Brother Bernard's final words had been enough to drive Stephen away to seek solitude.

He entered the library and was surprised to find someone there. Someone or some ... thing. It appeared that someone had dumped a man-sized and vaguely man-shaped puppet in his reading chair, a man-sized puppet with shiny red skin, long skinny limbs which ...

... was reading one of his books, licking its fingertips as it turned each page.

The creature's huge, glistening eyes lifted to look at Stephen. It had rather arresting eyes, set between ears that stuck out at a jaunty angle. There was the brief rustle of a paper bag and the thing popped a jelly baby into its mouth.

Stephen's mind simultaneously crashed through several possibilities – TV prank show, a child in fancy-dress, the onset of schizophrenia – but the sight of the thing munching on jelly babies drew an immediate response from him.

"No!" yelled Stephen. "How dare you! Those were for Brother Bernard! You can't just eat them now he's dead."

The creature didn't move, but the eyes seemed to take on an expression of mild curiosity.

"Who's dead?"

"Brother Bernard."

The thing shrugged.

"Show me someone round here who isn't."

Stephen goggled.

"Am I dead?"

"Well, you're in Hell, so ..."

Stephen frowned.

"No, I'm not."

The creature blinked.

"What?"

"We're in St Cadfan's. And you're trespassing!" said Stephen.

"This is Earth?" said the red creature. It stood up in surprise, its weight on those stick-thin legs.

"Oh, God," said Stephen. "You can stand. You're real."

"Of course I'm real."

"And, you – you're a demon! Are you a demon?"

"I'm in your book, madam," he said, pointing at the page.

"I'm not a madam. I'm a man."

"But the dress?"

"I'm a monk and you ... you ..."

Stephen ran for the shelves, searching frantically for a book he knew he had seen there at some point. Rutspud sat and ate jelly babies, watching him.

"Dammit!" shouted Stephen, unable to locate his copy of *Rituale Romanum*, and dredged from the depths of his memory what words he could remember.

"Right. Here goes, demon. I command you, unclean spirit, by the mysteries of the incarnation, passion, resurrection and ascension of our Lord Jesus Christ, by the descent of the Holy Spirit, by the coming of ... something or other. I command you to obey me to the letter. You shall not be emboldened to harm in any way this creature of God or –"

"What creature of God?"

"Bugger! You're not possessing anyone, are you? You're just ... there."

Stephen made the sign of the cross for good measure. Rutspud gripped his stomach and frowned.

"I cast you out, unclean spirit," Stephen shouted, "along with every Satanic power of the enemy, every spectre from Hell and all your fell companions, in the name of our Lord Jesus Christ. Be gone. Go on now, go! Walk out the door! Just turn around now, 'cause you're not welcome anymore ..."

Stephen stopped and saw the demon creature curled up, clutching its belly.

"That really hurts," said Rutspud.

"Really?"

Rutspud grimaced and then farted loudly. "Beelzebub's beard!" he groaned. "Did you do that?"

Stephen reeled from the sulphurous stench. "I might have done," he said, unable to tell what had been achieved through the power of prayer and what had been achieved through the power of jelly babies.

"Well, don't," said Rutspud, glaring at Stephen. "You've given me a really bad tummy ache. What did you do that for?"

Stephen looked at Rutspud.

"To be honest, I don't really know. Instinct." He sat down in a chair opposite Rutspud and stared at him for a few minutes. "So, what are you going to do to me?"

Rutspud shrugged and farted again. "I'm not here to do anything to anybody. I've got enough on my plate."

"Well, you must have come to me for a reason."

"Hell! Is everyone on Earth as self-centred as you, or is it just the ones in dresses?" He pointed down the corridor. "If you must know, I found a staircase. I was just having a look. Who knew it came up here?"

Stephen sat up straight and swivelled his head between the demon and the door.

"Wait, there's a staircase in that bit of corridor down there that leads down to Hell? Good grief! We weren't wrong when we said it was unsafe. Talk about health and safety issues."

"Trust me, I'm equally surprised," said Rutspud.

"Well, it's all too much for me today. I've had enough, I can't be doing with this as well. Bodies and plague rumours and poor, dead Bernard. This place is going properly to the dogs."

"Do you always whine this much?" said Rutspud, getting up, giving one last, gusty fart that seemed to restore his composure, and pacing around. "Your existence is really that bad, is it? What's the worst thing that might happen to you, hmmm?"

"You. Dragging me off to Hell and tormenting me for all eternity?"

"Apart from that."

Stephen shrugged.

"Mostly it's the boredom and the sense that I have no real purpose in life," he said. "The feeling that I could completely lose my mind and it just wouldn't matter. Nobody here would notice."

Rutspud gave a small snort.

"Boo shitting hoo, lady. Do you live with the daily threat of being minced into little pieces?"

"Well, of course not."

"Oh, well maybe there's an entire hierarchy of malevolent despots who want to find excuses to punish you?"

"I wouldn't call Manfred or Father Eustace despots – actually, I don't know what we'd call our new abbot – and we don't have a hierarchy really. That's possibly part of the problem."

"Right," said Rutspud, "so keep your whining for someone with fewer problems than you. Saving my skin takes every ounce of my considerable cunning and energy, and the better I get at doing it, the more enemies I make."

Stephen stared at Rutspud and gave a small shake of his head.

"What's happening here? Am I supposed to be feeling sorry for you?"

"You can if you like."

"You're a demon! I didn't dedicate my life to the service of God to go round feeling sorry for demons."

Stephen broke off with the sudden thought that he might be sleepwalking. That would explain a lot. He looked at his feet and saw that they weren't muddy, but what did that really mean? He pinched his arm and it definitely hurt, but he wasn't sure what that meant either. He was only sure that he needed to bring this conversation to a close.

"No. No, no, no," he said to Rutspud. "You need to go. You can take your staircase and go straight back to Hell."

"It's not my staircase. I think it's Escher's," said Rutspud with a small pout.

"Go!" yelled Stephen.

Rutspud shrugged and sauntered towards the door.

"And don't even think about taking those jelly babies!" shouted Stephen.

Bastian hesitated before he picked up the phone. He felt bad about undermining Manfred's authority, but someone needed to do something. Every single one of the monastery's upcoming visits had been cancelled now, and they were facing serious cash flow problems if he didn't take this opportunity. He dialled the number, knowing it would be early in Texas, but the email *had* said any time of the day or night.

"Hello," he said. "Chuck Katzenberger, please?"

"The very same," came the leisurely drawled reply. "Now, would this be Brother Sebastian in England?"

"We're actually in Wales, Mr Katzenberger."

"And that's in England, right?"

"Sort of tacked onto the side, really."

"Now, I hope you're going to be able to make me a happy man, Brother Sebastian. I've spent my life and a personal fortune trying to prove I'm descended from Sir Gawain, one of Arthur's knights. Now, I know it's true in my heart of hearts. My past-life regression therapist in Austen has shown it to me. But now, having read the compelling internet testimony of your countryman, Mr Ewan Thomas, I realise your skeletons might just give me the chance to run a DNA test to prove what I already know to the rest of the world. Do you believe in past lives, son?"

Bastian coughed.

"It's not about what I believe, is it, Mr Katzenberger? Er, just to be clear, the sum that you mentioned in your email, you're prepared to offer that much for each complete skeleton?"

"I am," said Katzenberger. "I told y'all, this is real important to me. If we have a deal, I've already arranged for your boat guy in Aberdaron to pick them up tonight and send them on."

"Tonight! So soon?"

"I got where I am today by making things happen, and making them happen fast," said Katzenberger. "Now, do we have a deal?"

"Yes, we have a deal," said Bastian. "I'll email our bank details so that you can arrange the transfer, and I'll get the skeletons packed up right now."

"Father Eustace." Stephen tapped on the wardrobe door. "Father Eustace, can I talk to you please?"

The door cracked open enough for Stephen to see a pair of wild eyes and a whiskery face. It had been generally concluded that shaving in a dark wardrobe was probably going to be messy and unsafe, and Manfred and Brother Gillespie had concluded that the abbot was to be kept away from sharp objects.

"Trey, er, TREVOR!" croaked Father Eustace.

"No, it's Stephen, Father Abbot," said Stephen. "I really need someone to talk to about all of the things that have happened today. If I try to talk to Bastian or Manfred, they'll just think I've gone mad, but you ..."

"Dead," said Father Eustace without expression.

"Yes, that's right," said Stephen. "We've all lost a colleague today. It's the first time that's happened since I got here, Father Abbot, and it's horrible. We need someone to help us with this. We need a leader."

"Season," came a croak.

"Yes!" said Stephen. "To everything there is a season. Ecclesiastes, isn't it? It's helpful to be reminded of that. Yes, thank you, Father Abbot, that's a comfort. There's something else as well. Bernard's death isn't the only thing on my mind."

Stephen paused, and put his face a little closer to the gap in the wardrobe.

"Father," he whispered, "you're going to think I'm losing my mind, but I met a demon today. In the library."

Father Eustace's eye gave Stephen a look that urged him to continue.

"I tried to exorcise him, but he took it badly."

"Temper," said Father Eustace.

"Well, yes. He acted as if I was just being mean," said Stephen.

"Christian!" shouted Father Eustace.

Stephen exhaled deeply.

"You're right, Father Abbot. I failed to act like a good Christian. Demon or no demon, I was wrong to act in hatred towards him. I was expecting, I don't know, tricks or torments or something. He seemed ... he seemed as if he just wanted to have a chat."

"Legion!"

"Of course. Even our Lord was willing to talk to demons, even to give them what they wanted. I handled it all wrong."

"Jelly babies!" crowed Eustace, although Stephen failed to notice the hand that extended from the wardrobe.

"How did you know about that?" said Stephen, standing up. "I wouldn't even let him have that small treat. Well, maybe I can make that better."

He left the room without hearing the faint keening sound from the wardrobe, and the plaintive cry of "Jelly babies!"

Manfred was in the almonry when Bastian found him. It had, long ago, been a place where charity was dispensed to the poor. Up until last year, it had been a storage area which had contained a multitude of things, including Manfred's illicit apple schnapps. Then, after the apple-scented explosion, it had briefly been a pile of rubble, then finally rebuilt as a general purpose workshop. In this space, Manfred collected up anything that he thought might be reusable and attempted to breathe new life into it.

"Ah, Bastian!" said Manfred. "You're just in time to see the first test run!"

"Can I look later, Manfred? I'm in a bit of a hurry. Where are the bones?"

"Right here, my friend. Right here. Now, just take a moment. Nothing on Bardsey is so urgent that you cannot afford to take a little time to relax. Do you remember me saying that I had a plan to make a unique ossuary, something that has never been seen before?"

Bastian nodded impatiently, knowing he'd get no sense out of Manfred until he'd had his say.

"Well, this is my proof of concept for an animated ossuary. It's not complete, but you'll certainly get the idea. What we're going to show in this little tableau that I've designed is Jesus driving the moneylenders out of the temple."

He picked up an orange power cord and plugged it in.

"This skeleton here is Jesus. You'll see him pushing towards these other skeletons here who are the moneylenders. I have used a motor from an old strimmer which is mounted on the back of this board, and it is connected to some cams and linkages that I made myself."

Manfred gave a wink and switched on the power. The motor whined into action and sure enough, Manfred's cam translated the rotary movement of the strimmer into a rocking movement, and the Jesus skeleton, wired together with old coat hangers, tipped forwards and backwards, hands outstretched to drive off the frankly indifferent moneychanger skeletons that lounged around on chairs or sat in pieces on the floor.

Bastian chuckled, in spite of himself.

"Lovely effort, Manfred. Is it meant to make that clunking sound?"

"Oh, dear," said Manfred. "Something has slipped, I think."

There was an abrupt change in the pitch of the motor as it revved faster. The Jesus skeleton had stopped rocking and, to Bastian's horror, was now completing a full rotation, feet twirling through the air, as though Jesus had suddenly decided to take up breakdancing as a means to chasing off the moneychangers. As the Jesus skeleton's path was clear, the second rotation was faster, and the next faster still, the skeleton rising up like a fairground centrifuge as it span.

"No. Wait," shouted Manfred and would have thrust himself into the blades of that bony propeller if Bastian hadn't held him out of its reach. Jesus's feet sliced through, ground against and generally dashed the moneylenders to pieces. Wires tangled, mangled limbs flailed about, and the skeletons were obliterated by the impact of the spinning bones smashing repeatedly against them at high speed.

Manfred dived under the lethal Jesus's range for the power switch, just as the last remaining pieces of the skeletal son of God flew off and smashed against the wall.

Bastian was speechless, and gaped at Manfred, who nodded briefly and then inspected the back of the board.

"Yes, I can see what's happened here," said Manfred. "I'll need to adjust –"

"Manfred!" bellowed Bastian. "I sold those bones! They're worth thousands to the guy that wants them! The boat's on its way over to collect them."

Manfred raised a quizzical eyebrow.

"... and you were going to mention this when?"

"I'm mentioning it now! He only wants complete skeletons though. Look at the state of these." He kicked through the tiny white chunks on the floor. "We haven't got a single one."

Manfred surveyed the pile of smashed bones.

"Oh, I don't know. I have some strong adhesive here. If we get a diagram of how a human skeleton goes together I'm sure we –"

"We don't have time for jigsaw puzzles!" shouted Bastian. "The boat's on its way now."

Bastian briefly wondered whether he could use the body of Brother Bernard, but aside from the legal and ethical problems, he really wasn't sure how quickly it was possible to render all flesh off a body. Right now, he mused, if he had the means, he'd happily render down Manfred's bones to hand over to Chuck Katzenberger.

As the monks came to terms with the death of one of their own, the evening meal in the refectory was a subdued affair, although the dressing-gown clad Brother Henry wouldn't let go of his tasteless little joke.

"... but now, I don't think he was calling Huey," he was saying at the table across from Stephen. "I think he was retching."

He leaned forward, puffing out his cheeks theatrically, and made a protracted vomiting sound.

"Huu-eeeugh!"

Stephen tried to close his ears and his mind to Brother Henry's insensitivity. He looked away and saw Brother Huey, sat apart from his brothers, lost in his thoughts. Where was Manfred? It was at times like this that the monastery needed a strong leader, someone to steer them all through these difficult times.

"Monks!" came a shout from behind him. All heads turned to see Father Eustace in the doorway. He tottered forwards and leaned on a table. His eyes took them all in.

"Monks!" he repeated.

The brothers of St Cadfan's stared at him. He was a tall man, a scraggly man with a patchy mess of a beard which seemed to be an interesting inversion of the patchy baldness on top of his head. This was the first time many of them had seen their new abbot. It was the first time Stephen had seen him clothed. Father Eustace Pike's habit hung on his narrow shoulders, and it appeared that Father Eustace had to constantly readjust it to stop it slipping through the neckhole and ending up with it around his ankles.

"Monks on an island!" said the abbot.

There was a long silence. Father Eustace stood with his mouth open. The monks waited.

"When there's a whole world out there," said Father Eustace. "A monstrous, terrifying world." He eyed them all. "Could there be a better place to be than with monks on an island?"

There was a murmur of mild surprise and agreement from various tables around the refectory.

"Things change," continued Father Eustace, as his hand groped for a bread roll. "There's always change. Change, change, change. New challenges. Challenge, change, challenge." He bashed the bread roll on the table for emphasis. "We move on to the next phase of life. We can't stop change. It will always happen, however much we resist."

He dropped his gaze to the bread roll, pulled a chunk free and popped it into his mouth.

The monks watched him eat.

"Surrounded by kindness," said Father Eustace, "life is bearable. Change is bearable." He stared blankly into space for a moment. "We don't need wardrobes. Fraternity, brotherhood. That's what we need."

Then he sat down in a chair and beamed at the other monks.

Stephen looked around at the other faces. They all reflected the same emotions that he was feeling. A release of some sort, a realisation that they all had their problems, but that they were part of a strong, spiritual community. Father Eustace Pike had broken his five week silence, but had chosen a powerful time to do it. Stephen looked at his twenty-odd brothers: Clement sniffing thoughtfully, Henry silenced, Huey brushing something from his eye that he'd refuse to admit was a tear. Stephen smiled at the scene before him. Maybe this was the dawning of a new era, where St Cadfan's would put its troubles behind it, its days of madness a thing of the past.

Manfred and Bastian peered into the gloom. The boat was several feet out and didn't seem to be coming any closer. There was no sign of Owen.

"I hope there isn't a problem," said Manfred. "I was hoping he might have brought my pumpernickel with him."

Bastian counted to ten in his head so that he didn't use language that was unbecoming for a monk.

"Look, is that him? Oh."

They saw a figure totter forward in a huge plastic orange suit.

"What is that thing he's wearing?"

"I think it's a biohazard suit."

Owen raised a loudhailer.

"I'm not coming any closer," came Owen's voice. "They tell me you've got the plague here."

"There's no plague," called Bastian. "We're open for business as usual!"

"Yes, that's fine," said Owen, "I'll be sure to mention the plague to any birdwatchers that come asking for trips."

"He can't hear you," said Manfred. "Look, he's winching across a container. I think he wants us to put the bones into it."

"Well, all we've got is a box of bits!" said Bastian.

"Ah, we'll add a little note," said Manfred, pulling a notebook from his habit.

"What on earth will we say?" asked Bastian.

Manfred sucked thoughtfully on a pencil.

"So, this American, wants whole skeletons, yes?"

"Yes."

"How about this then."

Manfred scribbled for a few minutes and handed a note to Bastian.

Please find twelve skeletons, carefully dismantled for transport.

"Who knows?" breathed Bastian. "Maybe it could work."

They loaded the box, with the note, into the cradle on the boom arm that Owen had swung over, and gave him a wave to indicate that they had finished. Owen gave them a wave in return, tripped over the giant orange bootees that formed part of his biohazard suit and fell over the side. He bobbed in the water like a huge inflatable, angrily waving them back as they waded in to offer their assistance.

"No, get back!" he burbled, rolling in the waves. "I'm fine. No plague. Let me get back!"

Manfred and Bastian shrugged, and left Owen to scramble up the ladder on his own.

Stephen explored the still damp cellar.

"Hello-o?"

There was no sign of any demon, not even the lingering smell of his sulphur farts. Nor, at first, could he see any staircase. And why would he? There had been no staircase noted when the corpses were hauled out.

But then Stephen saw it. The staircase skulked in the darkness, blending in artfully with the furthest wall, as though it were an optical illusion, a sort of reverse *trompe l'œil* which made the three-dimensional stairs appear to be a flat pattern on the wall.

The stairs seemed to shimmer and twist kaleidoscopically before his eyes. He tapped the side of the torch that he carried. Clearly, he needed to get some new batteries.

Stephen decided that he'd leave his peace offerings at the top of the stairs, rather than risk a failing battery going any further. He placed the items carefully by the top step, so that Rutspud couldn't miss them if he made another visit. The book was not one from the monastery library, but one from Stephen's own bookshelf. It somehow seemed apt. On top of it, he rested the remainder of Brother Bernard's jelly babies, the bag folded over neatly.

Stephen regarded his gesture of Christian friendship, patted the bag of jelly babies as though bidding it farewell, and left.

Chapter 4 – The day the food ran out

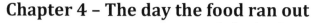

"What do you think?"

Manfred looked up from his notes at the large rectangle of card in Bastian's hands and the big letters in a variety of felt tip colours.

"'How Not To Die'?"

"It's for my presentation tonight on how not to die."

"I can see that."

"Look. I've drawn a picture of a monk. He's not dead. And he's smiling."

"Good."

"Because I'm trying to keep it upbeat. I thought a physical presentation on boards, rather than a powerpoint, would save on using up precious petrol in the generator."

Manfred considered Bastian's presentation board.

"And the content of this presentation?" he asked.

"Oh, the usual," said Bastian. "What's safe to eat, what's not. Basic hygiene, precautions against plague. You know, generally" – he waved his arms around vaguely – "how not to die in this time of crisis. How's the menu planning coming on?"

The largest table in the locutory was covered in papers: old manuscripts, scraps of frantic writing and small herds of screwed up paper balls. Manfred ran a hand through his curls and flicked through the paper ruins.

"Thrown out of kilter by the discovery that the rats have eaten all our remaining potatoes."

"So what have we got left?"

"Fat rats."

"I don't think the brothers are ready for a rodent-based diet."

"The Cantonese call it *jia lu* or 'super deer'. It's considered a delicacy."

"Yes. Well, reconsider, brother. Reconsider very, very hard."

"Brother Stephen has provided me with some useful texts from the library," said Manfred, and tapped a thick tome of the collected works of Flavius Josephus. "Did you know that, during the first century siege of Jerusalem, the besieged resorted to eating belts, leather straps and cooked tufts of grass?"

"Is that all?"

"And babies. But we're out of babies."

"And that's the best advice history has to offer?"

"No." Manfred shifted the Josephus aside and opened a printed volume. "From the histories of Joan of Arc, we have the siege of Orleans. Culinary delights included tree bark, shoes and rat droppings."

Bastian thought for a minute.

"Wednesday, there was spotted dick ..."

"The last of the sultanas, I swear," said Manfred, crossing his heart. "But we are certainly going to have to get imaginative with our foodstuffs from now on. Here."

Manfred pushed a list over to Bastian. Bastian read.

"Snails. Fair enough. Worms. Barnacles. Candles. Shoe polish? Really? Organic emulsion paint? Don't think I could stomach that."

"You recall yesterday's pasta Carbonara?"

"That wasn't really cream sauce?"

"That wasn't really pasta either."

Bastian held his stomach and concentrated on the list.

"Toothpaste, cough syrup and sawdust all crossed out."

Bastian groaned. "But I had seconds of last night's meringue pie. This is barbaric."

"You think I don't know that?" said Manfred. "As prior, refectorian and Westphalian Bake-Off Champion two years running, I am appalled and ashamed at what I have had to resort to."

"Don't blame yourself, Manfred."

"I don't," said Manfred with an uncharacteristic rancour that could only be attributed to hunger. "I'm not the one who's failed to secure another food parcel airdrop."

"Hey," said Bastian. "It's not *my* fault the last one rolled into the sea and was pillaged by gulls. That RAF commander was rather sniffy about our failed attempts to rescue the package. He's clearly never been dive-bombed by the vicious Bardsey birdlife."

"What about convincing Owen to bring us something?"

"Refuses to come over until Brother Bernard's remains have been tested for plague. *And* he said that Dylan Davies has taken up position on the roof of the Ship Hotel with a rifle and will shoot any monk who tries to row back to the mainland."

"Great. Are we even going to be safe going out for our fishing trip later?"

"It is to be hoped."

"Stephen is going out to collect wild bird eggs later and Brother Huey has been camping out on the hills hoping to catch rabbits –"

"Catch his death of cold more like."

"– but I am not overly optimistic," Manfred concluded. "If we do not get some fresh food soon then we are going be very hungry indeed. But on the plus side ..."

"Yes?"

"According to our *Medicinale Anglicum*, starvation is a good protection against the plague."

"Right. So not a course of antibiotics, then?"

"We must work with what we have, Brother Sebastian. Here's another cure. Drink a mixture of baby fox's blood and urine thrice daily in a silver goblet blessed by the king."

"And do we possess a goblet blessed or otherwise by the king?"

"We have some silver in the church. I thought that if Prince William happened to be visiting his old RAF base in Anglesey, he could do a fly-by blessing or something."

"Doubtful."

"Have faith, brother," said Manfred, sweeping the paper balls off the table. "I've been collecting the brothers' pee for more than a week in preparation."

"Those barrels in the cellar leak, you know."

"Cheer up. We shall have one last fine meal tonight. Marsh rabbit *a le pâturage*."

"Rabbit with grass?"

Manfred coughed.

"*Marsh* rabbit with grass."

"Marsh rabbit." Bastian thought and then put his 'How Not To Die' board down unhappily.

Manfred shrugged genially.

"Best not to think about it, brother."

In the library, Stephen looked up from his copy of *Gaudio Ex Coquere*. There was that sound again, a lugubrious rumbling sound accompanied by tiny popping sounds. He stepped out into the corridor. Three barrels of monk piss stood beneath the explosive bird mural created by Brother Huey and the late Brother Bernard. One of the stinking barrels frothed and sloshed as though it was reaching some urinary critical mass and was about to explode.

Stephen held his nose and peered down into the golden murk.

"How long have you been there?" he asked.

The reply sounded something like, "Blub Ub."

"Sorry," said Stephen. "I was only asking."

Rutspud emerged slowly, a morose look in his over-sized eyes.

"You could drown in there," said Stephen. "Couldn't you?"

"If only," said the demon, licking his lips slowly. "What a way to go. Monk's piss. Delicious."

"I'll take your word for it. I can bottle some for you to take home if you like."

Rutspud froze for a second and then burst into a frenzied bout of wailing and gnashing of teeth. Stephen had never actually seen a person gnash their teeth before. It was a common enough phrase but quite bizarre to see in practice. It took Stephen several seconds to realise that Rutspud was crying.

"There, there, buddy," said Stephen, tentatively patting the demon's wet shoulder. "What's the matter?"

"It's terrible!" he howled. "I'm done for! Scabass has always had it in for me and now ..."

Rutspud sank back into the barrel and gargled in anguish.

"What?" said Stephen. "Is someone going to kill you?"

Rutspud's bubbly reply indicated that demons couldn't die and that Stephen was an idiot to think they could.

"Whip you then?" said Stephen. "Spit roast you? Poke you with those three-pronged pointy things?" He thought quickly. Demons were creatures of the perverse. Perhaps they found pleasure in pain and vice versa. "Give you a pay rise? Invite you round for a cup of tea? Give you their blessing?"

Rutspud stood up, spitting out a stream of piss.

"He does that."

"Who? Does what?"

"Lord Peter. He offers benedictions to those he hates. And if you've really annoyed him, he makes you say Hail Marys."

Rutspud had mentioned this Lord Peter before, but the politics and situation in Hell made no sense to Stephen. He chose to ignore it; it took his entire grip on sanity to accept that this creature before him was one of the denizens of Hell. His mind didn't dare consider much more.

"What happens when demons say Hail Mary?" Stephen asked.

"I don't know but I don't think it's a pretty sight."

"And that's what's going to happen to you?"

Rutspud shook his head in self-pity.

"Worse. They're sending me to the kitten room."

Stephen looked at him.

"Does kitten mean something different in Hell to what it does here?"

Rutspud shook his head.

"Are these giant three-headed man-eating kittens?" said Stephen. "A sort of cat Cerberus?"

Rutspud shook his head. Stephen chewed his lip.

"I think you'd better hop out of there, dry off, and tell me all about it."

Nero ushered Rutspud into the office.

"Your six o'clock appointment is here, my lord."

Lord Peter swivelled in his office chair.

"Six o'clock?"

"Yes, sir. Oh." Nero scampered across to a large mechanism of cogs, levers and numbers on the wall, added since Rutspud's last visit, and hoisted one of the arms round. "BONG!" he declared. "Six o'clock."

Rutspud frowned.

Lord Peter smiled at him.

"Efficiency is a calculable measure. A matter of achievement divided by effort multiplied by time. A over E times T. One can't measure efficiency without actual time."

Rutspud shifted uneasily from one foot to the other. The touch of shag-pile carpet on his feet was nauseatingly sensuous.

"And so, I have invented it. Is it time for another 'bong' yet, Nero?"

"I don't think so, sir."

"Well, dash it all. How about some ticks and tocks?"

"Very good, sir," said Nero and, adjusting the laurel wreath of razor-blades on his bloody scalp, stood in the corner and began to quietly recite, "tick-tock, tick-tock, tick-tock ..."

"Now, Rutspud," said Lord Peter, "I hear nothing but good things about you. Belphegor constantly sings your praises."

"Thank you, lord."

"And you've also maintained responsibility for your cave of tortures in the sixth circle."

"I do my best."

"All is as it should be and yet ..."

Those last two words were like a blade slicing down into Rutspud's gut.

"And yet?" he asked, a quaver in his voice.

"Something disquieting has come to my attention. Enter!"

The door opened and Scabass strode in, an object clutched in his hands, almost skewered by his ice-pick fingers. Rutspud recognised the object at once, and Scabass grinned at him with a mouth full of metal spikes.

"I'm sure you can clear this up in no time," said Lord Peter. "Could you tell me what this thing is?"

Rutspud could not deny the truth in face of the material evidence.

"It's a cushion, my lord."

Lord Peter held out his hand and Scabass passed it to him.

"Very soft," he commented.

"Woven from the shorn hair of vain women and stuffed with the dried guts of dieticians," said Rutspud. It was a lie. It was made, inside and out, from the cut-offs of old monk habits from St Cadfan's.

"And do you know where Scabass found this?"

Rutspud nodded nervously. Lord Peter leaned forward over his desk.

"Care to explain?"

"Shipton – that's one of the damned in my cave – has piles."

"Piles?"

"Haemorrhoids, sir. She complains about them a lot, between making predictions of woe and gloom."

"And so you made this to ...?"

"Actually, I had Cartland and Nightingale make it," said Rutspud. "I did whip them while they sewed and stuffed it," he added quickly.

Lord Peter's expression had taken a turn for the perplexed, going from a mask of feigned managerial concern to genuine bewilderment.

"You had this made – *specifically* made – to ease the pains of one of the damned?"

Rutspud took a deep breath. Right, he told himself, time to play the trump card, his only card.

"Hell's role is to provide high quality torture provision within the framework of a theologically didactic universe," he said. "The damned must be punished, be seen to be punished, and that punishment must serve Hell's overall strategic pathway. We do not torture all the damned in the same way. That's why we have Individual Torture Plans. In fact, one should go so far as to say no two damned are tortured in exactly the same way."

"Ye—ees?" said Lord Peter in the tones of one who was willing to humour Rutspud a little longer but only a *little* longer.

"Shipton's ITP indicates a course of hangings, gouging and general abuse. Her piles are not a factor in our plans for her."

"But her piles hurt," said Scabass. "We are *meant* to hurt them."

"Of course, sir," said Rutspud without taking his eyes off Lord Peter. "But it is my professional opinion that the piles are noise, interfering with the signal message we are trying to communicate to this individual."

"You are proposing that the painful piles are distracting her from her true torture?" asked Lord Peter.

"But torture is torture!" Scabass snarled.

Rutspud shook his head at such naivety whilst sharing a knowing look with Lord Peter.

"And let's not forget Pirithous," he said.

The looks of confusion on Scabass's and Lord Peter's faces were wonderful.

"King of the Lapiths," said Rutspud. "Friend of Theseus. We have him in the fourth circle, condemned to sit on a giant stone for all eternity for his hubris."

"Oh, *him*," said Lord Peter.

"He's our piles guy," said Rutspud. "He's Hell's Mr Haemorrhoid. Hell only has one Sisyphus, one Tantalus, one Pirithous. To allow Shipton to *revel* in her piles is to damage part of our important brand."

Lord Peter was nodding. He was actually *nodding*.

"That is truly commendable, Rutspud," he said.

"Thank you, lord," said Rutspud, fighting to keep a grin from his face, particularly while Scabass was standing there, stunned, mouth agape.

"To put such thought and effort into your torture plans ..."

"I only exist to serve," said Rutspud.

"Of course, you're over-thinking it," said Lord Peter.

"What, my lord?"

"It's *de trop*. It's perfectionism taken to excess."

Rutspud's mind stumbled.

"I'm ... I'm trying too hard?"

"One is flattered, of course," said Lord Peter. "But I don't want one of our very best burning out in his prime. You need to take things down a notch or two. Uncoil those springs."

"Sir?"

"You need to relax."

Rutspud reeled as though punched. He turned on the spot and found himself facing the poster next to Lord Peter's inverted crucifix. The kitten dangling from the branch, looked back at him.

"Hang in there," said Scabass with a dark chuckle. "Shall I escort him to the Relaxation Centre now, sir?"

"I think it's in use at the moment," said Lord Peter. "What's the time, Nero?"

Nero swung the arm of the clock.

"BONG! It's seven o'clock."

"Already?"

"Er, time flies like an arrow, sir," he said.

Lord Peter stood.

"Very well, Rutspud. You are to report here at, um, twelve o'clock for some intense relaxation."

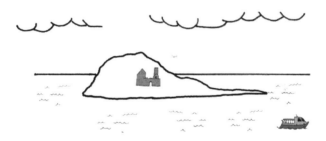

"And that's it," said Rutspud to Stephen. "I've got until the twelve bongs and then I'm going to be stuffed into a room full of kittens until I am 'better'."

"And these kittens, they'll ... what?"

"Sit there and look cute." Rutspud shuddered within the folds of the habit that Stephen had loaned him. "Or rub themselves up against me. I might even be required to stroke them."

Stephen suppressed the urge to laugh. The demon was clearly distressed. Stephen didn't regard Rutspud as anything like a friend. He looked upon the demon as something partway between a personal outreach project and a schizophrenic delusion. Whatever the case, it seemed both impolite and unwise to laugh at one of Hell's minions.

He found the entry in the *Librum Magnum Daemonum* he had been looking for.

"Here," he said. "This is the entry for Scabass. Let's see what it says. Shredder – is that shredder? Yes, shredder of souls. He is a merciless ..."

"Your Latin's rubbish," said Rutspud, turning the book towards him. "He is a tyrant with no mercy, who can identify and exploit the most subtle of faults to condemn those who oppose him."

"He sounds quite horrible."

"You really don't know the half of it," said Rutspud.

Stephen closed the book with a fat, papery slam and shrugged.

"So, don't go back," he said.

"What?"

"Stay on Earth. Run free in the Welsh countryside. I mean, I suppose you could even stay here. We could try to pass you off as a new monk. A short, very ugly monk. In fact, we've already got a few of those so ..."

"No," Rutspud whined. "I can't. They'd find me. They'd send someone. And then they'd drag me to Hell, my own private Hell. I'm sure Escher's cooked up some weird recursive fractal Hell. You've heard the phrase, 'the devil's in the details'. Well, that'll be me. In a Hell within a Hell within a Hell." He rolled his eyes at the futility of it all and looked around him. "Maybe that's all this place is: another level of Hell."

"Ah, you've been to Wales before, then," said Stephen. "Come on, we'll sort something out."

"Why?" said Rutspud.

"Why?"

"Yes, why would you want to help me?"

"Just being friendly and charitable," said Stephen. "Goodness is its own reward."

"Are you trying to make me puke?"

"Hey, if you don't like me being nice to you, you don't have to come here."

Rutspud shook his head firmly.

"This" – and he gyrated his hands to figuratively cover the situation – "this is a ... a trade mission. Give and take. Tit for tat. You've given me the books – Wilde says thanks, by the way – and the material for the cushions and what have you."

"By the way," said Stephen, "that business of hangings and gougings for Old Mother Shipton you mentioned. You don't actually ...?"

"No. No need," said Rutspud. "That woman wails on cue when the inspectors come round. It actually makes a break from her awful predictions."

"So, if this is purely a business relationship, what have you given me in return?"

Rutspud clicked his tongue in thought.

"I could bring you and your boys some food from the banqueting hall of surprisingly large cutlery."

"Food from Hell?" said Stephen and tried to imagine what effects, physiological and spiritual, such sustenance would have on the brothers. "I don't think so."

"Maybe I could bring you back a couple of kittens?"

"I don't think we're in much of position to keep pets," said Stephen as he crossed to the bank of cabinets beneath the largest library shelves.

"I wasn't thinking about pets," said Rutspud. "I was thinking roasted, broiled, barbecued."

"Thanks but no thanks," said Stephen.

He pulled out two empty stoppered bottles from a cupboard.

"Now, let's bottle up some of that monk piddle for you for later and see if we can't come up with a solution to your little problem."

Bastian clutched the side of the rowboat as it rolled in the tide. The idea of taking to the water to catch some food had seemed a good one, but the boat that Father Eustace had brought to the island from the mainland was cramped, with four monks aboard and, between them, Brothers Bastian, Clement, Lionel and Henry had about as much sea-sense as a drunken Cockney on a lilo.

They were carrying out a plan that, at the moment of its conception, when they were huddled round the warming room fire with very little in their bellies except quantities of Brother Manfred's inexhaustible camomile tea, had seemed quite ingenious. They had several lengths of fishing line strung with hooks and pieces of silver from the church altar. According to the one fishing text in the library, mackerel were drawn to shiny objects, mistaking them for tasty sandeel.

In their fireside planning, they had pictured mackerel positively sacrificing themselves on the hooks for the monks' continued survival. However, after an hour at sea, albeit no more than twenty yards from shore, there had not been so much as a nibble, and the waves and the constant fidgeting of the brothers continually threatened to capsize them.

Brother Clement, as sacristan, had insisted on coming along to guard the church silver. However, he was using the outing as a method of delivering a discursive sermon on all things spiritual to his trapped audience.

"Our usage of the communion chalice and paten in this vulgar enterprise is a rich analogy for man's materialism and short-sightedness," he said.

"Really?" said Brother Henry, hunkering down in the well of the boat in his dressing-gown and trying to concentrate on his Sudoku book.

"Like the man who throws away the apple seeds because he cannot eat them, we are ignoring the rewards of eternity in search of short-term gain. We should turn to the Lord for our sustenance."

"Oh, God," said Brother Lionel, thrusting his arthritic fingers together and bowing his head. "Please send us two dozen juicy steaks. Oh, and a new set of teeth for me to eat them with," he added, whistling through his gums as he spoke.

Brother Lionel opened one eye to stare at the sky.

"No steak!" he declared crustily.

"God's sustenance is spiritual, not merely physical," said Brother Clement. "We should be in the church, not here."

"You're right," said Bastian abruptly. "Why didn't I think of that before?"

"See?" said Brother Clement, gesturing at Bastian's sudden piety.

"There's six months' supply of communion wafers in the sacristy," said Bastian. "It's not much, but it's something."

Brother Clement frowned.

"I must object. Communion wafers are not to be devoured like some midnight feast."

"Best bit is, they're not really communion wafers," said Bastian.

"What?"

Bastian coughed.

"I know this man in Caernarvon. He did me a deal on ten thousand ice-cream wafers. And you know the price of those communion wafers. It's extortionate."

"We've being using ice-cream wafers!" sputtered Brother Clement.

"Since the Christmas before last, actually," said Bastian. "I'm surprised no one noticed."

Brother Clement closed his eyes and shook his head.

"It matters not. As with the transubstantiation of the wine, the blessing of the bread – be it communion or ice-cream wafer – makes it suitable for the liturgical act. I am put in mind of a miracle which is most pertinent to our current situation."

"Oh, goody," muttered Brother Henry.

"The miracle of the herrings," said Brother Clement.

"I could eat herring," said Brother Lionel. "Mush it up with my gums."

"I don't recall that particular miracle," said Bastian.

"It is truly astounding," said Brother Clement. "That wisest of monks, St Thomas Aquinas, lay dying in his bed and, as a last request, asked his brothers to bring him some herring. The monks did not imagine they would find any, as they were far from the coast, but went out into the street to buy some. They found a fishmonger with his basket of wares and asked him if he had any herring. The fishmonger was doubtful, and said that he only had sardines. The fishmonger opened his basket to check and – lo! – there were herring within and St Thomas was able to enjoy his final meal."

Brother Clement looked to his fellow monks for their reaction.

"Is that it?" said Brother Lionel.

"What do you mean, 'Is that it?'" said Brother Clement. "It was a miracle."

Brother Henry looked up from his puzzles.

"The miracle was that the fishmonger – a man whose job it is to sell fish – happened to have some fish?"

"Yes, but he didn't think he had any herring."

"Oh, so it's the miracle of 'sorry mate, I haven't got any of them. Let me check. Oh, I have. My mistake'?"

"Such scepticism!" Brother Clement snorted. "There are none so blind as those who refuse to see. There are holy signs and wonders all arou– Oh, my goodness! Look!"

Brother Clement stood up in the boat, pointing.

"What?" said Bastian.

"There! On the water! Isn't that a pelican?"

"I think it's a gull. A big fat gull. Sit down before you tip us over."

"No," Brother Clement insisted. "It's a pelican."

"We don't get them round here."

"Christian symbol of sacrifice and sustenance. It's a sign."

"It's a sign it's lost," said Brother Henry. "The nearest pelicans are in Africa."

"No. No. Did not St Thomas Aquinas himself in his hymn describe our Lord as 'loving divine pelican, able to provide nourishment from his breast'?"

"Did he?" said Bastian.

"We are truly saved, brothers. This is a sign! This –"

In the act of declamation, Brother Clement put a foot on the gunwale, slipped and pitched forward into the sea.

"Well, that shut him up," said Brother Henry.

Brother Clement surfaced in a burst of spray and loud gasping.

"Are you all right there, brother?" called Brother Lionel.

Bastian looked down at the floundering monk.

"Does anyone know if Brother Clement can swim?" he asked.

"Can you swim, brother?" called Brother Lionel.

Brother Clement gave a watery cry that didn't settle the matter one way or the other.

"Looks like someone will have to save him," said Brother Henry without much urgency.

"Oh, Hell." Bastian gathered up the hem of his habit to disrobe.

"Don't leap in after him," said Brother Lionel. "He'll drag you down. Well-documented fact. Best to save someone who's already unconscious. It's dangerous otherwise."

"That's soon sorted," said Brother Henry, knelt up in the boat and raised one of the oars like a club. "Oi! Clement!"

The drowning sacristan glanced upwards and Brother Henry struck downwards.

"Is it always this bright?" Rutspud attempted to shield his eyes from the glare of 'outside'.

Stephen, rechecking the harness around his waist, looked up at the rolling clouds above.

"This is what's called 'overcast'," he said. "Fairly normal for the UK, but sometimes it clears."

"Clears?"

Stephen nodded and clipped the rope and descender to his harness.

"You know, the clouds clear away."

"And what's above them?"

"Nothing," shrugged Stephen. "The sky. The sun."

"Sun?"

"Yeah. A big ball of flaming gas half a million miles across. You know, the sun."

"And beyond that?"

"Space, the galaxies, the infinite universe."

A shiver ran up Rutspud's knobbly spine. He was vaguely familiar with the cosmology of the mortal world, but he couldn't quite cope with the notion of places without ceilings. He felt a terrible vertigo, the sense of a massive abyss above him.

"What is all this stuff?" Rutspud kicked at the equipment on the ground to distract himself.

"Abseiling gear. Helmet. Ropes. Flare gun. Manfred insisted."

111

"And all this to collect some piddly 'bird' eggs?"

"We're hungry. A few guillemot or gull eggs could save us from starvation."

Rutspud peered down the cliff that edged the cove. Surf ebbed through sharp, angled rocks at the base.

"Seems like a lot of effort for very little gain," he said.

Stephen grunted and, slowly feeding the rope through the descender device at his waist, lowered himself over the edge.

"I mean," Rutspud called down to him, "if they were big eggs, I'd understand. You ever seen the egg of the Ziz?"

"Ziz?"

"Monstrous bird. Supposedly going to be the main course at the banquet at the end of time."

"And it's real?"

"Mate, I was there when one of its eggs broke. Five dozen castles of Hell washed away in a flood of rotten egg gubbins."

"You're making it up. There's no such bird," shouted Stephen.

"Sure," Rutspud muttered. "Eggs big enough to squash a forest are stupid, but big balls of burning gas, oh no, they're perfectly sensible."

Bastian, soaking and panting for breath, hauled Brother Clement up onto the stony beach. Brother Clement was pale but for a surprisingly square bruise blossoming on his forehead.

While Brothers Lionel and Henry brought the rowing boat onto the shore, Bastian pulled away a strand of seaweed and put his ear to Brother Clement's chest.

"Thank God," he sighed, eyes closed with relief. "He's breathing. He's breathing!"

"Of course he is," said Brother Henry. "I didn't hit him that hard."

"No," said Bastian, "but you can still run up to get Brother Gillespie and tell him why you saw fit to clonk a drowning man over the head."

Brother Henry tutted at this additional chore but, nonetheless, with a soggy-hemmed dressing-gown wrapped about him, began to walk up the path.

"Well, I think I'm all done here," said Brother Lionel with a pout of his gummy mouth. "Fishing was a failure. Always said it would be."

"You're going nowhere," said Bastian. "You're going to wait until Brother Clement comes round and give him the bad news."

"What bad news?" said Brother Lionel in pretend surprise.

"That you let go of the fishing line and that our church silver is currently at the bottom of the Irish Sea."

"Pah. Always with the negativity, you young uns. What about the good news?"

"Good news?" said Bastian.

Brother Lionel gestured to the dozen spider crabs that were still latched onto Brother Clement's sodden habit.

"It's crab for tea!"

Stephen grunted and sidled further along the cliff face. Those crevices and cracks, which had looked like promising nesting sites, had proved to be either unused or abandoned. From his position between the clifftop and the sea, he could now see there were a number of nesting birds on the opposite cliff, but he couldn't access them without climbing back up and repositioning his tether on the other side of the inlet.

"How many have you got so far?" Rutspud shouted down to him.

"None!" Stephen replied.

"None? As in not one?"

"Yes," Stephen yelled. "Not a single one."

"What's the problem?"

"The problem?" Stephen readjusted his footing on the rock, putting all his weight on the line. "The problem is there are no eggs!"

"Well, you should look for some!"

"Oh! You think?"

"Yes!"

Stephen swore under his breath and inched along further, struggling to maintain purchase on the wet, mossy rock.

"Wait a moment," he said. "I think I've found something."

It wasn't much of a nest. For a start, it was in a poor location, on a jutting ledge rather than in any sort of protective nook. It was surprising that the wind hadn't already whipped it away. The construction materials were an unusual combination. The base of the nest seemed to be formed primarily from the top half of a sheep's skull, the walls resting upon it composed of scraps of paper, fragments of plastic, shreds of car tyre and a bizarre assortment of spoons, pencils, fish remains and a single rubber glove. The whole thing was held together with artlessly placed globules of mud.

Stephen climbed a little and peered down into the nest. Two mottled green eggs sat in the base of the sheep skull, rolling back and forth as the wind buffeted the pathetic nest. They weren't the eggs of any species Stephen recognised.

He hesitated and found himself weighing up the pros and cons of taking the eggs.

Con: There were only two eggs. It hardly seemed worth it.

Pro: A spoonful of omelette for each of the brothers was far better than no omelette at all.

Con: It seemed oddly heartless to steal the eggs from such a plainly rubbish nest. A mother bird with such awful nest-building skills deserved every bit of help she could get.

Pro: Clearly the builder of that nest was an unfit parent. It would be a kindness to end this tragedy now.

Con: If this nest-building was typical of the species then the species was, in all likelihood, endangered.

Pro: Any bird which was such a piss-poor nest-builder after millions of years of evolution probably deserved to go extinct.

Con: But look at them! Aw! Little eggs! Soon to be cute little chicks! The circle of life!

Pro: Stephen was hungry.

Stephen reached down but, as his fingertips brushed against the lip of nest, a white and yellow blur dove down out of the sky at him. Orange feet slapped him in the face and he instinctively pulled away from the squawking and frantic uncoordinated flapping of large wings.

"Did you find something?" shouted Rutspud.

Stephen lost his footing and he fell away from the cliff edge. The rope at his harness tightened but, as he pitched back, he felt the entire harness slipping.

"No! No!" he shouted, as he flipped over, head downwards, and the harness, perhaps never designed to be worn over monk's robes, slid off Stephen's hips and down his legs. Some still-functioning sliver of his terrified mind made the life-saving decision to bend his legs and the loose harness caught under Stephen's knees.

Stephen screamed as he dangled upside down above the rocky surf while the demented, shrieking bird flapped around his knees.

"Oh, God!" he yelled. "Help me! Help me!"

"What?" shouted Rutspud.

"Jesus! Help me! Pull me up!"

"Have you found any eggs?" said Rutspud.

"Just do it!"

Manfred looked at the haul from the fishing trip, his eyes agleam.

"It certainly beats marsh rabbit," he said, poking playfully at one of the crabs in the tub of water. "Yes, you do, Mr Snippy. You certainly do."

"Anything beats roasted rat," said Bastian. "In fact, nothing beats roasted rat. Literally having nothing is better than roasted rat. You can cook these up?"

"Absolutely. I'm thinking of a Hawaiian recipe with coriander and basil, flaked ginger, pepper, breadcrumbs and a little oil."

"We have those things?"

"Or something a bit like them, I'm sure. Get the gas-fired barbecue out in the cloisters, brother, and put on your best grass skirt."

"Eh?"

Manfred grinned.

"We're having a luau!"

Stephen lay out on the ground, his fingers clutching instinctively at the grass beneath him. He was still breathless and a tiny bit terrified but, mostly, he felt an exhilaration and gratitude at his continued survival. The late afternoon sky, cloudy and grey though it was, had never looked more beautiful.

"So," said Rutspud, squatting beside him and methodically pulling apart a clover, "I notice that prayer doesn't work."

"What's that?" said Stephen.

"Prayer. There you were, shouting out for the Almighty – 'Help me, help me' – and nothing happened. The Big Guy didn't step in to save you."

"I'm alive, aren't I?"

"Yeah. That's because I pulled you up."

"Maybe God sent you to help me."

Rutspud blew the remains of the clover off his palm.

"Are you trying to piss me off?"

Stephen sat up and looked at Rutspud. I'm chatting with a demon, he thought to himself. A real, red, sort of scaly demon. With little horns and everything. It was a continual surprise, one he was unable to get over.

"Prayer works," he said. "Maybe not in the way some people might think. It's not like magic wishes. It's not a demand that God bend the laws of nature for our personal gain. Prayer is the opening of oneself to the divine, spiritually accepting there is something beyond this merely physical world. I think I should pray for you."

Rutspud sprang to his feet.

"Woah, puny human scum! Pray for *me*? Pray *for* me?"

"Worth a shot. You've got kitten-shaped worries. Maybe this is your only solution."

"No, it's not," said Rutspud fiercely. "It sounds like an invitation to blow up the universe. Pray for a demon? That's like matter and anti-matter, water and electricity ... er, zippers and male genitalia."

"Have faith," said Stephen and put his hands together.

"Fine!" snapped Rutspud. "But don't expect me to stay in the blast radius. I'm hiding behind that rock."

Rutspud scuttled away rapidly, towards a large outcrop of stone. Stephen waited until he was out of sight.

"Okay?" he called out. "I'm going to start now."

"Er, Stephen?" Rutspud replied.

"Yes?"

"I think you'd better come see this."

"What is it?" said Stephen.

"I don't know. Possibly dinner."

The Hawaiian luau had started out so promisingly.

Manfred had fashioned grass skirts for the brothers and a surprising number agreed to wear them. Brother Henry had produced a pair of Hawaiian print shirts from his personal trunk and given one apiece to Manfred and Father Eustace. Brother Vernon had set up the poles for a limbo competition in the centre of the cloisters. Brother Clement, the mildly concussed father of the feast, had been placed in a deck chair, a half coconut containing nothing but fresh water and a cocktail umbrella placed in his hand. The only problem was Manfred's inability to get the barbecue started. While he fiddled with gas valves, knobs and lighters, the prepared crabs sat cold and uncooked on the grill. Monks circled hungrily and Manfred's promises that they would be cooking in no time at all and that there was a surprise dessert for afters did little to appease the ravenous men.

Bastian decided it was time to provide some welcome distraction. He rested his display boards against the nearest stonework balustrade and got out his laser pointer pen.

"Brothers!" he said loudly. "While Brother Manfred gets our feast underway, I would like to deliver a short presentation."

Two dozen starving monks turned unhurriedly to look at him.

"Presentation?" said Brother Lionel.

"How Not To Die!" declared Bastian grandiosely. "Thirty minutes of edification that could save your life."

"I'll be dead in thirty minutes if I don't get any food," said Brother Henry.

"First up," said Bastian, revealing the next presentation board, "what's safe to eat and what's not."

"Beard!" shouted Father Eustace apropos of nothing at all.

"No, Father Abbot," said Bastian. "Lichen and moulds. Did you know there are any number of moulds, fungi and lichen growing in and around St Cadfan's?"

"You want us to lick rocks for our supper?" said Brother Henry.

"I'm game," said Brother Lionel. "I like food you can lick."

"But which are safe?" asked Bastian. He played his laser pointer over his presentation board. "Look at these two pictures. One of these is perfectly nutritious, the other poisonous. But which is which? Hmmm? Anyone care to take a guess?"

Brother Huey sat cross-legged in the lee of the rock. A piece of string ran from his hand to a stick propping up the edge of a cardboard box some six yards away. Underneath the box, an unperturbed rabbit sat munching on a chunk of carrot.

"Can we eat it?" said Rutspud.

"If you can catch it," said Stephen faintly.

"I didn't mean the long-eared kitten monster. I meant this one."

"No," said Stephen with a quiet forcefulness.

He approached Brother Huey. The old monk's robe was damp with condensation. His skin was the same grey as the clouds above. His eyes were closed. He looked like he was just taking a nap although his face looked more peaceful in death than Stephen had ever seen it in life.

"Do you think he's started to go off?" said Rutspud.

"No, that's just his feet. They've always smelled like that."

"So he's still good for eating?"

"We don't eat the dead!"

"Oh. I see. Why?"

"It's not healthy. It's not respectful. And ... and it might be the plague."

"Plague?"

"A horrible way to die that we might all catch," said Stephen, feeling a knot of panic begin to unfold in his chest. Two monks dead within weeks of one another. Two close associates. If it wasn't something infectious, what could it be? Brother Huey wasn't exactly the type to die of a broken heart.

"We have to tell the others," said Stephen.

He looked round. They were almost as far from St Cadfan's as it was possible to get on the small island. Sure, the monastery was

118

only a five minute jog away, but Stephen felt a sudden and irresistible need to do something, do something now.

He rooted through the climbing gear Manfred had given him.

"Woah," said Rutspud. "Are you going to fire that?"

"You think I shouldn't?"

"I was going to ask you if I could do it."

Stephen gave him a look, pointed the flare gun at the heavens and squeezed the trigger. A pink bolt of fire flew up over the island. They watched it slowly arc towards St Cadfan's.

"Not respectful to who?" said Rutspud.

"Sorry?"

"If we eat him, who are we disrespecting?"

"Brother Huey, of course."

"But he's dead."

"I know! And we respect the dead."

"But he's no longer here," said Rutspud. "He's gone. His spirit has fled."

Stephen nodded reflectively.

"At peace in Heaven."

"Or the other place."

Stephen glared. "Shut up!"

"What?" Rutspud kicked a stone at the rabbit under the box and it fled, taking the carrot with it. "You think we don't have any monks in Hell? We have whole pits of them."

"Brother Huey was a good man," Stephen insisted. "He was always nice to ... well, actually, he was a miserable sod most of the time. But he devoted his life to helping ... I'm not sure what he spent his life doing. He was a fine artist."

"We have artists in Hell too," said Rutspud.

Stephen sighed irritably. "Then we'd best pray for his soul."

He knelt beside the seated corpse of Brother Huey and put his hands together.

"I think I'll stand over there," said Rutspud.

Stephen grabbed Rutspud's wrist and dragged the demon down beside him.

"You can sit with me. And I'll pray for you as well. Heavenly Father ..."

Bastian was in full flow, pontificating on the importance of hand washing and the all-round benefits of soap. Manfred was still struggling with the barbecue. The gas bottle was clearly full and the valve open. He had twisted the barbecue gas intake knob more times than he could recall, and he was pumping the lighter button constantly. There was hiss and smell of gas but no flame.

In the presence of a band of monks who were probably ready to eat the crabs raw, Manfred retained his patience, got down on his knees and inspected the underside of the barbecue. There was the canister and the rubber tube connecting it to ...

"Ah."

There was a hole in the tubing, an age-worn gap in the cracking rubber, through which gas was leaking.

"Not good," he said, and made to turn off the gas at the bottle.

The valve wouldn't turn. Manfred grunted to himself and put further pressure on it. The valve would not budge. With an increasingly nervous urgency, Manfred picked up his barbecue tongs and sharply rapped them against the valve.

With a solid 'thunk', the valve mechanism sheered away from the gas canister. Natural gas whistled from the resultant hole and the canister rattled with the force of it.

"Definitely not good," said Manfred, and backed away rapidly.

He coughed away the stink of gas and turned to the other monks.

"Brothers! Brothers!" he shouted.

"I'm nearly done," replied Bastian. "I am sure we will be ready to tuck into your food in just a minute or two."

"There's a bit of a problem," Manfred said. "Um, a bit of a gas leak."

The nearest monks scattered. Some stepped briskly into the protective corridors of the surrounding cloisters.

"I'm sure that I'll get it under control in just a tick. But if we could all back off a bit and check that there are no naked flames about."

The monks moved rapidly, but Bastian was stood still, gesturing at the sky with his laser pointer.

"What's that?"

Manfred looked up at the descending distress flare. His first thought was of Brother Stephen. His second was of the incandescent pink ball and the escaping gas.

He opened his mouth to shout a warning.

Rutspud was pleased to discover that Stephen's prayers did not instantly banish him to Hell, turn him inside out or do something equally horrible. He was, however, disappointed to discover that prayer seemed to involve little more than closing one's eyes and talking to the Almighty in the hope that he might be listening.

"... and please help Rutspud in his time of need," said Stephen. "Yes, I know he is a demon, Lord, one of the fallen ones, but I guess that since you are the creator of all things, he too is one of your creations. Give him strength to overcome his trials and the courage to do what is right."

"Fat chance of that," Rutspud muttered.

"Please don't interrupt," said Stephen, eyes still closed. "I'm talking to God, not you."

"I'm just saying that –"

There was a far off sound, an explosive boom, muffled and yet enlarged by distance.

"What was that?" said Stephen.

"Was it God?" said Rutspud.

Stephen scowled at him.

"I thought it might have been his signal to say your time's up. He's not angry, is he?"

Something small fell end over end out of the sky and smacked Rutspud on the head.

"Ow!" he declared. "Praying hurts."

He bent and picked up the object. It was warm to the touch and slightly scorched at one end.

"That's Bastian's laser pointer," said Stephen, clearly confused.

"His whatty-what-what?"

Rutspud pressed the button on the side of the tubular device. A red dot of light appeared on the grass.

"Actually," said Stephen, "that could be the answer to your prayers."

"You're shitting me."

"I'm not."

"Nah. You're shitting me."

"I defecate you not, demon. You see, kittens are very playful creatures ..."

By nightfall, Brother Huey had been laid out in the monastery crypt, in an alcove next to Brother Bernard. The monks gathered in the cloisters afterwards.

Manfred and Father Eustace stood in the slight crater at the middle of the scorched and blackened lawn. Most of the monks had red faces, as though they had been out in the sun too long. Some were missing eyebrows, lending a surprise air to their already stunned looking faces. None of the brothers had been seriously injured in the gas explosion, although Bastian had apparently lost his laser pointer and Brother Vernon had had his glasses smashed by a flying crab.

The monks looked to their leaders for leadership. Many of them weren't particularly hopeful.

"Father Abbot," said Manfred and nudged his superior in the ribs.

The rarely focussed abbot seemed to mentally surface.

"Fires," he said ponderously. "The eternal fires await."

He paused. The brothers waited.

"But, in Hell," he said, "are there crabs? Are there crabs?" He scrutinised them all. "I think not."

He fell into silence again and, once he realised that this was the end of the abbot's speech, Manfred stepped forward.

"Brothers," he said, "I know all our thoughts are with Brother Huey. And Brother Bernard. And, yes, I too share your concerns. They have told us there is no plague on the island but, if there is not, we are facing a disturbing coincidence."

There were mutters of unhappy agreement from many of the monks.

"Some of you have asked if you can sleep somewhere other than the dormitory that you previously shared with Brother

Bernard and Brother Huey. I can understand that. And so we will set up some temporary beds in the church."

"The church?" said Brother Clement indignantly.

"The church is, above all, a place of sanctuary, is it not?" said Manfred and gave Brother Clement his firmest gaze.

"Of course, brother," said the sacristan humbly. "But I suppose I will have to stay up all night to guard the communion wafers from any midnight snackers."

"Not at all," said Manfred and waved Bastian over.

Bastian came forward with a tray of dishes.

"Lemon sorbet," said Manfred. "Garnished with the last of the wafers. It's no feast, but at least we can eat, enjoy and remember our brothers who have passed on."

"Lemon sorbet?" said Brother Lionel. "Where did you get the lemons from?"

"Strangest thing," said Manfred with a smile. "I was in the visitors' centre and discovered in a cupboard two bottles of limoncello liqueur."

From the back of the crowd, there was a cough.

"What is it, Brother Trevor?"

"Stephen."

"Stephen."

"Are you sure that's limoncello? It couldn't be anything else?"

Bastian handed out bowls and spoons to the hungry monks.

"That's what it looked like to me," said Manfred. "Do you think it might be something else?"

Stephen looked at the monks tucking in to their desserts. He'd need to fill replacement bottles for Rutspud.

"Nope," he squeaked. "No, I'm sure that's what it is. No, thanks, Brother Sebastian. I'm not hungry."

123

"BONG!" declared Nero loudly. "Twelve o'clock."

Lord Peter smiled at Rutspud. So did Scabass, but there was a world of difference between them. One was a smile of a fool who believed he was doing good. The other was the smile of a git who relished the pain of others. Rutspud wasn't sure which one he hated more.

"Looking forward to some well-deserved relaxation therapy?" said Lord Peter.

"Absolutely," said Rutspud, feeling the shape of the laser pointer in his clenched fist.

"Enjoy," leered Scabass and opened the Relaxation Centre door for his underling.

"What is that unholy moaning?" said Rutspud. "It sounds like a whale trying to mate with a pipe organ."

"Oh, that'll be the Enya," said Scabass. "Don't worry, you'll totally forget about it once the kittens get to work on you."

With that, he propelled Rutspud roughly inside and shut the door.

Rutspud looked across the pastel carpet at the mass of mewling, furry creatures stumbling towards him.

He quickly turned on the laser pointer and found that the kittens halted their progress to chase the little light. He swept the light briskly over to the wall and the fastest of the kittens ran face-first into the wall and fell back with a small kittenish "oof".

Rutspud smiled.

This might actually be fun.

Chapter 5 – The day the cargo container washed ashore

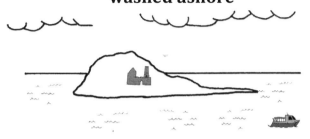

"Shhhh! We really don't want to wake the others," said Stephen.

"What is all this stuff?" Rutspud pulled out a hinged metal implement from one of the refectory cupboards. "Some sort of finger-crusher, surely?"

"I doubt it."

"Toe-mangler?"

Stephen held up his candle to take a look, and shrugged.

"I believe Manfred uses it to mash potatoes," he said. "Not that we've had potatoes for a while. We've had seaweed mostly. A lot of seaweed." Stephen indicated a large smelly bucket next to the sink. "That's just for our breakfast fry-up tomorrow."

"Smells like the pool of Yan Ryuleh Sloggoth," said Rutspud.

"Who?"

"Elder demon of the impenetrable depths. Nice guy. Likes oil company executives," said Rutspud.

"Likes them?"

"For lunch. I've told you, Stephen, I can bring some food from Hell if you like."

Stephen sighed.

"To be honest, I quite like seaweed," he said. "Manfred made cake from it yesterday. Don't ask me how, but it was nice. What we could really do with is fuel of some sort. We haven't had hot water for a fortnight. That and fuses, they all blew when Manfred tried to wire up that old tractor battery after the generator ran dry."

"Fair enough, mate. I'll see what I can do," said Rutspud, and emerged from a cupboard holding some battered enamel plates. "Let's go!" he grinned.

The two of them crept quietly outside and stole down the hillside. It was a clear night and the moon cast a helpful glow.

"Everything's more exciting at night, somehow," said Stephen.

"Less frightening," agreed Rutspud and gave an involuntary shudder. The intolerable glare of the sun had not only been painful on his skin, but also a constant reminder that there was no sensible roof on this place.

"That spotlight," he said.

"The moon," said Stephen.

"How far above us is it?"

Stephen looked at him.

"What kind of answer wouldn't freak you out?"

"Ooh, I think I could cope with the idea that it's a hundred feet above us."

"Yeah, that's about right," said Stephen cheerily. "All this sneaking about reminds me of when I was young, staying up late."

"Staying up?"

"When you're a child, a human child, all your parents want is for you to stay in bed and get a good night's sleep," explained Stephen.

"Parents. Those are the people who hatched you out?"

"Something like that – but when I was about ten, I really, *really* wanted to see a badger, so I'd go outside after midnight and look around the garden. It always seemed like a different place in the moonlight."

"Did you ever see a badger?" asked Rutspud.

"No," said Stephen. "I don't think there are any in Erdington, but it was the most exciting thing, to be sneaking around outside when I was supposed to be in bed."

Rutspud gave Stephen a sideways look.

"So there's a part of you that likes to break the rules then?" he asked. "Even you, a monk?"

Stephen shrugged. "I think there is. I wouldn't be human otherwise."

"There's so much I don't understand about humans," said Rutspud, with a rueful shake of his head. "Why do the good ones have bits of bad in them? Why do the bad ones have bits of good in them? Why do some men have boobs?"

"It's all part of God's mysterious plan, I guess," said Stephen.

"Speaking of which, I checked the arrivals board for those friends of yours, Huey and Bernard. They're not down there with us."

"Well, that's a relief," said Stephen. "I'll rest easier knowing that. Now, shall we?"

They had arrived on a flat piece of scrubby grass.

"Right, I know how this works," said Rutspud. "I've seen it on the internet. I'll stand here, you go over there. I throw the frisbee and you jump up and catch it in your mouth."

Stephen frowned.

"That's dogs you're thinking of. I won't be catching it in my mouth. I probably won't be catching it at all to be honest."

"Oh," said Rutspud, a little disappointed. "Can we get a dog from somewhere?"

"There aren't any on the island," said Stephen. "Apart from a collie who visits from the mainland sometimes. Let's just try throwing it for now."

Rutspud tried an experimental flick of his bony wrist and then unleashed the upside-down enamel plate towards Stephen. It sailed past him and continued for a considerable distance before it clattered to the floor.

"Yes! Did you see that?" crowed Rutspud, and he skimmed another plate through the air.

A few minutes later, Stephen puffed back to Rutspud, having run back and forth, collecting plates.

"My turn now."

Rutspud found that his long, skinny arms and lightning-fast reactions made him adept at catching the frisbee-cum-plate. He capered with joy as he stretched up to catch one that looked as if it was going to elude him.

"I'm a frisbee natural," he declared. "I think I win at this game. So, we're doing football tomorrow, yes?"

Stephen nodded.

"We need something for the day after. Are you absolutely sure you haven't got a unicycle?" Rutspud said. "I mean, maybe you just forgot where you put it?"

"No, I really don't have one. I'm utterly certain there are no unicycles on Bardsey."

"Shame. Right, I'm just going to have one last go with this, see how far I can throw it," said Rutspud.

He stepped back and put everything he had into one final throw. The plate disappeared across the grass, over towards the rocky shore.

"Come on," said Stephen. "You need to help me find that."

They trotted over the rise and clambered over some rocks before they found the plate.

"Hey, what's that?" said Rutspud, pointing towards the shore.

A large shape loomed against the skyline.

"It looks like a container," said Stephen as they approached it.

"Well, duh," said Rutspud, "everything's a container if you try hard enough. Take it from me, when demons get bored they can stuff *anything* into *anything*. Oh, the fun they have in the pit of gluttons."

"Not sure I want to know about that," said Stephen. "I still can't believe that Hell's really a place, you know. It seems so wrong."

"You believe in God, why wouldn't you believe in Hell?"

"I always just imagined it was an absence of God. A spiritual thing. More of a concept than a reality. Not a place where demons actually torture people. For eternity."

He shuddered with distaste.

"Hey, don't get shirty with me," said Rutspud. "I just work there. Now apart from being a container, what do we think this is?"

"A cargo container," said Stephen. "That's what they're called. They're like big boxes that can fit on the back of a lorry, and they get piled up on ships. This one must have fallen off a ship."

"What's inside?" said Rutspud. He splashed into the water and rapped on the door. It made a hollow, metallic clanging sound.

The big metal box was more than twice his height and three times longer than it was tall.

"It could be anything," said Stephen, stepping in with the hem of his habit held high. "I suppose we'd better wait until the tide's fully out before we try and open the doors, it's going to be tricky with the water up here like it is."

"I won't get to see," said Rutspud with a small pout. "I'm going to miss all the fun. Well, make sure you let me know if there's a unicycle in there, won't you?"

Stephen led the other monks down the path just after dawn.

"Well, our restless, early-rising brother has found something interesting here," said Manfred as they took in the sight before them. The container was completely clear of the water now. "I estimate that we have around two hours before the tide will turn and make things difficult for us."

"We need to see what treasures lie within as quickly as possible," said Bastian.

"Treasures?"

"There could be something really valuable in there," said Bastian, with a glint in his eye. "Electronics, antiques, high-end fashion."

"I was hoping there might be something we could eat," said Manfred with a raised eyebrow.

"Oh yes, of course. That would be nice," said Bastian with a distinct lack of conviction.

"I think we should say a few words."

The other monks looked at Brother Clement in puzzlement.

"Beg pardon?" said Brother Lionel.

"The Lord's bounty has been delivered to us by his mysterious hand," said Brother Clement. "The least we can do is offer our thanks."

"Fine." Manfred hefted a sack of tools from his shoulder. "Heavenly Father, we are thankful for this unexpected offering in our time of need. We receive this gift as your humble servants. Could you please bless these bolt croppers so that we can be sure of gaining entry?"

Some fraught minutes later, filled with shouted instructions, some slightly sweary disagreements and the screams that followed Brother Vernon stubbing the toe of his brothel creepers on the container door, the brothers of St Cadfan's (aided by the blessed bolt croppers) managed to gain access.

The monks all crowded round as Manfred pulled the doors open. One of the doors jammed against an outcrop of rocks, but through the other they could see that the container was filled with boxes.

"What's inside?" said Stephen his voice squeaking with excitement and curiosity.

"A little calm, please," said Manfred.

"Sorry. It's just like Christmas, isn't it? Wondering what's inside."

"Oh," said Brother Clement condescendingly. "Of course. Christmas is all about the presents, isn't it? Not about our Lord, Jesus Christ."

Stephen gave him an apologetic look.

"It is about the presents a bit," he whispered to no one in particular.

"Listen everybody!" said Manfred firmly. "We do not have time to be distracted by peeking inside these boxes. If we wish to make sure we get them out of the way of the sea and the weather, we will need to form a human chain and get them all up to the monastery before we examine them properly. Can I please count on your discipline and energy?"

There was a slight grumbling, but the monks got to work and they managed to clear the last of the boxes as the advancing water began to slosh inside the container. Most of the boxes had been of a manageable size, but there was one oversized package that was wrapped in opaque plastic and affixed to a pallet.

"What do you suppose this is?" asked Henry, who was holding the middle of the pallet, while Manfred and Stephen struggled with the ends. "Let me check the other side."

Henry let go of the pallet and walked around to the other side and put his hands underneath to support it again, as he scrutinised the mysterious package.

"Henry," said Stephen, puffing with exertion, "I didn't notice any difference at all when you let go just then. You're not actually helping."

"Well, that's not very nice," said Henry. "Sometimes I think you're not much of a team player, Stephen." He tugged at the plastic that wrapped the contents. "Maybe it's a karaoke machine. I like a bit of karaoke. Or bingo, it could be one of those machines with the balls."

"Brother, I think you may have dropped the cord to your dressing-gown," said Manfred, nodding over Henry's shoulder.

Stephen ignored Henry's retreating blather as he went off to look. Manfred winked briefly and the two of them continued to negotiate the rocky path with the awkward load.

Manfred made sure that the boxes were piled safely indoors in the refectory and then ushered Father Eustace forwards to preside over things.

Father Eustace plucked ineffectually at the plastic covering the pallet. Manfred stepped forward with a paring knife and used it to slash through the plastic covering. There was a brief silence as the monks all absorbed the sight before them.

"Is it a go-kart?" Brother Lionel eyed the vehicle's chunky wheels and cherry red paint job.

"It's a mobility scooter," said Bastian. "You know, for lazy people and sometimes the disabled and old people."

"This may be disappointing to some of you," said Manfred. "We cannot expect that everything we find here will be useful."

Father Eustace was climbing stiffly onto the scooter seat as he spoke.

"We should open some more packages to see whether – ah Father, I think these things are transported without a battery," said Manfred. "It's most unlikely that it will – oh."

Eustace pulled sharply forward on the scooter. It crashed down off the pallet and the crowd of monks parted rapidly as he zipped across the refectory floor.

Brother Clement pushed forward and held up his hands for silence.

"Brothers, I think we have just been shown the way to deal with this."

"Have we?" said Stephen.

"Care to explain?" Manfred asked.

"I would liken our situation to the parable of the talents," said Clement. "If you recall, Matthew tells of a master who, upon going away for some time, entrusts his property to his servants. The first servant was given five talents, the second two talents and the third was given one talent. I'm given to understand that a talent is quite a lot of money, by the way."

"Yes, do continue," said Manfred.

"Well, the parable tells how the first two servants made a healthy return on the money by investing it in some way, which pleased the master greatly. The third servant merely buried it, so that he handed back exactly the same amount, untouched. That servant was punished for being lazy."

"Ah yes," said Bastian. "The parable of rampant capitalism. One of my favourites."

Clement gave him a sour look.

"I rather think that it's intended to show how we are each expected to make the best use of what we are given," he said. "Father Eustace has demonstrated that we can find a use for each and every gift that has been sent to us in this most unusual benefaction. It is our duty to trust in the wisdom of our Lord and find the means to benefit St Cadfan's with the contents of these boxes."

Manfred nodded enthusiastically.

"Brother Clement, that is a fine idea. Surprisingly. We distribute the boxes amongst us all, unopened. Each of us must use our creativity to find a constructive use for what's inside."

He caught a small cough from Clement.

"We use our creativity and the *power of prayer*, yes, of course," corrected Manfred. "In that case, let us form an orderly queue and we can hand out the boxes."

The monks jostled for position in the queue, as they craned their necks to see which of the boxes looked most promising. Manfred heard whispered comments drifting towards him as he did a count of the boxes.

"Those metal boxes look as though they're protecting something valuable. We could be talking custom-made guitar."

"There's a special seal on that box there. Gotta be something good in there."

"See the writing on the side of the red cartons? Do you think it's Chinese for nougat?"

Manfred ignored the fantasies and speculation, and started to hand out the boxes.

"Move back please, brothers, once you've got your boxes! I know you want to see what's in them, but please move back so we can keep things going."

The refectory soon turned into a frenzy of box opening.

"Who's got nails? I can't get this tape off!"

"Where are the scissors?"

"I've found a woman!"

At once, all of the monks stopped scrabbling at packaging and silence fell.

"Come again?" said Brother Henry.

"What did you say, Brother Lionel?" asked Manfred.

"There's a woman in my box. Look!"

Bald and ancient Brother Lionel held a plastic woman high up in the air, turning so that everyone could see.

"Why's she got no arms or legs?" asked Henry.

"Because it's Annie," said Brother Gillespie.

All heads turned to him.

"You can't possibly know her name," said Lionel, clutching the doll to his chest defensively.

"She's a Resusci-Annie," sniffed the infirmarian, stepping forward. "Look, her chest goes up and down. She's been saving lives for generations."

"Is it one of them marital aids?" said Brother Lionel.

"It's for practising CPR," Brother Gillespie explained.

Gillespie gave his ever-running nose a preparatory wipe, took the doll, placed her on the floor and showed the monks the life-saving technique. Manfred noticed that Lionel scowled throughout at the violation of his new friend.

"Look! Look what I got!" shouted Henry.

Everyone turned to see what he had. Henry's face glowed with pleasure as he slotted together the vertical sections of pole.

"Is that an IV stand?" asked Manfred."

"Yes! I've wanted one of these for as long as I can remember," said Henry, whisking it back and forth on its wheels.

"But why?" asked Manfred.

"I was in hospital, as a child, with a broken arm," said Henry. "All the cool kids had these. They went everywhere with them, like faithful dogs. I really wanted one too, but they said *no*. Oh, I'm so happy, I've got my own at last!"

Henry danced and twirled with his new toy.

"Now remember, brothers, the challenge is for each of us to find a way to use these things to benefit the *whole monastery*," said Manfred. "What do you have there, Bastian?"

"I think it's antiseptic handwash," said Bastian, holding out a pump bottle.

Manfred sniffed it critically, detecting an alcoholic base.

"I wonder if it might serve as a useful marinade."

"Manfred," said Bastian, "there is a skull and cross-bones and a large warning that says it's not for human ingestion."

Manfred made a dismissive hand gesture as he continued to sniff the intriguing liquid.

"That's just to cover themselves. It would probably be fine in moderation."

He handed the bottle back to Bastian and turned his attention to his own box. He pulled out a handful of plastic tubing with a nod of approval. Now here was something he could work with! It looked vaguely medical. In fact, it struck Manfred that everything they'd opened so far seemed to be medical supplies of some sort. He delved further and found some sturdy-looking bags that seemed designed to fit onto the tubing, presumably for intravenous drips and the like. Manfred's mind raced with the possibilities. He had promised that he would not make any further attempts to distil alcohol after last year's explosion, so he scrubbed that idea with some regret. He was wondering if it might be possible to construct some rudimentary bagpipes when a shriek of pain went up.

"There's scalpels in that one, watch out," came Stephen's voice.

"Ah, best get Brother Gillespie," said Manfred absently, blowing into an IV bag. It made a small farting noise, rather than any musical note.

"I don't think so," said Stephen. "It was Brother Gillespie who stabbed his hand. He seems to have fainted."

The office of Quilldust, the census-taker, was fitted with shelves from floor to ceiling, and every shelf was laden with folders, their spines inscribed with neat handwriting. Rutspud saw that there was a sleek black computer on the desk, but for some reason, Quilldust chose to write everything down in longhand in a huge book.

When Rutspud had asked him why he kept the machine if he wrote everything out, Quilldust had replied, "The computer is for underlings who displease me."

"You mean you write reports about them, log details of their transgressions?"

Quilldust had shaken his head and simply pointed at the blood encrusted along the edge of the monitor.

Rutspud had so far answered questions about his name, place of residence and occupation. Quilldust had written down his answers with excruciating slowness, using real ink. Each time he came to the end of a line, he carefully blotted the words, to be sure that he didn't smudge them.

"Next question," said Quilldust. "What is the size of your cave? You may give the answer in square metres, square yards, hectares or acres. An estimate is fine, as long as we find it to be accurate to plus or minus five per cent if we choose to carry out a spot check."

Rutspud had no idea.

"How often do you carry out a spot check?" he asked.

"Approximately one answer in a hundred will be selected for further verification," said Quilldust.

"And what happens if I'm wrong?" asked Rutspud.

"You carry out the next hundred spot checks," said Quilldust.

Rutspud concentrated. He could do this. Shooting from the hip was what he excelled at. He pictured the cave, and the things within it. The snooker table would account for about a tenth of the floor space. How big was the snooker table? Say three and a half by two metres. Seven square metres.

"My cave is seventy square metres," he said confidently.

Quilldust wrote down the answer, taking so long that Rutspud wanted to tear the pen from his hand and write it himself, but he sat and waited.

"Do you exist in any other dimensions?" asked Quilldust eventually.

Rutspud tried to imagine what that question meant. Did they somehow know about his visits to earth? Did that count as another dimension?

"Apart from the usual ... three?"

"Yes."

"Would I know about it if I did?" he asked, cautiously.

"We're just trying to build a complete picture of the whereabouts of all demons," answered Quilldust. "If we're likely to find you manifested elsewhere, we could do with some warning so we don't double-count."

"Right. No. I'm only ever in one place at once," said Rutspud, and waited while the pen scratched slowly across the surface of the paper.

"I need to ask you about some of your underlings," said Quilldust. "Do you keep any imps?"

"Yes. I command a horde of the Tiny Blue Innumerables."

"I see. And how many of them are there?"

Rutspud blinked. He had large eyes and he blinked big.

"Well ... they're innumerable. You can't count them."

"You haven't bothered?"

"No. I have tried. But they are innumerable, uncountable. It's part of their nature. It's metaphysically impossible to know how many of them there are."

"Yes. And when you have tried to count them, how many did you count?"

Rutspud shrugged.

"Seven? Twelve? Thirty-two?"

"Which is it?"

Rutspud groaned inwardly.

"Twelve," he said. "Put twelve."

Quilldust did just that. Slowly.

"I also need to ask you about a demon called Frogspear. Where might we find him?"

"Ah," said Rutspud. "It's a bit complicated."

Quilldust looked up at him, his pen poised.

"Yes?"

"Frogspear doesn't actually exist anymore. He was chopped up, at the same time as Bootlick. Parts of him are in the demon Lickspear."

Quilldust took a very long time to write this down, word for word.

"And what happened to Bootlick?" he asked.

"Parts of him are in Lickspear too," said Rutspud.

"Where is the rest of him?" asked Quilldust, as he finished transcribing.

"The rest?"

"Two demons were chopped up, but you have only accounted for half of the pieces. Is there another demon who comprises the remaining pieces?"

Rutspud's mouth opened and closed.

"Well, Lickspear is slightly bigger than either Frogspear or Bootlick, so it's more like sixty percent."

Quilldust stared at him.

"I'm afraid I don't know," said Rutspud.

Quilldust recorded, in his careful handwriting, that the interviewee was unable to account for the whereabouts of the remaining demon parts.

"You could try asking Scabass," said Rutspud. "I'm responsible for my group of damned souls, not any demons. Don't you want to ask me about them?"

"No, this census is for demons only," said Quilldust, "and don't worry. We'll be asking Scabass. We'll be asking *every* demon."

"What's the reason for all this?" asked Rutspud. "Have we lost some demons?"

Quilldust ignored the question.

"I need to ask you about another associate. What do you know about the whereabouts of the demon Lugtrout?" he asked.

"I never actually met Lugtrout," said Rutspud. "I'm his replacement in the R&D lab, but he left before I got there."

"How convenient for you," said Quilldust, and wrote down what Rutspud had just said.

Rutspud frowned at this.

"What do you mean by –"

"You do *know* the penalty for harbouring a fugitive demon, don't you?" asked Quilldust, fixing him with a penetrating gaze. "It's a one-way ticket to Hell."

Rutspud wasn't sure if he was supposed to laugh. A nervous smile played on his lips.

"But we're already in, ah, Hell, aren't we?"

Quilldust shook his head as if Rutspud shocked him with his hopeless naivety.

"You surely don't imagine that we wouldn't keep something back? A place much, *much* worse, where we could send those who can't adhere to the rules?"

Rutspud held up his hands to indicate that he was innocent of imagining anything, but Quilldust continued to fix him with that unnerving stare.

"There are demons who think that they can outsmart us. Who think that they can drop out of sight and we might forget about them. We forget *nobody*."

Rutspud mouthed wordlessly. He had committed none of these crimes! He'd done lots of things that he was sure Quilldust wouldn't approve of, but he was entirely innocent of this ... of what, exactly?

"Where do they go?" he asked, curiosity getting the better of him. "The demons who try to drop out of sight."

"We've had a number try to hide out in Limbo," said Quilldust, with a malicious smile. "They don't tend to last long. There are 'things' in Limbo. We've had some defect to Heaven, of course, but most of them think they can find a quiet corner in a quiet cave off one of the more inhospitable plains. We always find them. Never failed yet."

Rutspud escaped from Quilldust's office after another page and a half of questions that ranged from the mundane to the uncomfortable and bizarre. He went through Hodshift's maintenance tunnels to return to the lab, but made a deliberate detour by the furnaces.

The thick door, warm to the touch, had a long lever handle. Rutspud pulled it down and the door flew open, bringing a blast of superheated air.

"What you doing?" squawked a demon, hobbling over, his eyes white against the blackened, melted ruin of his face. "Shut the door! Shut the door!"

Rutspud scrabbled forward into the boiling furnace room and dragged the door closed behind him.

"Precious heat lost! Precious heat lost!" the demon twittered to himself.

"Sorry," said Rutspud. "I just came to ask you if I could have some coal?"

"Hmmm?" The demon had reclaimed his dropped shovel and waved it threateningly at Rutspud. Rutspud backed up against a soot-encrusted bank of machinery.

"I just want some coal, please," said Rutspud.

"The precious fuel source?" said the demon. He attempted a frown but, with his melted forehead drooping down to his cheekbones, it was a barely effective expression. "Why would I give you that?"

"Because you've got loads?" said Rutspud. "I just need a bucketful, for the R&D lab."

"What's in it for me?" hissed the demon. "I could get into trouble."

"I've got a bottle of monk's piss," said Rutspud. "How would that be?"

He pulled out a bottle of the clear yellow liquid. The demon's sunken eyes grew wide with longing.

"Let me get a bucket," he said, licking his lips or, at least, the flesh where his lips had once been.

Rutspud looked at the array of instruments and dials behind him. Among the grimy readouts and switches were relay switches, valve tubes and, in their brass brackets, some ceramic-encased fuses.

"Fuses," he said to himself. "Hey! Mate! Can I have a couple of these fuses too?"

But the demon had limped away in search of a bucket and did not reply.

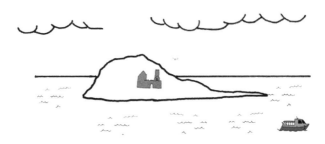

Manfred was pleased with his morning's work. He prepared the last two boil-in-the-bag crab and seaweed meal pouches, which were carefully enclosed in IV bags, ready for later. When food was in such short supply, it was important to seal in all of the nutrients, so that they wouldn't be lost in the cooking water. When the crabs were cooked, he would siphon out the delicious cooking liquor, to make a nourishing broth for lunch the next day.

A whooping sound came from outside, and he went to look. Brothers Vernon and Gillespie were behaving most oddly. Their faces were smeared with mud and blood. They carried strange spear-like weapons and were performing some primitive dance of celebration.

When they saw that Manfred was watching them, they stopped cavorting and whooping. Vernon straightened his robe, patted his Elvis quiff, and walked over to Manfred.

"We have made good use of our boxes," he said. "Brother Gillespie and I joined forces. I had a portable ultrasound machine, which we have used to locate moles underground."

"You can do that?"

"Yes sirree! And we used our spears to stab them through the turf."

He illustrated this by stabbing his spear vigorously up and down.

Manfred looked at the spears in astonishment. They were scalpels lashed to bamboo canes from the shed.

"You've been hunting moles?" he said. "I had no idea there *were* any moles on the island. You caught some?"

"Yes!" said Vernon, with a triumphant grin. He displayed another pole with seven moles hanging off it from their short tails. Brother Gillespie whooped and danced on the spot which was as much exercise Manfred had ever seen the perennially ill monk do.

"Don't take this the wrong way, brothers," said Manfred, "but I think a little quiet meditation might be a good idea to counter the *distress* of hunting."

"Oh, we're not distressed, daddio," said Brother Vernon, his eyes ablaze. "Quite the opposite. We're off to see what else we can hunt. Something bigger, perhaps."

Manfred was about to caution the two of them against this path, when a shout came up from beyond the wall.

"Did you hear that?" he asked.

"No," said Vernon.

"What did you think you might hunt?" asked Manfred carefully.

"Oh, this and that," said Vernon, without meeting Manfred's eyes.

"We're hunting *the Beast*!" said Brother Gillespie with a wild grin.

"What beast is that, brothers?" asked Manfred, wondering if the interesting mushrooms had cropped again.

"No-one's seen it," said Vernon. "But Lionel's building a trap. We want to catch it and stab it with our spears!"

Brothers Vernon and Gillespie had started up their spear dance again, when Manfred heard the shout for a second time. It sounded quite urgent, so he left the spear-wielding monks until later and went through the stone arch to see who was shouting. He knew that Bastian had been tinkering with the generator, with the idea that he might be able to run it with the alcohol-based hand gel.

He came across Bastian rolling on the floor, his habit ablaze. He was trying to put out the flames, but the pungent smell of the hand gel told Manfred that he was well-doused in an effective accelerant, and the flames leapt back up every time he succeeded in partially quelling them. Manfred ripped apart the IV bags that he carried in his hands and spilled the liquid onto Bastian, along with the crabs and seaweed that they contained.

"Thank you!" gasped Bastian as he staggered to his feet, his habit smouldering.

Manfred looked at his blackened face, eyebrows completely gone, and the livid flush on his cheeks.

"I think we must get some burn gel applied to you as quickly as possible," he said. "You're lucky not to be toast, my friend."

"I can go and find Brother Gillespie in the infirmary," said Bastian.

"Perhaps not," said Manfred. "I think he's a little preoccupied. I shall treat you myself."

Brother Henry had taken the rowing boat. He'd teamed up with the beanpole that was Brother Terry, who had been fortunate enough to find that his box contained many yards of medical gauze.

"I don't know a lot about fishing," said Terry slowly. "Do we just drag this behind the boat?"

He held up a bundle of gauze in his long arms.

Henry sat back with a smile.

"Just row us out a little way and I'll show you what we need to do. We're going to do it the smart way. You know me, if there's a way of working smarter, not harder, I'm your man."

Brother Terry was extraordinarily tall and skinny, all elbows and knees. As he rowed the small boat, Henry relaxed and trailed his hand through the water.

"Right, this should be far enough," said Henry, peering into the murky depths. "Let's make a scoop from your gauze."

He pulled out a wire coat hanger and the metal pole used for opening windows. He winked at Brother Terry, who watched him with furrowed brow.

"So we make a circle from the coat hanger by pulling out the sides and, look, we'll use the top here to fix it to our fishing rod."

He wrapped the straightened-out hook around the top of metal pole, but frowned as it wobbled a bit too much for his liking.

"Tell you what, I will donate my dressing-gown cord for the good of our fishing trip," he said, untying it from his waist and wrapping it around the joint. "Here we go, nice and firm. Just get your gauze and knot it round the wire."

Brother Terry managed to attach a large piece of gauze by pulling threads from the weave of the loose fabric and knotting them around the wire. He dropped it into the water and sloshed it back and forth a few times.

"It's quite heavy now it's all wet," he reported. "You might have to help me when it's full of fish."

He looked back at Brother Henry.

"How will it get full of fish?" he asked. "Are they just going to swim into it?"

"Watch and learn, Terry, watch and learn!" said Henry, tapping the side of his nose. "What would you say if I told you that you're in the company of a fishing guru?"

"I'd say 'who else have you got in the folds of your dressing-gown?'" said Terry, eyeing the soggy net.

Henry leaned forward and opened the box at his feet. He pulled out two paddles attached to the case with curly wires.

"It's a defibrillator," he explained.

"I can see that," said Brother Terry. "Are you sure this is wise?"

Brother Henry pressed a big red button on the case, which glowed with a lightning bolt symbol. There was a brief electric squeal.

"Frying tonight!" he cried, dropped the paddles over the side and grasped the end of the cane to help Terry haul in the soon-to-be-electrocuted fish.

The results were startling. Brother Henry felt as though he'd been kicked by a horse. His hands were rigidly locked onto the metal rod. He was unable to move or even breathe for a long, long moment, and he could sense panic rising from Brother Terry, who was frozen in place before him. After what felt like an eternity but was probably just a few seconds, he felt his muscles relax and he collapsed to the floor of the boat, Brother Terry sprawling before him. They both lay, panting with relief to be alive.

"That was horrible," said Terry. "What happened?"

"We just got an electric shock," said Henry. "It's all right, it won't happen again unless someone presses the button."

"What? Where's the button?" said Terry, rolling over to look.

"It's just th – no, stop!"

There was a jolt and everything went black.

Stephen looked up as Rutspud flicked through the contents of his given box with a grimace.

"It's a bit boring, isn't it?" Rutspud complained. "What are these cards with pictures of humans on them?"

"They seem to be forms for ordering medical photographs. The doctor puts a mark where he wants the photo taken. I don't quite know what to do with them."

"Are they men or women?" asked Rutspud, indicating the line drawing.

"I think they've deliberately drawn it so that it could work for either," said Stephen.

"That would be a great improvement to humans, if you ask me," said Rutspud. "I still think you could have done much better with your box."

"We get what we're given."

"Come on. Why don't we go and steal that scooter and go joyriding?"

"No, definitely not. Father Eustace has fallen off it several times already just going round the cloisters. I don't think it would work too well on rocky paths. Anyway, I'm rather pleased with my efforts so far with the sticking plasters. Look."

Stephen stepped back from the section of stained glass he'd been mending on the library floor. Numerous windows had shattered as a result of the unfortunate barbecue incident the other week, but Stephen was halfway through reconstructing a large angel with flesh-coloured plasters.

"I can see that you're quite enjoying that," said Rutspud, "but it's not much of a spectator sport watching you do a jigsaw. I don't suppose we can be a bit more creative with the next one and give them dogs' heads or something?"

Stephen shook his head. It would be nice for them to work together on something, but that sounded like a recipe for disaster.

"Boring!" said Rutspud. "Let's go and see if we can make a unicycle out of that oxygen trolley."

"I need to check the corridor first. Brother Lionel has been out there for ages making some weird contraption. We don't want to run into him."

Rutspud jumped up onto the table.

"What would happen if the other humans found me?"

Stephen hummed in thought.

"Scientists would want to dissect you."

"Been there, done that. Had my entire innards rearranged during the Great Harrowing."

"Most of the monks would attempt to exorcise you."

"Well, I don't fancy that. That one you tried gave me a real gut-rumbling bellyache."

"In truth, I think most people would vomit, faint or run screaming."

"Now, that sounds like fun."

"No, it doesn't. You wait here a moment."

Rutspud shrugged, and lazily tossed some pieces of glass about.

Stephen went out into the corridor and found Brother Lionel standing on a stepladder, securing a rope to the ceiling. From the rope hung a ghoulish apparition that somewhat resembled a monk. Its upper body was formed from Resusci-Annie doll, those pale, sightless eyes sweeping across the corridor as the thing swayed slightly. A monk's habit hung down from Annie's shoulders.

"What is that thing?" asked Stephen. "It's a bit creepy."

"It's a trap," said Brother Lionel. "Make sure you don't stand on that bit of floor down there."

Stephen peered at a noose that was puddled on the floor just underneath the decoy.

"What are you hoping to catch?" he asked.

"I don't really want to say," said Lionel, winding some bungee cords around a cable drum. "But I bet you I catch *something* tonight."

Stephen wondered if someone had indeed seen Rutspud creeping around. Could he be the intended target?

"I really don't think you're going to catch anything more interesting than a cold standing around here," said Stephen.

"I'm fine," said Brother Lionel.

"Sure you don't want to head off to the warming room for a nice cup of cocoa?"

Brother Lionel's gaze snapped up.

"We've got cocoa?"

"Not really, though Brother Manfred does this thing with ground seaweed, barrel sweepings and pepper. It *looks* like cocoa. It's certainly warming. Brr!" he added pointedly, by way of emphasis, wondering if he and Rutspud would ever get past.

"I'm nearly done now," said Lionel. "You're wrong, though. I bet I do catch something. Tell you what. If I don't, then I'll let you in on a secret."

"What secret?" asked Stephen.

"I'll tell you if I don't catch anything."

"You might as well tell me now. Nothing's going to get caught in this thing, unless it's a clueless monk who's not looking where he's going."

"Don't be so sure!" said Lionel, stepping back to admire his handiwork. "Here's the deal. If I catch nothing, I'll tell you my secret. I'm out of here when the quarantine lifts anyway."

"What do you mean?"

"I've had enough of island life."

"But this is your home, Lionel."

"It's a drafty hovel."

"What will you do if you leave?"

"I'm seventy-three, boy. I'm going to find me a nice nursing home to die in. Anyway, the other side of the bargain is this. If I do catch something then you need to pay a forfeit."

"What? No!" Stephen thought for a moment, and curiosity got the better of him. "What's the forfeit?"

Lionel looked him in the eye.

"I've got these painful, scabby corns on my feet," he said. "I need someone to trim them for me."

Stephen recoiled in horror at the thought.

"I don't do feet," he said. "Even when they *haven't* got scabby corns on them."

"Shame," said Lionel. "They cause me a lot of pain."

Stephen hesitated. He was a monk, wasn't he, and a good Christian ... What was a little bit of minor body horror if he could help to ease someone's suffering?

"All right," he said, turning away. "As long as you wash them."

Stephen went back into the library to find Rutspud had stuck together a stained glass angel with its head upside down in his absence.

"Nice, eh?" said Rutspud. "I bet you'll fix it when I've gone."

"Nah," Stephen said with a shrug. "It would be more work to take it all apart again now – nobody will notice."

"You're lucky you haven't got someone looking over your shoulder the whole time," said Rutspud. "There's a census going on downstairs at the moment, and they're making everyone sweat. They want to know everything about *everything*."

"Oh no, you're not going to get into trouble for bringing us that coal and stuff, are you?" said Stephen. "I mean, we're really grateful, but I'd hate to see you get, er, dissected or whatever on our account."

"I don't think so. I picked those up on the way back from my grilling by the census demon, Quilldust, but I'm sure I wasn't followed."

"Quilldust?" said Stephen with interest. "I'm sure I saw him in here."

He went over to the bookshelves, shifted aside a copy of *Clara et Praesentis Periculi* and opened the *Librum Magnum Daemonum*. Stephen turned the pages until he found what he was looking for.

"Here we are, Quilldust. Ah, look, why don't you read it, you'll only moan about how bad my Latin is." Stephen turned the book towards Rutspud.

"Quilldust," read Rutspud, "Recorder of the Damning Details. Pit-brother to Treyvaw, the hunter of demons. It is said that he is able to bring forth evidence of *any* lifetime that would take a *hundred* lifetimes to read."

"Huh?" said Stephen. "What's scary about that?"

"He brings atrophy and inertia by the means of his scratching quill. The fall of empires has been preceded by those who sought a recorded history and expired before their completion."

Rutspud slammed the book closed.

"Let's just say he's detail-orientated."

He shuddered in recollection.

"The coal was a fair exchange, anyway," he said. "That reminds me, I'll take some more of that monk piss when I go back."

"Hm, it might have all gone," said Stephen. "Manfred found it in the cupboard and told the others it was Limoncello. Most of us aren't very well-travelled, so I think they've been supping away, thinking it's Italian booze."

"Italy! I've seen that on the internet," said Rutspud.

"You have the internet in Hell?"

"In Belphegor's department, yes. Surprisingly good Wi-Fi signal too. Italy's the one with the winding mountain roads, tiny cars and buses full of gold bars, isn't it?"

"Yes," said Stephen, smiling.

"I'd love to go there."

"I've heard it's beautiful."

"There or Niagara Falls."

"Apparently also very impressive."

"Or the pyramids in Egypt, or the Amazon rainforest, or Australia, or Jurassic Park."

"Er, that last one doesn't actually exist," said Stephen. "It's made up."

"I saw it. All those dinosaurs."

"Sorry. Made up."

"Oh, that's a shame, it looked interesting," said Rutspud. "Made up, huh?"

"Sorry."

"Like Disneyland."

"Actually, Disneyland is real. You can go there."

Rutspud laughed. "Yeah right. I bet there are giant talking mice there and everything."

Stephen opened his mouth to answer, but thought better of it.

"Which is your favourite?" asked Rutspud.

"I quite like Goofy."

"No, I meant place you've visited. Where would you recommend?"

"Well, I told you, I'm not very well-travelled. I haven't been to the rainforests or the Himalayas or ... any of those places." He clicked his fingers. "I did go on a school trip to Calais once. But I didn't like the food."

"Frogs' legs? Snails? Roast starling?"

"No, I had a bad sausage roll on the ferry. Never went back. No, I like it here at the monastery. It's peaceful and we have everything that we need. Well, normally we do, when we haven't run out of everything."

Stephen rocked back on his heels, deep in thought. "Most of all though," he continued, "most of all, I really love the men I live with."

"Ah," said Rutspud slowly, with a knowing look.

"What?"

"It's a sex thing, isn't it? I've seen that on the internet too."

"No, no, *no*! It most certainly isn't a sex thing! I'm talking about the friendship we have. More than friendship, more than colleagues. We're like each other's family. It's taken the loss of Huey and Bernard to make me realise how much this family of monks really means to me."

Stephen glanced at the photograph-ordering forms. An idea was forming as to how he might use them. He discarded the top one, where Rutspud had doodled a curious mixture of secondary sexual characteristics. It simply bristled with boobs and penises.

Rutspud was quiet for a moment. "Am I your friend?" he asked at last.

"Hmm?"

"Am I your friend, Stephen?"

Stephen looked at him. Rutspud's large and surprisingly expressive eyes conveyed a powerful blend of confusion, hope and fear.

"We meet up and have fun. We've both run risks to help each other out. I always look forward to seeing you. I'd say we're friends, wouldn't you?"

Rutspud looked as though he'd been punched.

"Wow," he said softly.

"What?"

"I've never had a friend before. You know, just enemies I didn't hate that much. A friend ..."

"Are you okay with that?" asked Stephen.

Rutspud nodded slowly. "I think that I am."

Stephen woke suddenly in the night. That wasn't so unusual. What was unusual was finding himself hanging upside down. Something had a tight and painful grip on his ankle. He couldn't see a thing, but then he realised that his habit was covering his head. He wrestled it away and immediately understood what had happened.

"Lionel!" he called. "LI-O-NEL!"

Lionel was indeed first to arrive, most of the other monks close behind him. Stephen couldn't be sure, but it looked as though there were a couple of them at the back with their faces painted and weapons of some sort. "I caught something," said Lionel. "I told you all I – Oh. It's only Trevor."

"Stephen," said Stephen tiredly.

Stephen saw their faces turn from shock to recognition and then slowly to mirth. It suddenly occurred to him that his body was largely uncovered, as his habit flapped uselessly around his head.

"It is Stephen," agreed Brother Clement.

"Would you all stop pointing and staring like that?" snapped Stephen. "Just get me down!"

He wrestled some more with his habit, which only made things worse, as his view was obscured once again. He heard a noise that sounded suspiciously like a camera.

"Bastian, you'd better not be taking pictures," he yelled.

"Just a quick one, for the year book," said Bastian.

"We don't have a year book!"

"We do now."

"Let us help you down," said Manfred, carrying the stepladder towards Stephen. "Can I suggest that you try to catch him as he falls please?"

Moments later, Stephen was in a crumpled heap on the floor.

"Oops," said Manfred from above.

Stephen breathed a sigh of relief to find that he was unhurt, and looked up just as Resusci-Annie plummeted onto his head

"Saving lives for generations," muttered Stephen as he slipped into unconsciousness.

Manfred was serving breakfast. He looked up to see Stephen walk in.

"Ah, so good to see that you're up and about," he said. "I made sure that we kept you something after the ordeal you suffered in the night."

Manfred slipped some fritters onto a plate.

"What are these?" asked Stephen. "Looks like meat. We haven't had meat for ages."

"It is indeed meat," confirmed Manfred. "Everyone has agreed that mole is tastier than, ah, some of the alternatives we've tried."

Stephen sat down, and Manfred was pleased to see that his pupils were equal and reactive.

"So, Stephen. It appears that some of us have received a small *gift* in the night," Manfred said. "Little cards. We were just reading them out. Brother Henry, let's hear yours."

Manfred hadn't liked to ask why Henry had chosen to model his hair in the style of Einstein. If he didn't know better, he might be inclined to think that he'd suffered a large electric shock. Wherever he'd got his styling product from, he'd evidently shared it with Terry. Manfred shook his head. Even an island of monks had its fashion victims.

"Mine is like some of the others," said Henry. "It's got this little picture that has been modified. Mine is wearing a dressing-gown and carrying a Sudoku book. Hmph."

"Continue, Henry, what does it say?" said Manfred.

"It says 'You're admired by everyone for your laid-back attitude. Nothing would ever cause you to panic.'"

"That is a most admirable quality indeed," said Manfred. "Father Eustace, did you get a card?"

Eustace picked a card up from the floor and dropped it onto the table.

"Cock!" he shouted.

Heads leaned forward. Manfred looked at the card himself. It did indeed depict a person liberally covered with ... cocks and other rude symbols.

"Father, I couldn't help noticing that you got that one off the floor," said Manfred. "Did you get one slipped under your door like the rest of us?"

Eustace pulled another card from the basket on his motorised scooter and thrust it at Stephen who was sitting next to him. Stephen picked it up and, glancing at Eustace for confirmation, read it aloud.

"It says 'You're not afraid to say the unsayable. You're not afraid to say nothing at all. Please don't change.'"

Manfred nodded in approval.

"Bastian, perhaps you would read yours out again for the late arrivals?"

"Certainly," said Bastian. "It says 'Your careful ways with money make the most of our funds, which enables us all to live here. We are extremely grateful for your expertise.'"

"I will read you mine, also," said Manfred. "'Your generous spirit and unstoppable creativity nurtures us all.' The picture also features the curly hair, if you can see?"

He held the card aloft.

"Lovely. These cards are a very good idea, whoever created them," he said, looking around the room. He wondered if the person who had written them would have had the foresight to write one for themselves. "Stephen, did you get a card yourself?"

"Yes, I did," said Stephen, pulling one out of his robe. "Mine has got a Resusci-Annie bouncing off his head, which is a nice touch."

"Topical," agreed Manfred.

"It says *'You have made the library into a resource to be proud of, and you continue to grow into the kind of well-rounded monk that this monastery needs.'*"

Manfred beamed round at the table.

"I am truly delighted to see the constructive and creative ways in which we have managed to use the meagre resources at our disposal. I think we can all agree that this idea with the cards is nourishment for our very souls."

There was a murmur of approval.

"Which is fortunate, as we have experienced a shortage of actual nourishment, so this should sustain us, with a warm glow, through a long day without food."

There was silence as the monks processed this disappointing yet inevitable piece of information.

Manfred looked around at their faces then began to smile.

"Oh, guys, look at your faces! It was just my little joke. Of course I made sure that you won't be hungry."

He uncovered a large bowl on the side table.

"It's seaweed surprise. Enjoy."

"What's the surprise?" asked Stephen.

"There's nothing but seaweed," suggested Brother Henry with a scowl. "Oh, look. I'm right."

Chapter 6 – The day the boat came back

"I tied a knot in my handkerchief to remind me," said Belphegor, and held up a green, stained rag that was more a series of knots than an actual handkerchief. "But, as soon as I got near enough, I forgot why I was there. I even tried tying a knot in my tail as a more emphatic reminder."

Belphegor reached into his wheelchair seat and waggled something at Rutspud that definitely was not a tail.

"Okay, chief," said Rutspud. "So, how can I help?"

Belphegor gestured across the rocky slope to the sluggish river at the shallow cavern floor.

"The level of the River Lethe is going down. So are the levels of three of the other rivers of Hell. Look, it's barely a trickle. I wanted to get down there and take a depth measurement with this measuring rod and some water samples, so we could work out what was going on."

"Fair enough," shrugged Rutspud.

"But," said Belphegor firmly, "there are clearly fumes rising off this river of forgetfulness. I need you."

"To devise some breathing apparatus for you to use."

"No, to remind me what I'm supposed to be doing when I forget."

"Oh, okay."

"Ready?"

Rutspud gave his superior a thumbs up. Belphegor pushed a lever and his mechanical chair trundled away and down the slope. The heavy chair crushed smaller stones below its fat wheels and simply rolled over larger rocks. Belphegor stopped some distance from the river.

"Are you all right, sir?" Rutspud called.

Belphegor spun round.

"Ah, Rutspud! Glad you're here. I seem to have got lost."

"You were going to take a measuring from the river," Rutspud shouted.

"Was I? Why?"

"Because of the reduced water flow."

"I see."

Belphegor rotated and rolled down until his wheels were several inches deep in the water.

"What's going on?" he shouted. He looked back at Rutspud. "Hey! You! Did you put me here?"

"Just measure the river!" shouted Rutspud.

"What?"

"The river levels are falling!"

Belphegor frowned.

"Get out your rod!" yelled Rutspud.

"I hardly think that's going to help," muttered Belphegor. "Hey! There's a knot in this thing. Have I forgotten something?"

"Yes!" yelled Rutspud. "You need to take a sample. Use the jar! That one!"

Belphegor peered at the jar in his hand, seeing it for the first time. Rutspud watched him struggling with his thoughts and the jar.

"No, sir!" he yelled. "A sample from the river!"

"What?"

"From the river!"

"What is?"

"The sample!"

"What sample?"

Rutspud groaned, took a gulp of air, and ran down to the riverside. As his feet splashed in the shallows, he realised that the water was hot, almost boiling, and that a fine steam was rising off it. He snatched the jar from Belphegor's hand, scooped up a quantity of water and presented the vessel to his wizened boss.

"There!" he said.

Belphegor looked at the jar.

"Er, thanks," said Belphegor. "I am a bit thirsty actually."

Rutspud gasped as Belphegor drank it.

"What?" said the inventor demon. "Did you want some?"

Rutspud blinked and looked about himself as though waking from a troubling sleep.

"Er, yes, please," he said. "It's quite hot here."

He took a deep, satisfying gulp. He looked down at the water running between his feet.

"What's going on here? Did one of us have an accident?"

"Don't look at me," said Belphegor. "I've tied a knot in mine."

"Why'd you do that?"

"No idea."

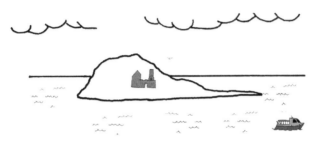

Stephen woke from a troubled sleep. As he stretched, his fist collided sharply with a stone wall and he sat up at once. Fully awake, he cradled his banged hand. His camp bed was positioned across the corridor, side to side, blocking the door to the guest room in which Brother Lionel had spent what he had declared to be his last night in the monastery.

"It's morning," Stephen called through the door. "The quarantine's lifted and, if you're lucky, the first boat should be here in a couple of hours."

There was no reply from the monk within. Understandable, really. Brother Lionel was old; old men were entitled to be a little hard of hearing and slow to rise. He had also become more than a little eccentric in his dotage. The bizarre trap which had ensnared nothing apart from Stephen was evidence of that.

"And, look," said Stephen, "no one's tried to kill you in the night."

He stood, propped the camp bed up against the wall and, knocking softly first, entered the room. Lionel lay still beneath his sheets. His bald and wrinkled noggin poked out from the top.

"Come on," said Stephen. "You don't want to miss your chance to escape Death Plague Island."

He gave Brother Lionel a little shake. And then a poke. And a pinch.

"Oh, Lord!" swore Stephen under his breath.

Manfred couldn't help but be swept up in the carnival atmosphere that had gripped St Cadfan's that morning.

Owen the boatman, reassured by fresh scientific tests by the disease control bods at Bangor University, was returning for the first time in far too many weeks. Even Manfred, maintaining a cool head in his role as prior and as de facto leader of the monastery while the abbot's sanity continued to circle the airfield, could not help but mentally picture Owen's boat as laden with tonnes of supplies. Crates of fresh food and much missed luxuries danced in front of his imagination.

And so, when Stephen bounded into the almonry, babbling at speed and almost tripping over the intravenous tubes and demijohns that formed part of Manfred's seaweed-fuelled microbrewery, the prior assumed that the young chap had merely become infected by the general monastic excitement.

"You'vegottocomeitsBrotherLionelIcan'twakehimHewon'tget up!"

"And good morning to you too," said Manfred.

"ButIthinkhesdeadandIwasoutsidehisroomallnightandIdidn't hearanythingbutIthinkhe'sdead!"

"Now, now," said Manfred, taking Stephen's arm and patting it gently. "Calm down. Slow down. Is something amiss?"

Stephen nodded breathlessly.

"Okay, brother. Now, I'm sure it's not as bad as you think. I mean," Manfred laughed, "it's not as if another one of our brethren has died in mysterious circumstances."

Stephen's face froze.

"Who?" said Manfred, alarmed.

"Lionel!"

"How?"

"I don't know!"

Manfred took a shocked step back.

"No. The boat is due within the hour. If Owen finds out someone else has died, he'll never come back again!"

The parade of fruit and vegetables, of soap and toiletries, of spices, herbs and other delights that Owen would bring faded in front of Manfred's inner eye.

"We can't have this," he said, quietly.

"I know," said Stephen. "It's terrible. What do we do?"

Manfred swallowed hard.

"We have to cover it up."

"What?" said Stephen.

"No one must know that he died here. We have to hide Brother Lionel."

"Well, this is new," said Rutspud, standing at the top of the ash dunes and gazing down at the Lake of Fire.

"Most disconcerting," agreed Belphegor.

Four jars of Hellish river water sloshed in Belphegor's lap. They had, finally, managed to get the needed samples from the River Lethe, although Rutspud couldn't quite remember how they had ultimately achieved it.

"I think we can assume that Hell is getting hotter," said Belphegor.

"Well, Hell is meant to be hot," said Rutspud. "I don't think you can be certain it's getting any hotter."

"I rather think the evidence is compelling."

"Really?"

"Consider," said the purple inventor demon, "the four watery rivers of Hell are drying up."

"Well, yes ..."

"The pool from which the fifty Danaides are forever doomed to carry water in their useless sieves –"

"Is empty, yes. I know, but still ..."

"And now, this," said Belphegor gesturing.

"This is evidence of nothing," said Rutspud, convinced that if he accepted there was a problem, he would be dragged into fixing it.

"Then do please explain," said Belphegor, "how might it be that half of Hell has apparently descended on the Lake of Fire to *cool down!*"

Rutspud watched the demons frolicking in the shallows.

"It's always been a popular spot," he said.

"And the floating pontoon and diving board?"

Rutspud watched demons gleefully propelling themselves off the springboard and into the depths. On the furthest shore, the thousands of human souls damned to burn in the lake squatted sullenly on the banks, evicted from their own corner of Hell.

"It's a puzzler, true," Rutspud agreed, "but I don't think we should assume that this means Hell is –"

"Iiiice cream! Dig your righteous ice-cream!" cried Lickspear, strolling by with a tray on a strap around his neck.

"Oi!" Rutspud shouted.

Lickspear strolled over cheerfully.

"Might I procure a goodly ice-cream for you and the foxy lady?" he drawled.

"Lickspear, what in the blue blazes of Hell are you doing?"

"Selling ice-cream," said the badly-stitched demon.

"Why?"

"Mammon told me to. He gave me this swell tray, said 'make some money, my boy' and entreated me to come down here."

"But who's in the cave? Who's looking after the gang?"

Lickspear shook his head at Rutspud's appalling lack of faith.

"Over there, handing out deckchairs. The joint's jumpin' my lord."

Rutspud looked along the shore to see Mama-Na and Boudicca handing out folding chairs while Bernhardt and Cartland collected money.

"I can't believe you did this without my permission," said Rutspud.

Lickspear grinned unfazed.

"It surely is an agreeable frolic, pops. Showing my initiative, as 'twere? Now, good friends, can I lay an ice-cream on you?"

"No, you bloody can't!"

"Is that a bile sorbet?" said Belphegor, pneumatically raising his seat to get a better look at Lickspear's wares.

"Directly from the ninth circle of Hell, you dig that?"

"Ooh, and are those sulphur sprinkles?"

"Assuredly, man."

"Sir," said Rutspud reproachfully. "Do not encourage him."

"What?" said Belphegor. "I like sorbet. Pay the fellow, Rutspud."

Rutspud sighed. It was a heavy sigh that started in his knees and took an age to reach his mouth.

"Fine!" he snapped. "Make that two sorbets, Lickspear."

"Sure thing, gentlemen," Lickspear beamed.

"And no skimping on the sprinkles."

In the end, more than a dozen monks from St Cadfan's came down to the rocky beach to meet the boat from the mainland. The monks had been cut off for less than six months but, with their flag-waving, ecstatic hollering and ill-advised jigging, they acted as though they had been cut off from all civilisation for decades.

Barrels, bags and boxes were stacked at the aft of Owen's sturdy boat but, apart from Owen himself, there was only one passenger. Bastian furrowed his brow and stared at the tiny blonde woman who, he was convinced, was specifically waving at him.

In their haste and joy, the monks made a well-meaning and inadvertent hash of helping the boat moor up. Ropes tangled, monks stumbled in the surf, and Brother Vernon was very lucky not to have been crushed between the hull and the shore. A cheer went up when Owen finally lowered the gangplank and stepped down.

"It's like the bloody arrival of Jesus in Jerusalem," muttered Brother Henry.

"Blasphemy," said Brother Clement.

Bastian shrugged. Actually, it was fairly apt. Give them a few palm leaves and a few 'Hosanna's and maybe a donkey for Owen, and it would have been a reasonable recreation of Palm Sunday.

"Bread, he's brought bread!" cried Brother Desmond. "Real bread!"

"And toothpaste!" exclaimed Brother Terry.

"I'm happy as long as he's got my back issues of *Monks, Monks, Monks*, the journal for the modern monk," said Brother Clement.

The tiny distant blonde woman resolved into a tiny up-close blonde woman, and one Bastian was surprised to recognise at that.

"Ms Well-Dunn!" he said.

"Carol," she smiled. "Brother Sebastian, I'm so pleased to see you."

Bastian, who had not had a woman of any age particularly pleased to see him in a long time, could not help but smile in return.

"I can't say we were expecting you," he said.

"I phoned and e-mailed."

"No electricity for at least four weeks," he said, gesturing generally at the monastery on the hill behind him.

"And I wrote."

Bastian pointed at the tub of undelivered letters and packages that Owen was now bringing down the gangplank.

"I'm surprised that you would want to return at all after the ... incident."

"I must admit," she said wryly, "that I had to answer some difficult questions from the school governors, but the children loved it. I am often asked if we can go back to the island with 'the Jedis and skeletons'."

"Well, due to some overactive imaginations and unfortunate mentions of plague pits, we've pretty much been in an informal quarantine ever since. Owen said that one of the mainlanders had taken up post on the pub roof and threatened to shoot any plague-infested monk who dared to cross over. Joking, of course."

Owen gave Bastian a blank stare and a raised eyebrow.

"Still, you are our only visitor in months, and we're all delighted to see you," said Bastian, despite the fact that no other monks had even noticed Carol's appearance, so engrossed in the forgotten delights of crisps, shampoo, monk-themed periodicals and the like were they.

"Not your *only* visitor," said Owen and nodded along the beach.

A spritely black and white border collie dog was gambolling at the sea's edge.

"You brought Jessie?" said Bastian.

"I didn't bring her deliberately and you know that," scowled Owen.

"Jessie?" said Carol.

"She lives on the mainland," explained Bastian. "Ridiculously precocious creature. Oi, Jessie!"

The dog looked up.

"Clear off and go bother someone else!" he shouted.

The dog bobbed its head and sprinted off up the hill.

"Did that dog just nod?" asked Carol.

"Best not to think about it," said Bastian.

"I am unhappy," said Lord Peter with a smile.

The dissonance between his words and that smile made the quill-like hairs stand up on the back of Rutspud's neck.

"Deeply unhappy," said Lord Peter, his smile widening.

He looked around the table, at Mulciber, Hell's architect, at Hodshift, the ear-covered maintenance demon, at Belphegor, and at Rutspud himself. The only person who didn't get treated to a penetrating stare was Nero, who was taking the minutes.

"Hell is getting hotter," said Lord Peter. "It's an undeniable and thoroughly inconvenient truth. The question I have called you together to answer is why it's happening and what's to be done about it."

"Tha's two questions, boss," said Hodshift.

Rutspud attempted to surreptitiously move his chair further away from Hodshift's.

"What makes me particularly unhappy," said Lord Peter, speaking to all, but keeping his eyes utterly fixed on Hodshift, "is that the Celestial City has got wind of our little problem and has declared that it is 'interested'. When Heaven's delegation come to speak to us about this, I want to have answers and a solution already in place. Perhaps, Hodshift, you should begin by explaining exactly what problem we are facing."

"Right-o, boss," said Hodshift chummily. "Yer see, Hell is like a delicate ecosystem. It's almost entirely cut off from the rest of the metaphysical universe and what 'appens in one place impacts on everyfing else. We've always had a problem wiv the heating. You add more and more souls to a closed system then the pressure an' heat is bound to go up. It's a size slash pressure thing, yer basic Boyle's Law, so-called because if we don't do nuffing about it, we're boiled to buggery. That's the law."

"But why has it suddenly worsened now?" said Belphegor.

"Simple. Like I said, it's a delicate ecosystem. Like if a butterfly flaps its wings, there's a hurricane on the other side of the world."

"What's a butterfly?" said Rutspud.

"No idea," said Hodshift. "Anyway, the fing is, we have some pretty complicated heat regulators in the furnaces. Cut a long story short, someone shut one of them down by removing an electrical fuse."

Rutspud's innards lurched. The furnace room. A faint whimper escaped his lips.

"Problem, Rutspud?" said Lord Peter.

Rutspud forced his face to adopt a less panicked expression.

"I don't think it is much of problem," he said. "Surely, all we need to do is put the fuse back and everything will be hunky-dory."

Hodshift sucked through his teeth.

"S'not that simple, mate. Yer dealin' wiv a positive feedback system. The whole fing's running out of control now. Putting a fuse back in would be like shutting the stable door once the horse has bolted."

"What's a horse?"

"No idea."

"And, meanwhile, Hell is falling apart around us," said Mulciber. "The ninth circle of Hell is melting. The Frozen Hell of Traitors is now the Slightly Slushy Hell of Traitors."

"Well, hang on," said Rutspud. "Isn't that part of the answer? Hell has hot bits and cold bits. Let's just shut down the hot bits and let the cold bits chill everything else off. Turn off the furnaces."

"It doesn't work like that," said Belphegor.

"No?"

"It's a dynamic system, you see," said Hodshift. "We have fuel-burning furnaces at one end and carbon-capture centres for fuel reclamation and heat sinks at the other. Round an' round it goes. It's like a flowing river and we're the fishes. We shut it down and Hell stagnates and dies."

"So, to summarise," said Belphegor, "because of the foolish actions of an individual or individuals, our world is going to get hotter and hotter until it is utterly destroyed."

"Yep," said Hodshift.

"And we need to fix it."

"Yep."

"You know," said Mulciber, "if the humans had this problem in their world, they'd have it sorted out in no time. Resourceful bunch."

"Then maybe we'd better get some of our best damned working on it," said Belphegor.

"Very well," said Lord Peter. "Of course, there is another matter that we must also address here."

"Yes, my lord?" said Belphegor.

"Yes. The matter of blame. I always think it's important for each of us to acknowledge when we have erred and to face the consequences."

Rutspud quivered with fear.

"I have heard," said Mulciber, "that the demon responsible for the section from where the fuse was taken was seen to be consuming proscribed substances at the time."

"Proscribed substances?" said Lord Peter.

"Monk's piss."

Rutspud let out another involuntary whimper.

"Rutspud, you have something to say?" asked the ruler of all Hell.

"I was just thinking," Rutspud said, "I ought to go talk to this demon at once and see what can be learned."

"Excellent," said Lord Peter. "Most excellent. Please see to it immediately."

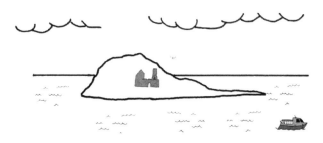

Stephen and Bastian clumsily carried Brother Lionel between them, Manfred with his hand hooked under the old monk's armpits, Stephen with Lionel's knees around his waist.

"This is wrong," said Stephen.

"Left turn," said Manfred. "To the refectory. It's not wrong. It's about the greater good."

"Since when were you a utilitarian?" said Stephen.

"I'm a pragmatist. One, we've only just had the first quarantine lifted. The physical and mental health of some of our brethren can't cope much longer. Two, another death could irreparably damage the monastery's reputation."

"Oh, and the fact that we're concealing deaths won't?"

"And, three, who's to say Lionel didn't leave the island alive and well and go find a quiet corner of Wales to die in?"

"But he's here."

"Who's to know? He has no family on the mainland. Not a single person. No friends, apart from us."

"Makes you wonder why he wanted to leave."

"We hide him for now and then – in here. Here! – we quietly bury him and, if anyone asks, tell them he took the boat back."

Manfred lifted the lid of the chest freezer in the kitchen larder with his elbow.

"In."

Stephen helped him lower the little man into the empty freezer. Manfred closed the freezer lid slowly.

"It's like that film," he said, with a weary shake of his head. "You know, the one with Sean Connery."

"*Goldfinger*?"

"No. The one where everyone's dying and he has to solve the mystery."

"*Murder on the Orient Express*?"

"No," said Manfred irritably. "The one where he's a monk. You must know the one. He visits a monastery and all the monks start dying and everyone thinks it's a sign of the end times. But it's actually a conspiracy involving a special book and a secret maze in the monastery library. You must know it. The thingy of the something, it's called."

"*Hunt for Red October*?"

Manfred sighed.

"I can't believe you haven't seen it. And there's that bit where the young monk meets a beautiful wild girl. Not that we get much monk/woman romance round here, thank God."

Carol closed the locutory door behind her, shutting out the noise and bustle of a monastery come back to life.

"I just had to come and see you," said Carol.

"You did?" said Bastian.

"It's been the only thing on my mind for weeks."

"Oh?"

She removed her waterproof coat and backpack and draped them over one of the few tables not taken up with Bastian's computers and IT equipment.

"I have something to show you," she said, unzipping her fleece jacket.

"Really, Carol?"

"I think you'll be surprised but very pleased."

She reached inside her jacket and whipped out a USB memory stick.

Bastian blinked.

"Let me show you," she said and, ramming the stick into one of the PCs, opened a window on the screen.

"This is footage from the children's camcorders, taken on our visit to you a few months back," she said. "I think you're going to see something quite amazing."

Bastian watched the jerky camerawork, accompanied by a soundtrack of static hisses, wind howls and two dozen students who could no more stop talking than they could stop breathing. The desolate landscape, the bedraggled figures and the atmosphere of misery and futility put Bastian in mind of that *Blair Witch* film Brother Vernon had suggested they watch a few years back.

"Oh, *that* is interesting," said Bastian.

"You don't think I came all this way to show you video of Peroni Picken pole-dancing with an umbrella, did you? No, wait. Now."

Carol clicked the pause icon.

"What?" said Bastian, seeing nothing.

Carol pointed at the screen.

"There."

Bastian squinted at the white blur.

"It's a bit of paper blowing across the hillside."

Carol shook her head.

"It's mostly wings but you can make out its legs trailing behind it. And that, that bit there, that's its comb."

Bastian wrinkled his nose and sniffed.

"It's a bird. So what?"

Carol grinned. Her eyes lit up when she smiled. There was a child-like expression on wonder on her face, a Christmas morning kind of face.

"It's not just any bird."

She opened her backpack and took out several printed sheets, each in a polythene pocket. One was an enlargement of the frozen image on the screen. Another was an illustration from an ornithological reference book.

"'The yellow-crested Merlin stilt,'" Bastian read. "Funny looking thing. I don't think I've seen one of them before."

"No," said Carol excitedly. "No one has. Not for at least half a century."

"Oh, it's rare, is it?"

"Not rare, Brother Sebastian. It's been declared extinct for over twenty years."

"So that fuzzy thing can't be it then."

"And yet one of your older monks included it as part of the mural in the visitors' centre."

"So," said Bastian slowly, "Bardsey Island is home to perhaps the only living specimens?"

Carol nodded.

Bastian stroked his chin.

"I'm guessing this would be a big deal in the bird-watching world."

"A very big deal," Carol agreed.

"The kind of thing that would even make the national newspapers?"

"Middle pages of the better kind of broadsheet, yes."

"And people would want to come and see it, wouldn't they?"

"Lots and lots of people," said Carol.

"People with money," said Bastian softly.

"Um. Sorry?"

Bastian cleared his throat.

"Did I say that last bit out loud? Scratch that." He made a show of looking again at the images Carol had brought. "I suppose what we really need is proof that this thing is alive and well and living here."

"I've brought my camera and binoculars."

"I'll grab my coat," said Bastian.

Rutspud ran like he had never run before. Demons were rarely built for high speed. It was only the damned who ever felt the need to run and, in a domain from which there was no escape, there was little need to chase them at speed. But Rutspud had a sensible number of legs, and they were a matching pair, so he could produce a decent turn of speed when required.

He did not run directly to the furnaces, but took a detour to Infernal Innovations first, to pick up a stoppered flask of water.

"Have you got any yellow paint?" he asked Bosch, who was leaning over a design painting for a new torture centre.

"Septic wound yellow or rabid eyes yellow?" the Dutchman asked.

"Sort of piss yellow," said Rutspud.

"Language please," said Lewis as he sanded down the door for his latest wardrobe.

"Fine. Urine yellow, please. And quickly."

As Lewis went back to his work, humming a ditty to himself, the painter passed Rutspud a pot. Rutspud emptied half of it into the flask and was running out of the room before it had even begun to settle.

A five minute sprint into the maintenance tunnels and then the furnace room had shaken up the water and paint sufficiently to give it a pleasing yellow tinge.

"Shut the door! Shut the door!" cried the shovel-carrying demon. "Precious heat lost! I'm in enough trouble as it is."

Rutspud saw that it was – Hell be praised! – the same demon as before; the same waxy, melted forehead, the same drooping, sweat-coated nose.

"I thought I'd just drop by and see my good friend," said Rutspud.

"You got me in trouble," said the demon.

"Me? No."

The demon nodded, bits of his face wobbling about as he did.

"You took that fuse, didn't you?"

"No idea what you're talking about. Did you tell anyone?"

"Tell them what? That I let you in? I just played dumb and hoped they'd blame it on someone else."

"Wise policy, friend."

The furnace demon wiped his sweaty forehead and tried to push some bits of his face back into place.

"They now reckon Hell's going to get hotter and hotter until it explodes and that will be the end of everything."

"Explodes?"

"You know. Pop!" Rutspud made an explosive gesture with his hands.

"That does sound awful," said the demon.

"I dunno. I can see an upside. I fancy a bit of oblivion, me."

Rutspud gave him his best consoling and friendly smile.

"Listen, friend, let bygones be bygones. I brought you a little something to cheer you up."

He passed the flask of dyed water to the demon. The thirsty demon took it without a word and drank. He pulled a face.

"It's not half as nice as the last stuff."

"Drink up."

The demon poured most of it down his throat.

"It's all right, I suppose," he said. "Where'd you get this stuff from anyway?"

"The Lethe, river of forgetfulness."

The demon frowned.

"The river of ... who are you?"

"No one," said Rutspud. "No one at all."

"OK, so who am I?"

Rutspud took the remains of the flask from the demon's hand.

"You," he said, retreating towards the door, "can be whoever you want to be. Welcome to oblivion."

With the furnace demon's memory sufficiently wiped, Rutspud legged it over to his own cave of tortures. It was as much of a home as he had anywhere. Tesla's scream-organ was producing a fine, many-voiced hymn of pain as he entered.

Wilde, Cartland, Bernhardt and Nightingale were playing cards at a small table. Potter, Whitehouse, Mama-Na and Boudicca were playing table tennis doubles at a much larger table.

Bridge and Ping Pong Mondays.

Shipton, who was not a fan of cards or table tennis, usually spent the Monday sessions writing out dire prognostications in her journal. She was slumped in an armchair, lazily fanning herself with a folded piece of paper.

"Greetings, team," said Rutspud. "I need Lickspear. Where is he?"

Bernhardt lowered her cards and peered at Rutspud.

"Oh, look everyone, it's thingy. That demon who used to work here."

"That fair-weather companion and all round ne'er-do-well?" said Shipton.

"I said, where's Lickspear?"

"Away, Mr Rutspud," said Whitehouse.

"Where?"

"Elsewhere," said Wilde. "Which, I hear, is delightful this time of year."

"Unlike this place," said Nightingale. She put down her cards, pressed down her short apron as she stood, and approached Rutspud with a small thermometer in her hand. "It's far too hot," she said.

"Hot?" frowned Rutspud. "Don't know what you're talking about."

"The air temperature in here is a few degrees below boiling."

"My reading glasses have melted," said Whitehouse.

"You're delusional. I think it's quite chilly in here. Brrr. Might even go fetch myself a scarf to keep warm."

Bernhardt was shaking her head.

"I can't believe it," she said.

"Believe what?" said Rutspud.

"Decades of Wednesday afternoon acting lessons and you are still the worst liar in Hell."

"Am not!"

Mama-Na slammed the ping pong ball off the table and into Rutspud's forehead.

"Vnnn urrr!" she growled angrily and wrung the sweat from her deer-hide tunic to make her point plain.

"I do not have to explain myself to you!" said Rutspud hotly. "Now, where is Lickspear? I need his help."

The scream-organ fell quiet, the last tortured cry fading slowly.

"Isn't it interesting," Telsa turned away from his mechanical creation, "that you only seek any of us out if you want something?"

Rutspud opened his mouth.

The words queued up in his brain. He knew what he needed to say. He was the boss. He was a demon of Hell and they were his victims, his playthings. He could have them chained, flogged, eviscerated and ground into mince with a simple word to his imp minions. He was in charge. They were nothing but the MEAT in his TEAM. If he said jump, they should ask which pit of horrors they should jump into.

But words didn't come. They no longer seemed right.

"Listen," he said quietly. "I think I'm in trouble. I think we're all in a lot of trouble. I would like your help ..."

His throat constricted, choking on something that couldn't quite make its way up to his lips. He screwed his eyes shut.

"Please," he said.

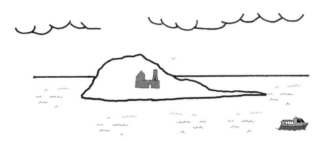

Rutspud stalked into the monastery library. Stephen was reading, slowly and aloud.

"'The demon-hunter ... Treyvaw ... is a general in the armies of Hell. He is tasked with bringing punishment to the punishers. In Hell, none shall go ... unscourged. Those devils who fail to deliver the most terrible of tortures to the damned will be taken to –'"

Rutspud prodded Stephen in the back. Stephen turned away from the *Librum Magnum Daemonum*.

"Oh, hello," said Stephen. "Wasn't expecting to see you until later."

"What have you done to me?"

Stephen gave him a funny look.

"What have I ... done?"

173

"Yes, you. You've cast some weird spell on me. There I was, in my cave of horrible tortures, informing the damned that I needed their help because Hell is over-heating and is, in all probability, going to explode or implode or melt or something, and they were giving me –"

"Sorry?" said Stephen. "Hell's over-heating? Is that why it seems warm in here?"

"Yes, yes. And it's your fault, by the way. And they were giving me a load of grief because I, apparently, don't spend enough time –"

"My fault?" interrupted Stephen. "How is it my fault?"

"You're missing the point," said Rutspud.

"I mean this sounds kind of serious. How is Hell going to explode or implode or melt or whatever?"

"They weren't listening to me," said Rutspud, "just like you're not doing now and I was going to give them an absolute carpeting and, you know what, I couldn't. I felt ... I felt ..."

"What?" said Stephen.

Rutspud growled and stamped his foot, angry with himself. "I felt *guilty*."

Stephen's eyebrows rose and his mouth twitched.

"You think this is funny?" said Rutspud.

"I think it's good."

Rutspud scowled.

"And I ended up – urgh! – apologising to them for being grumpy and then I promised them that I – Oh, Satan's balls! What's that?"

Rutspud stumbled back, a finger pointing in horror at the black and white creature sniffing around in the corner of the library.

"That's Jessie," said Stephen.

"It's hideous. It's like a one-headed Cerberus but it's all ... furry."

"It's a dog. She's from the mainland."

"It's like a giant kitten. Why's its nose wet?"

"Dogs have wet noses."

Rutspud shuddered. Horrible, fluffy looking thing! He bared his teeth and hissed. The dog-thing, Jessie, looked up at him. Its tongue lolled out the side of its mouth. There was a cheerful intelligence in its eyes.

"Can we kill it?" asked Rutspud.

"No, we can't," said Stephen. "Jessie is a soft old thing and she does anything you ask her. Jessie, come play with Rutspud."

The horrible creature bounced over. Rutspud began to flap his hands about to ward it off, but Stephen grabbed him by the shoulder.

"Damn it! There's someone coming. Under the table!"

Stephen thrust his demon pal beneath the central table and pulled the white table cloth down to properly conceal him. Jessie sniffed at its edges. Stephen straightened up in time to see three people enter the library: Brother Manfred with an iron beer keg, Brother Sebastian with a large clay demijohn, and, inexplicably, the schoolteacher who had visited some months before, carrying a fat plastic container of brown green liquid in her arms.

"Sorry, you've got the wrong place. The Messiah's in the stable next door," said Stephen.

"What?" said Manfred.

Stephen gestured at their burdens.

"Three gifts. Like the wise men. It was a joke. Um, hello."

"I see," said Manfred.

Bastian put his load down.

"Manfred's looking for a place to store his beer while it ferments. I told him that it's really quite warm down here."

"It is, isn't it?" said Manfred, surprised. "I wonder if Bardsey sits on some geothermal feature?"

"I'm sure it doesn't," said Stephen quickly.

"I thought we could store this in the warmest of the cellar rooms," said Manfred.

"I'd rather you didn't."

"You see, I seem to have made more seaweed beer than I have storage for. Admittedly, some of it will be depleted after tonight's celebration."

"Celebration?"

The schoolteacher – Carol – stepped forward.

175

"Brother Sebastian and I have some exciting news," she said, in the gushing tones of someone announcing an impending birth or nuptials. Neither seemed likely, so Stephen said nothing.

"Bardsey may be home to a bird previously thought to be extinct," said Bastian.

"Really?" said Stephen.

"Although we have yet to locate it," said Carol.

"Which is why we've come to you, hoping for some better maps of the island to aid us in our search," said Bastian.

Beneath the table, Jessie growled.

"I see that dog's here again," said Manfred.

"I didn't invite her," said Stephen. "Hey, Jessie. Go show Manfred somewhere *upstairs* where he can stick his beer."

There was a snapping sound from under the table and the sheepdog reappeared with something long and thin in her mouth.

"Is that a stick she's found?" said Bastian.

Jessie's bared teeth, gripped around the thing that Stephen realised was definitely not a stick, contorted her face into a mischievous grin. She huffed at Manfred and began to herd him out of the library.

"I'm not being bossed around by a domestic animal," protested Manfred, despite all evidence to the contrary.

Carol put her beer-filled container down on the table.

"Brother Trevor, isn't it?"

"Stephen," he said.

"Really? You look so much like a Trevor. Sorry."

"I know. So it's maps you're after?"

"We need to search all the cliffs and wondered if you had some maps among your collection. This is the bird we're looking for."

She withdrew a crumpled plastic wallet from her pocket and flattened it out on the table.

"It's the yellow-crested Merlin stilt," she said.

Stephen looked at the picture. He took a sideways step and looked through the door to the mural painted on the corridor wall outside.

"That bird?" he said, pointing.

"Yes. I hoped the artist had perhaps seen it on the island."

Stephen shook his head.

"Brother Huey, who is sadly no longer with us, painted that to Manfred's designs. And Manfred got the picture from JJ Audubon's 1828 edition of *Birds of Britain*." He pointed to a fat volume in a glass case.

"Oh," said Carol, clearly disappointed. "I thought a monk on the island had perhaps seen it."

"They have," said Stephen. "I have."

"I beg your pardon?" said Bastian.

"Blasted thing nearly took my face off when I was searching for eggs."

"You saw its nest?" asked Carol.

"Right in front of my face. Give me your map."

Carol unfolded an Ordnance Survey map. With no trouble at all, Stephen planted a fingertip on the cove where his egg-hunting trip had ended in near death.

"It's there."

"Are you sure?"

"Doubly sure."

Bastian grinned. Carol actually, physically, jumped for joy. Bastian took the map from Stephen and the pair of them ran from the room, like school children released for the summer.

"Do you not want to take your beer with you?" said Stephen to no one, and then remembered Rutspud. "Oh, my God! Are you all right under there?"

"What do you think?" grumbled Rutspud.

"I thought I saw Jessie take your ..."

Rutspud emerged from the under table, using his one remaining arm to pull himself upright against the table.

"You thought what, Stephen? Did you think, oh, there goes a bloody dog with Rutspud's arm? Did you?"

Stephen stared at the demon's stump.

"Does it hurt?"

"Pain is relative."

Stephen poked the ragged and bloodless wound. Rutspud looked at him coolly.

"Are you finished gawping?" he said.

"Could we reattach it?" asked Stephen.

"If that sodding monster hasn't eaten it, yes. Frankly, right now, this is just one more item on a very long list of things that have gone wrong for me. Before you shoved me under the table and into the maw of that beast, I was going to tell you that I sort of made a promise to my gang of damned souls."

"What sort of promise?"

"A treat to thank them for all their hard work on my behalf. A little jolly."

Stephen nodded.

"Did you promise to bring them up here, Rutspud?"

"I might have done."

A whole bunch of reasons to argue with Rutspud sprang to Stephen's mind but, standing in front of them all, was a single reason not to. Hell was Hell, Earth was better. Provide succour for the suffering was the greatest good a Christian could do. No one since the time of Christ had actually taken the damned out of Hell and offered them respite and even the stories of Jesus's harrowing of Hell were bloody apocryphal.

"Of course they can come up here," said Stephen. He put his hand on the beer Bastian had left behind. "We can have a little party here tonight."

"Brilliant," said Rutspud. "And if anything gets out of hand and one of your monky mates sticks his nose in, we can give him a dose of this."

Stephen looked at the large flask of yellow liquid.

"And how exactly will force-feeding them piddle help?"

The afternoon weather had turned grim. Although there was no rain in the air, a chill wintry wind blew across the exposed island. The seas were choppy with foam and the clouds above thick, white and heavy.

"I think it could snow." Bastian pulled his hood more tightly around his neck with his gloved hands.

"This cove is only a few hundred yards further," said Carol, consulting her map.

"So why is this bird so rare?" asked Bastian.

"Oh, the usual story," said Carol. "Invasion and destruction of its habitats. Hunting. Egg theft. The last breeding pair in Cornwall were shot by a local man who thought they were Nazi spies."

"Ah, that usual story."

"And possibly the fact that they are the world's worst parents and most suicidal of lovers."

"Worst parents *and* most suicidal lovers?"

"Mmmm." Carol turned the map in her hand and adjusted her course a fraction. "They are appalling nest builders. A love of shiny objects and a peculiar aversion to wood mean that their nests are gaudy, impractical things that, according to ornithological reports, frequently fell apart before the chicks were fledged. They're the footballers and WAGs of the bird world. If birds had *Hello* magazine, there'd be a regular feature in which the 'yellow-crested Merlin stilt shows us around their Cheshire mansion'. Awful."

"And suicidal lovers?"

"Oh, that's not uncommon. Birds are all about extravagant gestures. Birds of paradise waggle their enormous feathers. Adelie penguins give each other pebbles. And the yellow-crested Merlin stilt flies into rocks."

"It does what?"

Carol shrugged.

"To impress the girls, the male Merlin stilt flies headlong into the nearest cliff. I suppose from an evolutionary perspective, it started out as males flying close to the cliff edge to show their skill and prowess. But, yes, it evolved into flying straight into unyielding stone. I guess if you're the only male who can do that and not die, then that says something for your strength and stamina."

"I see."

"Doesn't stop it being stupid though."

"Come on, then. Let's find this bird before it makes itself extinct," said Bastian. "You look cold."

"I'm fine."

"You've got very rosy cheeks."

"Years of alcohol abuse, that's all." She grinned and then abruptly stopped. "Sorry, that probably sounds really sinful. I didn't mean to offend."

179

"No offence," said Bastian. "Alcohol abuse is one of the few vices we monks are positively encouraged to indulge in. If we get back in time, we can abuse our livers utterly with Brother Manfred's seaweed beer."

"Can't wait. Um." Carol pointed to a high ridge. "Is that that sheepdog up there?"

"Jessie?"

"It had this stick in its mouth."

"Uh-huh?"

Carol shook her head.

"A stick that was trying to slap it and escape from its mouth. Ignore me. Let's go."

"I do hope they will be having a finger buffet," said Cartland. "I think a high-quality finger buffet is the hallmark of all the best parties."

"I've always considered the hallmark of a good party to be my presence," said Wilde.

"A party?" said Shipton. "So t'is like a high feast day?"

"Urv arrr-arrgh!" said Mama-Na.

"Or one of those."

"I recall, from my many evenings with the Herberts, that the key to a successful social occasion is the quality of the conversation," said Nightingale.

"Polite conversation," agreed Whitehouse.

"I hope they're not using paper plates," said Cartland. "That would simply be a terribly bad show."

Rutspud stopped abruptly, halting the party of chained individuals.

"Look around you," he hissed, waving at their surroundings with a hand that was not currently there. "Where are we, guys?"

"The Fields of Turpitude," said Tesla.

"And more generally?"

"Hell?" suggested Bernhardt.

"Right," growled Rutspud. "We're in the domain of demons. And we're sneaking out for a little late-night party. I've chained you up so that, if challenged, I can tell the powers that be that I'm taking you off for some extra-curricular flogging. What will make it *less convincing* is if you're gaily discussing the importance of good manners and quality tableware!"

"Sorry, sir," said Potter.

"That's okay," said Rutspud. "Now, is there any chance we could have some moaning and wailing?"

Boudicca set up with some cries of anguish. Shipton, who could always be relied on, wailed heartily.

"Not the flogging!" cried Bernhardt dramatically.

"The horror!" screamed Whitehouse.

"Nnng Forrr!"

"Have mercy!"

"Paper plates!"

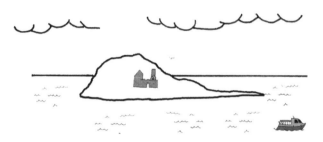

It had indeed started to snow, fat flakes falling from a darkening sky.

Bastian held onto Carol's wrist as she peered down over the cliff edge. The Welsh mainland was now a dark grey band of land between equally grey sea and sky. They were losing the light and, Bastian feared, were equally likely to lose their footing if they persisted for much longer.

"Nope, not here," said Carol. "So, tell me, what made you give up the big city life for this beautiful wilderness?"

"I think you've just answered your own question," said Bastian.

"You know what I mean."

Bastian nodded and the duo edged along a little further.

"Back in the day, I was as rich as Croesus but had a lousy life," he said.

"Oh, yeah. Being rich is an absolute drag."

"I was a lousy husband."

"You had a wife?"

"Once upon a time. A long time ago."

"I had me one of them once. A husband, not a wife."

"Not a lousy one like me."

"Oh, no. I'm sure he was perfect. That was why so many shitty women threw themselves at him. And you know what happens if you throw enough shit. Anyway, the one that stuck to him just happened to be younger than me, taller than me, and with perkier tits." Carol laughed. "Did you see how I segued seamlessly from mild-mannered primary school teacher to bitter old hag in under thirty seconds? I apologise."

"Don't," said Bastian. "It's hard to let go when people hurt you."

"Yeah, but I apologise for hijacking your story. You were saying you were a bad husband. Not that I believe you, by the way. Nope, not here. Move along."

"Believe it. My work. The money. The numbers. They were everything to me. It was an addiction. I was so blind to the greed, to the machine I had become, I barely noticed when she left."

Carol pulled on his arm as she leant further out. He tightened his grip on her wrist.

"We're going to have to stop soon," he said. "Look again tomorrow."

"So, what opened your eyes to the truth?" asked Carol.

"The global economic slowdown. The Credit Crunch. I happily let my private life fall apart. I didn't even blink. But the day the world decided that I was unimportant, that the work I was doing was not the vital cornerstone of industry I saw it as but was, at best, trivial and, at worst, downright evil ... Yes, that was the day I came to my senses."

"And that's why you became a monk?"

"Well, sort of. Careful, Carol, you're awfully close to the edge. Here on Bardsey, if I grow vegetables or farm chickens, I have produced something. Here, if I raise money for restoration work or charity, I have helped someone or made the world a marginally better place. Here. Here, I matter."

"Lie down next to me."

"What?"

Carol got down on her hands and knees and wriggled on her front until her head poked over the cliff edge.

"What do you reckon that is?"

Bastian gathered his habit, got down next to Carol and looked over the edge. He could see the wet cliff face and far below the almost invisibly dark wash of seawater in and out, in and out of the cove.

"Where?" he said.

"There," she said, a voice right by his ear. "Under this ledge."

"It looks like a pile of rubbish," said Bastian. "Like someone's spilled luggage."

"And the white frilly-edged thing?"

"An old towel."

The white towel-like thing shifted and turned its head. It clicked its beak and repositioned itself in its nest.

"Oh, my goodness," said Bastian.

Carol started to laugh and slapped her hand over her mouth, reducing her laugh to a delighted squeak.

"That's it?" said Bastian.

Carol rolled onto her side to look at him. Lines of delight creased the corners of her wide eyes.

"That's it," he said.

She put her hand on his shoulder.

"It certainly is," she said and planted a fast, hard kiss on his lips. She broke off almost instantly. "I'm sorry, brother. I really am. Totally inappropriate."

"No. No. I'm excited too. It's –"

Bastian's words were squashed as she kissed him again.

"Okay," she said. "I definitely meant to do it that time. I shouldn't have, I know but I ju–"

Bastian kissed her back.

The monks of St Cadfan's threw themselves into the celebratory evening meal like drug addicts loose in a pharmacy.

Their months of isolation and weeks of near-starvation were at an end, and the brothers had been queuing at the refectory door a full two hours before dinner was due to be served. Conversation and laughter echoed through the corridor while they waited, not waiting impatiently like the famished men they were, but contentedly like refugees who knew salvation was close at hand.

However, when Stephen helped Manfred usher them in, they had to step back hurriedly to avoid being trampled by the horde. For a bunch of mostly septuagenarian holy men, they moved pretty darn quickly.

"Form an orderly line, please," called Manfred.

The plea fell on deaf ears (some of them genuinely so).

"At least use a plate, Brother Terry!" Manfred shouted. "And the serving spoon!"

Stephen put a hand on the prior's arm.

"They're happy, brother," he said.

"True," agreed Manfred. "Although I'd rather Brother Vernon didn't drink the soup straight from the tureen."

Plates were piled high with fresh bread, meat and vegetables, including four types of potato.

"Where are the tankards for this beer you've promised us?" asked Brother Henry loudly.

"Put safely aside until Brother Sebastian and Ms Well-Dunn return," said Manfred. "Our feast tonight should, I hope, be a celebration of a miraculous discovery."

Stephen came down to the visitors' centre just as Rutspud was leading his party of Hell's prisoners out of the cellars. Stephen had not given much thought as to what he expected the damned to look like but, seeing them now in the flesh, he realised he had expected to see skeletons, zombies, ethereal shades – something that hinted at their deathly state. But, no, here they were, a band of ragged, muck-streaked and, above all else, tired looking human beings.

"– clearly a non-Newtonian structure," a moustachioed man with neatly parted hair was saying to Rutspud, "a helical stair that passes through dimensions other than the conventional four. Impressive."

"Greetings," said Stephen. Ten pairs of eyes turned on him. "I am Brother Stephen. Can I just say a big welcome to – Hang on, Rutspud. Why are they all manacled together?"

"Part of my cunning ruse to sneak them out," said Rutspud. "I'll have them off in a jiffy."

"Now," said Stephen. "I was going to suggest a spot of food and drink, but perhaps you would all care to come along to our guest dormitories – totally unoccupied at the moment – and make use of our showers. I might be able to rustle up some spare habits to replace your current ... vestments."

"Showers?" said an imperious looking woman with braided hair and an accent that drifted between Welsh and Irish.

"A washing closet, Boudicca dear," said a woman in horn-rimmed glasses.

"Boudicca? Queen of the Iceni?" choked Stephen.

"Yes, yes," said Rutspud tiredly. "I suppose some brief introductions are in order. Stephen this is Boudicca."

"Your majesty," he said, shaking her hand enthusiastically.

"Whitehouse."

"Mary? A pleasure."

"Shipton."

"As in Old Mother?"

"Ursula to me friends, boy."

"A pleasure, madam."

"Moving along," said Rutspud. "This is Bernhardt."

"A delight, Sarah."

Oh God, thought Stephen. I'm shaking hands with dead people. This is amazing!

"Wilde."

"Oscar," said Stephen. "Always been a fan."

"Cartland," said Rutspud.

"Dame Cartland. Another fine author."

Oscar Wilde looked at Stephen down his nose, clearly unimpressed at being linked by such association.

"This is Tesla," said Rutspud.

"Nikola, isn't it? I think I saw David Bowie play you in a movie once," said Stephen. "Greetings."

"Potter."

"Miss Potter, welcome."

"Nightingale."

"Florence?" said Stephen. "How could you possibly have ended up in Hell? In fact, how could any one of you be condemned to this? But Florence Nightingale? Madam, how is this possible?"

"Well ..." said Nightingale.

"Not a word," instructed Rutspud sharply. "Rule Number Three, Nightingale."

"But, Rutspud ..." she protested.

"Rule Number Three?"

Nightingale sighed.

"'Do not talk to anyone about your crimes or cause of damnation. No one is interested.'"

"Rules, Rutspud?" asked Stephen.

The one-armed demon nodded firmly.

"My little gang have been given some very clear rules for tonight's expedition. Don't want things going awry while we having our little away day. Well, you've now met my entire band."

"Grrr Nnhh!"

"Oh, yes. Sorry. The last one. Mama-Na."

"Good to see you too ... madam, is it?" said Stephen, shaking a massive grimy paw.

"Ha!" laughed Rutspud. "I knew you'd struggle with at least one of them. See, everyone? See? You all look alike."

"I think I can be forgiven," said Stephen, "given that Mama-Na here is some sort of Cro-Magnon or something."

"Nnnnf!" grunted the cavewoman and slapped Stephen across the head.

"Mama-Na!" shouted Rutspud. "We do not hit the nice man!"

Potter helped steady the dazed Stephen.

"She's a Neanderthal," she pointed out. "She gets touchy when people get it wrong."

"I'll remember that," said Stephen. "To the showers."

Bastian and Carol paused in front of the closed refectory door.

"Right."

"Right."

"This is it."

"It is. We just go in. Two ordinary people."

Bastian looked down to double-check that they weren't holding hands.

"We just go in. Tell them we've found the nest. They applaud. We get some food. Sit down."

"Separately?"

"Separately, but not suspiciously separately."

"How much is not suspicious?"

"One monk apart?"

"Best make it two."

"No one needs to know what happened," said Bastian. "Not that I'm ashamed of what we did. I mean I *am* ashamed, but I'm not ashamed because of you."

"Ditto."

"I've not got lipstick on my face or anything, have I?" he asked.

"I don't wear lipstick, Bastian."

"Oh. But I haven't got any ... you know ..."

"I think the word you're looking for is guilt," said Carol. "You're covered in it."

"Oh, crap, they're going to know," said Bastian. "They're going to find out."

"Not at all," said Carol.

He straightened his habit for the hundredth time and looked Carol up and down again, making sure that they hadn't left some incriminating sign such as a total lack of clothing or a tattoo saying 'I kissed a monk and I liked it'.

"Of course," he said. "It will be fine. I'm over-reacting."

Carol smiled.

"You don't think there's chance of a one last –"

Bastian gave her a peck on the lips.

"Let's do this."

He pushed the door open and strode in, almost leaping to ensure he was several feet ahead of Carol.

Two dozen heads turned to look and, as one, two dozen tankards were raised and a great ragged cheer went up from the men.

"The heroes return!" shouted Brother Vernon, fairly dousing Brother Gillespie with frothy drink.

"Thought you two were out for the night!" shouted Brother Desmond.

"Dirty pair!" sniggered Brother Henry.

Feeling their shameful secret bubbling to the surface so quickly, Bastian automatically reached out for Carol's hand for support and then stopped himself before he did something stupid.

Manfred wove through tables with three pewter tankards. He was wearing a cook's apron with the words 'HOT STUFF' stitched in sequins across it.

"I am so sorry, dear friends. We were going to wait for you before starting on the beer. Here, take a drink. But you were *so* long. It's dark out now. Were you successful?"

Carol nodded dumbly.

"Really?" said Manfred.

"A nest. Two birds. Two eggs," she managed to say. "A bit precariously positioned, but otherwise great."

Manfred grinned broadly.

"Hear that, brothers?" he called out to the room at large. "Ms Well-Dunn and Brother Sebastian have found the stilt nest!"

The cheer that came back at them was loud and hearty to the point of ecstatic. Tankards were chinked, cutlery was rattled and the buoyant and decidedly tipsy mood of the room went up a grade or two.

"A toast, then," said Manfred to the two embarrassed lovers. "To you two. Intrepid explorers of uncharted territory. Long may your partnership bear such magnificent fruit!"

"Er, yes," said Bastian. "Quite."

"Thank you," said Carol. "And perhaps it would be for the best if I left tomorrow morning so that I might go share the good news with the worldwide ornithological community."

She looked at Bastian.

"No," said Manfred. "Don't leave so soon. Surely you're staying for a little longer?"

"I don't know," she said. "What do you think, Brother Sebastian?"

The expression on her face made him want to hold her. It made him want to cry. He gazed down into the foam of his drink.

"I don't know, Caro– Ms Well-Dunn." He put on a smile he could barely sustain. "Let's leave such decisions until the morning. Cheers."

He drank deeply and shuddered.

"That is an interesting brew," he said.

Manfred nodded.

"Isn't it just? I'm not sure if I should call it beer or wine."

"Or some sort of hazardous industrial run-off," said Bastian.

"Mmm," said Carol, suppressing a cough. "You can really taste the, um ..."

"Meths?" said Bastian.

"Sea, I was going to say. Very, um, nautical."

"Well, don't just stand there," said Manfred. "Get some grub and have a seat."

"We need music!" shouted Brother Henry.

"Wheel out the gramophone!" shouted the geriatric Brother Cecil.

"We haven't had a gramophone since seventy-four," replied the equally geriatric Brother Roland.

Brother Cecil laughed and slapped his knee.

"The fight over who was better, George Formby or Max Bygraves. Brother Bernard broke the Max Bygraves record over Brother Lionel's head."

"And Brother Huey threw the gramophone out the almonry window," laughed Brother Roland in reply.

Brother Cecil launched himself drunkenly to his feet.

"Brother Bernard!" he yelled, hoisting his tankard in the air. "And Brother Huey! Great men and the best of brothers."

There was an uncoordinated reply as the monks held their drinks aloft and toasted their dead brothers.

Father Eustace clambered on top of his table, waved his drink in the air, shouted "Organ grinder!" and then ran from the room.

"Is that normal behaviour?" asked Carol.

Bastian shrugged.

"Insufficient data to say, really. Manfred, did Lionel leave this morning? I had hoped to say goodbye."

Manfred gave him a distressed look.

"Yes, well, you and I need to talk about that ..."

Stephen surveyed the damned souls, all dressed in fresh monks' habits, and made a decision that he suspected he would regret but wanted to make anyway.

"I've had a thought," he said.

"Yes?" said Rutspud.

"It would involve you putting on a habit too."

"Oh?"

"I had thought to have a little party down here in the library, sneak out a little beer and bread from the refectory upstairs. But, now that I think about it, the brothers upstairs have been at the booze for some time and they're probably ..."

"In their cups," suggested Nightingale.

"Three sheets to the wind," said Cartland.

"Absolutely trollied," agreed Stephen. "What would ten extra monks be in that great hall?"

"Are you sure?" said Rutspud.

Stephen shrugged.

"If we are to offer your ... your team a night off, then the least I can do is make it a good one. And, besides, you've got some of that magical forget-me juice, if things go pear-shaped. I think you all deserve a chance to experience our full hospitality."

"You are too kind," said Bernhardt.

"And where's the entertainment in that?" said Wilde. "Give me a stingy host any day. Begrudging generosity was always more fun."

"Ignore the man," said Whitehouse. "Lead on, Brother Stephen. I am sure a simply splendid evening awaits."

Stephen led the party out of the library, up from the refurbished wing and to the refectory.

"Okay," he said in hushed tones. "Go in, find a seat and I will bring some food and drink across to you. Hoods up everyone."

Mentally preparing himself for it all to go horribly wrong at any moment, Stephen led the way inside. As he had suspected, his fellow monks were deep in drink and deep in conversation and filling the refectory with enough noise for a hundred people. Maybe one head or two looked round as the line of new monks shuffled in, but none for more than a second.

Stephen waved his guests over to an unoccupied table and benches and made his way over to the side tables where an enormous feast had been mostly demolished. He gathered several plates and began piling the still plentiful remains onto them.

"S'Trevor!" said Brother Henry, wobbling over.

"Stephen," said Stephen.

"S'what I said," said Brother Henry drunkenly. "Where've you been hiding, eh?"

"Here and there," said Stephen.

Henry shook his head disapprovingly.

"You've missed a wonderful night. S'bastian and the little woman've found their bird."

"Oh, that's good news."

"And we've had *sooo* much food, it's been brilliant."

"Well, I hope to tuck in myself, so ..."

Henry grabbed his shoulder.

"It's just good to have us all here. You know, all the monks together. United." He hiccupped, momentarily looked like he was going to turn it into a retch, and then converted it into a belch at the last moment. "You do know that I love you, don't you, Trevor?"

"I do now," said Stephen.

"I mean I love all of you." He swung his hand wide, knocking the top off Manfred's fruit display. "All these men. It's like ... It's like ..."

Brother Henry squinted.

"How many monks are there at St Cadfan's?" he asked.

Stephen's stomach flipped.

"I don't really know, Henry."

"I thought it was like twenty or something but tonight ... tonight there's ... one, two, three, four ..."

Suddenly the lights went out, all but the long strip light between the kitchen serving hatch and the top table.

"What the ...?"

There was a loud, high-pitched and violent trill of plucked strings and Father Eustace was back on the table in the circle of light, a long-necked instrument in his hand.

"Where on earth did he get a guitar from?" said Brother Henry.

"I think it's a banjo," said Stephen. "And I've no idea."

Father Eustace strummed his way through a number of surprisingly tuneful chords.

"Oh, my God, he's going to sing," said Brother Henry.

Stephen took advantage of the diversion and bustled his many plates over to the party from Hell as Father Eustace launched into his song:

"Ol' Tom went up to Adam's cave to see the organ grinder.
And she was a comely wench with a fine career behind her.
Coin he brought, scrumpy fine, gold and sweet from Devon.
And she welcomed him, arms open wide, like the Gates of
Heaven."

It was a simple tune, with a few folksy embellishments, the sort of song that Stephen could picture someone singing with their eyes closed and a finger in one ear, indeed the sort of song most people would prefer to listen to with fingers in both ears.

Stephen placed the food on the table of the damned.

"I'll be back with the beer," he said.

Rutspud helped dole the food out but found himself distracted by the mad monk's singing.

"To Adam's cave I've come, my love, a place to rest my soul.
Let me lie with you till I moan no more and bury my bones in
your hole."

"I'd swear I've heard that tune somewhere before," said Rutspud.

"It's not like t'music they 'ad in my day," said Shipton.

"Nor mine," said Tesla.

"I'd lay down my tool, rest my head and drown myself in cider.
In your warm cave, I'll breathe my last and find sweet peace
inside 'er"

"It has a certain vulgar charm," said Wilde, smiling thinly.

"Vulgar is right," said Whitehouse unhappily. "But the food looks quite appetising."

"What is this?" said Boudicca.

"It's a roast potato," said Potter.

"Mmn pa-pa?"

"That's right. Potato. It's nice. Particularly with gravy."

"Ooh, I do love a good gravy," said Cartland. She prodded the food in front of her with a fork. "Do you know something?" she said.

"What, dear?" said Nightingale.

"I ... I can't remember when I last ate anything."

"I don't think I've actually had real food since I died," said Bernhardt.

"Well, now's your chance," said Rutspud. "Come on, tuck in."

"It seems odd," said Cartland softly.

"What?"

She put the fork down.

"I'm not hungry."

"Same here," said Tesla.

"Thou speaks true," said Shipton.

"Are you kidding me?" said Rutspud, flabbergasted.

"And what's this?" said Boudicca.

"That's also potato," said Potter. "Mashed."

"Mmn pa-pa," said Mama-Na.

"I see," said Boudicca and put it down again.

Rutspud, for reasons he probably could not articulate, found himself growing angry.

"What is this? Are none of you going to partake?" he said.

"If you tell us to, we will," said Potter dutifully.

"No. I want you to want to eat it. I'm not forcing you to."

"It seems like more than one pleasure of the flesh fades away with lack of use," said Wilde.

"We don't wish to appear ungrateful," said Whitehouse. "This all seems delightful, although the lyrics of the abbot's song seem more than a little suspect."

"*Pickled in drink they found him and they buried his bones in the hole.*

No Heaven's Gates for Ol' Tom, for he'd damned his soul."

Stephen returned to the table and loudly slid a tray of beers onto the table, sloshing foamy head into the tray.

"And *here's* your drinks," he said grandiosely.

"Don't tell me you lot don't want a drink as well," said Rutspud, passing them around.

"Of course not," said Tesla politely. "I am sure we'd all like to drink to the health of our host, Brother Stephen, and offer our thanks to Rutspud."

"Quite," said Cartland.

Bastian looked down at the contents of the freezer.

"Hmmm, I don't suppose you brought me here to show me that we're fully restocked with ice lolllies?"

"No," said Manfred.

"And, I'm just taking a wild guess here," said Bastian, "but I don't suppose you happened to come in here this morning and found Brother Lionel dead in the freezer?"

"No."

"Not done a little Walt Disney on himself and decided to freeze himself for future scientists to restore to life?"

"No. He died in his sleep."

"Like the other two?"

"Indeed."

"And your plans?"

The curly-haired German gave his friend a guilty look.

"I think we should bury him on the island. In secret."

"And tell everyone that he left on Owen's boat?"

"I'm sure we can pull the wool over Owen's eyes somehow."

"And thus spare the monastery further scandal and months of isolation?"

"That is right, brother."

Bastian nodded thoughtfully.

"Unless our illegal attempts to conceal a death are discovered. In which case the monastery will face further scandal, months of isolation, and see at least two of its members sent off to Cox's Farm Prison."

"Yes," said Manfred.

Bastian took a deep breath. Manfred watched him nervously.

"What do you think?"

"Beer," said Bastian. "I think I need a lot of beer."

It surprised no one that everyone was drunk long before midnight.

Firstly, the twenty-odd men of St Cadfan's monastery had been living on starvation rations for several months and were, to a man, several pounds underweight and ill-prepared for a night of raucous drinking.

Secondly, the damned of Hell drank on stomachs that had been empty for decades if not centuries (millennia in the case of Mama-Na, whose only previous experience with alcohol involved a pile of rotten and fermented mangos her tribe had found).

Thirdly, three monks drank in the knowledge that they had hidden their dead brother in a chest freezer and were already stepping across the line into criminal activity. Alcohol was, for them, a blessed escape from reality.

Fourthly, one of those three men (and his illicit lover) were drinking to numb the shock of what they had done and to help them process the emotional fallout that was certain to follow.

Fifthly, no one was surprised because Brother Manfred's seaweed beer had a startlingly high alcohol content and soon rendered them all incapable of surprise. They were drunk, the world was as it was, and, as drunks, they simply took the world as they found it.

"We'll burn Ol' Tom in our fiery hole – hey! – and there he'll moan and moan – hey!

Drown him in piss, gold and sweet – hey! – and feast on his throbbing bone – hey!"

A conga line had formed in the refectory, many habit-wearing figures weaving in and out between the tables to Father Eustace's improvised music. Some of the monks had picked up pans and trays and provided additional percussion.

"His heart and brains and lights beside – hey! – we'll feed into the organ grinder – hey!

And though he'll search 'cross Hell for his love – hey! – Ol' Tom will never find 'er – hey!"

195

Only three groups of people were not taking part at all: those who had stepped out of line to refresh their drinks, those who had passed out on the tables or benches from too much drinking, and Rutspud.

Rutspud, hiding his clearly inhuman face and lack of a right arm in the folds of his habit, was trying to spot faces beneath cowls and count up his party of damned. There was Cartland, who had managed to decant her beer into a wine glass that she had acquired from somewhere. There was Whitehouse who, tending to find sexual impropriety in all things, was nonetheless relishing the hip-wiggling dance, although perhaps not with the sinuous expressiveness of Bernhardt there. And ... there was Mama-Na, at home with the dance's simple rhythms, and Wilde, who was pretending not to be enjoying himself enormously. And even Shipton, hobbling along in the middle of the chain, was giving a raucous "Ha!" with every conga kick.

"And where are the rest of you?" he muttered.

Rutspud began exploring the darker corners of the refectory, occasionally taking hold of a table for support because the tangy seaweed beer affected even those of hardy demon stock.

A circuit of the hall revealed no extra bodies and, beginning to fear that one of his trusted damned had broken Rule Number One and fled, Rutspud began a hurried search of the adjoining rooms. Much to his relief, he found three of them in a room just off from the kitchens, gathered around an icy chest.

"What are you doing in here?" he said.

"Taking some scientific readings," said Tesla, waving a device of dials and gauges over the frozen box.

"It is a strange tomb of ice," said Boudicca.

"It's not a tomb," said Nightingale.

"Then why have they surrounded the dead man with food offerings?" asked Boudicca.

"It is clearly some sort of larder for keeping food cool," said Nightingale.

"A Frigidaire," said Tesla. "But this is most abnormal."

"I'll say," said Rutspud. "Stephen told me they don't eat their dead and yet here's one they're quite clearly saving for later."

"No," said Tesla. "The readings are abnormal."

"I think we'd all agree that poking scientific instruments at dead people is a bit weird, yes."

"That's not what I meant."

"You must listen to him, sir," said Nightingale.

Rutspud grimaced.

"What I must do is get you out of here. We're supposed to be keeping a low profile."

There was a loud scream from the refectory and the music came to a sudden halt.

"Mmm," said Rutspud, "I'm guessing we've entirely failed on the low profile front, haven't we?"

He darted back into the refectory to find Mama-Na swinging from the wooden rafters by her knees and a bunch of monks stunned gathered around a dazed man on the floor.

"It slapped me," muttered the prone monk.

"What is it?" shouted another.

"There *are* too many monks in here!" shouted yet another with a sense of vindication.

Stephen looked across at Rutspud and, panic written large on his face, was miming a throat-slicing action.

"Right," declared Rutspud loudly. "Party's over. My lot. We're off."

He tried to clap his hands for emphasis but failed because he had the wrong number of hands.

Stephen wildly directed the damned to the door while Rutspud prodded, propelled and generally rounded them up.

"Interlopers!" yelled a human.

"They're fake monks!"

"Fiery hole!" shouted the abbot.

Rutspud dug deep in his robes and tossed the flask of Lethe water to Stephen as he ran out the door.

"Maybe a nightcap for everyone, eh?" he said. "Onward! On! Go!"

Rutspud brought up the rear like a high-speed shepherd, shouting the occasional instruction when one of the damned took a wrong turn. Down into the cellar they ran, through the corridor of garish paintings, past Stephen's library and into the noticeably warm stone room.

Rutspud counted them down the stairs.

"One! Two! Three!"

Tesla stopped beside Rutspud.

"Sir, I have to tell you about that man in the Frigidaire."

"What? Now? Four! Five! Mama-Na, you and I are having words later."

"Gnnk Rrrrr!"

"He's not dead, sir," said Tesla.

"Seven! What? That's nonsense. You mean he's alive?"

"No, sir. I don't."

"Eight! Nine!"

Rutspud and Tesla were alone at the top of the stair to Hell.

"Wait!" said Rutspud, wide-eyed. "Nine. I counted nine."

"Sir?"

Rutspud gritted his teeth, infuriated.

"We've lost one!"

Chapter 7 – The day it snowed

Bastian had known hangovers before. In his younger days, working and partying in the Square Mile, he'd suffered many a Bollinger-induced brainburster, which he'd generally treated with a cornflakes and champagne hangover cure. However, he couldn't help thinking that the state of his mind and body right now went beyond the normal bounds of a hangover. A glimpse in the mirror had not been encouraging. A greenish tinge was something he'd seen before, but his complexion today was a greyish khaki. He'd been quite relieved to see that the others were the same colour. Perhaps some quality of Manfred's seaweed beer had caused this alarming transformation.

"Breakfast, anyone?" Manfred asked in the refectory.

Bastian gave a small shake of his head, and had to take a moment to recover from the pain that it caused him.

At the nearest table, Carol Well-Dunn seemed to quail at the very mention of food. Brother Stephen looked little better.

"Could I suggest a refreshing walk outside, then?" said Manfred.

"A walk?" said Stephen, who looked as though a mere stagger might kill him.

"I'm not sure I'm up to walking," said Bastian.

"But wasn't there something that you wanted to show us, brother?" said Manfred and then frowned. "But for the life of me, I cannot recall what it was."

"Was there?" said Bastian.

Carol wagged a finger at Bastian.

"Yes, it was very important," she said. "Very, *very* important." Her brow creased as she struggled to pursue the thought.

Bastian reached back into his recent memory. It was like plunging into a dark pool, full of nothing but uncertainty. A dark pool of slime and mud. A dark pool of slime and mud that burned his fragile brain with its acid touch.

He recalled he and Carol returning to the monastery, filled with excitement and burdened by a secret. Something ... shameful?

"I've never been so drunk that I completely forgot the events of the day before," said Bastian.

"What was in that punch that we had before bed?" Carol asked.

"We had punch?" said Stephen.

"It seems so," said Manfred. "We found you face down in it this morning."

"Oh," said Stephen, relieved, "*that* was why I was all wet and stinky this morning."

"If you like," said Manfred, kindly.

"Look at all the snow!" said Manfred.

There was general wincing as the band of morning walkers encountered the brightness of the morning sun and its almost deliberately offensive reflection off the snow that covered the island.

"My eyes are melting," whimpered Stephen.

Temporarily blinded by the brightness, Carol bumped into the back of Bastian.

"Oh, sorry," she said.

"Are you all right?" he asked touching her arm.

He snatched back his hand as a jolt of recollection shot briefly through him. He looked at Carol and saw something of his own confusion reflected in her eyes.

"The strangest thing just popped into my head," said Carol. "I think that punch must have given me some unusual dreams."

Bastian looked away and shook his head, trying to dislodge the deeply impure thoughts that had flooded his mind.

"Very strange dreams," he murmured.

"A brisk walk will soon restore us all to good health," said Manfred. "It's so very bracing."

"Painful," gasped Bastian. "The word you're looking for, my German friend, is 'painful'."

As though guided by a sense of déjà vu or, reflecting on Carol's words, as though re-enacting a vaguely remembered dream, Bastian found himself walking on automatic pilot to one of the furthest corners of the island and a rocky cove, cut like a steep V into the side of the island.

"We've been here before," said Carol.

"This was the place I showed you on the map," said Stephen.

"Did you?" said Bastian. "Blimey. I simply don't remember. It's like I've been given a shot of amnesia juice or something."

"Oh!" said Stephen, suddenly smiling. "Of course!"

"What?" said Bastian.

"Er, nothing," said the younger monk.

"Hmmm," said Manfred, crouching down at the cliff edge. "I can see that the snow is not so thick on the edge here. As though two people were ..."

Bastian looked at Carol and saw that she was looking at him. He wondered why his guts were churning with anxiety. Maybe they were simply churning with seaweed beer residue.

"It is possible that you were both lying here ..." said Manfred.

"What?" laughed Bastian, hearing instantly how horribly false his laughter sounded.

"To observe the bird, yes?" said Manfred.

"To observe the bird, yes," said Carol woodenly and coughed. "Er, what bird?"

"That one," said Manfred. "Well, those two."

They all shuffled carefully to the edge and peered over. A pair of creatures that looked like badly stitched glove puppets, each operated by someone without the requisite number of fingers, clicked, pecked and preened on their untidy pile of a nest.

"Magnificent," breathed Carol. "How could we forget our discovery?"

"Perplexing," said Bastian.

"So, this is the bird that will bring us many visitors?" asked Manfred. "It looks less impressive than I had imagined."

"It's an incredible opportunity for you," said Carol, straightening up, her complexion suddenly flushed with new vigour. "The excitement that it's going to cause on the birding scene – I can't begin to tell you how important this is. You just need to manage the visitors you're going to get."

"Managing excessive visitors is not a problem we've had to face before," said Stephen.

"Well, you definitely don't want the birds disturbed as they raise their precious young."

Manfred looked at the precarious ledge they were standing on.

"It's a tricky spot to be sure. We don't want to lose our visitors over the edge when they get too inquisitive."

"Can't we build a hide?" asked Stephen. "Somewhere we can let people see the bird, but in a controlled way, so they don't clamber about on the edge here."

"That's a very good idea," said Carol. "How quickly can you get something in place? I don't imagine Bardsey's a very easy place to get construction firms to come to."

"We can tackle it immediately," said Manfred. "We pride ourselves here at St Cadfan's on our ability to turn our hands to a multitude of practical things. I am certain that a simple bird hide is well within our capabilities. I can actually picture a very pleasing design where we can extend a viewing platform over the nest. I will draw up some plans when I have cooked some bacon sandwiches for our breakfast."

Bastian looked around the group and saw that everyone now seemed to be in the mood for something to eat and they'd mostly lost the greenish tinge from their faces. He smiled at Carol, and felt immediately guilty for some reason that he couldn't place.

"Well, the least we can do is to serve you a hearty meal before your journey home. And then on with the chores. Mind you, I've no idea what to make of all the dirty habits I've seen this past day."

Bastian flushed red and caught Carol's eye as he did so.

"What do you mean?" he squeaked.

"Great big pile of them in the laundry. I'd swear there are more habits to wash than we have monks at St Cadfan's," said Manfred with a shrug.

Stephen ducked his head down and hurried off as if he had something very urgent to attend to. Bastian breathed out with relief and wondered why he felt so very, very embarrassed.

Rutspud took a seat at the rear of the conference room. He did his very best to blend in with the background, but as the background was painted in a colour that he'd been told was *magnolia*, it wasn't an easy task.

"I had no idea magnolia was so very *unpleasant*," he whispered to Belphegor, who wheeled his chair next to him.

"It's supposed to be inoffensive to our Heavenly colleagues," said Belphegor with a shrug. "It's one of those compromise things. We promise not to decorate the place with priests' innards and they promise not to give us an uplifting pamphlet on God's love. What happened to your arm?"

Rutspud clutched his stump shamefully.

"Lost it in a fight."

"With who?"

"Er, Cerberus."

"And only lost an arm? Impressive."

"It might have been one of his smaller relatives. Not so many heads. I'm going to get it back later."

The conference room, temporarily conjured from pure nothingness in the Limbo lands between Heaven and Hell, was, if nothing else, decently air-conditioned and a blessed relief from the increasingly hot fires of Hell. Rutspud idly flicked through one of the neatly bound packs that was placed on the large table in front of him.

"So do you know who everyone is?" he whispered to Belphegor, eyeing the group of delegates from the Celestial City. "I know that's Joan of Arc. She and I are both involved in the annual Christmas present exchange thing."

"Really?"

"It's fun. They send our lot words of hope and comfort. We send them E Coli flavoured sweets and a short compilation video to remind them that every decent musician, singer and actor of the past one hundred years is down in Hell with us. Who's that guy?"

"Which one?" said Belphegor.

"The smug one."

"Narrow it down for me, boy."

"The cold-eyed one looking at us like we're the something he's just trod in. Next to the Archangel Michael."

"That's St Paul," said Belphegor. "A real piece of work. Loves quoting his own letters. And that's not Michael. Michael was the one with the lance. War in Heaven and all that tripe. Michael fell out of Heaven's favour during the 'unpleasantness'. *That* guy there is Gabriel. Insufferable bastard. Mouth like a foghorn and the brains of a hamster."

"And the two tonne tubster?"

"St Thomas Aquinas. Never get into an argument with him. He'll have you tied up in logic. The only thing he loves more than an argument is food. We always have to strengthen a chair just for him. One of my previous assistants got the chairs mixed up one time and he ended up on the floor."

"What happened to the assistant?" asked Rutspud.

"No-one knows," said Belphegor. "There's a Hell for those who transgress in our Hell. We all know that. I heard that Lord Peter arranged for him to go to *that* Hell's Hell. Nasty business."

"And why's Mulciber here?" asked Rutspud, nodding towards the fallen angel. "Is this an architectural issue?"

"We bring Mulciber to the table because he used to be one of *them*. Apparently they feel more comfortable with angelic faces to look at. Not accustomed to beauties such as you and I."

Rutspud shook his head and picked up his copy of the paperwork.

"Let's just hope that you and Lewis can prove adequate today. Keep us all out of trouble," muttered Belphegor as he paged through his own documentation.

Rutspud glanced over at Lewis, who seemed to be making detailed notes on the back of his copy, humming a folksy tune as he did. Rutspud leaned over and saw that the tweedy university don was, in fact, sketching an ornate wardrobe. It was one of those occasions, Rutspud decided, where coming out on top wasn't going to be an option.

On an open page of the meeting documents, a large graph showed infernal temperatures and a small spike as representation of the recent rises.

"This makes it look as though there's not really a problem," Rutspud said to Belphegor.

"Mmmm," agreed Belphegor, scratching his warty belly. "It's possible that Peter's involved the Pit of Statisticians."

"You mean these figures are lies."

"And damned lies. We'd best tread carefully in case we get *seasonally adjusted* if you know what I mean."

Rutspud didn't know what he meant, but understood an instruction to keep his head down and his mouth shut when he heard one.

Lord Peter entered the room, with Nero close behind.

"Game face," whispered Belphegor and grinned genially at all present with a mouthful of teeth that were not all necessarily his own, most having been haphazardly replaced over the millennia.

"Welcome, everybody," called Peter. "Thank you all for coming. Now, we've called this special meeting in order to get our finest minds focussed on the small environmental issue that we've noticed. I'd like to welcome our colleagues from the Celestial City who have graciously agreed to lend us their expertise."

"Agreed?" said St Thomas. "We are here at our insistence, fallen one."

Peter smiled without blinking and pressed on as though the obese saint had never spoken.

"I think we all appreciate what's been happening, but Hodshift here has made a brief presentation to summarise the key points. You've all got copies of his diagrams in your packs. Hodshift?"

"Right, Lord," said the demon engineer, getting to his feet and clicking a hand-held device. "This 'ere's a slideshow with some charts and so on."

The projector whirred into life and a diagram appeared on the magnolia wall.

"You'll see a rise in the temperature –"

"Well, this is strange," said St Paul, peering at the screen. "The graph you have there is in a similar *style* to the one we have here, but the spike in temperature is much larger."

"Oh. Aye," said Hodshift, his eyes wide with alarm. "Hold up a minute."

He clicked on a keyboard. A list of files appeared.

"Ah, yes. This is the one we want," said Hodshift clicking on DATA_APPROVED_BY_PETER.

The graph that appeared showed a much smaller spike.

"Peter, can I ask why you edited this presentation?" asked St Paul.

"Edited?"

"Edited. As in changed."

"Pfft," said Lord Peter, "I have merely provided some clarification. Hodshift is perfectly comfortable with my adjustments, aren't you, Hodshift?"

"Aye, very comfortable," said Hodshift, looking very uncomfortable indeed.

"So you found the figures that underpin the graph to be incorrect?" persisted St Paul.

"Not at all, it was simply a question of scale, of, shall we say, portraying a more accurate picture. Shall we move on?"

"Before we do, I'd like to take another look at the original," said Joan of Arc. "I think the scale was the same. Bring it up, Hodshift."

Hodshift glanced from Paul to Peter, a look of anguish on his face.

"Really?" said Lord Peter. "I'm not sure why you want to dwell on erroneous slides."

"Indulge us, Peter," said St Paul. "I'm trying to understand the journey you've been on. I offer only charity, which, as we all know, is patient, so let's take a moment to see the slide."

Hodshift was frozen with fear, his eyes swivelling back and forth.

"Well, proceed, man," said the Archangel Gabriel. "I think he wants your go-ahead, Peter."

"Very well," said Peter. "Hodshift, do show our guests the old, *invalid* slide."

A few clicks later, the original graph was back, with the enormous spike in temperature climbing up the right hand side.

"So, Hodshift, it appears that your original graph uses the same scale as the edited one, if I'm not mistaken, only it shows that the temperature is very much higher, and is still rising," said St Paul. He stood up and stabbed a finger at the graph. "So can you tell me if this figure here of five hundred degrees, for example, is accurate or not?"

Hodshift stared at the graph.

"That one, there? That one from three days ago? Well, ah. Actually," Hodshift swallowed as he saw an opportunity. "*Actually,* what happened was that it got so hot, the instrumentation broke, so we had to do some estimates. That's what we did, yes. After talking with Lord Peter, we realised that our estimates were a bit high, so we changed them. Yes."

Rutspud saw the tension lift from Hodshift as he glanced at Peter and got a small nod of approval.

"Interesting," said St Paul. "So what is the upper limit of your instrumentation?"

"It's calibrated to four hundred and fifty degrees," answered Hodshift promptly.

"Hmm," said St Paul, tracing his finger along the paper graph in front of him, "and yet according to the amended graph, the temperature hasn't yet risen above three hundred and eighty. I have a proposal to help move things along. In the absence of accurate figures, why don't we assume, for the sake of our discussions, that the temperature in Hell is rising very quickly, and to dangerous levels. Do you think that might help?"

Hodshift gave a tentative nod, with a glance at Peter for approval.

"In that case, I think I'm all done," said the quivering demon.

"Oh, I should say so," said Lord Peter coldly.

The Archangel Gabriel raised a hand.

"I do not care how badly your underling has presented your lies, Peter," he said. "We are here to find solutions."

"Quite," said Lord Peter. "And we'd be delighted to receive your wisdom on the matter."

Lord Peter rose, marker pen in hand, and stood before a flipchart.

"Let's brainstorm the matter," he said. "I'm sure I don't have to remind delegates that brainstorming must foster creativity. Remember, any idea has value. Don't be afraid to shout up."

Joan of Arc's hand was in the air.

"Joan," said the Lord of Hell.

"You shouldn't use the word 'brainstorm'," said the teenage saint.

Lord Peter blinked. "I beg your pardon?"

"It's offensive to people with epilepsy."

Lord Peter shrugged indifferently. "Are there any epileptics here?"

"I don't think that's the point. And you shouldn't call them epileptics. They are people who have epilepsy, not epileptics. They are not defined by their condition."

"Fine," snapped Lord Peter. "Let's not brainstorm the matter. Let's ..."

"Create a thought-shower," said Joan.

"Seriously? Not an idea-blizzard? Or a mind-drizzle? Nonsense. Come on, who has ideas?"

Rutspud looked around the table at a great many faces that were clearly too afraid to speak up.

"Lewis."

Satan's balls! thought Rutspud. The daft man had his hand up. Rutspud saw Belphegor try to activate one of the switches on his wheelchair, but the table was in the way. Was it the wheel-spikes or the electric cattle-prod? No matter; it was too late. Lewis was speaking.

"I think we can cool Hell right down with some natural resources from earth. All we need is the entire polar ice cap, which should bring our temperature down to what it was before this started," said Lewis.

Lord Peter froze, pen in hand.

"Riiight," he said, and wrote *ice* on the chart. "Did you have any thoughts on how we'd manage to get the *entire polar ice cap* here?"

"No," said Lewis.

"No," repeated Peter, in the tone of someone who would be returning to this later. "So do you have any further thoughts?"

"Oh, yes," said Lewis. "I've got another idea. If every inhabitant of Hell was to blow really hard in the same direction at the same time, we could create a strong wind and disperse the heat."

"Disperse it to where?" asked St Paul with a smirk.

"Somewhere else," said Lewis, rolling his eyes. "I don't have all the details, obviously. However, I am working on a wardrobe that could provide a portal –"

"Enough!" shouted Peter. "Who else has an idea? Hodshift, what would you recommend?"

"Me?" said Hodshift, quaking. "Me?"

"Yes, how should we prepare for the coming days? Tell us what you recommend."

"Well, if you really want my honest opinion," said Hodshift, "I'd be handing out hard hats to everyone, and evacuating them to the farthest reaches of Limbo for when the 'ole bloody lot blows."

"Unacceptable," declaimed Thomas Aquinas loudly. "The whole purpose of this meeting is to keep Hell's problems within Hell's borders. We don't want to shift any part of this problem into Limbo, least of all a bunch of infernal refugees!"

Lord Peter wrote the words *refugees* and *shift it into Limbo* on the board.

"Those weren't bloody suggestions!" shouted the rotund saint.

"All ideas are valid," said Lord Peter smoothly, "and your contributions are very welcome. Besides, I don't think we should take Hodshift too literally. I certainly wouldn't want to incite an unhelpful level of panic. I think we should take some other suggestions. Come on, Gabriel, do you have any ideas?"

"I think you've all clearly overlooked the most obvious solution," said Gabriel, "which is the power of prayer. It's a good job you called us when you did, quite frankly. We can get straight on with some concentrated praying."

Peter wrote *prayer* and *hard hats* on the flip chart. He circled the word *prayer* and nodded to the room.

"Well, that's clearly a quick win," he said happily.

"Who would they be praying to?" Rutspud whispered to Belphegor.

"The Almighty, of course."

"Well, He lives in Heaven, doesn't he? Why don't they just go to His office or whatever and ask Him?"

"I don't know. I'm just a demon," said Belphegor.

"I think perhaps we can form a focus group to take care of the praying," said Gabriel. "I think St Thomas is a must from our side. Perhaps one of your Research and Development team should be involved?"

Rutspud studied his notes carefully and tried to become invisible.

"Let's see. We could perhaps spare Rutspud. He's making quite a name for himself," said Lord Peter. "You'll find him a dynamic team player,"

Rutspud felt his world crashing down. He knew he couldn't withstand a concentrated onslaught of prayer, no demon could.

"With the greatest of respect, sir," he said. "I'd quite like to follow up on some solutions that I've been working on in the lab."

"What might these solutions be, Rutspud?" asked Lord Peter.

"It's a bit early to say," said Rutspud. "It involves, ah, non-Newtonian structures."

Peter stared at Rutspud for a long moment.

"Right, well perhaps *Lewis* could join the focus group," he said. "I shall be very interested to monitor the progress of your idea, Rutspud. I'll pop round tomorrow. Nero, be sure to add that to my schedule."

Rutspud smiled at Lord Peter and hoped sincerely that his eyes did not betray the panic that boiled inside him.

Manfred was at the head of a group of monks walking through the snow carrying timber and supplies. Apparently, the only supplies Brother Henry was capable of carrying were a kettle and a teapot which he carried one-handed on a tray. Brother Henry deftly unfurled an extension lead behind with the other hand as he walked. Manfred shrugged lightly. It would be at least encouraging for everyone to have hot drinks as they worked.

Brother Gillespie trotted over to Manfred.

"Do you really think this is the time to be working outside?" he asked. "There's snow on the ground. I can't have everyone laid up in the infirmary with a cold."

Manfred noticed that, as usual, Brother Gillespie was the only one who seemed to actually have a cold.

"Well, I hope you put on an extra layer, brother," he said. "We'll soon warm up when we start work. Quite honestly, I can think of nothing finer on a bright day like this! You should have seen the winters in Bayerisch Eisenstein. If we'd stopped work for a bit of snow, we'd never have gotten anything done!"

Manfred stopped and faced the others.

"Let us lay the supplies down here, brothers. I have the plans drawn up, and I will mark out the position of the base. Those of you with shovels, please be kind enough to clear the space that I indicate."

The monks spent much of the morning levelling the site and forming the base of what would, according to Manfred's designs, be a large shed-like structure. The interesting feature of this large shed was that part of it would project over the edge of the cliff, counterbalanced by the weight of the structure and several anchoring rods.

"Hey! Who threw that?"

Manfred looked up to see Brother Henry dusting snow from the back of his head. He saw Brothers Cecil and Roland clutching each other and laughing from the path. Henry looked around in confusion and bent back to the task in hand. Manfred saw Brother Cecil form another snowball and throw it with remarkable accuracy at Henry's head.

Henry looked at Brother Gillespie, who was sorting through a box of tools.

"Right," he said. "You asked for this."

"What?" sniffed the innocent infirmarian.

Brother Henry picked up a huge, unformed handful of snow and dumped it on Brother Gillespie's head. He shook the collar of Gillespie's robe to ensure that it went down his back. The high-pitched squealing and cavorting that followed drew everyone's attention.

"What's with Brother Gillespie?" asked Brother Desmond.

"Is he dancing?" asked Brother Vernon.

"A Beegees tribute," nodded Brother Terry sagely.

"Enough of that, that's not –" Manfred was cut off as a snowball erupted in his face.

By the time he could see again, there were snowballs flying back and forth in a frenzy. There were shrieks of shock, delight and general monkish glee. He wondered briefly whether to take the moral high ground, and then saw that Cecil and Roland were still throwing the snowy missiles from the path, apparently unnoticed by the other monks. He made himself a pile of neatly-formed snowballs and threw them in quick succession at the geriatric monks.

"Attack old men, would you?" shouted Brother Cecil.

Brother Roland stuck out his tongue and the two of them retreated down the path, heading for the warm fire in the monastery and laughing all the way.

"Let me have a go!"

Brother Henry was now sliding down the slope on his metal tea tray, while Brothers Desmond and Terry looked on with undisguised envy. Several monks glanced around for suitable toboggans. Manfred leapt sideways as Gillespie hurtled blindly down on Manfred's metal toolbox.

"Brother Clement, it's not like you to be so ... how can I say this, *playful*," said Manfred, as Clement sailed down the slope on a sheet of plywood.

"I'm enjoying a profound moment of religious contemplation," called Clement, from the bottom of the slope.

"No you're not, you're making a snow angel," yelled Henry, racing back up to have another go on his tea tray.

Manfred saw that Clement had tumbled off the plywood and was, indeed, flapping arms and legs to make a Clement-shaped angel in the snow.

"Come now, brothers," called Manfred. "Is this any way for men of God to behave? What if Father Eustace were to –"

"Shiny bottoms!" yelled the abbot, flying past on a large bronze plate, which Manfred suspected was the possibly priceless twelfth century platter from the church.

"I think we should perhaps take a break from the building work," said the prior, largely to himself.

"You've got to help me."

"Help you, Rutspud?" Stephen swivelled round on his chair in the library. "Help you? You gave us all a dose of your forget-me potion last night. I can't imagine what horrors you must have unleashed on us to resort to that."

Rutspud scowled.

"I didn't do that. You did."

"Did I?"

Rutspud nodded vigorously.

"We ran out, I gave you the potion and you must have –"

"What happened to your arm?" said Stephen.

Rutspud rolled his very expressive eyes. "I can understand why you gave some of the water to the other monks, but why did you drink some yourself?"

Stephen shrugged. "Don't know. Can't remember. But you need my help. What's the matter?"

"What's not the matter?" said Rutspud, and threw himself down in a chair in exasperation. "I've lost Potter, for one thing. I think she's wandering about up here somewhere."

"Oh, no," said Stephen. "That's not good."

"No," said Rutspud, "but that's not the worst thing. Lord Peter is coming to see me. He's coming because *I'm* supposed to have some sort of solution to Hell's overheating problem. Me!"

"Why you?"

"I told him I had. It was the only way I could get out of being on a praying focus group. Long story. Tesla's got a theory, but it depends on us getting some massive pipes up those stairs, and, yes, on top of everything else, I'm still missing an arm."

"I don't really know how demons, er, fit together. If we find your arm, can you just put it back on?"

"I'll get one of my gang to sew it on for me," said Rutspud. "We recycle demon parts all of the time, never known an appendage to stop working. I can sort of feel my arm right now."

"What? Surely not. What can you feel?" asked Stephen.

Rutspud concentrated.

"I can feel something like wind moving across it I think. Quite cold. The fingers are in the grass. It's definitely outside, somewhere on the island. High up probably."

"Oh. Let's go and look for it, then. Pop on a habit, you'll pass for a scrawny monk at a distance. Anyway, what pipes?"

"Eh?"

"Tesla's plan with pipes."

"Yes, he thinks we can use sea water to run some sort of heat exchanger. We need a pipe to take seawater down the stairs –"

"Seawater? As in *our* seawater?"

"Well, we certainly don't have much liquid water in Hell, mate. Yes, one pipe to pump the water down and another coming up to release steam."

"Really?" said Stephen. "It all sounds a little bit *noticeable*. A great big pipe with steam coming out of it is not going to escape detection round here."

"Tesla reckons he can time it so the steam won't come out until it's convenient. What time do you lot all go off and have a little pray?"

"Vespers is at sunset. That's about six o'clock at the moment."

"Six it will be, then."

"It's not going to be some great noisy trumpety blast, is it?"

"Nah. Strong but silent. Just like me."

"If you say so," said Stephen. "So, what are we waiting for? It sounds as though we can sort all of this out. We'll go and find Potter, and your arm, then you can get these pipes in place in time for Peter's visit."

"But what about Lord Peter finding out about the stairs?" said Rutspud.

"Why would he?" said Stephen.

"Well, he'd just go, 'Oh, where does this pipe go?' and he couldn't possibly miss them."

"Are you telling me that a demon of your cunning and expertise couldn't knock up a big box, with a pipe going into it and a pipe coming out of it, that looked as though it was doing all the good work *inside* it, with some sort of science or something?"

"A big box?" said Rutspud incredulously.

"Yes."

"I just paint up a magic box and tell him that all the amazing stuff is going on *inside*?"

"Yes," said Stephen.

"Well, it's so daft that it might work, I suppose."

Manfred found Bastian walking back up to the monastery after seeing Carol off on Owen's boat.

"You seem to get on well with Ms Well-Dunn," said Manfred.

"Do I?" asked Bastian, flushing slightly. "I hadn't noticed."

Manfred wondered what he meant by that, but it would have to wait.

"Now, Bastian, we have a small window of opportunity," he said. "The brothers have returned to the monastery for refreshments. I have made a new cinnamon cake to keep them distracted. It seems an ideal time to dispose of Brother Lionel."

"Yes," said Bastian, the colour wiped from his face. "Of course," he said heavily.

"I've left some shovels up by the bird hide," said Manfred. "We'll collect Lionel and then we can get digging."

Manfred had also positioned a wheelbarrow near to the kitchen door. They went inside and lifted the lid of the chest freezer. The dead monk lay within, a bag of garden peas wedged under his neck.

215

"That coating of frost he's got is really quite unnerving," said Bastian after a moment. "It looks as if he's been dusted with icing sugar."

"Yes, that is strange," said Manfred and then paused. Having a dead monk in the freezer was sufficiently strange; anything else was just decoration.

They struggled to prise Brother Lionel from the freezer, finding that he was all rigid angles locked into place with the existing contents of the freezer. With some effort, they finally lifted him into the wheelbarrow.

"Is that a leg of lamb?" asked Bastian.

"Yes. I can't seem to get it out from the crook of his arm," said Manfred. "We'll just have to take it with us."

Carrying Lionel in the wheelbarrow was not the simple task that it had sounded. His centre of gravity was off-kilter due to his frozen posture. Having slid into V between piles of frozen goods, Lionel was in something like the yoga position of *down-dog*, Manfred decided. The leg of lamb wasn't helping, either. Manfred wheeled, and Bastian crabbed alongside, hoisting the weight of Lionel's hips so that it didn't topple the wheelbarrow.

They reached a point on the hillside, which was far enough away from the bird hide to escape notice, and started to dig a hole.

"This is much harder than I thought it would be," said Bastian. "The soil's really hard."

Manfred nodded.

"Not too much more now, brother, but we really do need to hurry up, or the others will be returning. Cinnamon cake will keep them occupied for only so long."

Once again, Stephen found himself greeting damned humans in the cellars of St Cadfan's. Mama-Na and Boudicca pulled yard after yard of wide flexible piping up from the staircase, while Cartland (a woman who clearly possessed a head for figures and a mind of her own) argued over technical issues with Tesla.

"I've got Wilde and Nightingale working on the construction of the 'magic box'," said Rutspud. "Shipton and Bernhardt are on watch for nosey demons downstairs. We're not going to be interrupted by any of your lot, are we?"

"Manfred has made cinnamon cake for them all upstairs."

"And that will keep them occupied?" said Rutspud doubtfully.

"Until the cake is gone," said Stephen. "We're a community of simple tastes."

"Gnga pip hoo?" said Mama-Na, brandishing one end of the sinuous piping.

"That's got to go in the sea," said Rutspud.

"I'll show you the shortest path down," said Stephen. "And we'll have to camouflage it as we go."

"And while we're out, we'll go find Potter and my flaming arm," said Rutspud.

"I'm done in," grunted Bastian. "Do you think this hole is big enough? I guess we need to make sure the body is protected from predators."

"There are no large predators on Bardsey," said Manfred. "No foxes or anything like that."

"Maybe some ambitious rats though."

"If we protect him from birds, then all will be well," Manfred assured him. "Let's try him for size."

They upended the barrow and tipped the body into the hole. They both stood back and looked in dismay at Brother Lionel's bottom sticking up well above the ground as his limbs jammed awkwardly in the hole.

"This way round is no good at all," said Bastian. "I think we need to turn him over so that his bottom goes in first."

"I'll need to get down into the hole and hoist him up from underneath," said Manfred.

They struggled for some moments, Manfred pushing and Bastian pulling, and eventually succeeded in turning Lionel over.

"What are we going to do?" said Bastian. "It seems impossible to get all of his hands and feet below the level of the ground. I suppose it would be unseemly to, you know, jump up and down on them and squash them into place?"

"Yes, it most certainly would," said Manfred.

"Can you hear something?" said Bastian.

They both listened.

"Someone's coming!" hissed Manfred. "Jump up and down, squash these bits into place and get some soil over the body. Quickly!"

"There," said Stephen and pointed.

Potter sat on a rock, sketching in a book. With the hood of her borrowed habit drawn up around her neck, the wind swirling around her, she was the very picture of purposeful concentration and contemplation.

"She looks content," said Stephen, and felt a jolt of horrified realisation run through him. "Do you really want to drag that poor woman back down to Hell?"

"Want's got nothing to do with it," said Rutspud and then yelled, "Potter, what in the blue blazes are you playing at? I've been searching for you all over the place! You could have got us all in trouble!"

The elegant woman looked up from her sketching.

"Oh, is it time to go back down? I was coming right along, but I just wanted to capture the beauty of this place. Look at the views, sir!"

"Views? Views!" Rutspud gazed at the horizon. "No, much too empty in my opinion, which is of course the important one here. In case you'd forgotten, I'm the one in charge."

"Steady on," said Stephen, but Rutspud ignored him.

"If you'd be kind enough to tear yourself away from the views," said Rutspud, "we need to be getting back, just as soon as we've found my missing arm."

"It's over there, sir," said Potter.

"What?"

"It's over there," said Potter. "It's been helping me."

"Helping you?"

"Holding my spare pencils, pointing out interesting things to sketch, that sort of thing."

"Sometimes I think it's not really my arm," grumbled Rutspud. "What's it playing at, being nice?"

"Here it is," called Stephen, as he spotted it crawling through the snow.

"Grab it then. Be firm," called Rutspud.

Stephen looked at the spindly arm, and wondered if it could sense the slight tingling of fear and revulsion that he felt confronting an animated limb. It reared back, wiggled its fingers and lunged at his ankle, making him jump back with a squeal. Clearly the thing was toying with him. It seemed to quiver with mirth at his overreaction. He made a grab for it, annoyed now that it had made him feel so foolish.

"Hah! Got it!"

He wrestled it into a cloth bag that he pulled from his pocket.

Rutspud held Potter's sketch pad and flicked through it as they walked back down the hill.

"You've drawn everything," he said.

"Well, I'm always sketching, sir" she replied.

"Are you?" Rutspud murmured. "I never noticed you doing it before. Look! This has got to be a Meat and Mead Thursday, you can tell by the way Boudicca's grinning."

Bastian and Manfred were flattening the last of the soil and snow on top of the unfortunate Lionel.

"His foot's still sticking out!" hissed Bastian.

"Jump on it a bit more! Quickly now, those voices are very close," said Manfred, picking up the shovels, and moving off.

"I tried that, it's still sticking out!"

"Pile snow on it!"

"It's not working!"

Bastian looked around for anything that might help. He spotted a bucket, quickly upturned it over Lionel's foot and ran after Manfred.

"Into the hide!" Manfred hissed.

They both ducked into the partly-constructed hide, and crouched behind the skeletal supports that would eventually become the rear wall.

"Nice work, so far," whispered Bastian, looking round.

"Thank you," whispered Manfred. "The base is complete, I think that with another two days' work, we can have the rest of the structure in place."

"I see Brother Henry is making sure his home comforts are taken care of," said Bastian, holding up the jug kettle with a raised eyebrow.

They fell silent as they heard several voices from the path outside.

"One of them sounds like young Trevor," said Bastian.

"Stephen, you mean," said Manfred.

"That's what I said, wasn't it? Who's that with him? A very ... girly voice."

"Brother Terry?"

"Hmmm," said Bastian. "I know what you mean, but, no. What do you suppose 'Meat and Mead Thursday' is?"

"No idea," said Manfred from the other side of the hide, where he was sitting on the edge of the floor that jutted over the cliff. "This gives us an excellent view down."

"I think I'll be happier when we've glazed over that viewing hole."

"But look. Look!"

Bastian went over on his hands and knees to join Manfred at the edge. Bastian was not a man to be afraid of heights but, knowing that while he peered directly down through the hole in the floor there was nothing beneath his body but a couple of inches of plywood and some supportive batons, gave him a buzz of trepidation.

"One of them's on the nest," said Manfred.

"Can you tell which one?"

"I think it's the female. The male's comb is larger."

"It's really a special sight," breathed Bastian. "The birdwatchers will be thrilled to have such wonderful access."

"And you'll be thrilled to have access to their wallets," grinned Manfred.

"Hey, it's not always about the money." smiled Bastian in reply, and was surprised to realise that he meant it.

"Naturally, we'll have to strictly regulate access to this hide," said Manfred. "Even once we've got the counterbalance rods in place, this place won't be able to support more than three or four – ah."

Bastian heard the worry in that single syllable.

"Ah?" he said.

Manfred grimaced. "Now," he said slowly, "I don't want you to panic."

"Panic?" said Bastian. "Why would I panic?"

"My designs were carefully calculated. I was the assistant chief structural engineer on the Mönchengladbach Velodrome, you know."

"Why would I panic?" repeated Bastian.

The wind blew across the structure and the floor groaned loudly beneath them.

"We haven't put in the counterbalance rods yet. We're not pinned to the clifftop."

Bastian screwed up his face in an attempt to keep a lid on the fear and anger that had suddenly bloomed within him.

"Have you killed us, Manfred?" he croaked.

Manfred tried to give him a reassuring smile.

"All we need to do is move – very slowly – to the back of the – "

There was a sudden snap, and the floor tilted beneath them both. Their eyes met as they realised that the whole of the bird hide was pivoting on the cliff edge. They flung themselves back towards the other side, but the thing had already started its slow but unstoppable slide over the edge. The two monks managed an ineffectual paddle for a few moments before they dropped away, wood cracking, splintering and smashing against the rocks as they screamed and fell.

Bastian screwed his eyes shut. The hide fell apart around him. He heard parts of it smashing into the rocky cove below and ...

Bastian opened his eyes. He was surprised to find that he hadn't fallen to his death. There was a painfully tight pressure on his hands and wrist above him and a great weight pulling down on his habit but he wasn't dead.

He looked down at Manfred who was gripping the edge of Bastian's habit and swinging in the breeze.

He looked across at the female yellow-crested Merlin stilt in its nest which was eyeing him with interest.

He looked up at his straining arm and saw that his hand was still gripped tightly around the handle of the kettle and the flex, connected to a chain of extension cables leading over the lip of the cliff, was wrapped around his lower arm.

He started to laugh.

"Manfred! You'll never guess what's holding us up?" he shouted.

Manfred managed a grunt.

"Please tell me it's something solid and dependable," he said.

"It's the electric lead to the kettle," said Bastian.

"So, not particularly solid and dependable."

Stephen stood slightly behind Potter and Rutspud as they examined her sketch pad together. He found himself strangely reluctant to see the pictures of Hell, even though they seemed to be describing it with fondness. Ahead, Mama-Na and Whitehouse efficiently pulled foliage and patches of snowy turf over the pipe.

Stephen gave a start as a wet nose nuzzled his hand.

"Jessie! What are you still doing here?"

Rutspud turned and gave a low growl at the sight of the dog.

"I thought you'd left on Owen's boat," said Stephen.

"Why's it got that rope in its mouth?" asked Rutspud.

Jessie dropped the rope at Stephen's feet and tugged his sleeve with her teeth.

"She wants me to go with her."

Rutspud and Potter looked at Stephen blankly as he crouched and spoke to Jessie.

"Is there someone stuck down a well, or an old mine shaft?" he asked.

"That dog just rolled its eyes," said Rutspud.

"I need to go and see what she wants," said Stephen.

"Tesla should be switching the machine on any moment," said Rutspud. "I'll stay and oversee things here. But I'll have my arm back before you go."

Jessie eyed the wriggling limb as Stephen handed it over.

"Don't you even dare think it," growled the demon.

"What about the bird?" said Manfred from below. "Is it unharmed?"

"It looks all right," said Bastian from above. "Ooh, no. No, no, no."

The bird had flapped from its nest and fluttered barely a foot to come to rest on the top of Bastian's kettle.

"What?" wailed Manfred. "What's happening?"

"Go away," said Bastian. "Go on."

He tried clicking and even blowing at the bird, but it simply adjusted its position on the plastic kettle.

"It's pecking the plug connecting us to the extension lead," said Bastian. "It's coming loose."

"Brother?" called Manfred.

"Yes, brother?"

"I would normally say that my soul is ever prepared for death, but considering that we've just concealed the death of Brother Lionel and buried him in non-consecrated ground ..."

"My thoughts exactly. Oh no."

"Oh no?"

"I can see something shiny. I think it's exposed a wire."

"It probably shouldn't do that," said Manfred. "It could hurt itself."

There was a sharp electrical crackling sound, and a foul burning stench filled the air. Bastian was momentarily blinded by the flash and blinked to clear his vision.

"What was that?" called Manfred. "Oh. Something's fallen into your hood, brother. It looks like ... oops. That rare bird of ours, there seems to be a very good reason that it's rare."

Stephen looked down the edge of the cliff.

"Hello?"

At first all he could see were jagged chunks of wood tossed in the surf below.

"Hello?"

"Down here," called Bastian.

Stephen edged closer and saw Bastian swinging on the end of a thin cable. He realised that Manfred was hanging just below him. They were clearly in need of some urgent assistance.

"Hold on, brothers! I'll fasten the rope to something and help you as quickly as I can." Stephen looked around for something solid to use. "By the way, Bastian, I don't want to alarm you, but your habit seems to be smouldering."

A few minutes later, Bastian and Manfred were back up on solid ground, massaging their aching shoulders.

"I knew those abseiling workshops would pay dividends. Well done for your timely intervention," said Manfred, and then sighed. "I just wish we could report a happy outcome for the bird, which is most definitely dead," he said, examining the charred remains still inside Bastian's hood.

"There is *another* bird, isn't there?" asked Stephen.

"Yes, the male bird is still alive, I believe," said Manfred, "and the eggs as well, of course, which we may have to rescue."

"I saw a bucket back there," said Stephen. "Let's go and get it so we can put the eggs in it to carry them back."

Stephen saw a strange look pass between Bastian and Manfred.

"No, no, let's not do that," said Bastian. "That bucket is just not *right*. I even think it might have a hole in it. I think we should return to the monastery and prepare more carefully for the precious eggs."

"If you say so," said Stephen. "We'd best start looking for the male bird."

Much later, Stephen caught up with Rutspud, Potter, Mama-Na and Whitehouse on the slopes between St Cadfan's monastery and the sea.

"Where have you been?" said Rutspud.

"Bird-related emergency," said Stephen, and looked ahead. "I'm impressed. I can't even see where you've buried the pipe."

"Here," said Whitehouse and crouched with her palms on the snowy ground. "Feel it, young man?"

Stephen placed his hand on the snow and could indeed feel a soundless thrumming beneath his fingers. Gallon after gallon of seawater being pumped into an over-heating Hell.

Ridiculous, he thought happily.

"So that furry monster took you to rescue those other monks?" asked Rutspud with a shake of his head.

"Dogs can be noble and loving creatures," said Potter. "I had a beautiful spaniel with just the same warm, brown eyes."

"Horrible," said Rutspud with a shudder.

"Mmn arf arf nu!" declared Mama-Na exuberantly.

"And Mama-Na had one too," said Potter.

"Gng mmm."

"Until the winter her tribe were particularly hungry ..." Potter added quietly.

"Have you got your sewing things, Potter?" said Rutspud. "I want to get this arm of mine back on."

"Back in the cave, sir."

In the rapidly dimming light, the party made their way back up to the monastery. Potter fell into step with Stephen.

"Bird-related emergency?" she asked.

"The last male of a critically endangered species," said Stephen. "The yellow-crested Merlin stilt."

"Extinction of an entire species is such a tragedy," said Potter. "Sadly, in my day, we could see that man's encroachment on the land was causing problems for the natural world. I'd like to think that in the decades since, man has become a better steward and learned to look after his world."

Stephen shifted uncomfortably.

"Well ... er ..."

"No, of course," said Potter with a wry smile. "Man is man. I'll wager that the majority of Britain is not as tranquil as this lovely corner you enjoy as your home."

"No, that's certainly true. It is tranquil here. Perfect almost," said Stephen, gazing across the Irish Sea at the burnished red of the sunset.

"Rutspud was actually impressed with my artwork," said Potter. "He says he's got a painting project that will employ my artistic talents."

"Intriguing," said Stephen. "What's the project?"

"Some sort of box that needs to look as though it's packed with scientific marvels."

"I'm sure you'll do an excellent job," he said.

"The exhaust pipe's in place," called Rutspud, pointing.

"Keep your voice down," said Stephen. "Most of the monks should be heading for chapel, but we should still take care. You never know who we might bump into."

Stephen looked at the pipe filling the frame of the cellar window. Among the dark and shapeless stonework of the recently discovered cellars, this new addition was barely visible.

"It's actually quite discreet. I'm impressed," said Stephen.

"What's that sticking out of it?" asked Whitehouse.

"Where?" said Rutspud.

"It looks like feathers."

"It is! I can see its comb!" A smile barely made it onto his lips when it was dashed aside by a horrifying thought.

He looked at his watch.

"Would I be right in guessing that Tesla is a man of precision and careful timing?" he asked.

"Definitely," said Potter.

"Damn," he said softly. "Duck!"

A blast of steam erupted from the window. Even from a dozen yards away, Stephen could feel the heat on his face. Something bounced to the ground as they crouched there, but it was a few moments before the steam had died down enough for them to investigate.

"Oh no," Stephen said.

The steam had melted all the snow for yards around and had boiled the bird instantly. The few feathers that still clung to its carcass were clumped around cooked flesh.

"Well, that's it," sighed Stephen. "The last of a very rare breed of bird."

"Rare? Looks well done to me," said Rutspud, poking it hungrily.

"Shrn mm kuk-kuk," said Mama-Na.

"No, you're right," said Whitehouse. "It's not a duck."

"Hilarious," said Stephen miserably.

Chapter 8 – The day Rutspud got his new arm

In the cold light of morning, three monks inspected the corpses of the world's only yellow-crested Merlin stilts. The male and female lay side by side on the kitchen table, one steam-boiled and featherless, the other flash-fried and charred at its wingtips.

Manfred spoke slowly, morosely.

"I can't help but feel ..."

"Yes?" said Stephen.

"I can't help but feel stupid."

"I know what you mean. If we hadn't interfered, then maybe ..."

Bastian poked the male bird gingerly.

"And this one was struck by lightning, you say?"

Stephen nodded.

"That's right. A rumble in the clouds and then 'bzzt!'"

"Funny that. We didn't hear a thing."

"Very localised," said Stephen. "I mean, I had wondered if these birds had an, I don't know, affinity for electricity?"

Bastian frowned in an effort to understand.

"Evolutionarily designed to be killed by high voltage electricity?"

"God *does* move in mysterious ways."

"I think there is a difference between mysterious and downright baffling," said Manfred.

"Perhaps," said Stephen, "this is a punishment."

"For what?"

Stephen gave him a blank stare.

"Seriously? You don't think our treatment of Brother Lionel's mortal remains is worth a little divine wrath?"

"So God punished us with a lightning bolt?"

"And an electric kettle," said Manfred.

"Oh, I don't know," said Stephen. "I can't think straight. I'm shattered."

"Sleepwalking again?" said Bastian.

"I woke up in the library this morning, face down in the *Librum Magnum Daemonum*."

"You're not drinking enough camomile tea," said Manfred.

"Not sure about 'enough'," said Stephen. "Too much, perhaps."

"Nonsense," said Manfred, and put a kettle on the stove. He looked out of the kitchen window. "I suppose we will have to tell Mrs Well-Dunn about the birds."

"We don't have to tell her anything," said Bastian.

"Of course, we do. She's bringing her bird-watching friends here in three weeks' time."

"They can still come. There are plenty of beautiful birds here to see."

"They're coming to see the yellow-crested Merlin stilt."

"We have the eggs."

Manfred bent down to peer into one of the ovens where the recovered stilt eggs sat, nestled together, inside a sheepskin slipper.

"They're birdwatchers, not eggwatchers," said Stephen. "I think you'll have to call to cancel them."

"Turn away visitors?" said Bastian, appalled. "Even a handful? Are you mad?"

Manfred checked the thermometer tucked inside the slipper.

"Thirty-seven degrees."

"You do know this kitchen stinks of cooked wool and feet," said Stephen.

"The smell from the slippers will help the little birds imprint on me when they hatch," said the prior.

"You're going to be mummy bird, are you?"

"I can be whatever I want to be," said Manfred haughtily.

"Ha! Maybe we can persuade the birdwatchers to come and watch you."

Bastian sighed, pulled his mobile phone from his pocket and dialled.

"Carol," he said. "Hi, yes. You too. Look, I just needed to talk to you about your visit ... I know ... Well, that's very flattering. I'm sure Birmingham has its own charms but, yes, I can understand why you'd miss this place ... Mmm, anyway, about coming over to us. I've got something I need to tell you about the birds ... They *are* fascinating, aren't they? Such unusual behaviour ... Carol, there's been a bit of an accident. Me? No, I wasn't hurt. Bit startled actually when the hide collapsed. No, really. I'm here and whole and well ... That's very, very kind of you. It's just ... Yes, yes, we *could* build a new hide on the cliff top. I know your little band of twitchers would want somewhere from where to observe ..." He stopped and listened, nodding and occasionally giving Stephen and Manfred raised eyebrows in the universal, but unnecessary, sign for 'she's talking, I'm listening, I'm not just standing here, you know'. "Really?" he said eventually. "Thirty-eight of you? Wow, that's ... I think Owen can fit up to forty on his boat and ... Accommodation? We could sleep that many. Bed and breakfast?" Bastian looked into nowhere and counted and calculated figures on the fingers of one hand. "That's ... that's ... that's doable. Certainly."

Manfred and Stephen gestured silently but violently at him. Bastian winced like a wounded creature.

"Listen, Carol. The thing is ... about the birds ... Yes ..." Bastian's face took on an interesting shade and he half turned away from his brothers. "No, absolutely looking forward to seeing you too. Okay. See you then."

He hung up. He looked at the expressions on the other monk's faces.

"What? I tried to tell her."

"Tried how?" said Stephen.

"She's bringing thirty-seven people with her. Thirty-seven. That's got to put a different spin on the situation."

"Absolutely," said Manfred. "That's thirty-seven extra people who are going to be furious when they discover we've killed the bird they've come to see."

"Thirty-seven paying guests."

"Thirty-seven people who will demand their money back."

"But we have to make a return on this thing. I've already invested quite a bit of money in this venture."

"What money?" said Stephen. "Invested in what?"

Bastian smiled. It wasn't an inspiring smile.

"I know this Portuguese guy in the import/export business. He's getting me some novelty souvenirs."

"Novelty souvenirs?"

"Yellow-crested Merlin stilt toys, made from high-quality synthetics."

"How many did you order?"

"Two thousand."

The kettle began to boil.

"I think we all need a cup of tea," said Manfred.

"I think some of us need a slap," said Stephen.

"So what's the plan again?" asked Brother Clement, thumbing his rosary beads suspiciously.

Manfred looked down the length of the meeting table in the chapter house.

"We present to our visitors the ... illusion that the yellow-crested Merlin stilt is still alive and well on Bardsey Island."

"And how do we do that?"

"With models and decoys and that manner of thing."

Clement's beads stopped mid-click.

"So," said the sacristan, "you want us to lie."

"Is it a lie? Is it really?"

The monks present thought on this, and then Brother Gillespie sniffed mightily and spoke for all of them.

"Yes, brother. It is."

"Please," said Bastian, standing. "Allow me. Brothers, you know me as the procurator of St Cadfan's, but beforehand I worked in the heart of the UK's financial sector –"

"You were a scheming wheeler-dealer," said Brother Cecil, who possessed the natural propensity of the old to distrust anyone whose job didn't appear to involve any actual work.

"Were?" said Brother Roland, who simply thought Bastian was a sly and crafty bugger.

"– and we dealt in something called 'futures'," said Bastian. "Bankers and stockbrokers could buy, sell and trade in the future potential of products. Grain futures, pork futures, whatever.

Genuine, real and *honest* transactions were made regarding goods that did not yet exist, but would do in the future. The yellow-crested Merlin stilt is not gone."

"Looks like a goner to me," said Brother Henry, prodding one of the birds on the table with his Suduko pen.

"These two are, for sure," said Bastian, "but incubating in a pair of old slippers in the kitchen are two perfectly healthy eggs."

"That's it!" said Brother Vernon. "I understand!"

"Understand?" said Bastian.

"That's why my porridge tasted of feet!"

Bastian nodded.

"We have potential Merlin stilts, Merlin stilt futures, if you will. We wouldn't be lying to the birdwatchers. We'd be giving them a truthful glimpse of what the future holds."

"It's like the salvation of our Lord," said Brother Clement.

"Is it?" said Bastian. "I mean, yes, it is. Um, how exactly?"

"We are the salesmen or perhaps curators of salvation futures," said the sacristan. "When the faithful seek to be in God's grace, they are speculating on a salvation that is already offered, but also is to be achieved in the future. The Kingdom of Heaven is both now and yet to be."

Bastian smiled.

"What a beautiful analogy the yellow-crested Merlin stilt is for our own faith. How can we *not* do this?"

There were murmurs and nods among the monks.

"We could make some plaster of Paris models using those medical supplies from the cargo crate," said Brother Vernon.

"We could knit some too," said Brother Henry.

"That sounds nice," said Manfred, who did enjoy his needlecraft.

"We could set up an animatronic version using the strimmer engine you cannibalised for your failed ossuary," sniffed Brother Gillespie.

"We could capture seagulls and staple yellow feathers to their heads," said Brother Terry.

Everyone looked at him.

"Or paint their heads yellow," he said. "You know, either one works."

In the library, Manfred laid the female Merlin stilt down next to the open copy of JJ Audubon's *Birds of Britain*. Seeing the pathetic, lightly toasted corpse next to Audubon's vibrant and enchanting painting only served to highlight the loss that this dead bird signified.

"Here," said Stephen, pointing. "It's not much. Audubon was a painter, not a writer. Let's see. 'While other birds will sit upon the nest at all hours, the yellow-crested Merlin stilt leaves hers exposed to the cold air for long periods.'"

"I might be overdoing the warmth then," said Manfred. "But what about turning them?"

"Er. 'The bird is not a gentle mother but will knock her eggs from one side of the nest to the other with disturbing violence, screeching loudly at them all the while.' Is that any use?"

"Absolutely," said Manfred. "Very informative. Now, last thing, is this wool the right shade of yellow?"

The prior held a ball of wool next to the beautiful picture and made agreeable noises.

"Is that for one of the models you're making?"

"Oh, no," said Manfred. "This is for my costume."

"Costume?"

"Indeed," grinned the happy German. "Now, I must go down to the shore to record the sounds of the sea for our little babies and then it will be time to break out the sewing machine."

Manfred practically skipped out of the library and away up the corridor.

"He'll make a wonderful mother," said Stephen and then, more loudly, "You can come out now!"

One of the cabinets beneath the display cases swung open and Rutspud stepped out, munching his way through a bag of sweets. He was doing it quite skilfully, considering he still only had the one arm.

"What was all that about?" said Rutspud.

"Well, I only understood ninety percent of it," said Stephen, "but essentially we've got to look after the eggs of those two dead birds and convince a bunch of birdwatchers that the parents never died in the first place."

Rutspud compared the corpse and the book picture.

"I could find you a replacement," he said.

"A replacement?"

"In Hell."

"You have birds in Hell?"

Rutspud waggled his eyebrows. His large expressive eyes came with some fairly expressive eyebrows.

"Hell has almost infinite variety. If it doesn't already exist, we can invent it."

"You can invent birds?"

"I can certainly have a word with Bosch."

"The engineering company?"

"The Dutch painter. He works in our R&D department. If I could have some reference material to show what you need ..."

Rutspud reached for the antique book.

"Hang on," said Stephen. "I don't think you can take that. It's a very valuable book."

"I wasn't going to take the whole book, mate. I was just going to rip out the page."

Stephen felt his heart stutter and stagger for a moment. He swallowed.

"No, I don't think so."

"Fine. I'll just take the bird," he said, swiping the stilt corpse off the table. "But don't blame me if your replacement is slightly singed around the edges."

"Rutspud," said Stephen, as the demon was at the library door.

"What?"

"This is very *helpful* of you."

"Tit for tat," said Rutspud. "We're using your seawater to cool Hell."

"I know but ..."

"And you keep me well-supplied with jelly babies."

"Well, that's nothing. Seriously."

Rutspud gave him a long look. "You're my friend, Stephen. Okay? Simple as that."

"I know," said Stephen. "Thank you."

As he turned a corner in Hell's engineering corridors, a heavy iron hand fell on Rutspud's shoulder.

"Scabass. Sir," said Rutspud.

The larger demon squeezed Rutspud's shoulder and brought his unlovely face down to a level with Rutspud's.

"You've always struck me as a skulker," said Scabass.

"Really, sir?" said Rutspud. "I've always regarded myself as a purposeful loiterer."

Scabass pressed his spike-like nails into Rutspud's flesh, tenderly and meaningfully.

"And why are you loitering down here, Rutspud? You have a cave of tortures to oversee."

"And a post in Infernal Innovations, sir. And a pivotal role in Hell's emergency cooling measures. I was just off to check up on my invention."

"The magical box of cooling."

"The water-steam conversion matrix, yes. And why are you yourself here, sir?"

"To see your impressive device first-hand," said Scabass with the sharp-toothed grin of someone who had no intention of being impressed by anything. "Lead on."

"Of course, sir," said Rutspud, giving his loathsome superior a smile of subservient willingness that took a great effort to maintain, and set off along a pipe-lined conduit.

"What's that in your hand?" said Scabass.

Rutspud considered the dead bird.

"This?"

"Yes, that."

"It's my ... um ..."

"Yes?"

Rutspud's gaze travelled to his other arm or, rather, the lack of one.

"It's my new arm, sir."

"It's feathered."

"Yes, sir."

"And has wings."

"Always wanted to fly, sir."

"By putting wings on your arm?"

"Yes, sir."

Scabass scowled. "Never seen anything like it."

"Something one of the damned in R&D cooked up for me."

Rutspud led Scabass through a chicane of tunnels, all the while with those vile claws embedded in his shoulder, until they came to an innocuous chamber.

"And here we are!" said Rutspud loudly.

Potter leapt to her feet and, in a move that made Rutspud want to rub her belly or whatever it was humans did to demonstrate gratitude, whipped away her paintbrush and paints into her apron pocket and concealed all in a servile bow.

"This is it?" growled Scabass.

A stout square box stood at the back of the room. Two flexible pipes led out of the front and connected to larger existing pipes in the floor. The box itself had no other visible features. The exterior was a confection of cogs, wheels, dials and important looking labels. Of course, none of them did anything, apart from hiding the fact that the pipe entering the box travelled onward, through the back wall to a coal-fired pump, and the pipe exiting the box went up the Escher staircase to the mortal world.

"Who is this?" said Scabass.

"Potter," said Rutspud. "One of my damned."

Scabass scowled. "And you're letting it have a little holiday as your flunky? Where is the torture here?"

"It's just one soul, sir."

"Just one? *Every Damned Soul Matters*. Remember?"

"Of course," said Rutspud, quickly backtracking. "And it's worth mentioning that Potter here has an uncontrollable fear of ... pipes."

"Pipes?"

"Er, yes."

Potter burst into tears. "Please, terrible sirs, I can't stand it. There's so many of them. So many ... pipes. It's more than I can bear."

Rutspud grinned, a grin with a dual purpose. It showed Scabass how much joy he was taking in the torture of the puny soul and it was a genuine reflection of how impressed he was with Potter's progress in Bernhardt and Wilde's acting classes.

"Pull yourself together, man!" said Rutspud with a pantomime sneer.

"Woman," hissed Potter.

"Your label's fallen off. I couldn't tell."

"But what is she doing here?" said Scabass. "Does the machine require constant maintenance?"

"No, sir," said Rutspud. "It's self-sustaining. Potter's here because ..."

"I've brought the needle and twine you needed to sew your arm back on," said Potter helpfully.

"Exactly," said Rutspud.

"*Back* on?" said Scabass.

"On," said Rutspud. "She meant on."

"Very good," said Scabass. "Well, get to it."

"What?"

"The sewing. She can attach it while you explain to me how this thing works."

Rutspud sighed and passed Potter the dead yellow-crested Merlin stilt.

"What's this, sir?" she said.

"It's my *new arm*, of course," said Rutspud.

"But it's –"

"Amazing," said Rutspud, deadpan. "Oh, I know. It's just bloody marvellous."

While Potter worked to align the bird corpse with Rutspud's stump (an act that was made all the more difficult by being utterly nonsensical), Rutspud waved his free hand at the machine.

"Well, it's very simple, sir. The water comes out this pipe, is channelled through the hottest parts of Hell where it absorbs heat and converts to steam which is then returned to the machine through this second pipe."

Scabass nodded.

"Yes, but how does it work?"

"Hmmm, yes," said Rutspud, his mind rifling through a thousand hours of internet videos and earthly movies for something convincing. "The water-steam conversion matrix works by, er, reversing the polarity of the neutron flow which then, um, directs the heat through the flux capacitor."

"Flux what?"

Rutspud grimaced and let his brain go wild.

"It's a narrow beam of gravitons which fold space-time, consistent with Weyl tensor dynamics, until the space curvature becomes infinitely large –"

"In layman's terms," said Scabass.

"The steam gets turned back into water and the heat goes away."

Scabass nodded, as though he had successfully understood something deep and complex.

"Well, I am pleased to say that the areas of Hell fed by this machine have indeed shown a drop in temperature."

"Have they?" said Rutspud.

"Mmm. Unfortunately, they represent less than a thousandth of Hell's total area and, overall, Hell's temperature is rising at an accelerating rate."

"But at least I'm contributing to the solution," said Rutspud hopefully.

"Giving false hope," said Scabass. "And in a report that should have been titled *Fuck Me, I Can't Believe It Didn't Work, I'm So Shocked My Tits Have Dropped Off*, it has been revealed that praying for the heat to drop has not worked either."

"That's a shame."

"Is it?"

Scabass stretched, finally relinquishing his painful grip on Rutspud's shoulder. "So, I've been asked to lead a new initiative, one that will get real results."

"Really, sir? What's that?"

"I've been tasked with the heavy burden of apportioning blame."

"And how will that get real results?"

"Because, when our eyeballs are melting and our feet fused to the ground by the inferno, it will be some small consolation that those responsible are suffering even more."

"It's a thought," said Rutspud.

"Now, I have been compiling a list of those who are blameworthy and I think it's only fair to tell you that your name appears on the list."

"Me?" squeaked Rutspud. "Sir! What have I done?"

"Oh, Rutspud. Dear Rutspud. Be assured your name is at the very bottom of the list."

"Okay," said Rutspud, momentarily mollified. "And it's a long list, isn't it?"

Scabass blinked at him, tinny eyelids audibly clinking. "What?"

Rutspud shuffled uneasily but Potter, needle and thread and dead seabird in hand, held him in place.

"How many names are on the blame list, sir?" he asked.

Scabass looked up and, for a long time, counted silently on his fingers. Eventually, he looked down at Rutspud once more.

"One."

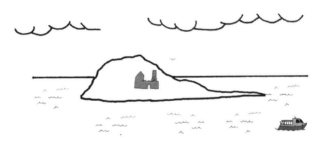

In the middle of the afternoon, a deep quiet came over St Cadfan's monastery. It was a dark, furtive quiet, as two dozen monks purposefully constructed a lie. Papier-mâché and clay models were inelegantly shaped and moulded. Wire devices were devised and tested and adjusted. And, on the hillside above the monastery, the gangly and optimistic Brother Terry sat alone with a small lasso and a pot of yellow paint.

But, in the monastery kitchen, there was noise. It was, for the most part, the gentle hiss and roar of the sea and the wind, played on a looped tape on an old reel-to-reel recorder. However, this was broken every hour or so by Brother Manfred screeching into the oven at the top of his lungs while attacking each orphaned stilt egg with a pair of wooden spoons. It was, he smiled, only what any good parent would do.

Satisfied, he returned to the kitchen table, where he had set up his sewing machine and his box of threads and buttons. He consulted the plan for his costume and continued to sew.

"Oi, you! I want a word!" shouted a red-haired man, stomping out of the stone labyrinth and up to the door of Rutspud's cave.

"Really?" said Rutspud, looking up from his conversation with Lickspear. "How about 'pitchfork' or 'scourging' or 'ten years with your goolies in a vice for forgetting your place, puny damned human'?"

"Ain't that fifteen words?" said Lickspear.

Rutspud stared at his badly-stitched friend.

"Since when could you count?"

"What can you mean by this thing 'count'?" said Lickspear.

"I've been told that you're the one responsible for this mess we're in," said the damned soul.

"And who are you when you're at home?" said Rutspud.

"Me?" The man straightened up. "I'm Judas Iscariot, taker of blood money, betrayer of our Lord and my one true friend."

"Ooh," said Rutspud, genuinely impressed. "A star inmate. But, wait, aren't you meant to be in the ninth circle of Hell, encased for all eternity in a solid block of ice along with the other great –" He stopped, already knowing the answer to his own question. "So, how is the ninth circle these days?"

"Empty," said Judas. "The whole thing has melted and everyone else, Brutus, Cain, the lot of them, have gone off to the Lake of Fire for a refreshing swim and an ice-cream."

"And that's where you should be. Now, hop it."

Judas wagged an angry finger at Rutspud.

"I was sent to Hell for a reason. I betrayed my brother, Jesus, and I deserve to be punished. I don't expect to be thawed out ten minutes after arriving because of your error."

"Ten minutes," said Rutspud thoughtfully. "Do you know how long you've been here, Mr Iscariot?"

"What?"

Rutspud grimaced and looked at Lickspear.

"Makes you wonder if cryogenically freezing someone is punishment at all."

"What are you talking about?" said Judas.

"Crying Jenny. The chick's got him all busted up," said Lickspear.

"Listen, I don't have time for your whinging, Judas," said Rutspud. "I've got some major arse-saving to do if I want to get off Scabass's shit list, I've got to help a friend, and – you may have noticed – I currently have a bird for an arm, so either piss off or take a number and sit down."

"I will not be spoken to like this," spat Judas indignantly.

"It's happening, carrot-top. Trust me."

"Pray, what's the story with your arm?" said Lickspear.

Rutspud raised up his new limb, which looked like the saddest hand puppet imaginable except that there was, of course, no hand within to operate it. Demon physiology being what it was, Rutspud could feel his new wings, his pathetic new feet, his new little beak, all plugged into his own nervous system. As his body adapted to the attachment, he was even beginning to gain fresh sensory input from his new tiny eyes, ears and nose. It wasn't a pleasant sensation.

"Glad you noticed," he said to Lickspear. "I need you to find a bird that looks just like this one."

"This very one?"

"This one. A bird that looks just like it."

"Needs a buddy, huh? That the deal?" asked Lickspear.

"Just do the job, okay?"

"Sir means perhaps to procure a matching arm on the other side? Lookin' sharp boss."

Rutspud clouted him round the ear with his good hand. Unfortunately, this caused the ear to drop off, although Lickspear seemed not to notice.

"Just find a bird for me, Lickspear," said Rutspud. "A white bird, yellow feathery bits on the top. Looks like this. Get the gang to help you if you must."

Rutspud angled the bird's head round and clicked its beak.

"Sure thing," said Lickspear, and then looked down. "Forsooth, an ear! Lay a spare on me. Mine keeps dropping off."

Rutspud dashed into the Infernal Innovations department far below the Fortress of Nameless Dread and into the office of Particulars.

On the rack, Torquemada groaned. Rutspud gave him a wave of greeting.

"Looking good, Tomas," said Rutspud. "Have you seen Bosch around?"

Torquemada groaned again.

Rutspud held up his bird-arm. "Long story, mate. Another time."

He pressed on in.

Lewis was in one of his workshops, screwing brass hinges onto a pine door and humming as usual.

"What're you up to?" said Rutspud conversationally.

"Narnia business," said Lewis.

"No need to be rude. You know, there is more to life than wardrobes."

Lewis looked at him.

"You laughed when I told you I was building a wardrobe gateway to the land of fairy."

"Did it work?"

Lewis gave his screwdriver a vicious turn.

"Don't want to talk about it. But this one will be an utter success."

"Yeah?"

"Wardrobe to Atlantis."

"Of course," said Rutspud. "How could it fail? Where's Bosch?"

"The spares room," said Lewis. "Looking for inspiration."

"Excellent."

Rutspud dashed through from the sawdust-strewn workshop to a warehousing area, which could have done with a spot of sawdust on the floor, to soak the blood up if nothing else. On wire shelves and iron chains hung body parts, carcasses and the miscellany of bones, organs and general unidentifiables that made up all living things.

Rutspud pushed through a dangling collection of legs, calling for the damned painter.

"In here," came the reply.

Rutspud rounded a carousel stack of various eyes to find the Dutchman squatting on the floor, a hoof in one hand and a large talon in the other.

"Which scares you more?" asked Bosch.

Rutspud shrugged.

"Which would you least want inserted in you?" said Bosch.

Rutspud reflected that, in an existence as long as his, he had experienced almost all imaginable scenarios of torment himself and was well-placed to offer an opinion. In other circumstances, he would have related the 'Satan's slippers' incident, but he was a demon on a mission.

"Forget that," he said. "I need your help. I need you to construct a creature for me."

The flabby painter's face lit up.

"A commission? I've been left to my own devices for such a long time: you've got something specific in mind?"

"Very much so," said Rutspud and held up his bird-arm. "I want you to make one of these."

Bosch looked at the yellow-crested Merlin stilt. Rutspud, with newfound control, tilted its head left and right.

"So, a demon-creature inspired by this bird," said Bosch.

"Absolutely."

"I can see it now. I shall give it a lizard's tail and the countenance of a plague doctor. Perhaps it will carry a spear. No, a trident."

Rutspud shook his head.

"I want it to look just like this one."

"Of course," said Bosch. "You wish to keep its innate birdness. Totally understand. Sharp-eyed. Cruel. I will give it the arms of a prostitute and it shall feed the damned through a clothes-wringer. I think I've got some beetle carapaces somewhere that would really work with this."

"No, no, no, no," said Rutspud, trying to remain calm and patient. "I don't want it to have beetle bits or prostitute arms or a trident. I want *this* bird."

Bosch nodded slowly, trying to understand.

"A demon of feathers and beaks and, and webbed feet."

"Exactly."

"I see. I could mount its feet on its chest, like raptor talons and transform those wings into a vile headdress."

"No," said Rutspud firmly. "Don't move any of it around. Everything where it should be. I want you to construct a demon that is the spitting image of this bird."

"So," said Bosch, slowly and with difficulty, "its head would be ..."

"A bird's head, like this one."

"And its body ..."

"A bird's body, just like this. Exactly the same. Wings and all."

"But the feet?"

Rutspud waggled the bird's feet.

"A perfect replica of these."

Bosch stared for a long time, nodding.

"I don't understand," he said, eventually.

Irritated by having his time wasted, Rutspud stomped back to his cave of tortures in the sixth circle. Tesla was belting out a few classic numbers on the scream-organ as he approached but, through the hideous heat haze that now permeated all of Hell, Rutspud could see that all was not as it should be.

Wilde and Cartland were remonstrating with that red-haired idiot, Judas.

"What's going on here?" Rutspud demanded.

"He's refusing to leave," explained Wilde.

"My torture has been stolen from me and I am not leaving until I am properly punished."

Rutspud punched him in the gob. "That should tide you over for now."

Judas sat on the floor, clutching his jaw.

"He's been absolutely intolerable," said Wilde.

"Intolerable? Really?" said Rutspud. "Careful how you use words like that or I'll have to re-evaluate how soft I've been on you over the years."

"Frozen in ice!" mumbled Judas indignantly. "Pressed. Crushed. Immobile. That's what I was promised."

Rutspud sighed wearily.

"Hasn't Lickspear done anything about it?"

"You sent him on that errand to find a bird."

"Oh, yeah. Where's he got to?"

There was a shift in air pressure, a sudden gale as thousands of cubic feet of air were displaced and a foot larger than a castle came down on the ground outside the cave. The impact drove a crater into the ground and knocked Rutspud and the members of his gang to the ground. The scream-organ was abruptly silent.

Rutspud sat up, wide-eyed.

"What the …?"

Cartland helped Wilde to his feet. There was no sign of Judas, the vast scaly claw covering the spot where he had previously stood.

"How you likin' my groovy ride?" came a tiny voice from on high.

Rutspud stepped back and tried to see past legs higher than the tallest towers of Hell, past a body that was as distant, white and wide as a skyful of cloud. A beak beyond scale swung back and forth across the red ceiling of Hell. A barely visible figure, more dot than anything else, waved vigorously at Rutspud.

"Lickspear?"

"Mellow, wouldst thou say?" shouted Lickspear from atop the bird's head.

"You've brought the Ziz!" yelled Rutspud.

"I brought the Ziz!" said Lickspear.

"You're an idiot!" bellowed Rutspud.

"Sweet match, ain't it?" replied Lickspear.

The largest bird in all creation flapped its wings, briefly pinning Rutspud to the ground with its hurricane force.

"It's too big!" yelled Rutspud.

"Get outta here," shouted Lickspear. "I thought it might be too big!"

Rutspud swore to himself.

"It's not even got the yellow feathers!" he shouted.

The almost imperceptible figure waved something about.

"Dig this, I got some paint!"

Rutspud looked at his bird-arm. The yellow-crested Merlin stilt looked back at him.

"I sometimes think I've only got myself to blame."

The bird-arm gave an involuntary honk and blinked. Rutspud couldn't tell if his arm was agreeing with him or not.

Chapter 9 – The day the birdwatchers came

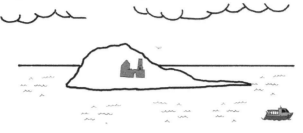

Brother Sebastian stood on the slipway, letting the ice-cold surf wash over his sandals.

"This is going to fail utterly," said Manfred, next to him.

"Trifle ..." said Father Eustace.

"It's going to go brilliantly," said Bastian.

"... and macaroons ..." said Father Eustace.

"It's going to be a PR disaster," said Manfred.

"... and lesbians," said Father Eustace.

Owen's boat rocked over the swells of the Irish Sea, navigating the waters with well-practised caution.

"We're going to offer our visitors the experience of a lifetime," said Bastian. "Isn't that right, Father Abbot?"

"All mixed together with a big spoon," agreed Father Eustace.

One of the figures on the boat, blonde haired and almost swamped by her orange life vest, waved at the monks.

"I don't think a PR disaster is possible," said Stephen.

"There speaks the voice of confidence." Bastian waved back at Carol Well-Dunn.

"I mean," said Stephen, "after the near drowning of the school children, the dead monks, and the plague rumours, our PR stock is at rock bottom. I don't think it can go any lower."

"See?" said Bastian. "Confidence."

"No," Manfred concluded. "I can't do this."

"I'm not getting cold feet," said Bastian. "You shouldn't either."

Manfred nodded.

"I am familiar with this idiom," he said, contemplating Bastian's feet in the sea. "It is an apt play on words. Well done."

"I'm just saying you need to relax."

Manfred patted his friend on the back.

"I will leave our guests with you. I have chicks to attend to. One of them pipped its shell last night and I must get dressed before they hatch."

"Dressed. Of course" Bastian watched the prior walk back up to the monastery. He gave Stephen a sideways glance. "This is going to work, isn't it?"

"It's worth a shot," said Stephen. "Seriously, the phrase 'nothing to lose' pretty much describes us."

"And your part in the deception?"

"Mmm," said Stephen thoughtfully. "Not what I expected, but I can assure you it's a most lifelike display."

Owen drew up by the island and tossed a rope to Bastian. Once tied up, Owen lowered the gangplank.

Carol practically bounded down the gangplank and nearly tripped into Bastian's arms. Bastian found himself bizarrely disappointed that she hadn't, which was an entirely impure thought for a monk to have and quite unlike him.

"Glad to be back?" he said.

"Wish I'd never left," she grinned. "But here we are."

"All thirty-eight of you."

"Thirty-nine now, actually."

"Thirty-nine?" said Stephen.

A broad-shouldered and jowly figure wearing a many-pocketed fishing jacket and what looked like snakeskin boots strode down the gangplank and enveloped Bastian's hand in a meaty handshake.

"Chuck Katzenburger," he said. "And you would be Brother Sebastian."

Bastian was stunned.

"*The* Chuck Katzenburger?"

"I should hope so. I took out copyright on my own name when I opened my first shop."

Katzenburger laughed at this but Bastian couldn't tell if he was joking.

"Oh, you know each other?" said Carol.

"This is Chuck Katzenburger," said Bastian unnecessarily. "Possible descendent of King Arthur."

"Sir Gawain, please," said the Texan. "I have some modesty."

"How did those skeletons work out for you?" asked Bastian, and had to forcibly stop himself from automatically declaring that it was too late for a refund.

"The guys at MIT say the DNA tests are inconclusive, but what do those wet liberals know? I've shipped them off to a science lab in France. Expensive, for sure, but they promise positive results. Say what you like about the French –"

"Armpits!" shouted Father Eustace.

"– but they don't screw around when it comes to science. They invented that black hole machine, didn't they?" He stamped his foot on the beach. "So, this is Wales, is it? Do I need to show someone my passport?"

Bastian swung his arm to indicate the mainland.

"This is all Wales."

Katzenburger grunted to himself.

"Don't reckon much to the border security. Didn't even notice it."

"I'm not sure they're particularly worried about people trying to sneak in and out of Wales," said Carol. "We met Mr Katzenburger in Aberdaron."

"Came to my ancestral homeland and couldn't pass up the opportunity to see your rare bird," said the American.

"Well," said Stephen with a nervous grin, "the yellow-crested Merlin stilt is quite an elusive bird."

"Dead!" declared Father Eustace.

"Dead hard to spot," Bastian agreed without a pause.

Katzenburger laughed throatily and patted a large pouch at his side.

"Not with these bins, brother. Sixty mil lenses and fifteen times magnification. Would have cost me at least three grand even if I'd bothered to haggle."

"Oh, good," said Bastian. "High powered binoculars."

"Great," said Stephen.

"Gangway!" called Owen and strode ashore with a fat, square cardboard box. He placed it down between Bastian and the abbot. Owen looked Father Eustace up and down.

"Hello. You're a new face. Don't recall bringing you across."

"Well, you didn't," said Stephen. "You remember, this is –"

"What is this?" said Bastian, looking at the box.

"It's marked Oporto," said Owen. "I've got another four boxes on the boat."

"Ah!" exclaimed Bastian. "They've arrived."

"What?" said Stephen.

Bastian ripped the box open.

"My Portuguese business partner has come through. Two thousand souvenir models."

He thrust his hands into the packing foam and pulled one free.

"Rubber chicken!" declared Father Eustace which was, unfortunately, a more than accurate description of what Bastian held in his hand.

"No, this can't be," whispered Bastian. "Scale models of the yellow-crested Merlin stilt made from quality synthetics. That's what I ordered."

Katzenburger leaned over his shoulder.

"Rubber chicken, brother," he concluded. "I hope the real thing is more impressive."

"Me too," said Bastian sadly. "Now, if everyone would care to follow me. Brother Stephen and the abbot have other matters to attend to."

The second chick had indeed pipped and, on the kitchen table, each in its slipper cocoon, the two yellow-crested Merlin stilt chicks were slowly but surely breaking out of their shells. Tiny beaks appeared at the holes they had made, nibbled at the shell, and disappeared again.

Manfred did not have long to wait. He shucked off his robe and began to pull on his mother bird costume. It was a one-piece outfit, not wholly dissimilar in form to his habit. However, the similarity ended there. Manfred's bird costume was made from white linen and covered in more than three hundred feather-shaped tassels. He had hand-stitched all of them, adding silver thread and sequins to more than a few of them. His hood was topped with an outrageous comb of yellow woollen dreadlocks. His arm sleeves, far longer than his arms, ended in sealed feather-trimmed wingtips. His hands poked through embroidered slits in the undersides of the wings and it was with these that he placed his balsawood beak mask over his face.

He admired his reflection in the base of a hanging saucepan.

"Just like the real thing," sighed Manfred happily, whilst inwardly admitting that his glittery confection wouldn't look out of place at a Rio carnival or a Gay Pride parade.

One of the eggs cracked further and one of the chicks cheeped.

"Don't worry," he called. "Mummy's here!"

Brother Vernon peered over the ridge and looked down. Several dozen assorted birdwatchers were wending their way along the island's coastal path. At Bastian's distant cry of "Look over there!" Vernon turned to Brother Gillespie.

"That's the signal, daddio. Launch Robo-Bird."

"I thought we agreed on Aviatronic One," sniffed the infirmarian.

"It was always Robo-Bird," said Brother Vernon.

"Only in your head. Look what it says on the plans."

Brother Gillespie pointed at the drawing sketched on a paper bag and some indecipherable scribble in one corner.

"Just press the bloody button," said Brother Vernon.

"Look over where?" said Carol.

"Oh," said Bastian, scanning the ridge. "I'm sure I saw something." He cleared his throat and bellowed. "Look! Over there!"

A shape pinged up from ground level and began circling the island hilltop. There was a collective intake of breath and the sound of thirty-plus binoculars and cameras being brought to bear.

"What's it doing?" said a twitcher, behind Bastian.

"Hard to say," he replied.

"Its wings are barely flapping at all," said Katzenburger.

"I'm sure they are."

"And it's just going round and round over that one point."

"Maybe it's spotted some food."

"Doesn't it eat fish and the like?" said another birdwatcher.

"Who can say?" said Bastian. "We are the first to study its behaviour in decades."

"Damn odd behaviour," said Katzenburger.

"Go on," said Brother Vernon. "Don't be a square. Give it some welly!"

Brother Gillespie wiped away a runny nose with the back of his hand and dutifully turned up the power on the dismantled strimmer. The engine spun faster, spooling out more strimming wire and sending the papier mâché bird higher, wider and faster.

"That's more like it," laughed Vernon.

"I'm getting dizzy just looking at it," said Gillespie, taking a much-needed lie down, safely out of the reach of the spinning wire.

"That is astonishing behaviour," said Carol.

"Isn't it just?" said Bastian.

"What could be its purpose?" asked a birdwatcher.

"Maybe it's riding on volcanic thermals," suggested Katzenburger. "Staying in the one spot to gain height."

"I'm not sure there are any volcanoes in this part of the world," said Carol.

"No," agreed Bastian, "otherwise that would have been a believable explanation."

The bird whirled round in ever faster circles, pushed outwards by centrifugal forces.

"It can't keep doing it forever," said a twitcher.

"No," said Bastian. "I suppose eventually it must –"

He hoped that he imagined rather than heard the snap of the wire tethering the bird but certainly everyone saw the bird cease its crazy gyrations and shoot off in a high arc across the island.

"Blimey! Look at the speed of that thing!" exclaimed someone towards the back.

"Where did it go?" cried another.

"To the other end of the island perhaps," suggested Bastian. "Maybe we might be able to spot it again if we go to the hide."

A shape wheeled over Rutspud's head and smacked against the rocks behind him.

"What was that?"

Stephen picked up the pulverised model.

"I guess it means it's our turn."

Rutspud's bird-arm pecked absently at an outcropping of grass.

"I'm not a gifted puppeteer, you know," he said.

Stephen stuffed the papier mâché evidence in his habit pocket.

"You're the best we've got," he said. "You'll be great."

"So, this is your second hide?" said Carol as they approached the cove.

"Yes," said Bastian. "We rebuilt it after deciding that the original simply wasn't robust enough for our needs."

"I thought you said it fell down," she said.

Bastian see-sawed his hand as he led Carol, Katzenburger and half dozen others inside.

"More sort of fell off than fell down," he said. "Some bits of it are still washing up on the island."

The new hide was indeed a sturdier and more safely secured affair than its predecessor, but Bastian, rocked by one bad experience, still felt uneasy inside it. Carol fearlessly approached the viewing window in the far floor of the hide and looked down the cliff side.

"It's amazing that the collapse didn't strike the nest, destroying the eggs or killing the birds."

"Yes," said Bastian, finding himself oddly able to tell the truth for once. "The hide completely missed the nest and, in no way caused the death of either bird."

"There are eggs in the nest," said one of the birdwatchers.

"Indeed," said Bastian. "Due to hatch any day now."

"For the life of me, I can't help but think that they look like ping pong balls with splodges of blue paint on them."

"They do, don't they?" agreed Bastian, laughing.

It was only then that he spotted a small tin of blue paint and paintbrush among some rags and tools in the corner of the hide. He shuffled sideways, ostensibly to make room for others, and placed himself in front of the incriminating tin.

"There it is!" said Katzenburger and pointed out of the front viewing slit in the hide. "Over on the other side!"

Bastian felt his chest tighten. This would be Stephen's puppet bird, a creation that Bastian had not yet seen or had the opportunity to approve. He knew in his heart that if Katzenburger could focus his super-binoculars on it for more than a second, the ruse would be uncovered and the game would be up. Bastian crouched, grabbed, and stood again, preparing to 'accidentally' throw paint on the lenses of the Texan's binoculars.

"My God!" said Katzenburger. "Are you guys seeing this?"

Bastian offered up a silent prayer and brought his arm back in readiness to throw.

"Truly magnificent!" said Katzenburger.

"What?" said Bastian.

"It's beautiful, isn't it?" said Carol.

"Is it?" said Bastian and scrabbled for his own binoculars that he had been previously afraid to use.

On the western side of the cove, Rutspud and Stephen lay down beneath a rocky outcrop, Rutspud with his bird-arm held up over the edge of the rocks. Rutspud paraded his resurrected bird appendage back and forth, bending, pecking and preening in a remarkably lifelike display. For no discernible reason, in a throaty voice from the corner of his mouth, Rutspud provided a little ventriloquist commentary for the bird ...

"Oh, what's this? I'm going over here. Peck, peck. Mmmm, delicious grass. What's that? Is it another bird? Look up. Is it a female? I'm so lonely since those sodding monks electrocuted my mate. Sigh. Peck, peck."

"You've clearly missed your calling," said Stephen.

"I should have been a bird?"

"You should have been a puppeteer."

"No thanks. We have whole pits full of puppeteers, shadow players, and Punch and Judy men down in Hell."

Stephen considered this.

"Is this because puppetry is a mockery of life and only God has the right to create true life?"

"No," said Rutspud. "Because they're horrible and nobody likes them."

"What about clowns?"

"Don't get me started."

By late afternoon, the birdwatchers had been on the go since their arrival and, having had at least one good sighting of that rare and beautiful bird, were ready for a break.

Bastian led them to the monastery, through the walled gardens, and down to the visitors' centre and the new dormitories. Once settled, they were directed up to the refectory for an early tea.

"Ambient sea sounds?" said Carol, cocking an ear to the sounds emanating from the kitchen.

"The prior's an old hippy," said Bastian. "It'd be all joss sticks and chanting nonsense too, if we let him have his own way."

"Isn't being a monk all about joss sticks and chanting nonsense?" said Carol.

Bastian was about to rebuke her and then saw the smile on her face.

"It's called incense, Miss Well-Dunn," he said. "Incense and prayer."

The birdwatchers found their own tables, or slotted themselves among the monks who had come in for tea. Chuck Katzenburger sat down on a table of brothers, taking up space enough for three monks, not because he was a big man, but because he had a certain presence and a way with his elbows that generated room around him.

"Hi guys," he said. "Or toodle pip or whatever you Englishmen say."

"Afternoon," said Brother Henry. "A successful day out on the hills?"

"Saw the rarest and most beautiful sight," said Katzenburger and patted his binocular pouch. "But there's not much that escapes these bad boys."

Brother Desmond, on kitchen duty, came out and laid plates of rough bread chunks and bowls of brown soup down on the table.

"And what have you been up to today?" asked Katzenburger. "Illuminating your manuscripts or something?"

"Painting seagulls yellow," said Brother Terry, sniffing at the soup.

Katzenburger frowned.

"And why you do that?"

Brother Cecil kicked Brother Terry's knobbly knees under the table and grinned gappily at Katzenburger.

"Brother Terry here is an impressionist painter. He likes to sketch and paint the local wildlife. And, it turns out, he's painted the seagulls ... yellow."

"Ah," said Katzenburger and tucked into his soup. "Interesting flavour."

"It is," said Brother Roland. "Not had this one before."

"Meaty," said Brother Cecil.

"And yet earthy."

"And this bread," said Katzenburger. "Is it baked with Parmesan or something because it smells of ..."

"Feet," said Brother Cecil. "Almost as though it's been cooked in the same oven as a pair of old slippers. Funny that, huh?"

Brother Roland turned toward the kitchen and called out, "Manfred, what soup is this?"

"Mealworm," said Brother Desmond, returning with further bowls.

Manfred leaned out of the kitchen swing doors and gave the monks a questioning thumbs up.

"I think he's trying out recipes for foodstuffs for the chicks," said Brother Desmond.

"Ah," said the assembled monks, utterly mollified, and tucked into their food.

Katzenburger put down his spoon.

"And you're happy eating mealworm soup and foot-flavoured bread?"

Brother Cecil looked the American in the eye.

"There were whole months when we had nothing to eat but seaweed cake and camomile tea. Bread and worms? This is bloody luxury, mate."

"Fair enough," said Katzenburger gamely. "But another thing ..."

"Yes?"

"That man in the kitchen. I couldn't help but notice that he was dressed up like a giant bird."

"No, he wasn't," said Bastian, drawing swiftly near.

"I think he was," said Carol.

"Ah, yes. There's a perfectly reasonable explanation for that."

"Is there?"

Bastian's mind had gone into freefall and even he was surprised at where it landed. "He's on an exchange visit."

"He's what now?" said Katzenburger.

"Brother, um ... Popo. Brother Umpopo is on an exchange visit from Papua New Guinea. He's simply wearing the traditional garb of his local order of monks."

"My!" said Katzenburger, impressed.

"But wasn't that Brother Manfred in there?" said Carol. "He's from Germany, not New Guinea."

"Was it?" said Bastian. "No. Definitely not. That would mean I was lying to you and that's clearly not the case."

Carol folded her arms. The otherwise delightful lady was turning into a small compact block of angry woman.

"Maybe you ought to bring Brother Umpopo out here so we can discuss the matter with him."

"Afraid not," said Bastian. "Brother Umpopo has taken a vow of silence –"

From the kitchen, there came a stream of happy squawks, interspersed with some 'cootchie coo's of delight.

"– and can only communicate with squeaks and baby sounds," said Bastian.

"What's going on here?" Carol demanded.

Bastian took a deep breath. He had been lying all day and the truth was hard to find. However, he was interrupted before he could utter a word.

"Distraction tactic!" yelled Father Eustace, mounted a table, and began to strum loudly on the banjo that had appeared from nowhere.

"Dinner and a show," said Katzenburger approvingly.

"That tune," said Carol dreamily. "I remember it from somewhere."

"Me too," said Bastian. "It was night, there was a party ..."

"... and there was beer and ..."

Carol looked down and saw that she and Bastian were holding hands.

Bastian saw it at the same time and the two of them pulled away as though burned.

"I'm so sorry," mumbled Bastian.

"No idea how that happened," said Carol.

The pair of them blushed in unison and neither knew where to look.

Rutspud and Stephen were crossing the cloisters, en route to the cellar, when Rutspud stiffened.

"What is it?" said Stephen.

"Can't you hear it?" said Rutspud.

"The appalling singing?" said Stephen, but Rutspud had rushed across the grass to the high windows of the refectory.

"It's that abbot of yours, isn't it?"

"Father Eustace," said Stephen. "It's not very good, I know, but there's no need to get into a tizzy about it."

"You don't understand," said Rutspud and leapt up and tried to grab at the window ledge to hoist himself up to look in. "I thought I'd heard it somewhere before."

"And?"

"It's the same tune that Lewis hums to himself all the damn time."

"Lewis? Lewis who?"

Rutspud made an exasperated noise.

"Wardrobe boy. Works in R&D."

"So what?" said Stephen. "Maybe they both heard it from the same place."

"That's exactly what I'm thinking."

Stephen's brow furrowed.

"What are you on about, Rutspud? I really don't understand."

"Nor me," said Rutspud. "Not yet. But I'm starting to get a really bad feeling. Damn it. Why are these windows so high up?"

He leapt again, but Rutspud's legs were designed for sinister sneaking and creeping, not defying gravity.

Much to Bastian's relief, Father Eustace's turn on the banjo diverted everyone's attention away from the prior in the bird costume.

"*We'll burn Ol' Tom in our fiery hole,*" sang the abbot, "*and there he'll moan and moan.*"

"This is traditional English music, yeah?" said Katzenburger doing his best to tap along in appreciation.

"I couldn't possibly say," replied Bastian.

"*Drown him in piss, gold and sweet and feast on his throbbing b –*"

"Oh, my God!" yelled someone. "It's the Merlin stilt."

Bastian looked up and saw that, beyond all reason, they were quite correct. A bird's head kept appearing at the refectory window, tapping momentarily before disappearing below the ledge again.

"It wants to get in," someone shouted.

"But why?" said Carol.

At that moment, the kitchen door was flung open and Manfred all but skipped into the refectory and declared with glee, "They've hatched! They've hatched!"

"Who has?" said Carol.

"And where did that bird come from?" said Bastian.

Manfred looked at the yellow-crested Merlin stilt at the window and, for a moment, their eyes met.

"She's come back from the dead to see her dear chicks," he said.

"That *is* Manfred in a bird costume!" said Carol firmly.

"Zombie!" bellowed Father Eustace and launched into a banjo solo.

In the chaos, Bastian heard Brother Clement say conversationally, "I'm sure there's a religious allegory or parable that explains this situation."

"Really?" said Brother Henry.

"Nope," said Brother Clement, "I've got nothing."

Chapter 10 – The day Stephen went down the stairs

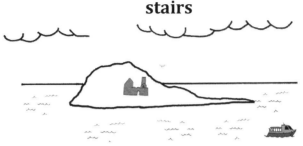

Stephen woke up with his face stuck to the *Librum Magnum Daemonum*. He peeled his cheek away and checked the page for drool smudges. This was no way for a responsible librarian to treat the manuscripts entrusted to his care, and it was becoming something of an unfortunate habit.

He looked at the page that was open. His Latin had improved considerably over the months.

"Flay ... shard. Flayshard, the demon-woman who is most ... highly skilled in the art of ... what's that? ... torture. She is renowned for her ... for her zeal in her work, taking the ... craftsman's pride in the suffering of others. She breeds ... *pulices?* ... parasites that will eat the victim's ..." Stephen stared at the words and then held it suddenly away at arm's length when he worked it out. "Urgh!" he said. "Nasty horrible thing."

He was feeling queasy and it wasn't even breakfast-time yet.

He had that unmistakeable tiredness that came after a night of sleepwalking. He could even see the footprints he'd made as he returned to the library. Always muddy. Did his sleeping mind simply crave a few nocturnal rounds of the cloisters or something? Nonetheless, out of curiosity, he followed them. The trail led him to the Prior's House and Father Eustace's room. He looked at the door thoughtfully. There were a number of vertical marks, gouges almost, on the door. Stephen checked his hands. It looked as though it was he who had inflicted the damage. He stared from the door to his broken fingernails.

He knocked.

"Father Eustace!" he called through the door. "It's me, Stephen."

Eustace opened the door and, unbidden, poked a bony finger into Stephen's stomach.

"Bacon?" he asked.

"We'll ask Manfred what's for breakfast," said Stephen, always wary of what on earth was in Eustace's mind or, indeed, what planet Eustace's mind was currently orbiting.

"Sausage for the abbot?" said the abbot.

Stephen shrugged.

"Father Abbot, could you tell me, was I here in the night?"

"Old man's sausage?"

"No, it's just I think I might have been sleepwalking again."

Eustace nodded thoughtfully and cast an arm around the room.

"Mmmm," said Eustace.

"Mmmm?" asked Stephen.

"Fried bread!" said Eustace triumphantly, and beamed at Stephen, clapping his hands.

Stephen sighed, realising that he wasn't going to get any useful information from Eustace.

"You're right, it's wonderful that we can have such luxuries. I really don't miss Manfred's melon and boiled egg special at all. You know, with the glace cherries on top? Even he realises that the visitors prefer bacon and eggs. Long may it last!"

Eustace's face had lost its look of beatific contentment. He was focussing on something behind Stephen, with a look of faint horror.

"Not spiders!" shouted Father Eustace.

Stephen turned to see that Rutspud's hand (still unattached to the rest of Rutspud) was crawling towards them down the corridor.

"Not spiders! Too crunchy!" bellowed the abbot.

He pushed past Stephen and ran down the corridor, swatting an arm in the general direction of the hand as he edged round, stomping his foot viciously to make it back away as he passed. The hand scuttled off in the other direction, leaving Stephen wondering what he'd just witnessed.

"What did you say is in this delivery?" asked Manfred, as he and Bastian stood waiting for Owen to put the gangplank in place.

"Merchandise, brother," said Bastian with a grin. "We can provide a better service for our visitors with our expanded range."

"You mean make more money from them?" said Manfred with a raised eyebrow.

"Tomayto, tomato," said Bastian.

"Do you realise that you're rubbing your hands together?" asked Manfred.

Bastian looked down at his hands and clasped them in an attitude of monkish prayer instead.

"This is new, Owen," said Manfred as the boatman wheeled a sack truck down a newly enlarged gangplank. "Very efficient."

"Saves my back," grunted Owen. "You seem to be ordering more and more supplies from the mainland."

"Our visitor numbers continue to rise," said Manfred. "Our Merlin stilt chicks continue to delight the birdwatching community."

"And Carol Well-Dunn is singing our praises to the twitching community near and far," said Bastian.

"Not complaining about that at all," said Owen. "Every visitor is putting pennies in my pocket. Well, nearly everyone."

"Nearly?" asked Bastian, looking up from the box that he was opening.

"This one never pays," said Owen, as Jessie sprang from the gangplank. "I keep a tally of her bills, in case I ever work out who her owner is."

"It's those people on the headland," said Bastian. "Live next door to that Arthurian nut, Ewan Thomas, and his dragon of a wife."

"No," said Owen. "Moved away before Christmas. This dog is ownerless, as far as I can see."

They watched the dog trot off towards the monastery.

"Part of me thinks no person has ever owned that dog," said Manfred. "Probably more the other way round."

Father Eustace advanced down the path in the opposite direction, a garden rake braced rifle-like against his shoulder.

"Oh, these will go down a storm!" said Bastian, pulling out an oversized t-shirt, which bore the legend *I heart Bardsey.*

"It's rather large," observed Manfred.

"We have a range of sizes," said Bastian, "kids included."

"Really?" asked Manfred. "Because I can see twelve boxes that say XXL and, er, none that say anything different."

"What?"

Bastian frantically opened boxes.

"Hah! Vermin!"

Manfred and Owen turned to see Father Eustace, running up and down the path, swiping the rake from side to side. Every now and then he thrust it forward with a vigorous swatting motion.

"What's he doing?" asked Owen, as he unloaded the final box.

"I don't know what it was, but it's dead now," observed Manfred.

"Bit odd, that new fellow of yours, if you ask me," said Owen.

Bastian opened the top of the latest box. His shoulders sagged as he realised that it was filled with giant t-shirts like the others. He thrust a manifest towards Manfred.

"Look, it says *various* on here! Surely various can't mean just one size?"

"No, you've got this one as well," said Owen, locating one box marked with XXXL. "You see? Various."

"They're not bloody T-shirts," shrieked Bastian. "I could wrap a hippo in one of these."

Manfred continued to watch the abbot's battle with apparently invisible foes.

"Father Eustace has enriched our lives with his eccentric ways, it is true," said Manfred with an indulgent smile at the savage pantomime.

"Another Eustace? Wow, what are the chances of that?" asked Owen.

"Another Eustace here?" asked Manfred. "No, there has been no other Eustace in the monastery in the years that I've been here."

Owen shook his head.

"What about that Eustace feller?" he said.

"I think you might need to be a bit more specific," said Manfred.

"You know. The one that was going stir-crazy in The Ship months back while I couldn't make the crossing?"

"Eustace Pike. That's him," said Manfred, indicating the figure receding into the distance, swatting rocks with a clearly mangled rake.

"Nah, this guy was enormous. Big fat man with a red beard," said Owen.

"But –" started Manfred.

"And what's this?" groaned Bastian.

He pulled open a fresh box.

"Them would be your bird glasses," said Owen. "Says it here on the manifest."

Bastian gave a little whimper.

"No, no, no, no …"

"What's the matter?" said Manfred.

"Bird glasses," muttered Bastian morosely. "Decorative glasses. Tumblers. Crystal. Etched with fine representations of our birds. That's what I wanted."

"And what have we got?"

Bastian ripped open a packet and slapped the sunglasses onto his eyes. He looked at Manfred. Pink plastic feathers, dotted with sequins, sprouted from the corners of the glasses.

"Bird bloody glasses!" he squeaked.

"Very Dame Edna whatserface," said Owen.

"I like them," said Manfred honestly. "I like them a lot."

"Great," Bastian sniffed, gesturing angrily at the boxes of useless merchandise. "And maybe one day we'll have a boatload of morbidly obese transvestites come to Bardsey and we'll be able to shift this lot!"

In the library, Stephen attempted to confront the maverick arm. The arm seemed to be in a playful mood. Perched upright, on the stump that would have been its elbow, the arm was attempting a mime.

"Prod?" said Stephen. "Beaks? Awkward giraffe?"

It flipped on two fingers and moved them in a walking motion.

"Walking?" suggested Stephen, not even certain whether the hand could actually hear him, and how that would even be possible.

The arm sped up the walking motion.

"Running? Chasing?"

The arm gave a thumbs up.

"Er, what's that one?" asked Stephen, as the arm made a gentle beckoning gesture. "Come here? Come hither? Chase me? What? You want me to expand? Right. So there's chasing. Someone has been chasing. Was Rutspud chasing you? Why don't you want to go back?"

The arm looked exasperated. Stephen had no idea how, but it definitely did. It started a new mime. The hand flipped over, and wriggled like a stranded turtle.

"Dead spider! Dying fly!" yelled Stephen, caught up in the game.

The hand wriggled on.

"Ill? Desperate? Helpless?"

The arm sprang to attention and gave the beckoning motion again.

"Oh, right. Helpless. Someone's in trouble?"

The arm nodded.

"Rutspud's in trouble?"

It nodded even more vigorously, and it was then that Stephen noticed that something was tied to the wrist.

Stephen untied the note, while the arm waited patiently. He frowned when he saw that it was one of Potter's sketches. Why had the arm been so keen that he should take another look at Meat and Mead Thursday? Then he turned it over, and found that the back was covered in Rutspud's slanted, but strangely neat, handwriting. It was misaligned and overlapped in places, as though he had written it in the dark and with some unusual ink. Stephen sat down at a table and started to read.

Can't be sure that this note will get to you. Being held captive in the Fortress of Nameless Dread. Know you can't do anything about that, but am very worried about my gang who came to your party. Afraid that something unpleasant will happen to them now that I'm not there. Only have myself to blame ...

Stephen read on, anxiety gnawing at him as he realised that his friend was in terrible trouble.

The conference room in the Sixth Circle Management Centre had become even more unpleasant a place in recent times. The lava that provided the room's underfloor heating and lighting had, in the present crisis, transformed from a comfortingly sinister red glow to a superheated white plasma that instantly carbonised the soles of any demon who let his feet rest on the grille flooring for more than a second.

Scabass gazed around the table at his team. Rutspud thought his flinty eyes held even more disdain and malevolence than normal, which was a surprising feat.

"We shall begin with the first item on the agenda," said Scabass.

"But, surely, we're not all here," said Codmince, who was taking the minutes. "Where is Pigcrack?"

"He's carrying out a special mission for me," said Scabass. "His report on new and exquisite torments from the seventh circle will keep for next time. Now, item one concerns complaints that we've had from some of our residents. I'm afraid that Tantalus has been most distressed to find that the apple tree which was supposed to be permanently out of his reach has cracked with the excess heat and he has been able to pick fruit from it. He has submitted a missive."

Scabass plucked at a sheet of bloodied paper.

"Here we are. *'Never, in all the years of my torment, have I seen such a lack of care and managerial oversight. I expect this situation to be remedied immediately, as I am eating delicious apples (baked apples no less!) whenever I want them. This cannot go on unless you wish to change all the dictionaries of the world so that 'tantalise' now* means 'put everything one wants in easy reach!' I would come and complain about this is person, but the pool of water in which I stand (and which is supposed to be just out of my reach!) has dried up and my lower regions are encased in dried mud.'"

He tossed the paper aside.

"We have a great many other such complaints," Scabass said, "and I want to know what each of you are doing to improve things. Bapslime, have you addressed the matter of the imps that have been disappearing?"

Bapslime opened his mouth and closed it again. Rutspud recognised the dilemma he faced, as they all knew full well that Scabass had been rounding up the imps himself. It was widely acknowledged that imps were able to regulate their temperature with the cooling properties of their blood, and rumour had it that Scabass was blending imps into some sort of refreshing cocktail.

"Sir, it has proven difficult to get accurate figures on the number of imps affected," said Bapslime carefully. "Everyone knows it's impossible to count imps, so it is very likely that *no imps at all* have actually disappeared."

Scabass grunted with satisfaction.

"Good work. Have you got that down in the minutes, Codmince?"

Codmince nodded as his pen scratched rapidly across the flesh of the damned soul kneeling at his feet. Minute-taking seemed an almost futile activity, in Rutspud's opinion, as it seemed likely that the damned soul would be turned into a lump of charred flesh long before the meeting was over.

"Next item on the agenda concerns the census," said Scabass. "Some interesting results. Quilldust has joined us to present them."

With a dry creak, the census-taker demon emerged from one of the room's few shadows and stood before the table. His feet smouldered on the iron grille flooring, but he didn't seem to care.

"The census has been a resounding success," he intoned. "The target of one hundred and ten per cent response rate has been surpassed."

Nobody expressed any surprise at this. They all had their targets. It was the way of the world.

"The usual rate of demon recycling is being maintained. I have taken stock of all spare parts, including those that have been described as artwork, foodstuff and mechanical devices by Belphegor's R&D department. Nonetheless, overall we have seen a net decline in the number of demons."

"Decline?" said Codmince.

"In short, we have some escapees," said Quilldust. "I have here a list of demons who have been found to be entirely absent from Hell." Quilldust opened a large ledger in his hands and read. "Spoongut, Toeflange, Crotchwatch, Lugtrout, Gufftit –"

"How is this even possible?" said Rimpurge. "It's not as though demons can just walk out. It's tough enough to get a pass out to Limbo."

Rimpurge's gaze swivelled across to Rutspud.

"The only one of us who's been to Limbo is Rutspud," he said with a nasty grin.

"What?" said Rutspud.

"You're involved with that dubious gift exchange thing each Crispmas," said Rimpurge.

"It's called Christmas," said Rutspud, "and I'm not the one who authorised it."

Quilldust gave him a penetrating stare.

"The Heavenly Host send bandages, food packages and words of comfort to the damned," Rutspud explained. "We send the blessed dead a selection of carnivorous flowers and shit chocolates."

"Where would we get chocolate from in Hell?" asked Scabass.

"We don't, sir. As I said, they're shit chocolates."

"We might consider the possibility that someone forged a pass," suggested Rimpurge.

"What if they've gone to earth?" asked Codmince.

"Could they have been summoned by a ritual, perhaps?" suggested Bapslime.

"Enough!" growled Scabass. "We can speculate all day –"

"And we have taken full account of summonings, transfers, and demons on extra-dimensional missions," said Quilldust with a soft insistence.

"The numbers are not important," growled Scabass. "The point is clear. Some demons are trying to shirk their duties, here and elsewhere. It must stop."

Rutspud was among twelve demon underlings who were acutely aware that Scabass's spikey fingers had automatically strayed towards the controls of his mincing machine. The feathers on his bird arm ruffled with fear.

"Just know this," snarled Scabass. "There will be no more soft touch management from me."

The demon team were very careful not to exchange glances at that.

"I can promise you a tough new regime," he said. "Every demon will know his place and every demon will know what will happen to him if he's found lacking in any way. This is my department and I am responsible for everything that goes on here. Hell is undergoing challenging times, but I want everyone to know that every move made by my team is subject to my scrutiny. Every thought that even crosses your minds becomes my personal responsibility. Do we all understand one another?"

Heads nodded around the table.

Scabass grinned.

"In light of that," he said happily, "there are some questions I have for you, Rutspud."

Rutspud froze.

"Some interesting pictures have come into my possession," said Scabass. "I don't understand exactly what they're showing me, but I'm quite sure there's a reasonable explanation. Let's start with this one."

Scabass pulled out a sketchpad that Rutspud immediately recognised as one of Potter's.

"'Meat and Mead Thursday,'" read Scabass from the top of the first picture, holding it up for the entire team to see. "Tell us all about what that is, would you Rutspud?"

The others craned forward to get a good look at the pictures, but even at a distance it was possible to discern quite clearly that this was a picture of damned souls cheerily raising glasses in a silent toast to the artist. Scabass flicked over to the next page as Rutspud burned under the accusing looks from his colleagues.

"I think I recognise the souls in this picture, Rutspud. That's the one called Wilde, isn't it? Looks to me as though he's playing some sort of game with the wrinkly one called Shipton. That rack of yours, with the unusual green covering doubles up as a gaming table, unless I'm mistaken."

"It's snooker sir," Rutspud said, in an attempt to recover a situation that was almost certainly lost. "An approved method of torment. It's in the guide."

"I believe you're right, Rutspud," smiled Scabass, "but only where we are able to relay it to television viewers in black and white. I don't see any television in this picture. What I do see is the woman Cartland chalking up the score, and looking as if she's rather enjoying the game."

"Sir, there's a completely reasonable explanation for everything that you see here," said Rutspud, his mind racing.

"Is there? Is there really, Rutspud?" Scabass leered at him, clearly enjoying the chance to make him squirm. He sat back, settling his bulk into the chair. "Please, do explain. This should be most enjoyable."

In Rutspud's cave, Lickspear was trying to persuade Potter to reattach his ear.

"I'd be very happy to sew it on," explained Potter, "but I need something solid to sew it onto. As far as I can see, you're a loosely organised collection of demon parts. You're more jelly than flesh. None of you is joined together properly."

Lickspear's face fell.

"Of course, that's what makes you special," said Potter, quickly. "No other demon can ever be quite the same as you."

"Lickspear!"

Potter shrank back into the cave as another demon rounded the corner.

"Well met, Pigcrack!" said Lickspear, trotting over to see a fellow demon who was clearly not as special as him. He gave a quick waggle of his laughing stick. "Tell on thy mind, we make good with those pictures?"

"What?" said Pigcrack.

"You offer'd that should your master admire them we might score us a neat prize."

Pigcrack gave Lickspear a smile. It wasn't a particularly nice smile. Lickspear noticed that and thought that it was such a shame that Pigcrack's smiles looked like he was being devious and evil instead of just plain friendly. Lickspear gave Pigcrack a big friendly smile to show him how it was done.

"As a matter of fact you did win a prize," said Pigcrack. "A special holiday for everyone in here."

"Dig that! Where to?" said Lickspear. "Is it Heaven? I heard Heaven is a real jumpin' joint."

"They all need to come with me now," said Pigcrack, and waved a hand towards Potter. "You first, with the apron. Don't be shy now."

Potter hung back.

"If it's all the same to you, I think I'll wait until Rutspud's back. He might wonder where we've gone."

Pigcrack smirked, as the other residents of the cave filed out to see what was going on.

"Rutspud? You'll be waiting a long time for him to come back. Fact is, I doubt anyone will be seeing him again."

Pigcrack dealt Potter a vicious backhanded blow that sent her stumbling across the room.

"And *that* is for addressing a demon directly. Don't let it happen again."

Rutspud pointed at the damning picture of the snooker game and tried to force his devious brain to come up with something that would convince Scabass of his innocence.

"I've been researching the effects of expectation on the human soul," he said eventually. "The theory is that I treat these subjects well. Allow them some hope and *then* crush it. If we simply torment these souls, day in and day out, then it's all part of a routine. They know what to expect and they accept it. I believe that if we show them a glimpse of a more pleasant existence, then the descent into hopeless torment can be made *so* much more extreme."

He glanced around the room, trying to gauge whether this was working.

"I'm working on a research paper as part of my role in R&D," he offered as a last effort.

"That would be your former role in R&D," said Scabass, gathering the pictures together in a way that indicated that there would be no more discussion.

Of course. Rutspud realised he was wasting his breath. It didn't matter if he could come up with something convincing or not. Scabass would seize any opportunity to get him out of R&D, so that he could the seize the role he had himself coveted. Rutspud was screwed.

"So, all that remains is the matter of your punishment," said Scabass. His finger strayed to the button that activated the demon blending device. "No ... we can come up with something much better than that, I think."

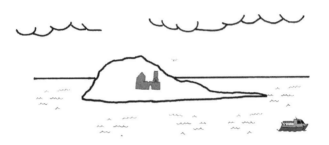

Stephen's hand ruffled Jessie's fur, as he stood at the top of the staircase. He gazed down.

"What's there to be afraid of?" he said, forcing a laugh from his unwilling throat.

Of course, there was a lot to be afraid of. There was a staircase that seemed to occupy not only the three regular dimensions, but some extra bonus dimensions that made Stephen want to rip his own eyes out. And then, after that, there was Hell ...

"I'm definitely going, Jessie," he murmured. "I can't leave Rutspud in the lurch."

Jessie looked up at him. Stephen stayed exactly where he was.

"This," he said, "is undoubtedly one of those situations where plunging straight in is the only way. You know, like, um, bungee jumping or sex. I think."

He risked being frozen rigid with fear if he waited any longer. Jessie licked her own nose and then nudged his leg.

"Are you coming with me?" he asked.

Jessie wagged her tail.

"Good," he said. "Thanks."

He looked down at the shimmering vortex of the staircase.

"Come on then, let's go."

They started down.

"Lord Peter." Scabass scuttled into the lord of Hell's office and bowed low. "I trust all is well?"

"Apart from the apocalyptic overheating and the missing demons?" Peter asked. "Just another day in paradise. Nero, can you please turn up the air-con?"

"Yes, Lord," said Nero, and with a preparatory adjustment of his toga and razor-blade crown, started to crank a handle. Scabass's eyes were drawn to the mechanism, constructed from human joints which articulated back and forth. It operated a large fan, which was a framework of flayed skin stretched over more bones. Ribs by the looks of it.

"A most ingenious device," observed Scabass.

"I'm afraid it's proving vulnerable to the heat," said Peter. "The bones keep melting. Now, what was the matter that you wished to discuss so very urgently?"

"It's Rutspud, sir."

"Rutspud?"

"The underling who you recently and – if I may be so bold – unwisely promoted to Belphegor's department."

275

"Ah, Rutspud. Spindly limbs? Very expressive eyes? Charming fellow. What's the little tyke been up to?"

"The most despicable crimes against your regime."

"Oh, really? What evidence do you have for me?"

The click of Scabass's fingers was like the ricochet of a bullet. The door opened and Codmince staggered in with a damned soul under his arm.

"I present to you the minutes of my team meeting. You will see inscribed here – yes, here, just above the kidneys – the detailed accusations made on the basis of some pictures that came into my possession."

Lord Peter scrutinised the damned soul's lower back.

"Rutspud has been allowing his damned souls to relax and enjoy themselves in between inspections," said Scabass. "Worse than that, he has colluded with them to deceive anyone who enters his cave, to convey the impression that they are being tormented."

Scabass paused while Peter read the minutes.

"I think we should definitely assume that Rutspud has abused his position in the R&D lab to enable some of these elaborate deceptions," Scabass added hopefully. "I imagine you will want to replace him with immediate effect."

"More than likely," said Peter, not looking up as he scanned through the rest of the minutes, right down to the buttocks.

"Someone who has demonstrated a talent for using their initiative? Someone with a persistent attitude and unquestioning loyalty?" suggested Scabass.

"Ye—ees, that sounds like a good idea," said Peter. "I must look around for someone like that. Now, these are very serious allegations."

"Oh yes," said Scabass. "And I'm certain that he is responsible for the overheating problem."

"Really? You have proof?"

"Unfortunately not, my lord, but the only reason that I can't prove it is that anyone who might have seen him has conveniently lost their memory."

"Oh?"

"This cannot be a coincidence. You will recall that Rutspud was involved in a study involving the River Lethe."

"The river of forgetfulness? Hmmm. I suppose that a cunning and resourceful demon might have made use of those waters. Nero, please make a note of this. One never knows when one might need such a thing. So, Scabass, what do you propose should be done with the person responsible for these crimes that you describe so very clearly in these minutes?"

Scabass rubbed his hands together, a sound not unlike the screech of car brakes, and grinned.

"I can't believe we've won a special holiday."

Lickspear trotted happily after Pigcrack and Rutspud's gang as they progressed through the Fields of Infinite Woe.

"Mama-Na, ain't you excited?" he asked. "Wherefore might we be headed?"

"Gaorgh mah," she said with a gloomy shake of her head.

Lickspear turned to Cartland, whose wide-brimmed hat kept snagging on the bones that protruded from the walls of the passageway.

"Reckon Rutspud's waiting on us? He sure loves surprises!"

"I always say that there's a fine line to be trodden between giving someone a nice surprise," said Cartland, "and accidentally wrong-footing them. It's a tricky thing, socially. However, in this case, I think it's safe to assume that Rutspud is preoccupied elsewhere, and the surprises that await us are likely to be less than pleasant."

Lickspear smiled uncertainly and moved forwards. He was often confused when Cartland spoke to him.

"Wherefore is our destination, Pigcrack?" he asked, when he caught up to the head of the group.

"The Pit of Appalling Horrors," said Pigcrack. "They behaving back there? You're supposed to be at the back, making sure there are no stragglers."

"Ain't seen no stragglers," said Lickspear. He'd check later with Wilde what a straggler looked like. "I bet the Pit of Appalling Horrors is a righteous joint!"

A short way off to one side, a man who was stuck knee-deep in the baking soil, plucked crisp apples from the withered tree above him.

"Look!" the man shrieked in disgust. "Another! I can just get fruit any time I like!"

"Take heed!" Lickspear called over to him. "We heading down to the Pit of Appalling Horrors. Get in, pops!"

"Oh, but you've not got there yet, have you?" sniped the man. "No! Your heart's desire is just out of reach. Mine? Mine?! It's right here! How bloody convenient!"

Pigcrack came to a sudden halt and Lickspear walked right into the back of him.

"What's hanging, man?" said Lickspear and then saw the robed and hooded figure appearing from a side passage. There were muted *oof* noises from the group behind them as the train of unhappy souls collided with one another.

"Identify yourself, stranger!" said Pigcrack. "This is a restricted zone!"

The robe hid the stranger's face. He held his hands before him, clasped together, but as Lickspear watched, a third hand appeared from the folds of the robe and pointed directly at him. It looked familiar somehow.

"My name is Jessephendor Clawbelly, and I demand that you hand over those prisoners to me," boomed the stranger in a deep voice.

"Clawbelly!" exclaimed Lickspear. "Never have I owned one of those. Cool, ain't it, Pigcrack? Man, he's got a tail as well!"

Lickspear indicated the furry tail that swished from side to side under the edge of the robe.

"Er yes," boomed Jessephendor. "You should take heed. When my tail wags, it means I'm ... I'm running out of patience. The prisoners, now!"

"By whose authority would you make such a demand?" growled Pigcrack.

"St Peter has sent me to review this case. I am an auditor. Um, I have spreadsheets and I'm not afraid to use them!"

Lickspear saw Pigcrack hesitate. There were muffled whispers from the humans behind him.

"I have heard mention of these spreadsheets," said Lickspear. "Devilishly evil."

"Show me proof of your authority," demanded Pigcrack.

"Very well, one moment," said Jessephendor. All three hands rifled inside the robes for a long moment. A document appeared.

"Here," said Jessephendor, flashing it briefly. "This bears the seal of St Peter."

"Pwhelli is not a name I have heard our Lord use before," said Pigcrack reaching for the document, "and whatever a library card is, it does not sound as though it carries sufficient authority –"

There was a brief electric crackle as Pigcrack's hand touched the stranger and a sound that was something like *foom*, and Pigcrack was gone without a trace. A faint glimmer hung in the air for a fraction of a second, as though all the light particles which had been bouncing off the demon were now confused as to what to do and were just hanging around in embarrassment.

"Well, I didn't expect that," said Jessephendor, as he pushed the hood back off his head.

"Brother Stephen!" said Potter, rushing forward. "I recognised Jessie's waggy tail."

She bent to fuss the collie who had appeared from beneath the hem of Stephen's habit.

"Gnarrgh hazargh!" crowed Mama-Na, slapping him on the back.

"Good work, young man," said Nightingale. "It appears that you have some startling powers down here."

"Powers?" said Stephen.

"My goodness, the man doesn't know what he can do!" exclaimed Wilde. "A holy man, in Hell. It appears that you can dispatch these demons with a single touch."

"Perhaps it is like the meeting of matter and antimatter," said Tesla. "A scientific concept I toyed with in another life."

"I'd warrant there are more deserving of a hearty handshake from you!" said Boudicca.

Lickspear stepped back in fear. These were words that he did understand and he wasn't sure whether he was ready to be dispatched.

"Not this one," chipped in Potter. "He's Rutspud's ... servant. Friend of a sort. Possibly pet."

Lickspear nodded vigorously.

"We need to find Rutspud," said Bernhardt. "What are we waiting for?"

"We don't know where he is, young lady," said Whitehouse.

"Yes, we do," said Stephen. "He's in the Fortress of Nameless Dread. But first, I'm to make sure that you're all safe. We need to get you to the R&D department, into the clock that Belphegor's making for St Peter. I'm then going to go rescue Rutspud."

"Mnn-ock?" said Mama-Na.

"Rutspud reckons you could all live in there quite nicely as long as one of you pops out every hour to announce the time. You might need to dress up as a cuckoo, that's all."

"Now, Stephen," said Cartland. "You can't honestly imagine that we'd sit aside like cowards while you took on the fortress alone?"

There was a discreet *woof* from Jessie.

"Sorry, not quite alone," acknowledged Cartland.

Scabass was really getting into the swing of it.

"Peel the skin from his tongue," he said. "Slowly, of course, making him chew a lemon as you go."

Peter nodded.

"Are you getting this, Nero?"

"Yes, sir."

"Good, carry on, Scabass."

"Those eyes of his ..."

Scabass suppressed a shudder as he recalled the many times that Rutspud had secretly mocked him. He always pretended to be so polite, so subservient, but it was his big googly eyes that gave him away.

"Ye—ees?" said Peter.

"Inject spiders' eggs into his eyeballs!" Scabass exclaimed with a burst of inspiration. "Make sure they are good, viable ones from a big, fat species that are certain to wriggle, hatch and emerge in the most unpleasant way possible." He cackled. "Just imagine the look on his face when he sees them pouring down his face."

Nero paused in his writing.

"How will he see them if the spiders have ... popped his eyeballs?"

"Good point, Nero," said Scabass. "Spiders in one eye. And then peel the skin from his torso!" Scabass realised that his voice was getting louder, but he didn't care. "Peel it slowly, just a few inches at a time. Plant the seeds of vigorous green weeds in the flesh and, and then introduce a family of guinea pigs. Yes! The cute furriness that all demons abhor, combined with the torment of them feeding upon the emerging greenery will be perfect!"

Scabass pictured the scene and sighed with happiness.

"There should be some audio-visual aspect. Obviously, you will remove his eyelids so that he is compelled to watch whatever we want. What *do* we want? Who's that man in the Pit of Bastards who made all those horribly cute films?"

"I know the one," said Lord Peter. "All twee cartoons with singing animals."

"Ach!" Scabass groaned as he laughed. "That one with the princess on helium who gets all the animals to sing while she tidies the house for the homunculus miners. I hear demons have vomited themselves inside out after watching that."

Peter nodded.

"And is that what you wish to be done?"

"I am a huge believer in personal accountability and responsibility, Lord. These punishments are no less than he deserves."

"Well said. I will make certain that all of these delightful torments are made available as you suggest. I must congratulate you upon your thoroughness. You will go to room four hundred at the Institute of Unflinching Obedience and present Nero's notes together with this letter of instruction. You can be certain that this punishment will be carried out to the letter."

Rutspud sat in a puddle at the bottom of a cell that was designed to generate slime. He'd seen Belphegor's original design for the engine that crushed waste from elsewhere in Hell and manufactured a green-tinted slurry that was pumped through tiny vents at the top of the walls to provide a constant cascade of foul-smelling effluent.

The fingers of Rutspud's one remaining hand paddled in the supposed puddle of slime. The overheating crisis had clearly interfered with the system, or evaporated much of the slime before arrival, as the puddle he sat in was semi-solid and steaming gently. It was surprisingly like one of those potted noodle snacks Stephen had offered him. Admittedly, the potted noodles smelled better.

"Oh, Stephen."

Rutspud hoped against hope (particularly tough given that, in no sense at all, was he allowed to pray) that Stephen had got his note and had done something – anything! – to help his gang. Certainly, it wouldn't be long before he himself would be subjected to all of the hideous torments that Scabass was certain to demand, but if he could at least save his damned friends from the same fate …

"You're a changed demon," he said to himself. "Or gone mad. Talking to yourself is definitely a sign of madness. Thinking potted noodles smell better than this gloop is another pretty big clue."

He tried to distract his mind from his evident descent into lunacy. One thing that certainly occupied his thoughts was the annoying mystery of how come he had heard Lewis humming the same tune that Father Eustace sang.

"Where could they both have heard it?"

They were not people he expected to move in the same circles, and the song that Eustace sang seemed to celebrate decidedly Hellish themes. What could Eustace and Lewis possibly have in common? He considered Lugtrout, the missing R&D demon.

"Maybe," he nodded to himself.

He wondered if it was possible that Lugtrout had left Hell by going up the staircase to the monastery. Could Father Eustace have met Lugtrout while he was out and about? If so, where was Lugtrout now?

Rutspud sat bolt upright, the realisation hitting him like a slap.

"Oh, Satan's balls!" he exclaimed loudly.

At that moment, the door to his cell swung open.

"Surprise!" said Stephen.

"Father Eustace?" Manfred said gently, as he and Bastian entered his room. "Father Eustace, we have an important matter that we need to discuss with you."

They crossed the room in the agreed non-threatening pincer movement, making no sudden moves to spook the unpredictable abbot. He no longer spent entire days in the wardrobe, but he did like to nestle in the space between the bed and the wall. He stared up from there, eyes swivelling between Manfred and Bastian.

"Bath time?" he asked.

"No," said Bastian. "We have questions."

"About who you are," said Manfred.

"Father Eustace isn't in right now," said the abbot. "Please leave a message after the tone."

"We know that your name is not really Eustace Pike," said Manfred, "or, at least, that you're not the same Eustace Pike we were expecting."

"Beep," said the abbot.

"Big fat bloke with a red beard, apparently," said Bastian.

"You have proven to be a unique and entertaining member of our community," said Manfred gently, "but my colleague and I lack understanding. We'd be very interested to know your story."

"And we'd also like to know what happened to the real Eustace Pike," said Bastian.

"If you can tell us," added Manfred.

Father Eustace eyed them both and then his shoulders sagged. He stood up and shuffled past them towards the door, indicating that they should follow with a brief flick of his hand.

"Beard," he said, sadly.

Rutspud looked on in astonishment, as his whole gang appeared, accompanied by Stephen and that shifty canine beast, Jessie.

Stephen gave him a huge grin, and Jessie trotted up to him, presenting his missing arm with a wag of her tail.

"We've come to rescue you!" hollered Boudicca. "By God, it feels good to be a warrior again!"

"We were just in the nick of time, by the looks of it. This cell has the most appalling décor," sniffed Cartland.

"Smells like Pot Noodle," said Stephen.

"I thought that," said Rutspud.

"I've no idea why slime must *always* be green," said Cartland. "They should really try it in pink one of these days."

"I don't understand," said Rutspud. "How on earth did you manage to find me and, even more incredibly, why did nobody stop you?"

"Finding you was the easy part," said Tesla. "I had the schematic of the tunnel system from when we connected up the pipes. It was a simple matter to plot a course to the Fortress of Nameless Dread."

"Yes, but it must have been miles coming through that way!" said Rutspud.

"I made us a chariot!" yelled Boudicca. "Stole a trolley, harnessed up the imps. Gave everyone the ride of their bloody lives!"

"That's *another* coin for the jar," said Whitehouse.

"Yes, it most certainly is," drawled Wilde. "She said 'lives' for goodness' sake. We haven't had those for a while, have we now?"

"Surely you met some of the guards, though? The fortress has those brutish scrowfrogs on duty. You know, the ones with the hands of a crab, the hide of a sea scorpion, and the brains of a cage fighter," said Rutspud, shaking his head at the recollection of the mindlessly violent creatures which were favoured in the more secure locations of Hell. "How in Hell did you get past them?"

"Bernhardt and I pretended to be Lord Peter and his oafish secretary," said Wilde. "Bluffed our way past."

"You did?" Rutspud was clearly unconvinced. "Isn't, er, one of you a woman?"

"We're professionals, Rutspud!" chided Bernhardt.

"And scrowfrogs have the brains of a cage fighter," said Tesla.

"A scrowfrog sold me a spare ear one time," said Lickspear. "Turned out to be a rock. One of my favourite ears ever, that one."

Rutspud got down on his hands and knees and stared at Stephen's feet.

"This is interesting."

The stone floor of the cell was heated to something slightly lower than the boiling point of water, making this one of the coolest areas of Hell by far.

"You should be screaming in agony," said Rutspud.

He put his hand on the stone by Stephen's feet. It was cool to the touch. Actually cool.

"How is this possible?"

"Some localised super-cooling process?" suggested Tesla.

"Maybe Hell can't hurt me," said Stephen.

Rutspud shook his head and got to his feet.

"You've *all* put yourselves in danger to save me," he said. "Stephen is a monk. He clearly gets special training or something but, the rest of you, this was stupid."

"I wouldn't say we exactly get trained for this sort of thing," said Stephen. "I'm actually a little freaked out, to be honest."

"We're a team, remember?" Potter said.

"You make that sound like a good thing," said Rutspud, puzzled. "Whereas we all know there's no 'we' in TEAM. There's ME and then there's the MEAT, all mangled up."

"But you've got it mangled up all wrong," said Potter. "Because you're also our MATE." She smiled at him primly. "If you're going to insist upon tortuous and twee anagrams, you'll find I'm rather good at them."

"We really are a team, Rutspud," said Nightingale.

"Like Malvern Girls' College under-15s hockey squad," said Cartland.

"Like a great horde of Iceni clansmen," noted Boudicca.

"Whatever," said Stephen.

Rutspud beamed round at them, and was about to say something when a cry went up from Shipton.

"By the stars, scrowfrogs approach! We must hasten from this place 'ere our doom arrive!"

"Wow, she really can see the future," said Stephen.

"No, she has exceptional hearing. She *notices* things before other people," said Potter.

Rutspud heard it then, the slapping sound made by a great many oversized feet coming towards them at a run.

"Come on!" he yelled to everyone.

Scabass strutted through the Institute of Unflinching Obedience and gazed at the portraits of famous demons that lined the walls. These were demons who had earned the admiration of their peers for their dedication to the art of torment. He stopped and read the caption below a particularly intriguing picture.

Flayshard demonstrates a level of tenacity to be proud of. She holds position without wavering, and allows her fingernails to grow into the victim's eyeballs.

Scabass nodded with approval. He was definitely in the right place.

He found room four hundred and knocked on the door.

"Come," came a voice of quiet command.

Scabass entered the room and stopped in surprise.

"Flayshard?" he asked.

The demoness nodded.

"I am deeply honoured that you have been assigned my case," he said, bowing low. "I was just admiring your portrait outside."

"Take a seat," Flayshard reached out for the paperwork that Scabass held.

She read the letter of instruction carefully, as Scabass gazed around at the tools of her trade, arrayed on the walls. Knives, pliers, scrapers and wrenches were immaculately maintained and all within easy reach. He sighed with satisfaction, knowing that a true professional would be taking care of Rutspud.

"These torments are most creative," murmured Flayshard. Her head was an inverted jellyfish, glistening poisonous fronds streaming upwards and away from her wound-gash of a mouth.

"Thank you, ma'am," he said proudly.

Flayshard pressed a button and restraints snapped around Scabass's wrists and ankles.

"Er ... what are you doing?" he asked.

"What am I doing?" Flayshard brandished the sheaf of paper and blinked in surprise. Her eyes were bubbles of cold bioluminescence beneath her jelly skin. "I thought you wrote this list."

"I did," said Scabass. "I mean, I dictated it."

"Then I believe you know what's in this list of torments."

"But they're not for me!" protested Scabass, a metallic squeak entering his voice. "They're for Rutspud!"

Flayshard read from the paperwork.

"The person *responsible* for the transgressions listed is to receive these torments." She looked up at Scabass. "And I quote from yourself directly here: 'This is my department and I am responsible for everything that goes on here.' And quoted again here: 'I am a huge believer in personal accountability and responsibility. These punishments are no less than he deserves.'"

"No!" cried Scabass. "Wait!"

"But this is a nice touch," said Flayshard. "Lord Peter says it's regrettable that you were unable to manage Rutspud, but is impressed that you are taking your punishment so seriously."

Scabass was speechless. His mouth worked but he could find no words to convey the wrongness of the situation. He thrashed at his restraints, his iron sinews straining but unable to make the slightest difference.

"Shall we begin?" said Flayshard, pressing another button. "We've got lots to get through." She flicked through the paperwork and giggled. "Lots and lots and lots."

Scabass's chair tilted backwards.

The ceiling was mirrored, enabling the victim in the chair to see everything that was being done to them. Scabass saw a mask of anguish and despair on his own face.

"Now," said Flayshard softly, "I, too, am a big believer in personal accountability and responsibility. We must do things right. So, I shall start with some rudimentary gougings and scorchings and will ask you to rate them on an agony scale from one to *merciful Hell no more, I beg you*. Super. Ready?"

They had clearly taken a wrong turning somewhere.

"What's this place?" asked Stephen.

"Hell's call centre."

There was a roar from some distance behind them.

"You. Not. Lord. Peter," called a deep and foul voice.

Rutspud had been dragged to the cells by the scrowfrogs on his arrival at the Fortress of Nameless Dread and had found them thoroughly intimidating. Then again, they were six times taller, wider and generally rounder than he was. He realised now, however, that an agile demon or, indeed, a human could outrun them with relative ease. What they had on their side was the sheer force of numbers and, of course, the brutish violence that they were extremely happy to mete out if they caught anybody.

Unfortunately, the call centre was wholly open plan, with no hiding place at all.

"Lord. Peter. Not. Woman," roared a scrowfrog as it burst through the call centre door.

Rutspud led the group onward, keeping to a low scuttle to hide behind the cubicle partitions. They could not help but catch tiny, one-sided snippets of conversations going on around them.

"That mess on your lawn? Your neighbour knows all about how it got there. Pop it through his letter box, that'll show him."

"Who would ring a call centre to ask about that?" Stephen whispered to Rutspud as they crept across the floor.

"It doesn't work that way. People who utter curses and profanities are put through here. They hear the conversation in their head, as if it's their own thoughts," said Rutspud.

Whitehouse had paused to whack an operator with her handbag, so Rutspud pulled her quickly away.

"What are you doing?" he asked.

"He said a rude thing. A *very* rude thing!" she protested.

"There. You. Are!" bellowed a scrowfrog.

"All of you, down the stairs!" shouted Rutspud. "Now!"

The stairs led to a level of the fortress with which Rutspud was utterly unfamiliar.

The walls were a softer shade of Hellish red than the rest of the building, and gentle music played, the muted screaming of souls that was clearly designed to lull. There were long rows of cots on either side of the room.

"What are you doing?!" hissed Rutspud.

Potter and Cartland looked guiltily up from the babies they were pulling silly faces and cooing at. Jessie was giving each of them a friendly sniff. Nightingale was investigating the medical charts on the end of the cots.

"They all have distinguishing birthmarks," she said. "Curious."

"Look, they have the number 999 upon their heads," said Potter.

"You're looking upside down. It's 666," said Tesla.

"The sign of the beast," moaned Shipton.

Whitehouse gave an exasperated sigh.

"There was a series of wholly gratuitous films on the subject, back in my day," she said sharply. "Quite, quite dreadful."

"Never imagine you'd watch *The Omen*," said Stephen.

"I didn't watch it!" said Whitehouse. "What kind of woman do you take me for?"

"So this is an antichrist nursery?" said Stephen, looking around. "Does that mean that each one of these babies has the potential to become the most evil person the world has ever known?"

"That's the plan," said Rutspud absently, looking around frantically for the most appropriate exit.

Stephen was stood is frozen contemplation.

"I feel as though I should do something about this," he murmured to himself. "It's like that whole travel back in time and shoot Hitler conundrum."

"They're dreadful creatures," said Wilde. "Just waiting to pollute the world with their evil."

"No," decided Stephen. "We can't judge them. They're not antichrists yet. They're just babies."

"Vewy, vewy sweet lickle babies!" said Cartland, putting her tongue out and getting a squeal of delight from a chubby infant.

"I know," said Wilde. "As I said, dreadful creatures. Vomit, wailing, yuck!"

"But where are the mothers?" asked Tesla.

Heavy and clumsy footsteps sounded from the stairwell.

"We need to go!" yelled Rutspud.

"But this one has an elevated temperature," said Nightingale. "I should monitor it."

"No! Come on everyone, through that door, now! That door!"

"And what are these dog kennels for?" asked Tesla as they bustled out.

"Not dogs, those are jackals," said Whitehouse with a shake of her head. "I'll tell you later."

"You said you never watched that film," said Stephen slyly.

"What I watched on TV after Ernest had dozed off on the coach is neither here nor there," she said, a twinkle in her eye.

"I'm going to feel a proper fool if this leads us nowhere," said Bastian.

"Have faith," said Manfred.

Manfred and Bastian had followed Father Eustace right across the island to the rockiest part of the shore. A blustery corner of land, too exposed and inhospitable for even the suicidal yellow-crested Merlin stilt to nest in. Bastian and Manfred stood in wary silence as Eustace clambered down to the shoreline, under an overhang of rock, and disappeared.

"I must admit, I'm not sure why we're here," said Manfred.

"I can see the headline now: Two Idiot Monks Watch Lunatic Abbot Drown."

Eustace's head popped out between two rocks and he beckoned for them to follow.

"My mistake," said Bastian. "Lunatic Abbot Leads Two Idiot Monks To Their Deaths."

The two of them climbed down carefully toward the sea, and Manfred was surprised to find that there was a cave just above the tideline. It was a smelly cave, with poor light, but definitely a cave nevertheless.

Bastian attempted to keep his habit off the damp floor. "Stinks in here."

"I think I can guess why," said Manfred, and pointed.

The source of the smell was a decomposing human body on the floor of the cave.

Bastian choked and coughed. Manfred pressed a spotty handkerchief over his nose and kneeled down to take a closer look.

"He's a monk," said Manfred, gently prodding his green, sea-sodden habit.

"Another dead monk," said Bastian. "I'm starting to think this line of work has unseen risks."

"This man was also, I think, on the rather large side. And do you think these wisps could have been a beard? A red beard?"

"Eustace Pike?" said Bastian.

"Didn't kill him," said Father Eustace suddenly.

Manfred rocked back on his heels.

"No," he said gently. "It was stormy when he attempted to cross – surprising he even got this far. I suppose he must have drowned."

"And when we saw the abbot's boat," said Bastian, "and this chap on the shore .... we put two and two together ..."

"And came up with five," agreed Manfred.

"Seven!" shouted Eustace.

"Of course, that leaves us one pressing question," said Bastian.

The two of them turned to Father Eustace.

"Who is this man and how did he suddenly appear – naked, I should add – on our island?"

"... Shipton ... Bernhardt ... Lickspear and this foul furry beast makes fourteen of us," said Rutspud. "In! In!"

Rutspud swept the gang in through the swing doors and down into the Places office of the Infernal Innovation Programmes R&D laboratory. Dante, Dore and Escher sat at their draughtsman's desks. Belphegor was puttering through in his poop-powered wheelchair.

"Ah, the prodigal son returns," croaked the purple demon. "I know this place is shrine to labour-saving devices and other forms of laziness, but you do actually have to turn up to work now and then."

"Sorry, sir," said Rutspud. "Got some friends I need to show around."

"Friends, Rutspud? When did this happen?" He peered at them from beneath wispy eyebrows. "Well, make sure they don't touch anything," he said.

"They wouldn't dream of it."

"Although, if any of them fancy giving my despairatron a test drive, I'd be interested in the results."

"Did you fix the blowing-up-all-of-creation problem?"

"Not sure, but what's life without a little risk?"

"Yes, sir," said Rutspud, and hustled the gang onward. "Oh, and sir, if you see any scrowfrogs, then we didn't pass this way."

"Scrowfrogs? What would they be doing down here?"

"Oh, you know, boss. Causing a ruckus, using their brawn instead of their brains. Trying to show that might makes right."

"Well, we'll soon see about that!" grumbled Belphegor.

Rutspud directed the gang through to the Particulars' office but, to his dismay, before the last of them were through, a pair of scrowfrogs burst through the entrance. Actually, they squeezed through, side by side, putting dents in the doorframe as they did. Rutspud shrank behind the doorway to Particulars.

Dore, Dante and Escher wisely hid under their desks, but Belphegor remained as he was and Rutspud realised that, though Lord Belphegor might be duke of Hell, he was still essentially a blob with arms, a wheelchair-bound blob with arms.

One of the scrowfrogs growled and knocked over a bookcase with a casual flick of his claw.

"What in the name of the Great Hoofed One do you think you're doing?" demanded Belphegor, and squared up before them, his chair puffing and clacking as he manoeuvred around.

"Search. For. Escaped. Demon. Rutspud," grunted a scrowfrog viciously.

"Well, he's not bloody here, so you can sodding well hop it!"

The scrowfrog leaned forward and prodded Belphegor in his belly with his massive claw.

"Don't. Take. Orders. From. Legless. Cripple," it laughed.

The scrowfrogs pointed at Belphegor and laughed openly.

Belphegor pulled a small lever on the side of his chair and a blade swung out from the chair, scything out in a wide arc at knee height and back again before disappearing again with an efficient 'snick'. The two scrowfrogs stared at each in confusion and then dropped to the ground, leaving their amputated feet exactly where they had been.

"Sorry, who's legless?" said Belphegor. "Hm, nice to field test these devices once in a while," he added, slapping the side of his chair with satisfaction. "On your way now, Rutspud."

"Thanks, chief."

The two scrowfrogs, undeterred by the lack of legs or the fact that they were bleeding all over the floor, rolled about and called after Rutspud.

"No. Escape."

"You. Will. Pay. And. Your. Cripple. Friend."

"Oh dear, oh dear," said Belphegor and pulled the lever again. The blade flicked out again at knee height, except of course that it wasn't the scrowfrogs' knees that were now at knee height. The scrowfrogs made wet sounds and then were silent.

"Brilliant device," said Belphegor. "Where did we get the idea from, Rutspud?"

"Boudicca," said Rutspud. "She had them on her chariot. I think it was to clear away the crowds when she went to the shops."

There was a scream from the Particulars' office. Rutspud raced off to find the rest of the gang. Shipton was on her knees, quivering with fear as she pointed at one of Bosch's creations.

"Foul demon," she screeched, "like unto a Scottish wolf but with the dead eyes of a halibut!"

"Thank you," said Bosch, wandering over. "It's one of my personal favourites. I do try."

"It's not real, dear," said Cartland, placing a hand on Shipton's arm.

"It's like something out of Dr Who," sniffed Whitehouse.

"Did you not approve of that either?" said Stephen.

"Tea-time brutality for tots," she said.

Jessie growled at the feet of the inert monstrosity.

"And what is this?" said Bosch. "It has the head of a hound attached to the body of a hound. Most strange!"

There were fresh bellows of anger from other rooms, multiple rooms.

"They're closing in on us," said Potter tersely.

"This way," said Rutspud and ran forward into Lewis's workshop area, not even pausing to give a wave of greeting to Torquemada on his rack.

"Woah," said Stephen. "Why has Hell suddenly turned into IKEA?"

Wardrobes lined the walls and almost every unoccupied space. Lewis looked up from a workbench at which he was planing a piece of timber.

"Everyone, hide in the wardrobes!" yelled Rutspud.

"I hardly think that's going to help," said Wilde. "First place they'll look, surely."

"You've got a better idea?"

Mama-Na let out a throaty yell as she opened a door and a large male lion roared at her from inside. She lifted her club, but Lewis sprang forward to stop her.

"No!" he said, and then rounded on the beast. "Calm down, Alan. The nasty lady isn't going to hurt you."

Potter opened a door that revealed a lush green forest.

"Interesting," she said. "Slightly unbelievable, though."

"This from the woman who wrote about talking rabbits in waistcoats," said Rutspud pointedly. "Just get in. Bernhardt! Tesla! Nightingale! Shift it!"

Lickspear opened a wardrobe.

"Neat!" he marvelled. "This one leads to a magical land that *looks just like the inside of a wardrobe!*"

Whitehouse pulled open another wardrobe and screamed out something most unladylike.

"Swear box!" shouted Boudicca.

The wardrobe opened onto a corridor within another part of the fortress, one along which were coming a dozen or more scrowfrogs.

"You built a wardrobe to another level of the fortress," shrieked Rutspud.

"Short cut to the vending machines," argued Lewis.

"Forsooth, snacks!" said Lickspear.

"Hide!" screamed Rutspud.

Stephen grabbed a door.

"Not the wardrobe to Atlantis!" yelled Lewis.

Jessie barked in warning but it was too late.

Stephen had already turned the handle. The wardrobe door shot back and was blasted off its hinges by a torrent of water that burst forth with such pressure, it was more like a foamy green wall. The initial blast picked up Stephen and slammed him against Lickspear and Wilde, and then bundled the three of them into an open wardrobe. The continuing surge of seawater rocked the Atlantis wardrobe onto its back, and the water now spouted upwards, pounding the ceiling with its titanic force.

Water quickly filled the workshop, spinning all around in a violent maelstrom. Rutspud (who was really not at home with swimming of any sort) flailed and sputtered his way to an overturned wardrobe that Stephen, Lickspear, Wilde, the furry dog and a bedraggled Whitehouse were using as lifeboat. Mama-Na, Shipton, Cartland and Lewis were similarly using another wardrobe to stay above the tide. Lewis leaned over the side of his vessel and plaintively called for Alan.

Stephen helped Rutspud over the side and into their wardrobe.

"Can people die in Hell?" asked Stephen fearfully.

"Dunno," said Rutspud. "I think we might find out."

The surging tide, which Rutspud noted appeared to also contain various fish, squid and misshapen things from the deep, had burst out through the doors of the Particulars' office and was no doubt flooding the remainder of R&D. Nonetheless, the swelling waters were constantly rising. The high ceiling was frankly not high enough, and they would soon be crushed against it.

"There!" Wilde waved a damp cuff across the way.

Rutspud looked. Water was pouring down and out through a large opening. Another of Lewis's wardrobes.

"It's our only exit," Rutspud agreed and, with Stephen's assistance, snapped off one of the doors and used it to scull their way towards it.

"But where does it go?" shouted Stephen.

"Out!" replied Rutspud. "And out is good!"

They did not have to get far before the wardrobe was pulled into the plughole opening. Screaming, they slammed down and were suddenly rafting along a corridor high up in the Fortress of Nameless Dread. Scrowfrogs and demons of all sizes bobbed in the surf about them.

"That's a bring down!" shouted Lickspear.

"What is it, demon?" said Wilde.

"We overshot the vending machine."

Nero ran breathlessly into Lord Peter's office.

"Lord ..." he panted. "There is a raging wall of water coming directly towards your office!"

Lord Peter frowned and looked at his diary.

"Does it have an appointment?"

"No, Lord?"

Lord Peter gave him a look.

"Then tell it to come back another time."

Scabass moaned and thrashed in anguish under Flayshard's expert ministrations. And they really were expert ministrations. While every fibre of his being contorted in agony, a tiny portion of his mind was able to reflect with some admiration at the attention she was putting into every single moment of the torture.

Flayshard straightened up.

Scabass opened one eye (the one without the spider's eggs in it).

"Why have you stopped?"

"This is very bothersome," she said.

"What?"

She consulted her notes.

"It says – you said, dear – that I was to employ a lion to rake the flesh from your shins, but we don't have any lions in at the moment."

"None at all?" said Scabass.

"Sorry."

"Do you have any other wild animals? Bears? Hyenas?"

Flayshard nodded.

"We do. But this was a specific request for a lion and I do want to get this *just right*."

Scabass could not help but smile, a smile in what he could now see in the mirrored ceiling was a bloody and toothless mouth.

"Mistress Flayshard?"

"Yes, Scabass?"

"Can I just say ...?"

"Yes?"

"The efforts you go to and the commitment you have to your work is just so very deeply impressive that I think I must say ..."

"Yes?"

"I ... I think you are ..."

An ominous grinding sound silenced Scabass. A quake ran through the room.

"Excuse me," said Flayshard and went to open the office door to see what was going on.

"Well, really!" she said and turned to Scabass. "You know you had 'crushed by a billion gallons of water' on your list?"

"Yes?" said Scabass uncertainly.

"Do you think we could skip to that bit now?"

Hodshift was on the roof of Infernal Furnace #235, checking the temperature measurements. The temperature gauges had evaporated into metal gases days ago, but he was a man of routine, who took comfort in making sure all the boxes were ticked. He looked up as he heard a strange sound. His head was covered in ears; he had a thing for noticing strange sounds.

Across the Plains of Perdition stood the Fortress of Nameless Dread and, bizarrely, it appeared to be on fire. Smoke – no, steam – was pouring from every window and door. It was as though the building was being pumped full of water.

"Bad idea," Hodshift grunted to himself. "The structural tensions of that building are designed to resist external forces, not internal forces. You pump that place full of water and soon enough it will –"

The Fortress of Nameless Dread exploded, cracking apart along three sides and disintegrating into an explosion of water and steam.

"That's what'll happen," said Hodshift.

The destruction of the fortress unleashed the water on the circles of Hell at large. A great, green, steamy sea swelled up, bloomed in mass, and raced outwards in all directions along the Plains of Perdition.

Hodshift's elevated position gave him a grandstand view of the approaching tsunami. He was a well-trained engineer and he knew what would happen when untold gallons of water came into contact with the superheated furnace beneath his feet. He pulled his hard hat down over his ears and whimpered gently.

The wardrobe rocked with an explosion that lit up the sea beneath them.

"What the Hell was that?" squealed Stephen.

"Bad things," said Rutspud, clinging onto the wardrobe edge with all his might. They had completely given up on the idea of steering. The waters were still rising, although more smoothly now they were away from the source. Wherever the seawater met Hell's white hot surfaces, the water boiled away, cooling all as it progressed. The air was thick with steam.

"Reminds me of a Turkish Bath in Soho," said Wilde conversationally, and then looked at the others. "Prettier company that time, though."

Tantalus, cursed founder of the House of Atreas, who murdered his own son and served him up for a banquet, continued to pluck apples off his ruined tree and complain about it to anyone within earshot.

"Oh! And another! All the apples I ever wanted! Would you like another apple, Tantalus? Yes, please! Well, have one, then! I will! Thanks!"

Of course, there was no one around to listen. Anyone who could move away from him had already done so. Trapped in his dried up pool, Tantalus had no one to complain to but himself.

"Actually, I don't really fancy apples today," he said. "You can get bored of one thing, can't you?"

He looked down at his knees and thought about the pool which he had never been able to reach to drink from and which had now disappeared completely.

"On reflection, I wouldn't say no to a drink. Just a bit of water."

A hot wind blasted him across the face. Tantalus looked up.

Across the distance, something dark and huge and foam-topped approached at speed.

"I mean, just a little bit," he said.

A large swell from behind threatened to tip the wardrobe over. Slurping, sucking whirlpools pulled them this way and that. A massive shape moved through the fog above them.

"It's the Ziz!" called out Lickspear. "Coo-Cah! Coo-Cah!"

Rutspud craned his neck to see past a leg larger than mountains to the underside of the largest bird in all creation.

"Can you get it to pick us up and take us to the steps?" he yelled above the sound of the bird-induced storm.

"Say what? I thought I might get it to pick you up and take you to the steps!" Lickspear yelled back. "Coo-Cah! Coo-Cah!"

A head larger than any sailing ship came round at them.

"Is that a bird?" said Stephen faintly.

"Er, it might be best if we all get up this end of the wardrobe," Rutspud said to the others. "I can see us being crushed otherwise."

In the event, the Ziz scooped the entire wardrobe up inside its beak and the gang were plunged into darkness. Someone sat heavily on Rutspud in the confusion. Jessie's bark echoed against distant walls. The smell of the Ziz's last meal hung about its cavernous mouth.

"What is that vile stench?" said Whitehouse.

"Rotting whale, at a guess," said Rutspud.

Hell is vast but not infinite and, within a surprisingly short time, the seas of Atlantis had found their way down through every circle. Furnaces exploded, lava fields solidified, and fires were extinguished. Boiling realms of superheated plasma became a sticky mess of melted slag and puddles. No corner was untouched by the waters, no sizzling stone uncooled. Much of the water evaporated, cooled against the ceilings of Hell and then fell as rain.

It rained in Hell.

A crack of light appeared in the darkness and then, suddenly, the Ziz's beak was open and the wardrobe was sliding down a broad velvet tongue and onto a smooth outcropping of rock. Stephen took a good long moment to collect his thoughts, realised his thoughts were an impossible and disgusting mish-mash of images and incidents and not worth collecting at all, and rolled out of the wardrobe onto the ground.

Jessie bounded out and licked his face. Stephen sighed. There was nothing like a damp dog to bring you back to some semblance of reality.

"You and I are going to need some serious therapy after this," he told her.

Jessie sneezed and shook herself in solemn agreement.

Stephen looked about. They were on a wide ledge, set above a huge water-filled valley.

Wilde groaned as Rutspud helped him out of the wardrobe.

"Oh, look, Oscar Wilde's coming out of the closet," said Stephen, but apparently no one was willing or able to appreciate the joke. Even Jessie treated him to a blank stare.

"Suit yourselves," he said.

In time, the waters receded. The wardrobe to Atlantis disgorged its last and, into Hell's sizzling foundations, the waters slowly drained away.

Demons and damned who had been fused into carbonised lumps by the heat were now merely damp lumps, Hellish dioramas sculpted in charcoal. The Lake of Fire became, briefly, an actual lake with actual water in it. The Plains of Perdition were awash with rubble, confused demons, and even more confused sea-life which now found itself in a far from hospitable environment.

Among the ruins there sat a chair of torment and, clinging to it against the draining waters, a demoness with a wound for a mouth and jellyfish fronds for hair.

"Hmmmm," she murmured reflectively. "That was certainly interesting, wasn't it? Now, where were we up to?"

Scabass sat, stunned, in his chair.

A bedraggled shape flopped, rolled and moaned piteously to itself a short distance off.

"Ah, a lion," said Flayshard.

The lion's coat was soaked and, as it struggled to its feet, it coughed up a large wet furball. Flayshard strode across to help the creature up and gave it a long appraising look.

"Well, it appears that we're in luck," she said, and used a pencil to make a tick on her sodden checklist. "Back to business, Scabass."

The Ziz, with Lickspear on its back and offering incomprehensible directions, returned in time with other wardrobes and other refugees.

Wilde, Whitehouse, Shipton, Cartland, Mama-Na, Tesla, Nightingale, Potter, Bernhardt, Boudicca and Lewis were eventually stood alongside Rutspud, Stephen and Jessie in their place of temporary safety. The valley below was no longer an inland sea, but

301

had drained to become a patchy bog through which demon and damned alike wandered in bewilderment.

"I think the over-heating crisis has been resolved," suggested Tesla.

"It's actually cold," said Potter, happily hugging herself against the chill breeze.

"Yeah, I don't like it," said Rutspud.

"Too hot, too cold," grinned Stephen. "You moan about the weather like a true Brit. Sure you don't fancy moving upstairs permanently?"

Rutspud gave him a wry smile.

"Speaking of upstairs," he said, "I think I recognise that doorway. If we can get down to there, we can find the stairs to St Cadfan's."

Thirteen bipeds followed the surefooted Jessie down the rocky valley wall. Once reached, the doorway indeed led to a series of damp corridors and, at last, to a set of stairs that were an offence to mathematics and logic and possibly liable to induce seizures in a visually susceptible portion of society.

"You are coming up with us, aren't you?" Stephen asked Rutspud, waving the eleven damned souls ahead.

"Oh, yes," said the demon. "Until I've worked out what to do about this mess I'm in."

Stephen trudged up stairs that still steamed lightly in the dissipating heat.

"I'm sure we'll find some way for you to blend in," he said.

Rutspud grunted in amusement.

"Oh, can't see why not. I wouldn't be the first."

"Oh yes?" said Stephen, frowning.

"I worked it out when I was in that cell. Your Father Eustace knows a weird song that Lewis hums to himself all the time. One of them picked it up from the other somehow."

"Well, maybe," said Stephen.

"And your Father Eustace is kind of new on the island, isn't he? Not really able to fit in?"

"You mean he's crazy as a box of badgers? Absolutely."

"And my predecessor in R&D –"

"Lugtrout."

"Lugtrout, right. He went missing."

Stephen's stomach twisted. He found himself wondering if he had swallowed some sea water.

"So, you're saying ..."

"That's right," said Rutspud. "Lugtrout is hiding out in Father Eustace's body. Can't say I blame him. Plenty of demons would do what he's done, given half a chance."

Stephen's innards gave a sudden and violent lurch. He groaned.

"What is it?" Rutspud asked.

"I feel a bit funny," said Stephen. "Maybe I caught a tummy bug from some pit of pestilence or something."

"The Pit of Pestilence doesn't tend to dish out tummy bugs, mate. Anyway, we're near the top."

Stephen grimaced and continued upward.

"So, you're saying Lugtrout has possessed Father Eustace?"

"Absolutely."

Stephen thought about this.

"Nah. Even after everything I've seen, I can't quite buy the concept of demonic possession."

As Stephen's foot touched the topmost stair, something stabbed through his guts.

"Good God!" he groaned and doubled over.

Rutspud's hands were supporting him as he went down on the stone steps.

"A little help here," the demon shouted.

"Nightingale!" shouted Boudicca.

"The man has been struck down by the flux!" wailed Shipton.

Stephen yelled out, stood straight again and arched his back as a fresh wave of agony tore through him. He had not known pain like it and was about to do his best to tell everyone that it was probably appendicitis, when a pair of talon-tipped claws pushed out *through* his stomach and his habit.

Stephen decided there and then that the best course of action was to scream, long and loud, and hope that context would make the details of his concerns obvious. Claws then arms and then a body that was surely bigger than Stephen's slipped out from the wound and onto the stairs.

Vile and sinewy and slick with slime and ooze, the horned demon glared around, crouching, then it rose up to its full height.

"Ow!" said Stephen, falling back onto his bum, exhausted and surprised but no longer in pain. "That really hurt!"

Rutspud looked up at the demon that towered over him. Matte black scales covered its shoulders and arms, while an olive green carapace spoke of military engineering. Rutspud had heard rumours that demons had given up body parts to have weaponry and special equipment put in their place. This was apparently such a demon. He looked up at the face with sudden recognition.

"Treyvaw!"

"Trevor?" said Stephen.

"I am," said the demon with an unpleasant grin, "and I've seen everything I need to."

"What?"

"You're coming with me."

The demon Treyvaw tucked Rutspud under his arm with ease and then turned his gaze on Stephen.

"Nice knowing you, kid, but it's time I moved on."

The demon flicked a claw in a line across the top of the staircase and it was gone. Simple as that, it was gone. Stephen thought that, for a moment, he saw Treyvaw and Rutspud shrinking away with impossible speed into the bowels of Hell, the staircase folding in upon itself as they went, a plaintive cry falling from Rutspud's lips. But then the moment passed and it was all gone and Stephen was sat on a cold cellar floor, staring at a perfectly ordinary stone wall.

The entrance to Hell was no more.

Chapter 11 – The day of judgement

Between them, Boudicca and Mama-Na carried Stephen into the monastery library and, once Bernhardt had swept the books from the largest table, laid him down so Nightingale could tend to him. Despite his protests that he was physically whole, they did not let him up until she had inspected his wound.

"There's nothing here," she said, prodding Stephen's pale belly through the massive rend in his habit.

"I told you," he said. "I'm fine."

And then he felt the weight of the world come down upon him because he was far from fine.

"It's gone. The stairway is gone."

"And we are on Earth," said Cartland.

"Earth?" said Lewis.

Potter nodded.

"Does that mean we're ... free?" she suggested.

"But dead," said Whitehouse.

"What is life?" said Tesla. "We move, we breathe, we think."

"No," said Whitehouse. "It won't do, us shuffling round the earth like the walking dead from some Hammer horror."

"We'll fit right in," said Wilde. "Trust me, half of London society is dead from the neck up."

"But the stairway is gone," said Stephen.

"And Rutspud is gone, too," agreed Bernhardt.

"Fnn grrr Naff?" said Mama-Na.

"That? That was Treyvaw the punisher," said Lewis.

"I have not seen his like before," said Shipton.

Stephen frowned.

"No, but I've heard that name before."

He swung his legs off the table, fetched the Big Book of Demons and turned back to a page he had read months before.

"'The demon-hunter, Treyvaw, is a general in the armies of Hell. He is tasked with bringing punishment to the punishers. In Hell, none shall go unscourged. Those devils who fail to deliver the most terrible of tortures to the damned will be taken to the furthest pit to suffer those torments they failed to inflict on others.' Oh, no."

"And he has Rutspud," said Boudicca.

"But it came out of me," said Stephen, dipping for a moment into hysteria. "That demon came out of me! The whole chestburster thing!"

"Most strange," said Shipton.

"What's this?" said Potter and pointed at a footnote.

Stephen read.

"For ... habitation? ... no, possessions by Treyvaw see *Periculosum Libro Puerorum*. We've got that! I've seen that on the shelves."

Seconds later, the slim battered volume was on the table. Stephen flicked through the pages.

"The black ... candle summoning of Meridiana, if performed incorrectly, gives ... entry? ... into the mortal plane for Treyvaw or any of the ... brood? ... of Shandor." He frowned. "That name does seem familiar."

"Meridiana?" said Cartland.

"Meridiana," said Shipton. "'Tis the succubus, the wanton hussy that tempted Pope Sylvester."

Stephen's face fell.

"Oh, poo!"

"Listen, mate," said Rutspud, "I'm sure we can come to some arrangement. I'm a demon of some influence."

Treyvaw laughed. It was the kind of laugh that someone might learn from an intensive week-long training course entitled How To Laugh When There's Nothing To Laugh At.

"I've spent months watching you, runt," he said. "You're a liar and a cheat. A fraudster and a manipulator who gets away with the most shameful behaviour by the skin of his teeth."

Treyvaw repositioned Rutspud under his arm as he stepped out from the maintenance corridor and down a scree slope to the soggy ruins of the fourth circle of Hell.

"Months?" said Rutspud. "You've been hiding out in Stephen's body for months?"

Treyvaw laughed again. He was getting his money's worth from that course.

"My man Stephen and I have been together for ..." – the demon made a sharp clicking noise while he thought – " ... nineteen years, three months and sixteen topside days."

"What? Why?"

"Because I needed him," said Treyvaw. "And he invited me in."

Stephen spoke slowly and uncomfortably.

"Look, me and my friend Darren Pottersmore were sort of into the occult when we were teenagers."

"Witches!" declared Shipton.

"No," said Stephen. "We just used to read crappy horror novels, listen to a lot of heavy metal – Megadeth, Slayer, that kind of thing – and mess about with books of spells."

"Sacrificing black cats at crossroads at midnight, that sort of thing?" suggested Wilde.

"Not really. We used to do it in Darren's bedroom and his mum wouldn't let me stay past nine at night and there certainly wasn't any animal sacrifice, unless you count popping out for some KFC when I got my paper-round money. Anyway, we did once attempt to summon a succubus, this Meridiana. Darren had a picture of her, I remember it very clearly. We drew the circle on the bedroom floor, lit the candles and everything, and performed this chant Darren had found."

"And?" said Bernhardt.

"Darren's mum came in and interrupted us at the crucial moment."

"She feared you were engaged in the devil's work!" said Shipton.

"No, she was just bringing us some squash and Findus crispy pancakes."

"The thing I do not understand," said Whitehouse, "is why two young men would want to summon a succubus."

Stephen blushed. Wilde sniggered. Mama-Na grunted and provided some hand gestures that were quite plain in meaning.

"But that was years ago," said Stephen. "And ... hmmm ..."

"What?" said Potter.

"It was about that time that people started getting my name wrong."

"How?"

"Calling me Trevor instead of Stephen. Trevor, Treyvaw? No. Really?"

"Did you have a burning desire to possess the body of a spotty teenager from England?" asked Rutspud.

"I was tasked by Satan with –"

"Satan? The Boss himself? Not Lord Peter?"

"This was before Lord Peter's reign. I was tasked with chasing down all demons who had escaped from Hell and into the mortal world," said Treyvaw. "His body was as good a vessel as any."

"And you just hung around in Stephen – which sounds a bit creepy if you ask me. I don't just mean 'I'm a demon' creepy but 'creepy uncle' creepy – and hoped to bump into some refugee demons?"

"No, fool. I guided him. I could not control his body when he was awake, but his mind ... I could plant ideas in his mind. I led him to Bardsey and the monastery."

"Why?"

"Why?" said Treyvaw condescendingly. "Why? Because of all the demons on the island, of course."

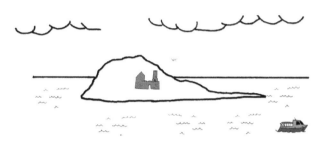

"So," said Nightingale, "this Treyvaw individual has been hiding out in your body all these years and has emerged now because ..."

"He saw Rutspud has been up to mischief," said Boudicca.

"No," reasoned Tesla. "Through Brother Stephen's eyes, he has seen our lord and friend breaking demon rules for months now. Something must have triggered this great unveiling."

"What were you and Rutspud discussing before Treyvaw appeared?" asked Cartland.

Stephen stood up straight.

"I didn't believe him," he said.

"Believe what?"

"He said a demon, Lugtrout, had possessed the body of our new abbot, Father Eustace."

Despite Manfred and Bastian's attempts to keep banjo and barrel out of reach, Father Eustace had taken himself to the refectory and sought solace in seaweed beer and song.

"*Pickled in drink they found him and they buried his bones in the hole,*" he sang morosely, accompanying himself with some downbeat plucking. "*No Heaven's Gates for Ol' Tom, for he'd damned his soul.*"

"Now, we're not upset with you," said Manfred, patting the old fellow on the back. "We just need to get to the bottom of this."

"There's no need to involve the authorities or anything," said Bastian.

Given all the quasi- and downright illegal things Bastian and Manfred had colluded in recently, up to and including the illegal burial of a dead monk, they probably had more to fear from the law than the identity-stealing Eustace. However, at the mention of 'authorities', Eustace gave out a terrible wail.

"We'll burn Ol' Tom in our fiery hole and there he'll moan and moan. Drown him in piss, gold and sweet and feast on his throbbing bone."

"I don't think there's any call for vulgarities," Manfred chided him softly.

"There he is!" came a call from the doorway.

Stephen hurried into the refectory with nearly a dozen people and one dog in tow. The men and women (and one shaggy lantern-jawed creature who might have been either) were dressed in dun-coloured and dirt-streaked rags like a bunch of extras from a particularly harrowing disaster movie.

"Who's this?" said Manfred. "Visitors?"

"Boat's not due back again until two o'clock," said Bastian.

"Step away from that man," said Stephen forcefully. "He's not what you think he is."

"We know," said Manfred.

"You do?"

"We're just sorting things out, calmly and in an atmosphere free from prejudice and accusations."

Stephen stopped in his tracks and screwed up his face, momentarily stuck for words.

Manfred smiled past him at the bedraggled visitors.

"I was just commenting to Brother Sebastian that we were unaware of any visitors on the island today. I'm Brother Manfred, prior of St Cadfan's."

"We've met," said a tall and forthright woman with dark hair tied back in an unruly bun. "Well, we passed one another on the evening of the feast, shortly before Tesla and I discovered the dead monk in your cooling chamber."

"Frigidaire," provided a man with rigidly parted hair and a neatly trimmed moustache helpfully.

"Dead monk," said Father Eustace.

"Actually, he wasn't dead," provided the well-groomed man, Tesla.

"Not dead?" said Manfred.

"As I tried to tell Rutspud at the time, he had never been alive."

"Of course Brother Lionel was alive," said Bastian. "Damn! I mean, I've no idea what you're talking about."

Stephen flapped his arms about to silence everyone.

"Enough!" he squeaked. "I've no idea what any of you are talking about, but we need to talk to this demon."

"I'd ask you to modify your tone, Brother Stephen," said Manfred. "An atmosphere free from accusation, remember?"

"But he *is* a demon," said Stephen and then stared at Manfred. "You said you knew."

"By which I meant I knew that this man isn't Father Eustace Pike."

"Well, no, he *is* Father Eustace but he's possess –"

"No, he's not Father Eustace, brother."

"Father Eustace Pike is dead and a-mouldering in a cave on the other side of the island," said Bastian.

Stephen looked about ready to explode with utter bewilderment.

"But then ... who is ... what is ... this ...?"

A tweedy fellow who had the absolute air of a university don (albeit one that had been attacked by a combine harvester equipped with a flamethrower) stepped forward and knelt beside Father Eustace. He took the mad and miserable abbot's hand in his own.

"Lugtrout," he said quietly, barely more than a whisper. "It's me."

Father Eustace's darting eyes met the man's. Father Eustace hiccupped.

"Monks!" he said.

The ragged academic nodded.

"I noticed. Lots of them."

Father Eustace leaned closer to the man, putting his mouth to the other's ear.

"Weird monks, Lewis," he said in a hiss that was probably meant to be a whisper but was nothing of the sort.

"All the best ones are," said the man, Lewis.

"You know Father Eustace?" said Bastian.

"I knew him when he was Lugtrout," said Lewis. "He was my superior – no, my colleague – in Belphegor's laboratories."

"Belphegor?"

"The name given to one of the dukes of Hell," said Manfred.

"That's right," said Stephen.

Bastian looked at him agog.

"In what universe can you say 'that's right' to such meaningless statements? Demons. Laboratories. Dukes of Hell."

"But it's true, brother," said Stephen. "Father Eustace – or whoever he is – is a demon in disguise. He worked in the R&D department in Hell. So did Lewis there. Although Lewis and these others aren't demons. They're members of the damned."

"What?"

"They're dead."

"No."

"Ninety years," said the woman with irrepressible curls in her hair. She swept a tattered shawl across her shoulder and somehow conveyed the impression that it was a luxurious velvet cape.

"Seventy two years," said Tesla precisely.

"Hrrnn Fafff-rrrn," said the vaguely simian woman.

"What was that?" said Manfred.

"She's says she died in the Winter of the Great Rhinoceros Hunt," said Lewis. "I think that might be around forty thousand years ago, knocking the rest of us into a cocked hat."

"This is insane," said Bastian.

"What is?" sniffed Brother Gillespie, coming into the refectory.

"We heard raised voices," said Brother Henry. "And now I see why," he added, pointing to the cask of seaweed beer beside Father Eustace.

It appeared that the commotion had drawn monks from across the monastery to the refectory, and the mention of beer caused the geriatric Brothers Cecil and Roland to hastily bring up the rear so they wouldn't miss out.

"Perhaps we need to discuss this in private," Stephen said to Manfred.

"Got something to hide from us?" said Brother Clement, clicking his prayer beads.

Stephen looked nervously from Manfred to Bastian and then to the damned and living around him.

"Have you?" said Bastian. "Or do you want to rethink this madness?"

"No," said Stephen and then cleared his throat. "Brothers, you may not believe me but I have come here today with these people, my friends – who happen to be dead and inhabitants of Hell, by the way – to speak to Father Eustace, who is not actually the abbot but a demon who escaped from Hell."

The monks were silent for a good long while and then Brother Vernon shouted out.

"The beer! Our brother's a square who can't hold his booze!"

This caused an eruption of laughter around the hall, much in relief.

"I haven't," declared Stephen. "It's true. And, furthermore, I can prove it. Shipton, please."

A ragged old woman whose clothes were the most ragged in the room by far, passed Stephen an open book.

"This incantation will reveal the demon that resides in the abbot's body," said Stephen.

"Really?" said Manfred.

"All those books have driven him mad," laughed Brother Terry, although there was a definite note of worry in his voice.

"He's watched *The Exorcist* once too often," said Brother Vernon.

"Well, we'll see," said Stephen, licking his lips to read.

"You would utter magic spells in this holy place?" said Brother Clement disapprovingly, clicking faster.

"Someone stop him before he embarrasses himself," said Brother Cecil, and pushed Brother Roland forward.

Bastian was aware of an inexplicable air of panic among the monks, their fear hidden behind their mockery, and was about to say something when Stephen began his incantation.

"Ego explorarent,
Cum meum oculus parva,
Quae incipit aliquid Dee."

Bastian had to admit that Stephen had performed it with some gusto, with even some wiggling of his fingertips, as though casting a sorcerer's spell. However, the effect of the incantation was, unsurprisingly, less than spectacular. Nothing had happened.

Stephen looked at Father Eustace and then, uncertainly, at the crowd of adult urchins behind him.

"Dear Stephen, the life of the monk can come with many unseen pressures," said Manfred kindly, "and our minds may become susceptible to certain ... delusions that ..."

Bastian gripped Manfred's arm tightly, causing the German to give a little yelp.

"What the ...?"

"Oh, good God!" said Bastian, pointing at Father Eustace's face, specifically at his eyes.

"The demon is revealed!" cackled the crone, Shipton.

She was right. Well, it made as much sense as any other explanation. Father Eustace sat there, banjo on his knee, his eyes glowing with a fiery red light.

"It *is* a demon!" said Bastian. "Brothers, are you seeing this? Come forward. Look!"

But now it was Manfred's turn to squeeze Bastian's arm.

"Behind you, brother," he hissed.

"What?"

Bastian turned and nearly fainted. Brother Henry's eyes were filled with a brilliant red light. Brother Gillespie's eyes were glowing too. And Brother Vernon's. And Brother Desmond's. And those of Brothers Cecil and Roland ...

Dozens of red glowing eyes.

"Even Brother Willie ..." said Manfred faintly, pointing to the smallest monk of all.

"All of them," said Bastian, equally faintly.

The two of them clearly hit upon the same thought at once and Bastian and Manfred looked in each other's eyes. Ordinary, lightless, human eyes.

"Not us," said Bastian.

"Or Stephen," said Manfred.

"But ..."

"Every other –"

"– bloody –"

"– monk on the island."

"Is a demon?" said Stephen.

Brother Clement cleared his throat, a full phlegm-laden clearing of the throat.

"I think, perhaps, we have some explaining to do."

Bastian was now holding onto Manfred for physical support. Fainting was a possibility about which his body had not yet made a firm decision. Dozens of demons with glowing red eyes surrounded them and, if Stephen was telling the truth, nearly a dozen dead souls who had somehow been dredged up from Hell itself. By that reckoning, there were only three actual living human beings plus one dog on the island, pitifully outnumbered by the possessed and the undead.

"What do we do?" he said to Manfred out of the corner of his mouth.

"I think," said Manfred quietly, "I should go put the kettle on."

"Really?"

"Well, I, for one, could do with a cup of tea right now."

"I'm a little parched myself," said the demonically glowing Brother Henry. "Are there any biscuits?"

Stephen helped Manfred with the tea things, although Whitehouse insisted on 'being mother'. Several gallons of strong, sweet tea were poured and then, following a small spat between Demon Clement and Demon Henry over whether fun-sized Mars Bars or Kit Kats were the ideal biscuit of the hour, everyone – human, demon, damned and dog – sat down in the refectory and took tea together.

"I was the first," said Demon Cecil. "I found the stairs in 1852, came up here, reanimated the body of some ancient sod in the crypt, and ingratiated myself with the monks who were here."

"No, you weren't, you silly fool," said Demon Roland. "I had been up here at least ten years before you arrived."

"Had not!"

"Had so."

"Is that possible?" said Stephen. "I thought Escher made the staircase. He wasn't even dead in eighteen fifty-whatever."

Demon Clement shook his head at him.

"There is no time in Hell. One point in history here does not have to correspond to events in Hell. There's no meaningful chronology."

"I was the last to come up the stairs," said Demon Terry. "1973. The eighth circle had converted from imperial measures to metric and I thought 'that's the final straw' and decided to run away."

"And these bodies of yours ...?" said Bastian.

"Dead monks," said Demon Henry.

"Other bodies," said Demon Terry.

"This is the fabled island of twenty thousand saints," said Demon Desmond. "There's plenty to pick from."

"Just dress them up with a bit of conjured flesh and Bob's your uncle," said Demon Terry.

"So, these monks aren't exactly possessed then?" said Bastian.

"Ooh, no," said Demon Henry. "Far too much hard work. That requires real effort."

"Were you this lazy when you were in Hell, Henry?" asked Bastian.

"Head of Infernal Efficiency in the third circle. Hourglass in one hand, pitchfork in the other."

"You had jobs in Hell?"

"Pit of Hypochondriacs," sniffed Demon Gillespie.

"Competitor Analysis and Counterintelligence," said Demon Clement.

"It does strike me as peculiar," said Manfred, returning from the kitchen with a fresh tray of tea and biscuits, "that you would take on not just the bodies of monks but their roles on the island."

"What do you mean?" said Demon Desmond.

"I mean, you could have left if you had wanted to."

"Why should we?" said Demon Gillespie. "We like it here."

"It's a life of quiet contemplation," said Demon Clement.

"The habits are very comfortable," said Demon Henry, despite the fact that he was actually wearing a dressing-gown again.

"And in a community such as this, daddio," said Demon Vernon, "people are perhaps a little more tolerant of one's eccentricities."

"Really?" said Manfred, offering around the biscuits.

"People don't seem too bothered by a little inadvertent ... kookiness."

"Can't say I've noticed any general kookiness," said Manfred.

"You are wearing a frilly apron," said Stephen.

"I'm on kitchen duties," argued the prior. "It's practical."

"And the sequins?"

"Health and safety. It's a hi-vis apron that says I'm a monk carrying hot stuff."

Stephen had always wondered why the sequins on Manfred's apron spelled out 'HOT STUFF' and now he knew.

"But doesn't all this religious imagery ... affect you?" asked Bastian.

Demon Henry pulled out the crucifix pendant he wore around his neck and regarded it.

"Odd that, isn't it?"

"But I destroyed a demon once, just by touching him," said Stephen.

"He did," said Boudicca. "It was mighty impressive."

"I've always thought that it's all a matter of choice and perspective," said Demon Clement.

"You can choose to ignore the power of the Almighty?" said Manfred.

"No one can do that," said Lewis, "but His power is like the tide; we can resist it and be destroyed or we can let it carry us to beautiful and wondrous lands."

"Or Wales," said Wilde.

"It's clear that we're not immortal," said Demon Terry. "Just look at Brother Huey and Brother Bernard."

"They were demons too?" said Bastian.

"Something destroyed them," said Demon Clement.

"Brother Lionel was certain he was to be next," added Demon Henry. "That's why he left the island."

"Ah," said Manfred and shared a decidedly shifty look with Bastian.

"He didn't?" said Demon Henry.

"The monk in the freezer," said Tesla.

"We didn't want to cause a panic," said Bastian. "People were worried about the plague."

"But he died of natural causes," Manfred assured them.

"No," said Demon Clement. "Demons cannot die."

"He was murdered," said Demon Gillespie.

"By the demon Treyvaw," said Potter.

"Who?" said Bastian.

"Me," said Stephen and bowed his head. "I did it. I killed them."

The great ocean of water that had washed Hell clean and doused the runaway fires had now gone. The global climate of Hell was returning some form of equilibrium. The Lake of Fire was currently a lake of small and individual, but definitely growing, fires. The ninth circle of Hell, whilst not quite a frozen pit of eternal torment, was certainly quite nippy with the promise of colder weather on the way. Hot, cold, light, dark, wet, dry; Hell was going back to business as usual.

There were some exceptions. Treyvaw dragged Rutspud past a great globular monster with tentacles the size of pine trees which was moaning unhappily in the rocky eyrie it had washed up in, far from its watery domain. Rutspud waved sympathetically at the Yan Ryuleh Sloggoth, although he couldn't tell if any of the waving tentacles was a form of reply.

"And what did you do with the demon monks when you caught them?" he asked Treyvaw.

"Sucked out their essences, of course," the demon hunter said. "Puckered up to their human hosts and – *sssccchlupp!*"

"Not sure if kissing monks is my bag, really. And, that's it, you destroyed them?"

"Nothing so soft as that," said Treyvaw. "Their workshy and traitorous essences have all been transferred down here to await punishment. You'll see them soon enough."

"I escaped from the Fortress of Nameless Dread once before, you know. I could probably do it again."

Treyvaw stopped.

"You're a funny one, little demon. I'd be quaking in my boots if I were you, not wisecracking like this is some jolly picnic."

Rutspud tried to turn his head to address Treyvaw but he was held in a particularly tight and restrictive grip.

"Oh, great and terrible demon, be assured that if I had any boots I would be quaking in them," he said honestly. "I am past terrified and in a far distant place where my mouth is running away with itself beyond all control. I can hazard a fair guess as to what lies in store for me."

"Is that so?" said Treyvaw. "Well, you're already wrong about one thing."

He shifted Rutspud around in his arms so the demon could look at the landscape ahead. Yes, much of Hell was back to normal, but there were exceptions. The Plains of Perdition were a wasteland in which demons wandered in the ruins left by the tidal wave. Where the Fortress of Nameless Dread had once stood there was now a jagged hill of shattered stone and brickwork. At the base, whipped into action by a team of demons, Sisyphus rolled the largest pieces of rubble away.

"At least he's doing something useful now," said Rutspud. "So, where are we going?"

"The Emergency Bunker of Accelerated Damnation," said Treyvaw.

"That does not sound very nice."

"Exactly," said Treyvaw. "Now, let's not keep Lord Peter waiting."

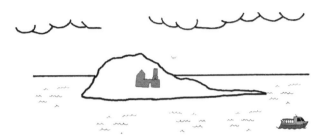

"All that bloody sleepwalking," said Stephen. "That wasn't me. I mean, it was me, but it was Treyvaw controlling my body. And whatever he did to Bernard and Huey and Lionel, that was through me."

"It wasn't your fault," said Manfred.

"Well, none of this would have happened if you hadn't tried to summon a sexy demon of the underworld," said Whitehouse.

"That's not a helpful comment, dear," said Cartland.

"I'm just saying."

"And all the camomile tea you had me drink to get a good night's sleep," said Stephen with a heartfelt irritation. "And that pumpernickel bread you had me eating."

"Both are marvellous for maintaining balance of body and mind," said Manfred defensively.

"I needed a sodding exorcism. I don't think grass-flavoured tea and bread you can break your teeth on is the answer. You're right, Whitehouse. It is my fault. And now Rutspud is going to suffer far worse than if I had never tried to rescue him in the first place."

"Now, this Rutspud character ...?" said Bastian.

"Is a demon," said Stephen. "He found me in the library. We became ... we became the best of friends."

"Friends with a demon," said Manfred approvingly.

"I did wonder what you were spending all those hours in the library doing," said Bastian. "So, this staircase from Hell, it comes up in the library?"

"One of the older chambers further down," said Demon Clement. "It was perfectly well hidden until the rains and those schoolchildren opened it up."

"It's incredible," said Manfred.

"Quite," said Bastian. "I think I'll need to see it before I believe it."

Stephen banged his head on the table.

"But it's gone. Treyvaw destroyed it, ripped it away. There's no way back."

Father Eustace put down his now empty tankard of seaweed beer, belched loudly and then moved immediately onto his cup of tea.

"What staircase?" he mumbled into his cup.

"The one you used to get up here!" snapped Stephen. "Our only hope of getting Rutspud back!"

"Now, the thing is," said Lewis, "neither my good friend Lugtrout nor I knew about the stairs when I agreed to help him escape ..."

Hell has access to almost infinite resources and, within its bounds, all things are possible. However, Hell tends to have a limited imagination and likes to fall back on familiar themes and popular tropes. Therefore, although the Emergency Bunker of Accelerated Damnation could have been a vast underground hall of gothic or baroque architecture lit in bright neon and served by an underground monorail, it was instead designed in a style that simply and unavoidably said 'bunker'.

Rutspud had been harangued and prodded down a flight of concrete steps, along an ugly and badly-lit corridor, and into a chamber of brutalist and functional design, the kind which any of the habitants of the Pit of Military Dictators would have been glad to call home. Perhaps they had even been brought in as design consultants or, more likely, cemented into the walls during construction.

Lord Peter sat at a high table, Nero at his side. Both looked somewhat soggy. Nero's laurel wreath of razorblades sat askew on his head. A gallery of high-ranking demons sat along one side. Apart from one dark-cloaked figure, all of them eyed Rutspud with hatred or hunger or both. Treyvaw shoved Rutspud onto a raised platform and manacled him with the chains rising from the floor.

"Let us begin," said Lord Peter. He addressed the gallery. "This court is gathered to pass judgement on those demons who have been found guilty of the most terrible crimes."

"Found guilty?" said Rutspud. "I think I missed that part, lord."

Treyvaw whacked Rutspud across the back of the head, nearly dislodging his eyes from their sockets.

"Demons," continued Lord Peter smoothly, "who have shirked their duties, abandoned their posts and fled to the mortal world. In short, demons who have given Hell a bad name."

"Bit harsh," Rutspud muttered, and was immediately rewarded with another bash around the ears.

"We will hear the evidence that has been compiled against them and then they will be punished with torments including, but not limited to, the despairatron."

Lord Peter gestured to a table in the centre of the room on which sat a simple silver box with a button at its centre. It didn't look at all impressive or frightening, but Rutspud had seen the schematics and knew exactly what it did and he was, as much as his mind had capacity for further fear, terrified.

"Bring up the other accused," said Lord Peter.

Around Rutspud, circular grates shifted aside and a small podium rose beside Rutspud's. At the centre of each was a demon. Spindle-limbed, pot-bellied and equal parts bewildered and petrified, they looked pathetically undeserving of the chains that bound them.

"Gufftit, Toeflange and Crotchwatch, my lord," said Treyvaw.

"Toeflange?" said Rutspud in recognition. "I haven't seen you in ages. Where have you been?"

The demon looked at him with rheumy and woeful eyes.

"Would you believe I've been taking a holiday in an elderly Welsh monk?" he said.

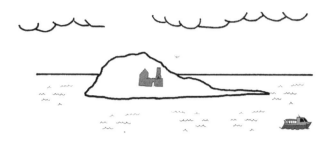

Father Eustace had finished his cup of tea and was inexpertly building a tower out of Kit Kat biscuits.

"Lugtrout was always a dear friend to me," said Lewis, "and I could see that the pressures of managing the R&D department whilst fulfilling his duties in the second circle of Hell were proving too much."

Manfred frowned in thought.

"A circle devoted to those who were lustful in life," he said.

"I think he found them quite a handful," said Lewis.

"Rampant todgers!" shouted Eustace.

"I had to help him escape before his mind snapped under the strain."

"Big flappy baps!"

"*Before* he snapped?" said Bastian.

"I can see he has flourished here," said Lewis with a fond smile.

"But how did you get him up here?" said Manfred.

"And can we get down to Hell the same way?" said Stephen.

"I should think so. Passage through the wardrobes is possible in both directions."

"Wardrobe," said Father Eustace.

Stephen slapped his forehead.

"A wardrobe! Of course!"

"Safe in the wardrobe," said Father Eustace, staring cross-eyed at the spoon. "Knotted pine."

"Sorry?" said Bastian. "Is there a doorway to Hell in Father Eustace's wardrobe? I think we would have noticed."

"Is that why he hid in there?" said Manfred.

"Or maybe he just associated wardrobes with escape, with safety," said Stephen. "Father Abbot, where did the wardrobe lead you? Where did you appear on the island?"

Father Eustace beetled his brow at the spoon as though trying to melt it with his still glowing eyes.

"Beard," he said.

"What?" said Stephen.

"Oh," said Manfred.

"That means something to you?" said Stephen.

"It does. There's a cave."

"Cave where?"

"We can show you," said Bastian.

"Then we go now," said Stephen, and stood up to show he meant business.

"We'll come with you," said Potter.

"No," said Stephen. "I'm not going to put any of you back in danger. The powers of Hell mean you harm, all of you," he said with a gesture to include damned and demon alike. "Manfred, Bastian and I will go."

"Sorry? Where are we going now?" said Bastian, somewhat perturbed.

"Hell, it seems," said Manfred.

"Then we need to get tooled up," said Bastian.

"Holy water."

"Crucifixes."

"Bottles of wee," said Stephen.

"Pardon?" said Bastian.

"For bribery purposes. Trust me."

"But what about the rest of us?" said Demon Clement.

"There's a boatload of tourists coming over this afternoon. Meet them, greet them, ply them with tea," said Manfred.

"And make sure they spend time and money in the gift shop," said Bastian.

"And will this have worn off by then?" sniffed Demon Gillespie, pointing to his eyes. They still blazed with a fierce red light.

"Hang on," said Bastian. "I've got just the thing."

He dashed out without further word and returned in a minute with a big cardboard box.

"Put these on," he said and dished out a pair of sunglasses to each demon monk. Soon enough there was a band of demon monks in pink, plastic-feathered sunglasses that certainly covered the glowing eyes but would undoubtedly raise many other questions.

Demon Gillespie coughed.

"Really not sure what kind of message we're sending out here," he said.

"I like them," said Manfred. "They're ..."

"Kooky," said Demon Vernon.

"Maybe *we* could help out with the visitors," suggested Cartland. "At least we look human."

"Why not?" said Stephen with some impatience at the delays. "All stay here. Deal with the tourists. Everything will be fine. Manfred, Bastian, we need to go. Now."

"There is no spoon," said Father Eustace.

"Exactly," said Stephen. "Now, let's go."

Even though he had already been found guilty in his absence, Rutspud discovered he was to be treated with a lengthy litany of accusations, bundles of evidence, and even character assassination witnesses. Perhaps Lord Peter relished the bureaucracy. Perhaps he imagined that the anticipation would only heighten Rutspud's suffering. Rutspud was only too glad to put off the inevitable and cherished every second that he stayed free of the despairatron.

On the central table of the grim hall were carefully labelled exhibits, including Potter's incriminating sketches, sample bottles of water from the River Lethe and Rutspud's internet search records.

Scabass had been wheeled in as the star witness. Taking time out from his busy schedule of constant and degrading torture at the hands of Flayshard, Scabass was brought in on his chair of torment with his torturer at his side. Rutspud took no pleasure in the deep scores in Scabass's steely flesh, the ravage of his toothless mouth or the fat eyepatch he wore over one eye which seemed to constantly wriggle and seethe. It wasn't that Rutspud felt any empathy for his former boss; he simply had no energy to feel anything for anyone but himself.

Throughout his testimony, Flayshard repeatedly poked and dug at Scabass's side with a variety of pointy, serrated and corkscrew implements.

"In truth," said Scabass, "we don't know how long – ow! – Rutspud has been lying to us, my lord. There's – oof! – probably been no torture of – hnnn! – of any sort in his cave of tortures for centuries. Shit, that hurts!"

"But your inspection records have consistently awarded him the highest grades," said Lord Peter.

"And the fact that – aargh! – he has not only shirked his duties but chosen to falsify evidence and – ow! – make a mockery of Hell's supportive performance management programme makes his – Satan's balls! – makes his crimes all the worse."

"Madam," said Lord Peter. "Do you really have to do that?"

"Just maintaining his levels of discomfort and suffering," said Flayshard, wiping her bloody fingernails on Scabass's shoulder.

"She's a true professional, my lord," said Scabass. "Don't stop."

Flayshard's bubble eyes blinked and then she rammed her hand into Scabass's open wound.

"Nnnn! Thanks!" grunted Scabass hoarsely. "Worse still, I believe that all the evidence presented today shows – oh, fuck! Are those my kidneys? – that this evidence proves that Rutspud not only caused the initial heating crisis by stealing fuses from Hell's furnaces, he also tried to cover it up by wiping the memories of witnesses with Lethe water – urnh! – and then attempted to undo his mistakes by, at first, illegally diverting water from earth through a pumping machine devised by one of his human allies and then – oh! No! Yes! – by unleashing a flood upon Hell that destroyed the Fortress of Nameless Dread."

Rutspud saw the deep anger that came over Lord Peter's face at this last comment. He could believe Lord Peter would put up with all manner of transgressions, but not anything that interfered with his precious corporate headquarters.

"Rutspud has not only failed in his duties," said Scabass, "he – ah! – has lied, he has cheated, he has tempted others to bad habits, shifted the blame onto others and caused almost incalculable destruction, misery and suffering."

Nero paused in his note-taking.

"Aren't these the kind of attributes we try to encourage in our demons, sir?" he said.

"Ye—ees, well, I'm sure that's not the point," said Lord Peter.

On the ruin-strewn Plains of Perdition, a pile of rubble shifted, rolled, and was still again. There was a muffled bout of swearing, a great thump, and then the pile fell away as three monks climbed up out of a buried wardrobe, lovingly crafted from knotted pine. Stephen led the way and cautiously glanced around before giving Manfred a hand up.

"This isn't Belphegor's laboratory," he said. "I'm guessing the wardrobe got washed out here in the flood."

Manfred put his hands on his hips and gazed round at the Hellish vista.

"Well, isn't that a sight?" he said.

"Not looking," said Bastian, his eyes screwed shut.

"It's okay," said Stephen. "I mean, it's Hell, but it's okay."

Bastian opened a single eye experimentally.

"It's, um ..."

"Yes?" said Stephen.

"It's rather like the Nevada desert."

"I know what you mean," said Manfred.

"Albeit at night."

"Yes."

"And with much of the desert on fire."

"Obviously."

"Hmmm."

"And with another desert directly above it," said Manfred.

Bastian contemplated the high ceiling of Hell.

"I think that's a bit more than I can handle," he said eventually.

"You're doing great," said Stephen. "Sure, this is Hell, but we're monks, men of God. We have nothing to fear."

"Fools rush in," said Bastian doubtfully, but followed the others out across the wasteland nonetheless. "Actually," he said, after some lengthy thought, "the real Hell is a bit ... well, this is all a bit of a cliché. Red light. Jagged rocks. Pools of fire. I can't help but feel I'm walking through a cheap TV production of Dante's *Inferno*."

"Dante's on the design team," said Stephen

Manfred made a dissatisfied noise and shook his head.

"You don't approve of Hell's aesthetic?" said Stephen.

"I don't approve of Hell full stop," said Manfred.

"Didn't you ever believe in Hell?"

"As a state of mind, sure. As an absence of God, absolutely. As a place?" He made clicks and squeaks with his lips as he thought. "I mean, Hell is *forever*, isn't it? What's the point of punishment if you don't get a chance to show you have changed?"

"But," said Bastian, "don't some people do things that are so bad, so terrible, that they can never, ever, ever be forgiven?"

Manfred looked at his friend.

"No, Bastian. I don't think I believe that at all. Forgiveness is love. And love is God's business. He's got a controlling share in all the love there is."

"And we're here because I love Rutspud," said Stephen, and then cleared his throat. "I mean, I don't *love* him. I mean I love him but not like *that*. That would be wrong on a number of levels. Um, obviously I'm a monk and we don't do ... that. And there's probably some inter-species thing. Monk on demon action would be quite inappropriate."

Manfred stopped his ramblings with a touch of his hand.

"You're absolutely right," he said. "'Greater love has no man than he who would lay his life down for his friends.'"

"'All you need is love,'" added Bastian helpfully.

"That's the Beatles," said Manfred. "Not the Bible."

"'I'll get by with a little help from my friends'?"

"Still the Beatles."

Bastian clicked his fingers.

"'All I do each night is pray, hoping that I'll be a part of you again someday. All I do is think of –'"

"That's Take That, Bastian. I'm starting to worry about your knowledge of scripture."

"Yeah, but it's a great song and you should never – Oh, God! What the Hell is that?"

From behind a high spur of rock a … thing rolled in front of them. To Stephen's eyes it looked like a haggis, a haggis the size of a warehouse, which had more than a dozen squid-like tentacles.

"Fhtagn dho-na ryuleh cthooloo!" it warbled as it flailed about.

"It doesn't look very happy," whispered Manfred.

"That makes two of us," trembled Bastian.

"I think that's something-something, the elder demon of the impenetrable depths," said Stephen. "Rutspud mentioned it."

"Then it should get back to the impenetrable depths and leave us alone."

"He's not going to hurt us." Manfred approached it slowly, half-crouched, hands held out in a gesture of friendship.

"What are you doing?" hissed Stephen. "You are *not* the demon-whisperer."

"I'm just going to say hi."

It was clear to everyone but Manfred that the great water demon did not appreciate the advances of a grey-haired German monk and reared in alarm and anger. Manfred didn't stop, but decided to respond by making soft shushing sounds and smiling broadly at it.

The demon gave a roar like a bubbling deep sea volcano and then swatted at Manfred with one of its vast tentacles. Despite its size, it moved with astonishing speed, and Stephen didn't even have time to blink or turn his head. If he had, he wouldn't have seen the demon vanish in a little shower of light and an audible inrush of air.

"Wow," said Bastian, amazed.

"What happened?" said Manfred, equally surprised.

"You destroyed it," said Stephen. "One touch and … *foom!*"

"I didn't mean to," said the prior apologetically.

"Did you sort of … I dunno, cast it out Jesus-style?"

"Were you thinking particularly holy thoughts at the time?" suggested Bastian.

"Don't think so," said Manfred. "And cast it out to where? We're already in Hell. This is where it's meant to be so ..."

"Blown him up," said a squat figure, wobbling towards them. "What you've got there is yer basic material disincorporation brought on by an encounter with the holy."

The demon was mostly man-shaped, apart from the sprouting ears that poked out from underneath his yellow hard hat. The hard hart was probably of little use given that a large hole had been explosively ripped through the top and much of the remainder had melted to the side of the demon's face.

"Are you all right?" said Stephen automatically.

"No," said the demon. "The explosion didn't destroy me, although I've gone deaf in five ears and I doubt I'll play the piano again. Not sure how many gallons of water I've swallowed, but I think there were a number of critters wiv pincers in it. All in all, it's been a rum bugger of a day."

"Is there anything we can do to help?" said Manfred.

"We're helping demons now?" said Bastian. "Not objecting, just checking."

"Well, technically, it is one of God's creatures."

"Are you trying to make me feel more miserable?" said the demon. "There is one thing you can do for me."

"What's that?"

"Take my hand."

Manfred was halfway to reaching out to the demon before he realised what he was doing. He snatched his hand back.

"What?"

"I won't lie to you, mate. I'm in a fair state of screaming bloody agony. Utter destruction is exackerly what the doctor ordered."

Stephen noticed that, from across the gloomy fiery plains, a number of other demons, large and small, were shambling, galumphing, and lolloping towards them.

"I'm not going to do that," said Manfred. "I want to help you, but not kill you."

The demon shrugged.

"Can't kill what ain't alive. Can't murder what ain't got a soul."

"Look, we'd love to help you," said Stephen, "but we need to get to the Fortress of Nameless Dread. Lord Peter has taken Rutspud prisoner."

"Nah, he's in the Emergency Bunker of Accelerated Damnation. You need to head about three leagues in that direction and take a left at the Pit of Gossip Columnists."

"Thank you," said Manfred.

"No problem. And if you see that arse of a fallen saint, Peter, tell him Hodshift said he's a right c –"

Hodshift's last words were lost as, while Manfred's guard was down, the demon lunged for his hand and vanished with a self-satisfied *foom!* of complete annihilation.

A collective gasp arose from the demons about them, at least those demons with the necessary mouths, breathing apparatus, and gross physical anatomy necessary for gasping.

"Me next!" yelled one.

"No, me!" replied another.

"I saw him first," added a third.

"I'm suffering way more than you."

"How can you say that? My leg's come off!"

"I'm psychologically scarred. S'all internal."

"Shurrup and get in line, you!"

"If you weren't arguing, he'd've been able to discombobulate a dozen of us by now!"

"Look," said Manfred in his sternest voice, which wasn't particularly stern at all, "I'm not discombobulating anyone."

"Me neither," said Bastian, whipping his hand away from the reach of an opportunist creature that looked like a cross between a monkey and a placenta.

"Move. Aside," boomed a scrowfrog, pushing through the crowds.

"Nothing. To. See. Here," bellowed its partner.

"Scrowfrogs. Just what we need," tutted Stephen and then he thought. "Actually, they *are* just what we need. Hey, you!"

"Stay. There," commanded the scrowfrog.

"You've got us. It's a fair cop," said Stephen. "Take us to your leader."

"You. Must. Come. With. Us."

"I know. That's what I said."

"Don't. Attempt. To. Flee."

"Wouldn't dream of it," said Stephen.

Treyvaw's evidence to the court was detailed, precise, and delivered with a level of wilful malice that few demons could sustain for long.

"Over the past year, Rutspud has been consorting with a human on Earth. Not just a human, but a Christian monk. By his own admission, Rutspud and the monk have become close."

"Now, listen here," said Rutspud. "Me and Stephen, it's purely platonic."

Treyvaw punched him in the side of the head to shut him up.

"Indeed, it is worse. The two of them are *friends*." Several demons in the chamber spat or vomited at the word. "This supposed demon of Hell, this torturer of the damned, has used his time and energies to help the fortunes of the monastery, provide food and energy to the monks at a time of crisis, and has even used the monastery as a getaway party retreat for a party of damned souls. They've been popping in and out of Hell with offensive regularity."

"Appalling," agreed Lord Peter.

"*I knew it*," hissed Scabass from his chair in the corner.

"My lord, whereas these other miserable demons fled their posts and took up residence in the mortal world, stealing fleshy bodies for themselves, Rutspud has used his powers and his status in Hell to deliberately counteract the work that Hell exists to fulfil. He should be fed to the despairatron without delay."

Lord Peter mulled this over thoughtfully, and Rutspud felt he could even see the words condemning him begin to rise from the man's throat. Rutspud's eyes flicked to the despairatron, that simple silver box. So innocuous, so terrible ...

The doors to the court room slammed open and two scrowfrogs thundered in, driving three figures before them.

"It's Brother Manfred!" exclaimed Gufftit.

"With Bastian and Stephen!" added Crotchwatch.

Toeflange waved at the three monks.

"Guys! It's me! Brother Huey!"

The monks could spare the demons little more than a cursory glance. A gloomy chamber crammed with hostile demons and the master of all Hell had seized upon their attention somewhat.

Lord Peter was on his feet.

"What is the meaning of this interruption?"

"Brought. Prisoners," said one of the scrowfrogs.

"Who are these damned?" asked Nero.

"We're not damned," said Stephen. "We're alive. We're from Earth. We're monks."

There were screams of terror, of outrage, and of fury from the demons in the gallery. Only the dark, cloaked figure remained still. Brother Stephen gripped at his fellow monks for support and the three of them stood firm.

"We've come to free my friend, Rutspud. Who's in charge here?"

"That would be *me*," said Lord Peter. "I am Peter, overlord and managing director of Hell, and you have no authority here."

"Where's Satan?" said Bastian.

"Got ousted in a management reshuffle, I think," said Stephen.

"Peter?" said Manfred. "As in St Peter? As in Jesus's disciple?"

"I am the rock on which His church is built," said Lord Peter grandly.

"Wow," said Manfred. "Can I just say I'm a big fan. Big fan. Loved your work. First bishop of Rome and all that."

Lord Peter smiled thinly.

"Thank you." He looked to the scrowfrogs. "Throw them in a pit. A deep one."

As the scrowfrogs attempted to round them up, Stephen protested.

"We demand to be heard."

"Demand?" said Lord Peter. "Make it a bottomless pit. Away with them."

The scrowfrogs were struggling. The monks weren't budging and the scrowfrogs were showing uncharacteristic intelligence by keeping their claws off the monks. They sidled around the three men like mimes pretending to battle an unseen force, waving their limbs and achieving nothing.

"Damn it!" shouted Lord Peter. "Grab them and drag them out."

"But. Lord."

"They're only human."

"If. We. Touch –"

"Now!"

There was a *foom!* and one of the scrowfrogs was gone. Manfred shook his head sadly.

"Apparently," said Stephen, "we are untouchable. We are – what's the word? – puissant."

There was some serious consternation among the demons around the room. Some cowered. Some froze. Some even made remarkable in-roads into pretending that they weren't there and never had been and that no one could prove otherwise.

Lord Peter raised an eyebrow.

"You intend to bully us, then," he said. "You would defy the authorities set in place by the Almighty Himself?"

Stephen shook his head.

"We only want to plead our case. We want to show you that what you are doing is wrong."

"Oh?" said Lord Peter. "Is that so? I was unaware that I had to justify myself to hoi polloi."

Manfred stepped forward.

"From what Stephen tells me, Rutspud has been of immeasurable help. When we were shivering and without power, Rutspud brought coal and other supplies to us."

"Yeah," said Rutspud out of the corner of his mouth. "I don't think that's actually going to help my case."

"And when the birdwatchers came," said Bastian. "His antics with a bird-puppet-thing helped distract and entertain them."

"Oh, he was entertaining visitors, was he?" said Lord Peter.

"And again," said Rutspud, "that doesn't really count in my favour."

"If Rutspud broke your rules," said Stephen, "it wasn't his fault. It was mine."

334

"Ye—ees?" said Lord Peter.

"He did those things for me."

"For you?"

Rutspud hoped against hope that Stephen was about to pull a blinding and brilliant argument along the lines of 'I summoned Rutspud with a magic ritual and commanded him to do those things against his will'.

Unfortunately, Stephen said, "He did them because he is my friend."

The gallery howled. If only Stephen had stopped there ...

"He did it out of love," he said.

The howls deepened. There was wailing and gnashing of teeth. The demon lord Berith attempted to eat his own head in disgust. Apart from the four accused, the only demons who didn't seem to be writhing in some state of anguish was the torturer Flayshard, who was busy taking notes on this new torture, and the cloaked figure in the gallery, who had remained immobile and unnoticed throughout.

"Enough!" shouted Lord Peter. "Condemned from the mouths of his friends who must themselves be Hellbound for consorting with demons. Bring him forth!"

Treyvaw unchained Rutspud and the remaining scrowfrog guard led him forward. Rutspud looked at the despairatron.

"Okay, joke's over," he said, pulling against the much stronger demon.

"You can't do this!" shouted Stephen and darted forward.

Foom!

The scrowfrog was gone. The gallery went wild with fear and fury.

With an athleticism Rutspud had never seen before, Peter's damned secretary, Nero, vaulted to the floor of the court and grabbed Rutspud. Stephen attempted to pull him away but Nero was neither a demon nor a small man. He shoved Stephen roughly to the ground and dragged Rutspud to the despairatron.

"What is that thing anyway?" asked Bastian.

"The despairatron," said Stephen. "All the pain and suffering experienced in Hell in one tiny box."

"Finger!" commanded Nero and now Treyvaw was there once more, squeezing Rutspud's hand until his joints popped and his fingers were splayed out in front of him. His fingertips were a hand's width from the despairatron, a hand's width from infinite suffering.

"**STOP!**"

In the gallery, a cloak was thrown back, a white light that was offensively bright by Hell's standards shone around and, suddenly, there were four familiar figures among the demonic throng.

"We have heard enough!" said the Archangel Gabriel with a voice that brooked no argument.

Demon lords and dukes backed away hurriedly from the archangel and the three saints who accompanied him: the dour-faced St Paul, the obese St Thomas Aquinas and the armour-clad teenager Joan of Arc.

"What is the meaning of this?" asked Lord Peter.

"A question we could ask you," said Gabriel.

"This court is presiding over a disciplinary matter relating to Hell's internal organisation and policies. You have no authority here."

The Archangel Gabriel spread his white wings and he seemed to bloom in stature. His halo blazed.

"There is no place where we do not have ultimate authority, Peter." He pointed at the three human monks. "And this goes far beyond Hell's internal affairs."

Behind him, Rutspud could hear two of the monks talking to each other in hushed voices.

"What do you call that thing in films where God pops up at the end and puts everything right?" whispered Bastian. "You know, the one I can't pronounce."

"Deus ex machina," whispered Manfred.

"Is that what's happening here?"

"Let's hope so."

Without so much as a waft of his wings, the archangel descended from the gallery to the floor of the chamber. One glare sent Nero scuttling away to the shadows.

"What we have here," he said, "is a debacle of appalling proportions. Demons taking on human form. Damned souls wandering the earth. Mortal men in Hell."

"I agree," said Lord Peter. "Which is why this demon is being punished."

"Is it his fault alone?" said the Archangel Gabriel. "Should he be the only one standing here?"

He swept his arm. There was a flash of lightning that left afterimages in Rutspud's eyes for several seconds and, at once, the chamber was much fuller. The damned he had left on the stairs, Lewis, Nightingale, Wilde and the rest of his gang, were now beside him. A clutch of demons, stunned and frightened, had also appeared behind them. Rutspud recognised Spoongut, Pencrust, and a number of others who seemed vaguely familiar but who he knew he had not seen in ages. So, these were the monks of St Cadfan's ...

"Yes, yes," agreed Lord Peter readily. "They should all be punished. If they hadn't tried to flee from Hell, none of this would have happened."

"Ah," said the archangel.

"But they wouldn't have been able to escape if not for the staircase linking Hell and Earth," said St Thomas Aquinas.

"Good point," said the Archangel Gabriel. "Who made the staircase and placed it there?"

"Escher," said Belphegor. "Transferred from Heaven on a secondment. He's been kept down here for losing the staircase in the first place."

"Lost it?" said Thomas Aquinas. "Where is this Escher?"

"Not here," said Belphegor, "and not seen since the flood."

"Most unfortunate," said Lord Peter.

"We can arrange to summon him, if we so wish," said Gabriel, but turned at the sound of a brief yip.

"Jessie!" said Manfred, smiling at the collie, as she entered, shepherding a rather surprised man into the middle of the room. "That dog really is a marvel."

"Escher?" said Gabriel, with a smile. "Good. Now, about the staircase you built ..."

"What staircase? Oh, that staircase?" said Escher.

"We're curious how it came to be lost," said Thomas Aquinas.

"I was so embarrassed," said Escher. "Lord Treyvaw had originally commissioned it, but then, shortly after completion, it vanished from the workshop and –"

"Treyvaw?" said Joan of Arc. "*This* Treyvaw?"

"That is interesting," said St Paul.

"A staircase that conveniently leads to Earth," said Thomas, "an escape route for any demon who chooses to take it. And a demon whose job it is to track down those who might do just that."

"I think that's called entrapment," said Rutspud.

"So, in fact," said the Archangel Gabriel, pointing a finger at the suddenly nervous Treyvaw, "it would appear that *this* demon is the architect of all your woes."

"Ye—ees, I suppose so," said Lord Peter slowly, clearly trying, and failing, to find a counterargument.

The Archangel Gabriel nodded in satisfaction.

"Then, there we have it," he said. "These damned shall go back to their pits, these demons shall be allowed to return – unmolested, I tell you – to their places of work, and these three men will be sent back to their earthly abode."

"And this Treyvaw character?" said Joan of Arc.

"Oh, yes, what about him?" said Rutspud, now cheered up immeasurably.

The archangel let his hand drop significantly to the table top beside the despairatron.

"Lord Peter, did you not earmark this contraption as punishment for the guilty?"

"I did."

"No!" yelled Treyvaw, and would have fallen back, but Gabriel had hold of him and, although the demon-hunting demon towered over the angel, Treyvaw did not stand a chance against him.

"Lords! No! This is not justice!" screamed Treyvaw. "Anything but this!"

Smoothly and inexorably, Treyvaw was hauled forward. But then, there came a shout from an unexpected quarter.

"Stop!"

All eyes turned to Stephen, human, demonic, and angelic.

"What are you doing?" said Rutspud.

"Just stop," he said. "Stop it now."

The Archangel Gabriel frowned.

"You have an objection, human?"

"I do," said Stephen. "This is not ... this is not how it should end."

"You would tell me what is right?"

"Um. Yeah." Stephen cleared his throat. "Seems to me, if we're looking for who is ultimately responsible, then it's really you, isn't it?"

"Me?"

"Well, more precisely ... Him."

Stephen jiggled an index finger upwards towards the metaphysical Heavens.

"Pssst," whispered Rutspud. "Don't go angering the angel. We've won, okay?"

"You should be careful what you say, monk, and who you say it to," said Gabriel, a threatening rumble in his voice. "Know your place and accept Heaven's judgement."

"I think, Brother Stephen," said Joan of Arc, "that you should tread carefully."

"Point is," said Stephen, "this situation is a mess. He" – and he pointed at Lord Peter – "wanted to inflict all the pain of Hell on my friend here. And you just want to do it to someone else. Why?"

"There must be judgement," said the Archangel Gabriel.

"Why?"

"Why?" spluttered the angel. "To distinguish good from bad. To reward one and punish the other."

"No," said Stephen. "It should never be like that. If we have any love in us at all ..."

He stepped forward and placed his hand over the despairatron.

"I would rather put my own hand on this thing than let you inflict it on anyone else."

Demons in the gallery leaned forward eagerly.

"That is the ultimate torture you're playing with there, little man," said Belphegor. "More pain than you can imagine."

"I know," said Stephen.

Lord Peter scoffed.

"You would regret your foolish decision the moment you touched the button. You would rather Rutspud suffer it for a century than you spend another second in contact with it."

"Exactly!" said Stephen, taking his hand away. "I would. I would do that. I'd change my mind, out of fear, because I'm only human. And that is precisely why torture in general, and Hell in particular, are stupid."

"Are you calling us stupid now?"

Stephen nodded.

"You. Me. All of us here. We're stupid. We're ignorant and foolish and frequently do the wrong things. And we do bad stuff because, in our ignorant and foolish way, we do short-sighted and selfish things. Do you think anyone can ever deserve endless punishment for being stupid?"

"This is a far more theologically complex issue than you realise," said Thomas Aquinas.

Manfred stepped forward.

"I am sure," he said, "that St Thomas Aquinas here – big fan of yours too, by the way – would point out that a transgression against the infinite majesty of God can only be met with a punishment of equally infinite magnitude."

St Thomas Aquinas's lips flapped wordlessly in the exact manner of a person who has had the very words stolen out of his mouth.

"But," said Manfred, "God is infinite love and forgiveness. Everyone can *and will* find their way to Him in the end."

There was a strange smile on Joan of Arc's face.

"Surely, Peter here, too, hopes that one day he might – just might – be allowed back in the Celestial City."

"But there must be punishment," said Lord Peter.

"God, yes," squeaked Scabass from his corner of continuing torture.

"There must be a Hell," agreed the Archangel Gabriel.

"Hell? Yes," said Manfred. "But does there have to be anyone in it?"

Chapter 12 – The day of the funeral

Bastian sat in the locutory of St Cadfan's, his unfocused gaze on one of the computer screens in the monastery's business hub. There was silence on the phone line and he abruptly realised that Carol Well-Dunn had asked him a question.

"What have *I* been up to?" he said, blinking hard. "Gosh, a bit of this and that. Wandering here and there."

"You're an enigmatic man, Bastian. What mysteries do you hide beneath that habit?" There was the indescribable audible equivalent of a blush of embarrassment. "That came out wrong. I mean, er, I mean, I didn't mean ... I was just saying."

"That's all right," said Bastian bluffly. "So, we're seeing you and your party on the fifteenth of next month."

"I imagine the yellow-crested Merlin stilts will be fully fledged by then. I'm looking forward to it."

"We're looking forward to seeing you too," said Bastian and, realised with some clarity, that it wasn't just her money he was looking forward to seeing.

"So, is there far to wander on Bardsey Island?" said Carol.

"Sorry?"

"You said you've been wandering here and there."

"Further than you'd think," he said.

In a place that was not Hell but, if it had an address, would certainly have the same postcode as Hell, there was a valley. The valley was not Limbo, but it was certainly a place of waiting. The valley was not Purgatory either; Purgatory did not bear a shocking resemblance to Near Sawrey in the English Lake District and did not have a substantial farm cottage on its slopes.

The cottage had ten human inhabitants. In the upstairs study, a woman looked over the graphs and charts for their upcoming Infernal case reviews. She tutted every so often, as the electric lights flickered, but she did not begrudge the man in the basement his esoteric and frankly dangerous experiments. In the library, a playwright and an actress sat reading much loved plays from all recorded history and occasionally attempted to good-naturedly point out how each was a superior aesthete to the other. In the cosy pink drawing room, three older women sat. Two of them wound yarn together, one proclaiming terrible events yet to come and the other telling her that everything would be fine if only people could be nice to each other. The third woman sat at an Olivetti typewriter and daydreamed. The remaining three inhabitants were out of the cottage. Two of them, wrapped in furs and carrying their weapons of choice, were out on the hills, pursuing rumours that there were other valleys and other people who had been given a reprieve from Hell – temporary or otherwise. One of them also hoped to spot a mammoth.

The final inhabitant sat on the back step of the cottage. She was stitching buttons onto the tiny waistcoat in her hands. It was fiddly work and distracted her from the dance routine she was also currently choreographing.

"No," said Potter. "Stop there."

The rats stumbled in their tracks.

"Lickspear," she said, "tell them it's step-step-turn and *then* jazz hands."

"T'ain't easy," said the patchwork demon. "These rats hail from the Pit of Carnivorous Rodents. They lack classic training, Miss Potter."

"Of course," she said kindly, "but they've got you to coach them, haven't they?"

Lickspear swelled with pride.

"Okay, boys. Dig what I'm puttin' down. Let us begin with the rudiments!"

"How do I look?" said Rutspud, stepping out into the yard.

Potter appraised him carefully.

"Well, you've got two arms again, if that's what you mean."

"That'll do then," he said.

"You off somewhere nice?"

"A funeral."

"Hope it goes well."

"Well, the dead man's going to read his own eulogy, so that should be a lot of fun."

Potter moved over to sit at the wooden bureau after Rutspud's departure, and worked on her sketches for the rats' outfits. She felt a wet nose against her knee.

"Hello, Jessie," she said, ruffling the dog's ears. The dog-sized flap swung shut as Jessie emerged fully from the cupboard at her feet, trailing a faint waft of brimstone and Welsh sea air.

In Hell proper, Lord Peter and Nero stood in what was currently designated as the Temporary Portakabin of Nameless Dread and looked over the plans.

"No, you see, I don't think I want to go down this route," said Lord Peter.

"No, lord?"

Peter regarded the drawings, the soaring spire of spike-covered stone, the skulls and the gargoyles.

"I inherited the previous fortress from the Fallen One himself, but it's really not my style."

"I see, lord. But this is classic Hell. It speaks of the darkness and the terror and the whole ..." – lacking the words, Nero pulled a scary face and growled.

"I understand, but I'd rather have an HQ that speaks of efficiency and order and the execution of watertight policies and procedures."

"Ah," said Nero. "Perhaps I should get in the NASA space toilet designers."

"That would be marvellous," said Lord Peter, clapping the former Roman emperor on the back.

Nero rolled up the plans.

"Sir?"

"Yes?" said Lord Peter.

"Did I ever say sorry for having you put to death? You know, on the cross."

"Several times," said Lord Peter. "Loudly and with tears in your eyes and everything."

"I meant, have I ever said it apart from during excruciating torture?"

Lord Peter thought on the question.

"No, I don't think so."

"Oh," said Nero. "Um, I am sorry. Just saying. Coffee, sir?"

"I'll get them," said Lord Peter. "You've got enough to do."

"Beard. Big beardy beard," said Father Eustace, placing his hand on the coffin that contained the remains of the original Eustace Pike.

In the monastery chapel, the assembled monks of St Cadfan's reflected solemnly on this wisdom. Brothers Bernard, Huey and Lionel sat in the front pews, looking no worse than usual for having spent considerable time in a state of disincorporation.

"We are monks," said Father Eustace. "And we are good monks. But are we men?"

The only three monks in the whole chapel who could truly be considered men in a deeply spiritual and biological sense sat at the back with Rutspud and considered this question.

"This was a man," said Father Eustace and thumped the coffin lid, nearly shaking it off the trestles. "But will you be a man like him? Hmmm?" He swung a finger out to take in the assembled monks.

The demon monks, who only wore the bodies of men for convenience's sake, nodded in agreement. Jessie the border collie, who had arrived a few minutes earlier, remained impassive.

"One day," sniffed Brother Gillespie (formerly the demon Spoongut).

"Aye," said Brother Henry (formerly the demon Pencrust).

"So," said Rutspud, leaning in to speak into Stephen's ear, "you're okay with most of your monastic order being demons?"

"I think so."

"It'll take getting used to," said Bastian. "But yes."

"And you're actually going to keep him as your abbot?" said Rutspud.

Stephen shrugged. "He's not a practical leader of men but, as a figurehead, he'll do."

"Certainly no worse than our last abbot," said Manfred.

"Really?" said Rutspud. "Blimey."

"And this new abbot plays a mean banjo," added Bastian. "Any community needs music."

"That's not what you said about my bongos," said Manfred.

"Bongos are an offence to the ears and you know it," said Bastian.

"Banjo!" shouted Father Eustace from the front of the chapel.

"Damn it, he heard you," hissed Manfred.

"Banjo! And beer!"

Father Eustace leapt into the nave and ran to the door. Several monks were already on their feet.

"And, apparently, the wake begins now," said Bastian.

"But I haven't laid out the sandwiches yet," said Manfred and hurried out.

Stephen and Rutspud ambled across the cloisters together. It was a clear day and Rutspud did his best to avoid looking at the horrible open skies.

"I'm not going to come in and join you," he said to Stephen. "I think you guys need time to get to know each other once more. You know, a bit of monk-on-monk bonding."

"No, that's fine," said Stephen and then, "You've never thought of joining us? Putting on the habit? It's a fine life."

"Thanks, but no. I've got work to do downstairs. And, besides, Hell has better Wi-Fi."

Stephen laughed. From the refectory came the sounds of a banjo striking up a merry jig.

"Listen," said Rutspud, "I have to tell you something. I've spiked the beer again."

"What do you mean?"

"Lethe water again. A lot."

Stephen frowned.

"I'm not sure your two friends are fit to cope with the knowledge that their brothers are not of this Earth."

"Really? I think Manfred and Bastian have taken it rather well."

"Okay, well maybe I've been instructed to tie up some loose ends."

"Ah, I see," said Stephen, understanding. "And are, uh, we one of those loose ends?"

Rutspud pulled a sad face. He had very expressive eyes and he did it well.

"I have my orders," he said.

"I see."

Rutspud's ear twitched. Apparently some bongos had joined in with the banjo – well, not so much joined in as set up in competition.

"Of course," he said to Stephen, "you don't *have* to drink the beer."

"I must admit I don't think I'm all that thirsty tonight," the monk replied.

Rutspud grinned.

"I'm pleased to hear it."

He gave Stephen a farewell wink and set out through the garden gate toward the far side of the island and a dank cave which led, against all probability, to the inside of a wardrobe in Hell. Rutspud strode like a man with a song in his heart. It was a silly little song with rude hand gestures and an excessive amount of bongo-playing, but it was a song nonetheless.

About the authors

Heide and Iain are married, but not to each other.
Heide lives in North Warwickshire with her husband and children.
Iain lives in south Birmingham with his wife and two daughters.

Heide Goody and Iain Grant are co-authors of *Clovenhoof*, the original novel about Satan's adventures in suburban England and the sequels *Pigeonwings* and *Godsquad*. They have each published solo works (available from Amazon) but seem to spend much of their time these days at festivals and workshops, explaining how two people can write a novel together and how much fun it really is.

The fifth book in the Clovenhoof series will be published in early 2016.

19497120R00205

Printed in Great Britain
by Amazon